**Electricity shot between them, so real Felipe could almost hear the crackle. It heated him too, making tiny jolts bounce on his skin, his heart thrum…**

His hand rose of its own volition, his fingers stretching towards Francesca.

A throb of need burst through him, so powerful he had to dig his feet into the floor to stop himself from hauling her into his arms.

'You are not leaving this suite.' His speech was long, drawn-out, ragged.

'I'm not staying with someone who can barely look at me and gets irritated every time I open my mouth.'

Without him knowing how it had happened his fingers closed around the delicate wrists. A moment later he'd pulled her to him so their bodies were flush, her breasts pressed against his chest.

'I don't dislike you,' he ground out, gazing down at the spitting eyes, the luminous skin, the lips that begged to be kissed… 'Don't you see that? I like you *too much*.'

For long, long moments they did nothing but gaze at each other, until the a... in her eyes softened to ... struck straight into his l...

# Bound to a Billionaire

*Claimed by the most powerful of men!*

Felipe Lorenzi, Matteo Manaserro
and Daniele Pellegrini.

Three powerful billionaires who want for nothing—
in business *or* in bed. But nothing and
no one can touch their closely guarded hearts.

That is until Francesca, Natasha and Eva are each
bound to a billionaire…and prove to be a challenge
these delicious alpha males can't resist!

Don't miss **Michelle Smart**'s stunning trilogy

Read Felipe and Francesca's story in

*Protecting His Defiant Innocent*

Available now!

Look out for

Matteo and Natasha's story in

*Claiming His One-Night Baby*

September 2017

and

Daniele and Eva's story in

*Buying His Bride of Convenience*

October 2017

# PROTECTING HIS DEFIANT INNOCENT

BY
MICHELLE SMART

MILLS
BOON

First Published in Great Britain 2017
By Mills & Boon, an imprint of HarperCollins*Publishers*
1 London Bridge Street, London, SE1 9GF

© 2017 Michelle Smart

ISBN: 978-0-263-92532-6

Our policy is to use papers that are natural, renewable and recyclable products and made from wood grown in sustainable forests. The logging and manufacturing processes conform to the legal environmental regulations of the country of origin.

Printed and bound in Spain
by CPI, Barcelona

**Michelle Smart**'s love affair with books started when she was a baby, and she would cuddle them in her cot. A voracious reader of all genres, she found her love of romance established when she stumbled across her first Mills & Boon book at the age of twelve. She's been reading and writing them ever since. Michelle lives in Northamptonshire with her husband, and two young Smarties.

Visit the Author Profile page
at millsandboon.co.uk for more titles.

This is for Nicky,
the best friend a girl could wish for. xxx

# CHAPTER ONE

'ARE YOU WITH ME?' Francesca Pellegrini tightened her ponytail and glared at the two men sitting opposite her in the small draughty room of the family castle. 'Will we work together and build the hospital in Pieta's memory?'

Daniele threw his hands in the air. 'Do we have to discuss this now, in the middle of his wake?'

'I am talking about building an enduring legacy for our brother,' she reminded him crossly.

Francesca had known Daniele and Matteo would need a little convincing but had complete faith she would get their agreement. Hurricane Igor had decimated the Caribbean island of Caballeros only ten days ago. Twenty thousand people had died and the island had been left with only seven working hospitals for a population of eight million. Pieta, the eldest of the Pellegrini siblings, had seen the devastation on the news and had sprung straight into action in the way she had always so admired.

Despite running an international law firm, he'd always looked at practical ways to help those suffering at the hands of natural disasters, donating money, hosting fundraisers *and* getting his hands dirty. He'd been famed and honoured for his philanthropy and she'd been so proud to call herself his sister. She could hardly believe she would never see him again, his life cut short when his helicopter crashed in thick fog.

'I'm not asking you for the moon,' she continued, 'I'm asking you to put your skills into building the hospital Pieta was planning for a country that has lost everything and to do it in our brother's memory.' Daniele earned a fortune—he'd just taken delivery of a brand-new yacht!—but what good did he do with it? Who did her brother serve other than the god of money?

Francesca knew she was being unfair to the brother who'd always doted on her but what did it matter? Pieta was dead and the only thing she could focus on to endure the pain was continuing with his plan and thus continuing his legacy.

'I'm not saying it's a bad idea,' he snapped back. 'Just that we shouldn't be rushing into anything. There are security concerns for a start.'

'The country has been flattened. The only concerns are dysentery and cholera.'

'Don't be so naïve. It's one of the most dangerous and corrupt countries in the world and you want me to send my men to work there and for Matteo to send *his* staff there.'

Matteo Manaserro, their cousin, owned private medical clinics across the western world, performing vanity services for people who refused to age gracefully. He'd also launched a range of youth enhancing products that had made him world famous *and* as rich as Croesus. Francesca's mother was an enthusiastic wearer of the entire range and swore she'd only had a couple of nips and tucks since using them. Pieta had often said Matteo could have been one of the greatest and most eminent surgeons in the world but that he'd thrown it away in the pursuit of money, just like Daniele.

'I'm travelling to Caballeros tomorrow. I'll confirm myself that your security fears are unfounded,' she informed him without dropping her stare.

Daniele's face went the colour of puce. 'You are not.'

'I am. It's all arranged. Pieta had already earmarked the site to build the hospital on and put aside money for it and arranged meetings with government officials and...'

'You're not going. You don't have the authority for a start.'

'Yes, I do.' She played her trump card. 'Natasha's given me written authority to act as her representative as Pieta's next of kin.'

Her sister-in-law, who had sat in on the meeting like a mute ghost, looked vaguely startled to hear her name mentioned. Francesca knew she'd taken advantage of her fragile state of mind to get the authority but squashed her conscience. This was Pieta's legacy and she would do anything to achieve it. She *had* to.

Maybe if she finished what Pieta had started her guilt-ravaged dreams would stop.

*I'm so sorry, Pieta. I didn't mean it. You were the best of us and I loved you. Forgive me, please.*

'It's not safe!' Daniele slammed his hand so hard on the old oak table that even Matteo flinched.

But Francesca was beyond listening to reason. She knew it but could do nothing about it, like a child thrown into the deep end of a pool and needing to use its limited strength to swim to the shallows. That's how she felt; that she needed to reach the shallows to find forgiveness.

'Come with me and keep me safe if you're that concerned. That hospital will be built with or without you even if I have to build it myself.'

Daniele looked ready to explode. Maybe he would have done if Matteo hadn't sighed, raised his hand in the gesture of peace, leaned forward and said, 'You can count me in. I'll work with Daniele, if he agrees, on how the basic set-up should work, and when the construction's complete I'll personally come in and get it up and running, but only for a month and only because I loved Pieta.'

'Excellent.' If her cheeks had been able to curve upwards, Francesca would have smiled.

'But I agree with Daniele that security is a major concern. You're underestimating how dangerous Caballeros can be. I suggest we bring Felipe in.'

Daniele straightened like a poker. He looked at Matteo and nodded slowly. 'Yes. I can go with that. He'll be able to keep Francesca safe when she's ordering dictators around and protect any staff we hire for it.'

'Wait, wait, wait,' Francesca interjected. 'Who is this Felipe?'

'Felipe Lorenzi is a Spanish security expert. Pieta used his services many times.'

'I've never heard of him.' She supposed this wasn't very surprising. She'd only started her traineeship in Pieta's law firm a few months before, after graduating. Up until his death she'd never had any direct involvement in his private philanthropy.

'He's ex-Spanish Special Forces,' Matteo explained. 'He set up his own business providing security to businesses and individuals who need to travel to places most right minded people run away from and earned a fortune with it. Pieta thought very highly of him and I imagine he would have brought him in to act as security for this project if he'd…'

*If he'd lived.*

'Then we bring him in,' Francesca said after a pause she could see was painful for all of them. She would never admit it but the thought of travelling alone to Caballeros did scare her a little. She'd never travelled alone before. But she would be brave, just as Pieta had always been. 'But I don't need a babysitter.'

'You might have to wait a few days for him to organise his men,' Matteo said, 'but whoever he sends will be ex-special forces like himself and trained to handle any situation.'

'I can't wait,' she told them. 'I'm not being difficult but I have a meeting set up about the sale of the land tomorrow. If I cancel it, I don't know when they'll let me rearrange it for. We can't afford any delays.'

The whole project rested on her getting the sale of the land agreed. Without it there would be no hospital and no legacy. She *had* to get that land.

Daniele's eyes flashed on her. 'And you can't afford to take risks.'

'Pieta did,' she informed him defiantly. 'I can decide for myself what risks I'm willing to take and personally I think the risks are exaggerated.'

'You *what*...?'

The fight between them was diffused by Matteo raising another hand for peace. 'Francesca, we both understand how much you want to honour Pieta's memory—we all want to—but you need to understand we are only concerned for your safety. Felipe has a large network of men working for him, I'm sure it won't be a problem for him to put something in place for your arrival in Caballeros tomorrow.'

She caught the warning look he gave Daniele.

Daniele must have understood whatever the look meant for he nodded shrewdly before turning his attention back to her. 'You will do whatever they tell you. You are not to place yourself at unnecessary risk, is that understood?'

'Does this mean you're in?'

He sighed. 'Yes. I'm in. Can we return to the rest of our family now? Our mother needs us.'

Francesca nodded. The cramping in her chest loosened a little. She'd got everything she'd wanted from them and now she wanted to find her mother and hold her tight. 'To summarise, I'll take care of the legal side, Daniele takes care of the construction and Matteo takes care of the medical side. What about you, Natasha? Do you want to handle publicity for it?'

Although only married to Pieta for a year, they'd been engaged for six years and she'd thought her shy sister-in-law should have the chance be involved if she wanted.

Publicity was important. Publicity brought donations and awareness.

Natasha shrugged her slim shoulders. 'I can do that,' she whispered.

'Then we are done.' Francesca got to her feet and rolled her shoulders, trying to ease the tension in them. Knowing she had Daniele and Matteo onside meant she could now, for one night only, mourn the brother she had loved.

From tomorrow, the hard work began.

Francesca clumped up the steps of the jet, shades on to keep the glare of the sun from her bleary eyes, to be greeted by the sombre flight crew. Her brother had been a man to inspire devotion and loyalty from his staff, and their obvious grief touched her.

If her heart didn't feel so heavy and her brain so tired from all the wine she'd drunk and the two hours of sleep she'd managed to snatch in the freezing room she'd always slept in when they'd stayed at the castle in her childhood, she would be excited to be on Pieta's personal jet. She'd never been in it before and it saddened her that now she would never travel in it with him.

The document Natasha had signed gave her carte blanche to do whatever was needed and use whatever resources were necessary from Pieta's foundation and personal estate for the project. She knew Daniele was angry with her for taking advantage of Natasha's fragile state and she did feel guilt for it but honestly, if she'd asked Natasha to sign over her house, car and bank account to her, she would have done so with the same glassy-eyed look. Before leaving the wake Francesca had pulled Matteo to one side and asked him to keep an eye on her. Matteo was more than just a cousin to them. He'd lived with them since he was thirteen and, being the same age as Pieta, had been his closest friend. Like the rest of the world, he'd been devoted to him. He would look out for Natasha.

Francesca was led into the main area of the jet, which was as luxurious as she'd imagined but before she had a chance to take it all in, she was startled to find a man sat on one of the plush leather chairs, a laptop open on the foldaway desk that covered what she could see were enormously long legs.

She stopped in her tracks.

Not expecting to be travelling with anyone, she glanced from the stewardess, who showed no surprise at his presence, back to the stranger before her.

The darkest brown eyes set in the most handsome face she had ever seen stared back.

Her breath caught in her throat.

It seemed as if an age passed before he spoke. 'You must be Francesca.'

The English was spoken with a heavy accent and from firm, generous lips that didn't even hint at a smile.

She blinked herself back to the present, realising she'd been staring at him. 'And you are?'

'Felipe Lorenzi.'

'*You're* Felipe?'

When Matteo and Daniele had spoken of the ex-special forces man she'd formed a mental image of a thuggish squat man with a shaven head and a body crammed with tattoos who wore nothing but grubby khaki trousers and black T-shirts.

This man was something else entirely. This man had a headful of thick hair that was darker even than his eyes and touched the collar of his crisp white shirt, which he wore with an immaculate and obviously expensive light grey suit with matching waistcoat and thin green checked tie.

He raised a brow. 'Were you expecting someone else?'

Unsettled for reasons she couldn't begin to decipher,

Francesca took the seat opposite him, fighting her eyes' desire to stare and stare and stare some more.

'I wasn't expecting anyone.' She pulled the seat belt across her lap, doing her utmost to sound together and confident and unaffected by his presence. 'I was told I'd be meeting one of your men in Caballeros.'

Daniele and Matteo had made the arrangements, working their phones like a whirlwind throughout the wake to ensure there would be protection for her when she arrived on the island. She'd hadn't been told to expect company on her flight. If she had she'd have made an effort with her appearance, not thrown on the first clothes that had come to hand. She hadn't had time for a shower or even to moisturise her face.

The face that stared back didn't moisturise, she thought, feeling rather dizzy. This face was intensely, masculinely beautiful. But battle-hardened. This was a face that had seen sights the horrors of which were etched in the lines around his eyes and mouth, in the bump on the bridge of his strong nose and in the white flecks in the thick untamed beard that covered his jaw. This man had an aura of danger about him that sent thrills she couldn't understand racing through her bloodstream.

'Caballeros isn't stable. It isn't wise to go there without protection.' Especially not for a woman such as this, Felipe thought. He would have risen to shake her hand but her appearance had thrown him.

Both the Pellegrini brothers were handsome so it was to be expected that their younger sister would be good looking too. He hadn't expected her to be so truculently sexy, in tight ripped jeans, a billowing white blouse, and glittery thongs on her small, pretty feet.

'I didn't know it would be *you* personally,' she explained warily. 'I was under the impression you supplied the men to undertake the protection.'

'That is the case but there are times, such as this, when I undertake it myself.'

In the years he'd provided protection for Pieta on his philanthropic missions he'd got to know the man well. Throughout his career Felipe had dealt with death and loss many times; had almost become inured to it. The shock of Pieta's death had hit him harder than he would have expected. He'd been an exceptional man, intelligent and for all his daring, naturally cautious. He'd known how to handle situations.

Felipe had been propped at a hotel bar in the Middle East drinking the malt whiskey Pieta had liked in his memory when both Daniele and Matteo had called to say Pieta's little sister was travelling to Caballeros, a country quickly descending into anarchy, first thing in the morning, and that nothing they said would deter or delay her. He'd known immediately that he owed it to the great man to protect his sister himself and had set into action. Within ten hours he was in Pisa, showered, changed and sat on Pieta's jet. The only thing he hadn't had time for was a shave.

Francesca removed her shades and folded them into her handbag. When she looked at him, he experienced another, more powerful jolt.

Her height was the only thing average about her. Everything else about her was extraordinary, from the sheet of glossy black hair that hung the length of her back to the wide, kissable lips and clear olive skin. The only flaw on her features were her eyes, which were so red raw and puffy it was hard to distinguish the light brown colour of her pupils.

She'd buried her brother only the day before.

He recalled Daniele's warning about her state of mind. This was a woman on the edge.

'I was very sorry to hear about Pieta's death,' he said quietly.

'Not sorry enough to attend his funeral,' she replied archly although there was the slightest tremor in her hoarse voice. Hoarse from crying, he suspected.

'Work comes first. He would have understood.' On his next visit to Europe he intended to visit Pieta's grave and lay a wreath for him.

'You were able to juggle your work commitments to be here now.'

'I did,' he agreed. He'd had to pull a senior member of his staff away from his holiday to take over the job he'd been overseeing to make it to Pisa on time for the flight. 'Caballeros is a dangerous place.'

'Just so we're clear, you work for *me*,' she said in the impeccable English all the Pellegrinis spoke. 'My sister-in-law has given me written authority to represent her as Pieta's next of kin on this project.'

Felipe contemplated her through narrowed eyes. There had been a definite challenge in that husky tone.

'How old are you?' At thirty-six he was a year older than Pieta, the eldest of the three Pellegrini siblings. He recalled Francesca once being referred to as the 'happy accident'.

'I'm twenty-three.' She raised her chin, daring him to make something of her youth.

'Almost an old woman,' he mocked. He hadn't realised she was *that* young and now he did know he was doubly glad he'd disrupted his schedule to be there as her protection. He would have guessed at mid-twenties. Sure, only a few years older than her actual age but those years were often the most formative of an adult's life. His had been. They'd been the best of his life, right until the hostage situation that had culminated in the loss of his best friend and a bullet in his leg that had seen him medically discharged from the job he loved at only twenty-six.

She glared at him. 'I might be young but I am not stupid. You don't need to patronise me.'

'Age isn't linked to intelligence,' he conceded. 'What countries have you travelled to?'

'I've been to many countries.'

'With your family on holiday?' Francesca's father, Fabio Pellegrini, had been a descendant of the old Italian royal family. The Pellegrinis had long eschewed their royal titles but still owned a sprawling Tuscan estate near Pisa and had immense wealth. Vanessa Pellegrini, the matriarch, also came from old money. None of Vanessa or Fabio's children had ever wanted for anything. When Felipe compared it to his own humble upbringing the contrast couldn't be starker.

'Yes,' she said defiantly. 'I've visited most of Europe, the Americas and Australia. I would consider myself well-travelled.'

'And which of these many countries have been on a war footing?'

'Caballeros isn't on a war footing.'

'Not yet. In which of those countries was sanitation a problem?'

'I've got water-purifying tablets in my luggage.'

He hid a smile. She thought she had all the answers but didn't have a clue what she'd be walking into. 'That would make all the difference but you won't be needing them.'

'Why not?'

'Because you're not staying in Caballeros. I've booked you into a hotel in Aguadilla.' Aguadilla was a Spanish-Caribbean island relatively close to Caballeros but spared by the hurricane and as safe a country as there was in this dangerous world.

'You did what?'

'I cancelled the shack you'd been booked into in San Pedro,' he continued as if she hadn't spoken, referring to the Caballeron capital. 'We've a Cessna in place to fly you between the islands for all your meetings.'

Her cheeks flushed with angry colour. 'You had no right to do that. That *shack* was where Pieta was going to stay.'

'And he would have hired my firm for protection. He wasn't a fool. You're a vulnerable woman...'

'I am not.'

'Look at yourself through Caballeron eyes. You're young, rich and beautiful and, like it or not, you're a woman...'

'I'm not rich!'

'Your family is rich. Caballeros is the sixth most dangerous country in the world. Things were bad enough when the people had roofs over their heads. Now they have lost everything and they are angry. You will have a price on your head the second you set foot on their soil.'

'But I'm going to build them a hospital.'

'And many of them will be grateful. Like all the Caribbean islands it's full of wonderful, hospitable people but Caballeros has always had a dangerous underbelly and more military coups than any other country since it gained its independence from Spain. Guns and drugs are rife, the police and politicians are corrupt, and that was before Hurricane Igor destroyed their infrastructure and killed thousands of their population.'

It was a long time before Francesca spoke. In that time she stared at him with eyes that spat fire.

'I was already aware of the risks,' she said tremulously. 'It's why I agreed for your firm to be hired to protect me. Not babysit me. You had no right to change my arrangements. No right at all. I will pay you the full amount but I don't want your services any more. Take your things and get off the plane. I'm terminating our contract.'

He'd been told she would react like this. Both Daniele and Matteo had warned him of her fiery nature and fierce independent streak, which her grief for Pieta had compounded. That's why Daniele had taken the steps he had, to protect Francesca from herself.

'I'm sorry to tell you this but you're not in a position to fire me.' He gave a nonchalant shrug, followed by an even more nonchalant yawn. *Dios*, he was tired. He hadn't slept in two days and could do without the explosion he was certain was about to occur. 'Your sister-in-law has made an addendum to the authority she gave you. If at any time I report that you're not following my advice with regard to your safety, her authority is revoked and the project disbanded.'

# CHAPTER TWO

THE SHOCK ON Francesca's face was priceless. 'Natasha did that? *Natasha*?'

'At Daniele's request. I understand he wanted her to cancel the authority altogether. This was their compromise.' As he spoke, the aeroplane hurtled down the runway and lifted into the air.

Now her features twisted into outrage. 'The dirty, underhanded...'

'Your brother and all your family are worried about you. They think you're too emotional and impulsive to get this done without falling into trouble. I am here to keep you out of trouble.' He leaned forward and spoke clearly. He needed her to understand that this wasn't a game and that he meant everything he said. 'I have no wish to be a tyrant but if you push me or behave rashly or take any risks I believe to be unnecessary, I will bring you straight back to Pisa.'

Her lips were pulled in so tightly all that showed was a thin white line. 'I want to see the addendum.'

'Of course.' He pulled it out of his inner jacket pocket. She leaned forward and snatched it from his outstretched hand.

The colour on her face darkened with each line read.

'That's a copy of the original,' he said in case she was thinking of ripping it into pieces.

She glared at him with malevolence. 'I spent five years working for my law degree. I know what a copy looks like.'

Then she took a deep inhalation before placing the document on her lap and clenching her hands into fists. 'Do not think you can push me around, Mr Lorenzi. I might be young but I'm not a child. This project means *everything* to me.'

'I appreciate that,' he replied calmly. 'If you act like the adult you claim to be there won't be any problems and the project will be safe.'

Her answering glare could have curdled milk.

Francesca was so angry she refused to make any further conversation. If Felipe was perturbed by her silence he didn't show it. He worked on his laptop for a couple of hours whilst eating a tower of sandwiches, then pressed the button on his seat that turned it into a pod bed.

Doing the same to her own seat, she tried to get some sleep too. She'd found only snatches since Pieta had died in the helicopter crash and that had been haunted sleep at best, waking with cold sweats and sobbing into her pillow. She didn't know which was the harder to endure, the guilt or the grief. Both sat like a hovering spectre ready to extend its scaly grip and pull her into darkness.

Had it really only been a week ago that her mother had called with the news that he'd been so cruelly taken from them?

For the first time since his death, tears didn't fill her eyes the second her head hit a pillow. She was too angry to cry.

She knew it was Daniele she should be angry with and not Felipe. Her brother was the one who'd gone behind her back and drawn up the addendum that effectively put Felipe in charge of her as if he were a teacher and she a student on a school trip. But Felipe, the hateful man, had signed it and made it clear he would enforce it.

It would be different if *she* were a man. He wouldn't be throwing his authority in her face and patronising her with her lack of worldliness if she were Daniele or Matteo. Her age and gender had always defined her within her family and it infuriated her to see it spread into the rest of her life.

She appreciated she'd been a surprise arrival, being born ten years after Daniele, twelve years after Pieta and their cousin Matteo, who had moved in with them when she was still a baby. The age difference was too stark not to be a factor in how they all treated her. To her father she'd been his princess, for her mother a female doll to dress in pretty clothes and fuss over. Daniele had fussed over her too, the big brother who'd brought her sweets, teased her, tormented her, taken her and her enamoured girlfriends for drives in his succession of new cars. She'd been his baby sister then and was still his baby sister now.

Only Pieta had treated her like a person in her own right and she'd adored him for it. He'd never treated her like a pet. His approval had meant the world to her and she'd followed his footsteps into a career in law like a puppy sniffing its master's heels.

*How* could she have reacted the way she had when she'd learned of his death? He deserved so much better than that.

She found her thoughts drifting back to the man whose care she'd been put under. Who cared if he had a face that could make a heart melt and a physique that screamed sex appeal? One conversation had proved him to be an arrogant tyrant. Francesca had spent her life fighting to be taken seriously and she was damned if she would allow him or anyone else to have any power over her...

She sat up sharply. She would call Natasha and get her to cancel the addendum! Why hadn't she thought of this sooner?

Phone in hand, she put the call through. Just as she was convinced it would go to voicemail, Natasha answered it, sounding flat and groggy.

'Hi, Natasha, sorry to bother you but I need to speak to you about something.' As quietly as she could so as not to wake the sleeping figure in the pod opposite her, Francesca explained her fears.

'I'm sorry, Fran, but I promised Daniele I wouldn't let you talk me out of it,' she replied with sympathy. 'It's for your own safety.'

'But it'll be impossible for me to be effective if this man can veto all my decisions.'

'He can't veto anything.'

'He *can*. If he decides it isn't safe for me to be somewhere or to do something he can put a stop to everything. Your addendum gives him all the power.'

'It isn't that bad.'

'It *is*. He can call a halt to the whole project if I don't do exactly as he says!'

Natasha sighed. 'I'm sorry but I made a promise. Daniele is very concerned about your state of mind. We all are. Pieta's death...' Her voice faltered then lowered to a whisper. 'It's hit you hard. Felipe will keep you safe and stop you making any rash decisions while you're there. Please, try to understand. We're only doing what's best for you.'

If Francesca didn't know how fragile Natasha's own state of mind was she'd be tempted to shout down the phone that she was perfectly capable of deciding what was best for herself. But shouting would only prove that she was unstable when right now she needed to convince them all that she was perfectly sane and rational.

Daniele had brainwashed her sister-in-law. It was him she needed to speak to. If she could convince him the addendum was unnecessary then Natasha would agree to cancel it.

'Thanks anyway,' she whispered.

Her next call was to Daniele. She wasn't surprised when it went to voicemail. The rat would be avoiding her.

She left a short message in as sweet a tone as she could

muster. 'Daniele, we need to talk. Call me back as soon as you get this.'

Proud that she hadn't sworn at him, she put her phone on the ledge by her pod bed. She had never failed to bend Daniele to her will before but this was a situation unlike any other. Cajoling him into buying her a dress for a ball— she was independent but not stupid—was one thing; persuading him to scrap a contract drawn up to keep her safe was a different matter.

'You won't get him to change his mind,' came the deep rumbling tone from the pod bed opposite, not sounding the slightest bit sleepy.

So the sneak had been awake all the time, listening to her conversations.

She threw the bedsheets off and got to her feet. 'I will. Just watch me.'

With no chance of getting any sleep she might as well have a shower and get herself ready for their arrival in the Caribbean.

Felipe ate eggs Benedict while waiting for Francesca to finish using the bathroom and adjacent dressing room. After nine hours on the plane he could do with another shower too. They'd be landing in Aguadilla in an hour, his Cessna at the ready to take them straight on to Caballeros and her meeting with the Governor.

He just hoped she was mentally prepared for what she would find there.

He understood her hostility. He'd never liked being subordinate to anyone either. Being in the forces had taught him obedience to orders but that had been a necessary part of any soldier's training. There was a chain of command and for anyone in that link to break it would see the whole chain collapse. He hadn't liked it but had seen the necessity of it and so had accepted it. Eventually he had climbed the chain so he had been the one giving the orders and now he commanded hundreds of men whose jobs took them all over the globe. Francesca would have to accept his authority in turn. Her safety was paramount. He wouldn't hesitate to pull her out if he thought it necessary.

Eventually she emerged from the dressing room.

'You look better,' he said, although it was an inadequate response to the difference from when she'd stepped onto the plane. Now she wore a tailored navy suit with tiny white lines racing the length of the jacket and tight trousers. Under the jacket was a black shirt and on her feet tan heels. Her lustrous black hair had been plaited and coiled into a bun at the nape of her neck. The effect managed to be professional and, he would guess, fashionable. It would certainly get her taken more seriously than the outfit she'd originally worn.

She answered with a tight smile and removed her laptop from the drawer a member of the cabin crew had put it in.

He got to his feet and stretched. 'I'm going to have a shower. Make sure you eat, we'll be landing in an hour.'

As he strolled past her he inhaled a fresh, delicate perfume and almost paused in his stride to inhale it again. Francesca smelled as good as she looked.

It didn't matter how good she smelt or how sexy she was, he reminded himself as he stripped off his suit, this was work where liaisons of anything but the professional kind were strictly forbidden. He had the clause written in all his employees' contracts for good reason. Their work was dangerous and needed a clear head. Any hint that the relationship between employee and client had crossed the line was grounds for instant dismissal.

Francesca could be Aphrodite herself and he would still keep his distance.

He switched the shower on and waited for the water

to warm. And waited some more. Francesca had spent so long in it she'd used all the hot water.

He shook his head as he realised it had likely been deliberate.

'How was your shower?' she asked innocently when he returned to the cabin.

'Cold.'

Her lips twitched but she didn't look up from her laptop.

'After eight years in the forces where bathing of any kind was rare, any shower's a good one,' he said drily. 'But that's irrelevant to the job in hand so tell me what the game plan is.'

'You're not going to tell me what it is now you're in charge?' She didn't attempt to hide her bitterness.

'It's still your project. I'm in charge of your safety. If you're prepared to accept my authority with that, I'm happy to follow your lead.' He wanted this project to succeed as much as she did and knew the best way to stop her doing anything rash was to let her think she had some control. 'You have a meeting with the Governor of San Pedro in four hours. What are you hoping to achieve?'

Looking slightly mollified, she said, 'His agreement for the sale of the land that Pieta earmarked.'

'That's it?'

'The Governor is married to the Caballeron President's sister and given the job directly from the President himself. If he agrees there's no one left to object and I can start organising everything properly.'

'And if he refuses?'

She grimaced. 'I don't want to think about that.'

'You don't have a contingency plan?'

She closed the lid of her laptop. 'I'll think of something if it comes to it.'

'Why didn't Alberto come with you? He's got plenty of experience with this.' He watched her reaction closely.

Alberto had been Pieta's right-hand man for his foundation. The pair had always travelled together, Alberto doing much of the legwork to get things moving. He knew his way around countries hit by natural disasters better than anyone and how to schmooze the people running them.

'He's taken leave,' she said with a shrug. 'You should have seen him at the funeral, he could barely stand. He's given me all the foundation's files but he's not capable of working right now.'

'Yet here you are, Pieta's sister, travelling to one of the most dangerous countries in the world only a day after you buried him, continuing his good work.'

Her jaw clenched and she closed her eyes, inhaling slowly. Then she nodded and met his gaze. The redness that had been such a feature of her eyes when she'd boarded the plane had gone, along with the puffiness surrounding them, but there was a bleakness in its place that was almost as hard to look at.

When she replied her voice was low but with an edge of steel. 'This project—doing it in Pieta's memory—is the only thing stopping me from falling apart.'

She had courage, he would give her that. He just hoped she had the strength to see the next five days through.

Francesca hardly had time to appreciate the beauty of Aguadilla before they stepped into the waiting Cessna. All she had time to note from the short car ride from Aguadilla International Airport to the significantly smaller airfield four miles away was the bluest sky she'd ever seen, the clearest sea and lots of greenery.

There were three men including the pilot waiting in the Cessna for them. Felipe shook hands with them all and threw their names at her while she nodded a greeting and tried to convince herself that the sick feeling in her belly wasn't fear that in twenty minutes they'd be landing in Caballeros.

'Are you okay?' Felipe asked once they were strapped in.

She jerked a nod. 'I'm good.'

'Is this your first visit to Caballeros?' the man who'd been introduced as James asked in a broad Australian accent.

She nodded again.

He grinned. 'Then I suggest you make the most of the beautiful Aguadillan scenery because where we're going is a dump.'

She gave a bark of laughter at the unexpected comment.

'Do these men all work for you?' she asked Felipe in an undertone when they were in the air.

'Yes. I've three more men posted around the governor's residence. All my employees are ex-special forces. James and Seb have both been posted here before. You couldn't be in better hands.'

'You managed all this in one night?' That was seriously impressive.

His dark brown eyes found hers. The strangest swooping sensation formed in her belly.

'While we're in Caballeros you're in my care and under my protection. I take that seriously.'

His words made her veins warm.

Francesca took a breath and turned away to stare out of the small window. When she put a hand to her neck she was further disconcerted to find her pulse beating strongly, and closed her eyes in an attempt to temper it.

During their last hour on Pieta's jet when she'd been working on her laptop, she hadn't been able to resist doing some research on Felipe's company. She supposed she should have done it before, when Daniele and Matteo had insisted Felipe's men be employed to protect her, but the thought hadn't occurred to her then.

What she'd learned had astounded her.

Matteo had said Felipe had earned a fortune from his business but she hadn't realised how vast his enterprise actually was. In one decade he'd built a company that spanned the globe, employing hundreds of ex-military personnel from dozens of nationalities. The company's assets were as startling, with jets of all shapes and sizes ready to be deployed at a moment's notice, and communications equipment reputed to be so effective the military from Europe to the US now purchased it for their own soldiers.

She could laugh to think of the macho meathead she'd imagined him to be. Felipe Lorenzi owned a business worth billions, and had the arrogance to prove it.

He'd struck up conversation with his colleagues who were seated in front of them. Their words went over her head. Her eyes drifted back to him.

He really was heavenly to look at. The more she looked, the more she wanted to look.

Coming from a wealthy family of her own, she'd met and mixed with plenty of wealthy, handsome men in her time, but none like him, none who carried strength and danger like a second skin.

As he gave a low rumble of laughter at some wisecrack of James's—shocking in itself as she hadn't thought he *could* laugh—she found herself admiring the size of his biceps beneath the expensive fabric of his suit jacket.

Her gaze drifted lower, to the muscular thighs. They had to be at least twice the size of her own...

As if he could sense her attention on him, Felipe turned to look at her and in that moment, in that look, all the breath left her lungs and her mouth ran dry. Fresh heat flushed through her.

It was like being trapped. She couldn't tear her eyes

away from the dark gaze before he gave a sharp blink and turned his focus back to his colleagues.

Francesca let out a slow, ragged breath and pressed her hand to her wildly beating heart.

Never mind being ruggedly handsome, Felipe Lorenzi was the sexiest man she'd ever laid eyes on.

What a shame he was also the most horrid.

Felipe had never thought he'd be pleased to land in Caballeros but as the Cessna touched down he sent a silent prayer of thanks.

He'd been busy chatting with James and Seb, the usual repartee, nothing important that couldn't be said in front of an outsider, when he'd suddenly become intensely aware *of* the outsider. It had happened so quickly it had taken him unawares, a thickening in his loins, an electricity over his skin, a lazy wonder of how her lips would feel beneath his, of what she would taste like...

Then, just as quickly, he'd pushed the awareness away and focussed his mind as he'd spent almost two decades doing, dispelling anything that wasn't central to the job at hand. An attraction to Francesca Pellegrini went straight into that category. Not central. Not even on the fringe. It couldn't be.

It was no big deal. He'd dealt with unwanted attraction before without any problems. It really was a case of just focussing the mind on what was important and the only thing of importance was her safety.

But there had been something in the look she'd returned that made him think the attraction could be a two-way thing. He could handle it.

Francesca Pellegrini was off limits as a matter of course. Never mind his no-sex-with-the-clients stipulation with his employees—and if he were to enforce a rule then fair play meant he had to stick to those rules himself on the occasions he went out in the field—but she was grieving for her brother. He'd seen hardened men lose their minds with grief. *He'd* almost lost his mind with it once, the pain excruciating enough to know he never wanted to go through anything like it again. And he never would.

He'd spent his childhood effectively alone and where once he had yearned to escape the solitude, now he welcomed it. All his relationships, from the men he employed to the women he dated, were conducted at arm's length.

'Ready, boss?' Seb asked, his hand on the door.

Like much of the island, Caballeros' main airport had been badly damaged. Pellegrini money and Felipe's own greasing of the wheels had ensured a safe strip for them to land on. Looking over Francesca's shoulder to stare out of the window he could see for himself the extent of the damage. The terminal roof had been ripped off, windows shattered, piles of debris as far as the eye could see. Feet away from them lay a Boeing 737 on its side.

'Are you ready?' he asked Francesca quietly. She was staring frozenly out of the window, taking in the horror. 'We can always rearrange the meeting.'

She lifted her shoulders and tilted her neck. 'I'm not rearranging anything. Let's go.'

# CHAPTER THREE

THE DRIVER OF the waiting car, another of Felipe's men, Francesca guessed, drove them carefully over roads thick with mud and so full of potholes she knew the damage had been pre-hurricane. Seb travelled with them, James staying in the Cessna with the pilot.

The Governor's residence was to the north of the island, far from the city he ran, an area relatively unscathed by the hurricane. To reach it, though, meant travelling through San Pedro, the island's capital, which along with the rest of the southern cities and towns had taken the brunt of the storm. She shivered to think this was the city she'd planned to stay in during her trip here.

They drove through towns that were only recognisable as such by the stacks of splintered wood and metal that had weeks before been the basis for people's homes. Tarpaulin and holey blankets were raised for shelter to replace them. People crowded everywhere, old and young, naked children, shoeless pregnant women, people with obvious injuries but only makeshift bandages covering their wounds. Most stared at the passing car with dazed eyes; some had the energy to try to approach it, a few threw things at them.

At the first bottle to hit their car, Francesca ducked into her seat.

'Don't worry,' Felipe said. 'It's bulletproof glass. Nothing can damage it.'

'Where's all the aid?' she asked in bewilderment. 'All the aid agencies that are supposed to be here?'

'They're concentrated to the south of the island. We just landed in the main airport and you saw the state of that. The other one is worse. They're having to bring the aid in by ship. The neighbouring islands have done their best to help but they're limited with what they can do as the hurricane struck so many of them too and the government isn't helping as it should. That airport should be cleared. There's much it should be doing but nothing's happening. It's a joke.'

By the time they arrived at the Governor's compound Francesca was more determined than ever to get the hospital built, not just for her brother's memory but for the poor people suffering from both the hurricane and its government's incompetence in clearing up after it. She felt she could burst with determination.

The Governor's residence was a sprawling white Spanish-style villa that made her hate him before she'd even laid eyes on him. There were armed guards everywhere protecting it, men who should be out on the streets clearing up the devastation.

As if reading her dark thoughts, Felipe stared at her until he had her attention.

His eyes were hard. 'Keep your personal feelings for the Governor to yourself. You must show him respect or he will kick you out and never admit you again.'

'How do I show respect to a man I already loathe?'

He shrugged. 'You're the one who wants to play the politician's role. Fake it. You've read Alberto's reports on Pieta's old projects. Think what your brother would do and do that. You're playing with the big boys now, Francesca. Or do I take you home?'

'No,' she rejected out of hand. 'I can do this.'

'You can fake respect?'

'I will do whatever is needed.'

Breathing deeply, Francesca got out of the car and walked up the long marble steps to the front door with Felipe at her side, leaving Seb and the driver in the car.

'Is there something wrong with your leg?' she asked, noticing a slight limp.

'Nothing serious,' he dismissed, his attention on their surroundings. She had a feeling nothing escaped his scrutiny.

After being frisked and scanned with metal detectors, they were led into a large white reception room filled with huge vases of white flowers and lined with marble statues, and told to wait.

The sofa in the reception room was so pristinely white that Francesca wiped the back of her skirt before sitting.

When they were alone, she said in an undertone, 'If this is the Governor's home I dread to think how pretentious the President's is.'

'Be careful.' Felipe leaned close to speak into her ear. 'There are cameras everywhere recording everything we do and say.'

She didn't know what unnerved her the most: knowing they were being spied on or Felipe's breath warm against her ear. She caught his scent, which was as warm as his breath, an expensive spicy smell that filled her mouth with moisture and had her sitting rigidly beside him to stop herself leaning into him so she could sniff him properly.

Clasping her hands together, she focussed on a painting of a gleaming yacht on the wall opposite.

She could not let her body's reactions to Felipe distract her from the job in hand. She'd spent her adult life rebuffing male advances. She'd turned down plenty of good-looking undergraduates at university, always with an appeasing smile and zero regret.

She hadn't wanted the distraction of a romance—not that romance itself played much of a part in a student's life—when she was determined to graduate with top honours. Sex and romance could wait until she was established in her career.

She sneaked a glance at the hands resting on the muscular lap beside hers. Like the rest of him they were big, the fingers long and calloused, the nails functionally short, nothing like the manicured digits the men at Pieta's law firm sported. Felipe was all man. You only had to look at him to know a woman's body was imprinted like a map in his memories.

A tall, lithe woman impeccably dressed in a white designer suit entered the room. The Governor was ready for them.

Pulling herself together, Francesca got to her feet, smoothed her jacket with hands that had suddenly gone clammy and picked up her laptop bag.

Her heart beat frantically, excitement and nerves fighting in her belly.

She could do this. She *would* do this. She would get the Governor's agreement for the sale of the land. She would make Pieta proud and, in doing so, obtain his forgiveness.

Felipe felt undressed without his gun, which he'd left in the car with Seb. He didn't expect any trouble in the Governor's own home but could see the bulges in the suits of the guards who lined the walls of the ostentatious dining room they were taken to.

The Governor himself sat at the dining table alone, eating an orange that had been cut into segments for him. The tall woman who'd brought them in arranged herself a foot behind him.

He didn't rise for his guests but gestured for them to sit.

Felipe hadn't expected to like the man but neither had he expected the instant dislike that flashed through him.

'My condolences about your brother,' the Governor said in Spanish, addressing Francesca's breasts. 'I hear he was a great man.'

From the panicked look Francesca shot at him, Felipe

guessed she didn't speak his native tongue. Without missing a beat, he made the translation.

'Thank you,' she replied, smiling at the Governor as if having a lecherous sixty-year-old ogle her whilst speaking of her dead brother was perfectly acceptable. 'Do you speak Italian or English?'

'No,' he replied in English, before switching back to Spanish to address Felipe. 'You are her bodyguard?'

'I'm here as Miss Pellegrini's translator and advisor,' he answered smoothly, avoiding giving a direct lie.

The Governor put a large segment of orange in his mouth. 'I understand she wants to build a hospital in my city.'

Felipe smothered his distaste at being spoken to by someone chewing food. 'She does, yes. I believe her brother had already been in contact with your office about the land it could be built on.'

He sensed Francesca's agitation at being cut out of her own meeting. She had the air of a pet straining at its leash. He shot her a warning look. *Calm down.*

Another segment went into the wide mouth, the gaze fixing back on Francesca's breasts as if he were trying to see through the respectable clothing she wore. From the gleam in his beady eyes he was mentally undressing her. From the angry colour staining her face she knew it too but the quick look she threw at him told him to say nothing.

'Two hundred thousand dollars.'

'Is that for the land?'

The mouth still full of orange smiled. 'That is for me. The land itself is another two hundred thousand. All in cash.'

Felipe stared hard at Francesca as he made the translation, sending another warning to her with his eyes. He would have spoken his warnings but was damn sure the Governor spoke perfect English.

To his incredulity she agreed without a second's thought or consideration.

'Done.'

'The hospital is to have my name.'

Here she hesitated. Felipe knew why—she wanted to name it after her brother.

The Governor saw the hesitation. 'Either it has my name or permission is denied.'

Felipe translated again, adopting a harder edge to his voice in the vain hope she would pick up on it, slow down and negotiate properly.

But she was too keen to get the agreement made to see the danger she was walking into.

'Tell the Governor we will be honoured to name it after him,' she said in a tone so grateful Felipe braced himself for the Governor to pick up on it and demand even more from her.

A full mouth of pristine white teeth beamed. 'Then it is a deal. I am having a party here next Saturday.' That was a full week away. 'Bring her to it. I'll have the documents ready for you. Tell her to bring the cash.' He snapped his fingers and the tall woman stepped forward. 'Escort my guests back to their car. They're leaving.'

As they stood, Francesca, full of smiles, said, 'Please give my thanks to the Governor for his co-operation.'

She virtually skipped with joy out of the villa.

Only when they were safely in the back of the car and out of the compound did Felipe turn on her.

'What are you playing at?' he demanded. 'Where was the negotiation? And what were you thinking agreeing to pay a bribe?'

The smile on her face fell. 'What's it to you?'

'You've agreed to pay a cash bribe. You've agreed to bring in four hundred thousand dollars into the Caribbean's poorest country. Can't you see what's wrong with that? Can't you see the danger?'

'I've done what needed to be done,' she said defiantly. 'Thank you for making the translations, but you're being paid to protect me and advise on my security. If I want your input with anything else, I'll let you know.'

This was exactly what Daniele and Matteo had warned him about. Francesca was so determined to get the hospital built in Pieta's memory that she was a danger to herself.

Francesca didn't understand why Felipe was being so negative. The meeting had gone a hundred times better than she'd expected. She'd expected to be drilled for hours about the hospital itself, its capabilities and the number of people they hoped to be able to treat. She'd made sure to have all the relevant figures and documents ready for him but in the end it had boiled down to one simple thing: money. And Pieta's philanthropic foundation had plenty of it.

Felipe was taking his job as protector too far.

'What about your career?' he ground out. 'Did you think about that? Do you want it ruined before it's even started?'

Excited that they were heading straight to the site the hospital would be built on, his words took a moment to sink in. 'What are you talking about?'

'If word gets out that you paid a bribe to the Governor of San Pedro your career will be over. Lawyers are supposed to be on the side of the law.'

Dear God, that hadn't even occurred to her.

She swayed in her seat as hot dizziness poured into her head. For one dreadful moment she really thought she was going to faint.

In her eagerness to get the site signed over to the foundation, it hadn't crossed her mind that she could be jeopardising her career by paying the Governor's bribe.

'Pieta paid bribes,' she said, more to herself and for her own mitigation.

'No, your brother was always smart enough *not* to pay them and not as openly as you're doing and not verbally with secret cameras recording every word said. He would never have put himself or his foundation in such jeopardy. He acted with discretion and had other people pay any bribe through intermediaries. You should know that.'

'I would if anyone had ever told me. It wasn't in any of the files.' But it wouldn't have been, she realised, her blood running colder still. Alberto had told her to prepare to 'grease the wheels' with the Governor but Alberto had been half crazed with grief and there had been nothing written down and for good reason; who would be stupid enough to leave a paper trail advertising law-breaking, even if for good reasons and intentions? 'Why didn't *you* tell me seeing as you know so much?'

She'd been so proud and relieved to have got the Governor's agreement that she'd been oblivious to anything else.

'I assumed you did know. I could hardly tell you in the middle of the meeting—'

'We're being followed.' It was Seb's voice that cut through their angry exchange.

Felipe turned to look out of the back window.

'Black Mondeo.'

'I see it.'

Felipe's left hand gripped Francesca's shoulder, preventing her from turning to look too.

'Keep down,' he said tautly.

'But…'

A silver gun appeared in his right hand.

'What do you need *that* for?' she virtually screeched.

'Someone's following us.'

'How do you know that?' she asked, her eyes on his gun. 'They might just be travelling the same route as us.'

His eyes were hard. 'It's my job to know and if I don't know then I don't take risks. Now hold on.'

The hand that had been holding her shoulder moved so his arm covered her chest like an additional seat belt. A second later she learned why when Seb put his foot down.

She only just held back a scream when she found them suddenly hurtling along the bumpy roads. Caballeros passed by in a blur, the roads narrowing and deteriorating the further south they travelled.

When they missed hitting an oncoming truck by inches, she squeezed her eyes shut and clung to Felipe's arm and didn't let go until with a squeal of brakes the car came to a stop.

'You can look now, we're at the airport,' Felipe said, his voice tight. 'We've lost them.'

She let go and was pleased to see him wince as he shook the arm she'd been holding with the grip of a boa constrictor. The gun was still nestled comfortably in his right hand.

'On what planet is travelling at a hundred miles an hour over potholed narrow roads keeping me safe?' she demanded, all the contained fear spewing out in one swoop. 'We could have been killed!'

Her door opened and James stood there, a big grin on his face. 'That looked like some ride.'

'Your colleague's a maniac.'

'Who? Seb? Don't worry about him, he's done an advanced motoring course.'

'Shut up, James,' Felipe bit out, then to Francesca said, 'I'm sorry if we scared you but I did warn you of the dangers.'

'You warned me of kidnap and robbery. You said nothing about a car ride turning into the rollercoaster ride from hell. You said nothing about being *armed*.'

'Would you have preferred we let them catch us? Should I have asked them nicely why they were following us and what they wanted? Should I arm myself with a feather duster to protect you?'

'Well…no…'

'Then let's get in the plane before they find us and tell us in person what they want.'

'We're supposed to be going to the hospital site.'

'That can wait.'

'But…'

The look on his face stopped her arguing further. It was a look that spoke plainly. If she didn't get out of the car and onto the plane *right now* he would carry her to it.

The adrenaline racing through her peaked to imagine what it would be like carried in his arms…

*Humiliating, that's what it would be, carted off like a recalcitrant child.*

Jutting her chin in the air, she twisted round and got out, snubbing James's offered hand.

'I don't know why you're ignoring me, I wasn't in the car,' he complained.

She couldn't help but smile weakly at his boyish charm even though he too had a gun in his hand. 'Shut up, James.'

'Yes, shut up, James,' Felipe muttered as he followed her, scrutinising their surroundings, his hand on her back, ready to throw himself on her should anything happen.

His heart still pounded from the adrenaline surge of the race back to the airport and he was as angry about that as he was about Francesca's idiocy. Adrenaline was part of the job—for most of them it *was* the job—but not like that.

Only when they were airborne did he put the gun back in his inside jacket pocket.

He'd seen Francesca's fear when he'd produced it.

Good.

Fear could be a useful tool provided one knew how to control it. She had controlled her fear well enough, he admitted grudgingly, but she had to learn her safety wasn't a game. There would be no compromises in that regard.

He closed his eyes and breathed welcome oxygen into his lungs.

He hadn't experience a charge like that since the hostage situation a decade ago that had ended in such destruction and his own medical discharge from the forces.

When they landed back in the safety of Aguadilla, Francesca found she could breathe again. Caballeros had frightened her more than she wanted to admit. The guns Felipe and his men carried frightened her too; a physical reminder of the danger Daniele and Matteo had been so keen to ram into her but which she had naively thought they were exaggerating.

Felipe took the wheel, taking them through rural byways where coconut sellers lined the road and men sat at tables playing board games. One minute they were driving through what looked like jungle, the next in the open air with the Caribbean Sea gleaming before them, then back into the jungle. Twenty minutes after they left the airport, they pulled up outside a pretty single-storey lodge.

'This looks nice,' she said, attempting a conciliatory tone at the rigid figure driving the car who hadn't exchanged a word with anyone since they'd left the airport.

Now that her adrenaline had settled she could appreciate that a combination of her fear and the awful realisation that she'd screwed up had made her come across as a spoilt brat. Felipe and Seb had done nothing more in the car than they were being paid for—keeping her safe. And Felipe *had* tried to warn her in the meeting, she remembered. But they'd been non-verbal warnings she'd ignored in her determination to seal the deal.

She would have to apologise.

'This is where we're slumming it,' James said, his eyes twinkling.

'Hardly slumming it,' she protested. 'It's charming.'

'Nah, not you. Seb and I have to slum it while you and grumpy here get to live it up in a seven-star paradise up the road. Don't party too hard.'

Both men slammed the doors behind them, leaving her in the back alone with Felipe up front.

He switched the engine back on.

'Hold on, I'll come and sit up front with you,' she said, but found the door wouldn't open. 'Have you turned the child lock on?'

He turned the car round, saying, 'Put your seat belt back on, we'll be there in a few minutes.'

She slumped back and folded her arms, her warmed feelings towards him disappearing in an instant at his arrogant highhandedness.

*'"Put your seat belt back on,"'* she mimicked under her breath. *'"Don't do this, don't do that, just do exactly as I say."'*

He could forget an apology.

Not even the long private driveway dotted with security guards that opened up to reveal their perfectly named Eden Hotel could lift her mood, or the thought of calling Daniele with the good news. When the contracts were signed a week from now he'd fly over and check the site and get the architectural plans, which he'd promised to get started on, finalised.

But she would have to tell him too about her foolishness. He would be rightly furious with her. She was furious with herself.

She followed Felipe out of the car and into the sweet air, and hurried to follow him into the hotel.

And what a hotel it was. Francesca had stayed in many luxury resorts with her family while growing up but nowhere that could compare to this. The Eden Hotel was like a tall, sprawling villa set back from its own private sandy cove, its pristine white fascia covered in all manner of colourful climbing flowers and vines.

It oozed money, a feeling compounded when she stepped into a giant oval atrium with a waterfall as a centrepiece that managed to be both bustling with life yet utterly serene, evoking the sense of calm she so desperately needed. It made the Governor's residence seem like a trifling town hall.

Felipe strolled to the horseshoe-shaped reception desk and used the time spent checking in getting a handle on the turbulence still coursing through him. All he wanted was to get into the privacy of his suite before he said or did something he regretted.

Once they'd been given their respective keys he said, without looking at the woman who'd caused all the turbulence, 'Your luggage has been taken to your suite. I'll meet you in here after breakfast on Monday...'

'*Monday*?'

'None of the officials you want to see will be available tomorrow. Not on a Sunday.'

'But Caballeros is in a state of emergency!'

'Have you made any appointments?'

'Not yet,' she admitted reluctantly. 'I didn't want to get ahead of myself before I got the Governor's agreement. I'm planning to call everyone on my list when I get to my room.'

'They won't see you tomorrow. For all its faults Caballeros is a religious country and Sunday is considered a day of rest so we will meet on Monday.'

'If I can get appointments made for tomorrow then we go back tomorrow.'

'We go back on Monday.' He stared hard at her angry

face. 'You can use tomorrow to do some proper research on what you're dealing with and be fully prepared.'

'Meaning?'

'The contract I signed was to provide you with protection for five days only. The Governor wants his bribe next Saturday, a week from now. If you want my agreement to stay the extra days then you need to stop acting like a brat, meaning you need to slow down and get your head straight before you make any more slip-ups. The deeds to the site aren't yours yet and the way I'm feeling right now I could call your brother and tell him his fears have come true and that you're a danger to yourself and should go home. *Buenas noches.*'

As he strode away, leaving her open-mouthed behind him, knowing perfectly well that only the threat of him calling her brother was stopping her from shouting at him and calling him all the names under the sun, he thought a day of rest would do him good too.

One day in Francesca Pellegrini's company and he was ready to punch walls.

# CHAPTER FOUR

A PORTER SHOWED Francesca to her room, where her luggage was already waiting for her.

She'd assumed she'd be staying in one of the cheap rooms—if a hotel of this magnificence had anything that could be regarded as cheap—but found herself in a ground-floor suite so large, airy and luxurious she could only ogle in wonder.

She'd thought James had been joking about them staying in a seven-star hotel and while she was thrilled to be here in this sun-drenched paradise, she was worried enough to temporarily forget all the ways she'd been imagining inflicting pain on Felipe Lorenzi, the horrible, arrogant, patronising man.

She knew what a blunder she'd made but he acted as if she were the only person to have ever made one.

In one respect he was right. She did need to slow down and get her head straight.

Pulling her phone out of her bag, she called Daniele. This time he answered. He took the good news about the agreement for the site with muted enthusiasm. The only real animation from him came when she asked—nicely—if he would sack Felipe and get another security firm to take over her protection. He laughed. 'I told you that you wouldn't be able to wrap him around your little finger. He stays.' And then he disconnected the call before she could confess about the bribe.

She rubbed her eyes. Maybe it was best to leave it a couple of days before telling him. She didn't think she could handle any more rebukes that day. But Felipe was bound to tell him...

She could scream. What a mess she'd made of things.

Had she really? She'd gone to Caballeros to get the Governor's agreement and had achieved it. The hospital would be built. And she understood the foundation *had* paid bribes in the past. She just needed to speak to Alberto and discuss how it could be done without endangering the foundation. Or her career.

Knowing her emotions were too charged to think clearly enough to make any further calls, she selected a bottle of white wine from the fully stocked bar, poured herself a large glass and took it into the bathroom so she could have a long soak in the enormous jetted bath.

It was too late to change hotels now. She might as well enjoy it for tonight and see about getting them moved to a cheaper hotel in the morning.

But instead of relaxing like she so wanted, her mind refused to switch off. Everywhere she looked, from the gold taps to the marble flooring, increased her worry. This hotel was too much.

With a sigh, she got out and dried herself, dressed quickly and put a call through to reception.

'Can you tell me what room Felipe Lorenzi's staying in, please?' she asked. 'We're under the same booking but I can't remember his number.' She crossed her fingers as she gave the little fib.

When the number was relayed she gave a little start. 'Room fourteen?' she confirmed.

That was right next to hers.

Her heart hammering for no reason at all, Francesca decided to just go for it and slipped out of her room to knock on the one next door.

He answered on the second knock, opening the door a crack. 'Is there a problem?'

'Can I come in for a minute?' she asked, matching his

frosty tone. All she could see of him was the shadow of his face.

He paused before answering. 'I'm about to take a shower.'

'I want to change hotels.'

'Why?'

'A hotel like this is expensive.'

'The cost of the hotel does not concern you.'

'It does. People work hard to raise funds for Pieta's foundation and give generously to it.'

'Do they give generously to pay bribes?'

'That's a necessity,' she protested. 'I know I went about it in the wrong way but you know as well as I that we wouldn't get permission to build the hospital without it. It isn't right to waste the funds on something as frivolous as a luxury hotel. Somewhere like where James and Seb are staying would be far more appropriate.'

The little of his face she could see darkened and when he replied it was in clipped tones. 'The foundation isn't paying.'

That alarmed her. 'Then who is? I can't afford it on my salary and I can't—'

'You're not paying either,' he cut in impatiently.

'Who *is* footing it?' It came to her in an instant. 'Daniele! He loves flashing his money and—'

'Was there anything else you wanted to discuss?' Felipe cut in again, not making any attempt to hide his irritation. 'Only I'm standing here without any clothes on and would like to take my shower, so if you don't mind...'

Francesca was unable to halt the mental image of him naked shooting like a spring lamb into her mind.

*Oh, dear heavens...*

*He was naked.*

'Was there anything else?' he repeated curtly.

*He was naked.*

'No.'

'Then I'll see you on Monday.'

Francesca stood before his closed door for a long time, her hand at her throat, her pulse beating like a humming-bird's wings beneath her fingers.

Felipe shaved his neck and trimmed his beard for the first time in three weeks.

It was guilt, he knew, that made his concentration waver enough for him to nick himself with the razor.

Guilt had been rising in him since he'd dismissed Francesca from the door of his suite.

He'd never had such problems with a client before and he'd had many clients and jobs that had been a hundred times harder to manage than Francesca and this partic-ular job. His last job in the forces had been a thousand times harder.

No, this was *him*. Like it or not, he damned well was attracted to her and somehow he had to find a way to man-age it without letting it affect their working relationship. It already was affecting it. Affecting him.

He expected his clients to obey him and his men without question. It was in the terms of any contract. Clients signed it knowing their lives were being placed in his hands. His clients, though, were, on the whole, heads of international organisations and other VIPs, the only common denomi-nator between them being that they were travelling some-where dangerous.

He had drilled it into his men that they were only em-ployed for protection. They were not advisors or aides. Their client's business was not theirs.

The risks Francesca was taking by agreeing to pay the bribe were none of his concern and she was correct that Pieta himself had paid them, although with far more dis-cretion than she'd employed. Felipe had turned a blind eye to much worse before and had no doubt he would turn a blind eye to much worse in the future.

He couldn't fathom why it angered him so much to see her taking the kind of risks that had never concerned him from anyone else.

She'd turned up at his door while he'd been buck naked, her long hair damp, her beautiful face free from make-up, a long blue summer dress on with her pretty toes peeking out at the bottom and a hint of cleavage showing...

He'd become aroused just looking at her. He'd had to grip the door handle with one hand and press the wall tightly with the other to stop himself pulling her into his room and throwing her onto the bed.

This had only fired the anger already coursing through him.

After he'd closed the door he'd stood there for too long, not moving, just trying to quell his arousal, trying to ignore that her suite was adjacent to his.

A day off from her would be a blessing, especially as their time together had been extended to a whole week. He had to remember she was grieving and that grief made people act in wayward ways. She needed his help and support, not his condemnation and anger.

But God alone knew how he was going to cope with a week of her company without either throttling her or bedding her.

The early morning was so bright that one peek through the curtains lifted a little of the despondency in Francesca's heart. The hotel's ground staff were already up and about, weeding and watering the abundant blooming flowers, hosing the pathways, many yawning.

She yawned in sympathy but didn't consider going back to bed. More sleep was the last thing she wanted. Sleep brought dreams and the ones she'd had during the night were still horribly vivid. Pieta had been sitting at the small kitchen table in her apartment in Pisa. She'd made him a coffee and laughed as she'd told him she'd thought he'd died. He'd laughed too and said it had been a misunderstanding. And then he'd stopped laughing and said he knew the truth about how she'd reacted when told he'd died.

She'd awoken muttering into her sopping wet pillow that she was sorry, sorry, sorry, over and over.

For some reason Felipe had been in the background of those dreams too.

She wiped fresh tears away with the palm of her hand.

She needed to get a grip on herself and get her head back to where it had been before she'd fallen asleep with her face buried in the thick file Alberto had given her before she'd left Pisa. She'd sat on the huge bed to re-read it, determined that from now on all her actions would be above board. She would be prepared for any situation that came her way. She would not do anything else that could jeopardise her career or Pieta's foundation.

After dressing she made her way to the main hotel restaurant, where she was the first to be seated for breakfast. She didn't want to be on her own. She'd ordered room service the night before and stayed in her suite. Now she craved company.

There was no company to be found here, though. All the other guests were still sleeping. Even if they'd been up she would still have been alone. This wasn't a hotel for the solo traveller.

There was one other solo traveller staying here too, she reminded herself glumly, but he didn't want her company. He didn't even like her, that much was patently obvious.

And she didn't like him. The less she had to do with Felipe Lorenzi the happier she'd be and today she didn't have to deal with him at all.

She managed to avoid him until early afternoon.

She'd returned to her suite to start calling the names of the officials she'd need to meet for the hospital development. Half the numbers were either wrong or their phone lines had been disconnected by the hurricane. The others were, as Felipe had predicted, taking a day of rest and had no wish to speak to her, telling her to call back tomorrow. Only the Blue Train Aid Agency, the only aid agency to be up and running in Caballeros, had been available to talk. The worker she spoke to, Eva Bergen, had been full of enthusiasm for the project and readily agreed to meet her the next day. Eva's experience in the country would be tremendously useful and Francesca ended the call feeling much better about everything. So much better that she decided to buy a swimsuit from one of the hotel's exclusive boutiques and go for a swim.

There were four pools to choose from. Opting for the huge rectangular one, she swam a few laps then settled on a sun lounger with her book, shades on to keep the glare of the sun from her eyes.

But she couldn't settle. The words on the page blurred into a mass as she found her thoughts constantly drifting, not to the forthcoming week and everything it entailed but to her protector. In truth he'd been in her thoughts constantly.

She was glad of the book, though, when she spotted the tall figure in the tight black swim-shorts walk to the other side of the pool to where she lay, a towel slung over his shoulder.

If she wasn't already on hyper-alert to any sign of him she would still have noticed him. She doubted there was a woman poolside whose eye he didn't catch, young and old alike.

Quickly she raised her book so it covered her face, hoping it was enough to hide her.

*Please don't let him see her.*

The next time she faced him she wanted to be fully dressed and feeling confident in herself, not wearing a two-piece swimsuit that would put her at a further disadvantage.

Like it or not, she was stuck with him for the coming week and had no idea how she was going to get through it without slapping his arrogant, handsome face.

Pretending to be engrossed in her novel, she couldn't resist a surreptitious glance and found him at the edge of the pool, testing the temperature of the water with his toes.

Even with the distance between them his muscular beauty made her breath catch in her throat. All thoughts of hiding disappeared as she drank in the magnificence Felipe's clothing had only hinted at.

His darkly tanned skin gleamed under the bright afternoon sun, his chest broad and muscular, a light smattering of hair across the pecs thickening the lower they went over an abdomen she just *knew* would be hard to the touch.

With a grace that belied his size and muscularity, he dived in.

She heard the distinct sound of a woman sucking in a breath. It took a few beats to realise the sound had come from her.

His arms powered him to the far side then he rolled in the water and swam fluidly back.

Back and forth he went, streaking through the pool as if he'd been born to water, born to swim.

She couldn't tear her eyes from him. It was as if she'd been hypnotised.

She lost count of how many laps he swam before hauling himself out.

The ache that had steadily formed while she'd watched turned into a throb to see water drip from his body and she almost forgot she was trying to hide from him.

Shoving her book back over her face, she closed her

eyes and took some long breaths in an attempt to get her heart rate back to one that didn't make her fear it would beat out of her chest.

Only when she opened her eyes again did she notice she was holding her book upside down. When she next peeked over it, Felipe had gone.

Fifty laps of the swimming pool and Felipe still felt wired.

Eight years in the forces had taught him to snatch sleep wherever he could. He'd slept without any problem leaning against jagged rocks, under prickly shrubs, in trenches of mud, with gun fire ringing in the distance, yet put him in a four-poster bed in a sweet-scented suite for a power nap and sleep remained stubborn. It had been stubborn all night.

It was that damned woman in the suite next door who was the cause of it.

He'd spent the morning working out tactics for the next few days, sending his plans over to James and Seb and his men situated on Caballeros.

He would feel better if he knew what those men who'd followed them had wanted but they'd proved harder to find than sleep.

Two more of his men were, at that moment, en route to Caballeros. When he returned there with Francesca in the morning there would be eyes and ears everywhere, keeping watch. Keeping her safe.

Felipe rubbed his eyes, sighed and swung his legs off the bed.

The guilt at his anger towards her had grown and his self-chastisement with it.

Control and discipline were the two most important elements needed for his job. He'd learned both in the forces and had carried it through to his business. He demanded the men he employed have the same qualities. When danger was rife, keeping a cool head was a necessity even when, as he'd learned to his bitter cost, it wasn't always enough.

He'd lost that cool head with Francesca.

He'd overstepped the mark. He would have to apologise. That had been his intention before he'd left his suite for a swim. He would do his fifty laps then seek her out and apologise.

She'd been at the poolside. He'd seen her the moment he'd stepped onto the tiles surrounding the pool, spotting her as she pulled a book over her face, pretending not to have seen him.

He'd swum his lengths with more vigour than usual, pounding the water as if the strokes could sweep away the image of Francesca on a recliner wearing nothing but a tiny pale yellow bikini.

*Dios*, she had curves that could make a man weep.

He'd sensed her watching his every stroke.

When he'd finished, he hadn't been able to resist another look while he'd dried himself. She'd been holding her book over her face again.

With the tell-tale tingles of arousal curling through his loins, he'd beaten a hasty retreat back to his suite and taken a cool shower.

Apologising could wait.

He couldn't entertain the thought of knocking on her suite door. That would be putting temptation in his path when he needed to divert around it.

It was standard practice to sleep in the adjacent room to the client. He'd arranged with the hotel manager to beef up the hotel's already tight security, the memory of the black Mondeo that had followed them hovering in the background of his mind a constant presence. Here, in this hotel, Francesca was safe. But not safe enough for him to contemplate changing suites to one on the other side of the complex, even though his every sinew strained to run.

Not wanting to be stuck with his own morose company and already bored with room service, he donned a pair of smart black chinos and a grey shirt, and decided to check out one of the hotel's many restaurants.

There were half a dozen eateries to choose from. The only one that appealed was the Mediterranean Restaurant and Bar, which seemed the most informal of them and promised live music.

If he could have chosen anywhere he would have found an American diner and eaten the largest burger on the menu but he didn't want to drive. He wanted to surround himself with people, eat and then sleep.

The restaurant was busy. A bar covered one wall while a small stage and dance area was set up on the wall opposite.

A waiter led him to an available table and as they went through the room Felipe spotted a lone figure sitting at a table tucked away in the corner, reading a menu.

His heart managed to sink and leap at the same moment, and in that same moment Francesca gazed absently around the room and found him. There was one quick blink before she put her head back down.

He rubbed the back of his neck. At the pool it had been easy for them both to pretend they hadn't see each other but now there was no avoiding her.

# CHAPTER FIVE

'DO YOU WANT some company?' Felipe asked when he reached her. She wore a pretty floral dress with tiny straps. He caught a glimpse of thigh.

Francesca eyed him warily then gave a small nod.

He took the chair the waiter held out for him and sat down, noting the tall multi-coloured cocktail glass with an umbrella and straw in it. 'What are you drinking?'

'Tequila Sunrise. Do you want one?'

'I'll stick to beer. Have you ordered?'

'I'm still making my mind up.'

The waiter scuttled off to get Felipe's beer.

Opening his menu, he watched Francesca studiously read hers, her teeth gnawing at her bottom lip.

'Have you had a good day?' he asked conversationally.

She shrugged but didn't look at him, reaching for her drink with a hand that shook. 'I've had worse.' She took a long drink through the straw.

'This isn't an easy time for you,' he observed, knowing it to be an understatement. She'd buried her brother only a few days before.

Her shoulders rose in another shrug and to his horror he watched her blink frantically in an attempt to hold back glistening tears.

She yanked her napkin and dabbed at her eyes, laughing morosely. 'Look, Felipe, you don't have to eat with me. I know you're just being polite. If you want to find another table, I won't care.'

'No.' Feeling like a complete ass, he ran his fingers through his hair and stared at her until she met his gaze. 'I'm sorry for the way I spoke to you.'

That surprised her. She took another drink of her cocktail, the light of the candle flickering off her eyes.

Eventually she said in a small voice, 'Have you spoken to Daniele about what happened yesterday with the Governor?'

'No.' He'd thought long and hard about it but had come to the conclusion that while she'd acted rashly, his condemnation had been too harsh. Francesca had been appalled when he'd pointed out the danger she'd put her career and the foundation in but it seemed she was far angrier with herself than he could be. She deserved the chance to see it through.

She closed her eyes. 'Thank you. I think I was overwrought yesterday. It's not an excuse but I've not been sleeping well since Pieta died and all that's been keeping me going is the thought of getting this hospital built. I promise I'll be considered in my approach from now on.'

'Why don't we draw a line through yesterday?' he suggested gently. 'Forget any cross words and start again?'

'I would like that,' she whispered. Reaching again for her napkin, she dabbed some more at her eyes then rolled her neck, took a deep breath, straightened and flashed him a smile that made his heart turn over. 'What are you going to eat? Seeing as Daniele's footing the bill, I'm going to select the most expensive items on the menu.'

Before he could correct her assumption, as he should have done the day before, she said, 'Have you met him?'

'Daniele?'

She nodded.

'I met him a few years ago in Paris with his girlfriend. Pieta introduced us.'

The bleak veil cloaking her since he'd joined her lifted in its entirety.

'Girlfriend? Daniele?' She leant forward, eyes alight.

'He's never had a girlfriend. Lots of scandalous flings, though.'

He shrugged. 'She was with him. I assumed she was his girlfriend. They acted like a couple.'

'Daniele with a girlfriend? That's amazing. Pieta knew they were together?'

'I assumed so.'

The waiter returned with Felipe's beer so they ordered their food and Francesca quickly finished her cocktail and ordered another.

'What were you all doing in Paris?' she asked when they were alone again.

'Attending a party at the US Embassy.'

'What did you think of Daniele?'

'Very different from Pieta.' He looked at her shrewdly. 'I would say you're more like him.'

'More like Daniele?'

'Pieta was intense and thoughtful.' At her darkening colour he added, 'You've an energy about you. You're impulsive and, I think, competitive. Daniele struck me as the same.'

She nodded slowly, her pupils moving fast as she thought. 'Yes. Daniele's highly competitive. He has to be first with everything and he *hates* losing.'

'And you? Am I right that you're also competitive?'

She grinned. 'I grew up wanting to be better than my brothers in everything.'

'Have you ever beaten them?'

'My aim throughout my education was to smash all their exam results.' She gave a mischievous smile. 'Which I achieved. It was very fulfilling. I even skipped a year. I like to tell people I'm the clever one of the family.'

Not so clever when it came to negotiating and agreeing bribes, he thought but didn't say. For the first time since they'd met they'd found relative harmony and he wasn't ready to break it.

'But when it comes to true competitiveness, Daniele's worse,' she continued. 'He's ferocious.'

'Has he always been like that?'

'As long as I've been alive. He grew up knowing the family wealth would pass on to Pieta—'

'*Only* to Pieta?'

'The oldest inherits the estate. It's always been like that, for centuries. Pieta inherited when our father died.'

'What about your mother?'

'She has rights to the income during her lifetime but the physical assets transferred directly to Pieta.'

'Will it go to Daniele now?'

'Everything that's family wealth will so long as Natasha isn't pregnant.'

'Do you think she could be?'

'I don't know and none of us can bear to ask her. It would be cruel. We'll have to wait and see.'

'So if she is pregnant…?'

'Then we have the first in the next generation of Pellegrinis.' A sad smile played on her lips. 'If it's a boy he will inherit, if it's a girl then Daniele will inherit.'

'That doesn't sound fair.'

'Natasha will inherit Pieta's personal wealth whether she's pregnant or not. She will have enough to provide for a child and we will all love and cherish it whatever its gender.'

'And what do you get from your family estate?'

'Nothing.'

'That's not right either.'

'Right or not, that's how it is.'

'Doesn't it make you angry?' He didn't know why he was asking. Francesca's personal life was none of his concern.

Her second cocktail was brought to the table and she took it with a grateful smile and immediately sucked half of it up her straw. Done, she put the glass on the table. 'It's not just the wealth that's inherited, it's the responsibility. I was glad not to have it as it meant I could do whatever I wanted with my life without having to consider anyone else and, believe me, the life I've chosen is very different to the one expected for me.'

'In what way?'

She pulled a rueful face. 'I was expected to marry young and have babies, like all the women in my family have done for generations. It isn't supposed to matter that us weak females don't inherit anything because we're supposed to be provided for by our husbands.'

'You didn't want that?'

'I wanted to provide for myself and have a career, like my brothers.' The thought of being a kept woman filled Francesca with horror. Her mother had inherited money but had blithely given it to her husband to invest for her, believing herself too stupid to manage it herself.

She remembered being a small child and her mother casually asking her father for money to buy some new shoes. It had been a nothing incident, her father going straight into his wallet and handing the money over, but it had crystallised in Francesca's mind as the years passed. What if he'd said no? What would her mother have done then? Why should her mother not manage her own money? And why should she, Francesca, not be expected to go out and make a living of her own just because she was born a girl? Why could she not be like her brothers?

'I've no idea how Daniele will handle having the future of the Pellegrini family on his shoulders if it comes to it,' she carried on, shrugging off the old memories. 'He was so competitive with Pieta that he drove himself to make a fortune that was twice what Pieta would have inherited just to show that he could, but was able to live his life as he wanted without the responsibilities Pieta had. If he does inherit he'll have to marry so he'll say goodbye to his freedom too.'

Francesca's chest tightened, all this talk of her family reminding her of her mother stumbling at Pieta's funeral. She'd spoken to her briefly the night before, letting her know she'd arrived in the Caribbean safely. Her mother had been too used to Francesca's stubbornness to try and talk her out of going but had made her swear she wouldn't put herself in any unnecessary danger.

'Forget your brothers, I'm curious about *you*. Do you even have a trust fund?'

'No, but all my education was paid for and I never wanted for anything when I was growing up. That's enough for me. I want to forge my own life.' One where she didn't have to ask for money to buy essentials.

'By following in Pieta's footsteps?' he said with obvious scepticism.

She paused, considering. 'There are—*were*—no better footsteps for me to follow in but don't think I wanted to make myself into his female clone. I saw the good Pieta was doing with his law degree and wanted to do it too.'

'Corporate law?'

She grimaced. 'No. I meant how he used it for the benefit of his philanthropy. Corporate law was a means to an end for him and that's what it is for me while I complete my traineeship.'

'What will you do when you're fully qualified?'

'I'm going to specialise in human rights.' She looked back up at him, straining to stifle the lump pressing in her chest. 'Can we stop talking about me and my family now? Just talk about nonsense? Otherwise I'm going to embarrass both of us by crying.'

A couple of hours later, Francesca's belly was full and her melancholy gone. The quick meal she'd intended to have before retiring to the unwelcome solitude of her suite had extended over three courses.

As time had passed, her animosity towards Felipe had melted, which she thought the handful of cocktails she'd consumed *might* have helped with.

A jazz band was playing on the stage, thankfully uplifting tunes, and there was a buzzing atmosphere she'd enthusiastically embraced. After the trauma of the past week it felt good to be letting her hair down. The gorgeous company helped.

Felipe was proving to be not quite the dictator she'd painted in her mind. But still arrogant, although not in the entitled way most men she'd come across in her life were. Felipe's arrogance came with an authority earned and built over an adulthood of having orders obeyed without question.

His apology had shocked her. She'd never known a man to apologise before, was quite sure the word 'sorry' didn't exist in any of the male Pellegrinis' vocabulary. Or her own, she had to admit.

She thought the more of him for it. A man who could hold his hands up when he was in the wrong without emasculating himself only soared in her estimation.

Francesca knew she could be pig-headed. It wasn't a part of her character she liked and, while in her head she would want to be saying sorry for whatever mishap or argument she'd caused or contributed to, her tongue would stubbornly resist.

Idly she wondered if Felipe's authority extended to the bedroom. What sort of lover would he be? She'd seen hints of fire beneath the calm, authoritative exterior— that fire had been aimed firmly at herself—and imagining those strong hands touching her made her skin tingle. What would it be like to have those intense dark eyes staring into hers in the height of passion…? Her lower belly clenched just to imagine it, the intensity of it shocking her.

She'd never had thoughts like these before.

Once their desserts were cleared away she ordered them Irish coffees.

She laughed at his arched eyebrow. 'It's not that late,' she defended.

'I'm more concerned about your head in the morning.'

She waved a hand airily. 'My head will be fine. I've not drunk that much.'

He fixed her with a stare that made her laugh when it should have quelled her.

'I might have drunk a little more than is good for me but I'm not drunk. And you've had as many as me.'

'I'm twice your size and have a much greater tolerance.'

'You are *huge*,' she agreed, leaning over to put a hand on his bare forearm. 'I bet you work out a lot.'

'Whenever I can.'

The dark hairs resting under her fingers were much finer than she'd expected, his skin smooth and warm.

'Are you married?' she asked impulsively.

'No.' Felipe moved his arm away from her touch and drained the last of his beer.

Her touch had felt too good for comfort.

'Have you ever been married?'

'No.'

'Ever come close to getting married?'

'No.'

'Do you have a girlfriend?'

He sighed. His love life was not a discussion he wanted with Francesca.

He should have gone to bed a long time ago.

'No. There's no room in my life for a relationship.'

'No room in your life? What a strange thing to say.'

Their Irish coffees were laid before them. Francesca

popped two sugar cubes into hers and gave it a vigorous stir.

'That spoils it,' he reproached. 'See? You've mixed the cream into it.'

'I need the sweetness.'

She would taste sweet. His weak-willed imagination that couldn't stop picturing her in that damned bikini was certain of it.

'Why is there no room for you to have a relationship? Do you need a bigger house?'

He almost laughed at the wink she finished her question with. As the evening had progressed she'd relaxed, her antagonism towards him now but a memory. Francesca had proven to be fun company, far removed from the spoilt brat he'd assumed her to be.

He had to keep reminding himself that she was his client—a grieving, vulnerable client—and that he needed to keep his guard up. This wasn't a date. It wouldn't end with a nightcap in one of their suites followed by...

He refused to allow his mind to wander any further.

'It's my life as a whole. When my job with you is over I'm going back to the Middle East and then on to Russia. I run a business with three hundred employees. It takes a lot of management.'

'Why does that stop you having a relationship?'

'I doubt there's a woman out there who would be happy with a man she went months at a time without seeing and weeks without any communication at all.'

'Natasha and Pieta often went months without seeing each other,' she pointed out. 'It didn't do them any harm and they were together for years.'

*That's what she thought.*

But Felipe wouldn't say anything negative about her brother when his coffin had only just been lowered into the ground. One day the truth he suspected—and he had no proof, only a gut instinct—about her brother would come out as the truth always did. He just hoped she was in the right mental space to cope with it when it did.

'Pieta was a very different man to me and when I disappear it's usually into danger. My business comes first. It has to. My men are deployed to the world's most dangerous hotspots where situations are fluid. Every eventuality has to be catered for. A call can come in at any time for an evacuation.'

'What if something were to go wrong with one of the jobs while you're here dining with me?' she asked reasonably.

He held his phone up. 'This is a satellite phone. It's standard military issue. All my men have one. They allow us to communicate with each other wherever we are in the world and the encryption means no one can hack them.'

'So if one of your clients or men were to get into trouble right now, you'd sort it all out sitting here with me?'

'My headquarters are manned twenty-four seven. There are protocols in place for every eventuality. But if anything untoward *were* to happen I'd be kept informed throughout.' Situations happened all the time. It was the nature of the job. People needed his protection for very good reasons and they hired his firm because they were guaranteed the best. In the ten years since he'd formed the firm, no client had ever come to harm.

'But if anything were to happen right now, you wouldn't personally be involved with solving it,' she persisted. 'So if you have the staff in place to keep everything running during your absences, there's nothing to stop you having a relationship.'

'I'm only ever absent from headquarters when I'm on a job. Being the boss means having all the responsibility if anything goes wrong.' He would not allow anything to go wrong.

Her eyes narrowed then began to dance. 'You sound like a man making excuses. Has a woman broken your heart?'

'No woman has ever got close.' And no woman ever would. During his army career he'd been happy to play the field—many women loved a man in uniform. He'd watched friends and colleagues settle down and seen the pressure starting families had had on them, how it could affect their focus and priorities, and had decided to wait until he left the forces before finding someone to settle down with. Then his unit had been flown in to handle a hostage situation, his life had gone to hell and thoughts of a family destroyed with it. He was better off on his own. Solitude was what he'd grown up with, what he was used to. Safer.

He thought of Sergio. He thought of Sergio's wife and unborn child. He thought about the hostages they'd been trying to save, half of whom hadn't made it out alive. Sergio hadn't made it out alive either, a memory that still had the power to sear him. His child was now a healthy nine-year-old growing up with a father he would only see in photographs.

Francesca didn't say anything, just stared at him with those beguiling light brown eyes that seemed to drink him in...

Without warning, she got to her feet, her face breaking into a beaming smile. 'I love this song! Let's dance.'

The jazz band had finished their set and now a DJ was playing to the full crowd.

'I don't dance.'

'Then I shall dance on my own.' And with that she finished her coffee and glided to the dance floor, her shoulders and hips swaying to the music he vaguely recognised, her long ebony hair shimmering in the lights.

Without an ounce of self-consciousness, Francesca threw her arms in the air and began to dance. The joy on her face must have been infectious because a couple of women hurried onto the floor to join her, the three of them immediately dancing and singing together as if they'd known each other for years.

He should leave her on the dance floor and go to bed. He wasn't her babysitter. His protection of her did not involve making sure she was safely tucked up at night. Judging by the animation on her face and in her body she'd found her second wind and wouldn't be going to bed any time soon.

Felipe sighed and signalled to a passing waiter for another beer.

He couldn't leave her.

And neither could he take his eyes from her.

He accepted his beer with a nod of thanks.

He sipped it slowly, watching her dance.

How could someone be so uninhibited? Did it come naturally to her or was it something she'd forced herself to be? He suspected it was the former, that this woman on the dance floor was the closest to the real Francesca he'd seen in their short time together.

It felt as if he'd been in her company for weeks.

She kept glancing at him, sometimes overtly, beckoning him with a finger to join her, to which he always shook his head.

Hell would freeze over before he'd dance with anyone, let alone Francesca Pellegrini. Watching her move and imagining her body flush against his own was enough torture to inflict on himself.

And sometimes her glances were fleeting, as if she couldn't help but look. Just as he couldn't help but look at her.

He shifted in his seat then smiled sardonically when a waiter brought the three dancing ladies a cocktail each. So much for his keen attention to detail—he'd no idea how or when she'd ordered them but seeing as they were Tequila Sunrises, he knew damn well they'd come from Francesca.

She met his eye again and winked, then drank her cocktail and returned to dancing with gusto.

The bubble of laughter swelling inside him died on his lips when one of her straps fell down her slender arm. She giggled and pulled it up, only for it to fall straight back down again.

The attraction Felipe had been trying to contain all night seemed to burst through him, the pulsing music dimming to a background noise as blood roared through his ears.

Shoving his chair back, he got to his feet.

It was time to call it a night before he did something he regretted, like joining Francesca on the dance floor and holding her so close she'd be able to feel his desire for herself.

# CHAPTER SIX

FELIPE MADE IT out of the restaurant and was halfway across the atrium when he heard light footsteps behind him.

'You left without me!' she accused.

He closed his eyes tightly and prayed for strength.

When he opened them he found Francesca's beautiful face gazing up at him, her skin glowing from her exertion on the dance floor. She didn't look upset at him leaving. If anything, she looked far too knowing.

'We weren't on a date and it's late,' he felt compelled to remind her. And remind himself. When she looked at him like that...

'Have I annoyed you again?'

He could laugh at her lack of guile. How many times had he heard his colleagues complain that women never made it easy for them, always expecting them to read their minds and know when something was wrong rather than just coming out and saying it? There was none of that with Francesca. Her emotions were always on the surface.

'No, you haven't annoyed me.'

'Good.' She tucked her arm through his. 'Then you can walk me back to my room.'

If she didn't look so unsteady on her feet he would shake her off.

He was annoyed enough with himself for allowing their meal drag on so long and for hanging around to watch her dance when he should have taken the earliest opportunity to escape.

His heart sinking in rhythm with his warming skin, Felipe took a deep breath and led the way.

'I've had a wonderful evening,' she said. 'Thank you for keeping me company.'

'No problem.'

'And you?' When he didn't answer, she prompted, 'Have you had a nice evening?'

That was a question he was not prepared to answer with anything more than a noncommittal grunt.

Thankfully they'd reached her door, allowing him to remove his arm from her hold and step back.

She rummaged in her bag and found her key card and immediately dropped it.

'Oops.'

'I'll get it,' he muttered.

He scooped it up and swiped the lock for her, then opened the door.

'Do you want to come in?'

He shook his head.

'The bar's got beer in it,' she said temptingly.

'I've had enough to drink.' He'd drunk only half of what she had but, as he'd reminded himself a dozen times throughout their meal, he was working. All that dancing had probably worked a lot of the alcohol out of her system but she was by no means sober. And she'd had the extra cocktail on the dance floor...

Yes, there was no way she was sober. Felipe was used to drinking with hardened men, not slender—but curvy, *Dios*, he could not get those curves out of his mind— women.

She bit her lip then tilted her head. 'Don't you find me attractive?'

*God give him strength.*

'I need to get some sleep.'

'You haven't answered my question. You didn't answer my last question either.'

The strap of her dress fell down again. He spoke through gritted teeth. 'I'm not going to answer it.'

Heavy footsteps trod towards them. He turned to see a man around his own age heading their way.

'Get into your room.' Felipe took hold of her wrist and walked her in. He didn't want to advertise the fact she would be alone in her suite.

The door closed quietly behind them.

Resolutely, he kept his back pressed against it. He would count to ten and then leave.

One. Two. Three.

'You *do* find me attractive,' she whispered, eyes shining as she stood before him.

Four. Five. Six.

She raised herself onto her toes and palmed his cheeks with hands as soft as anything he'd ever felt. 'I find you attractive too,' she breathed.

Seven. Eight...

He lost the count when her breath danced over his lips and her mouth found his.

Holding his breath, he clenched his hands into fists and willed himself not to respond.

He couldn't. He mustn't.

Francesca's lips didn't move. Not for a long time. He felt her breathe him in and fought not to inhale. Then she did move. Just a little. A turn of her head to cover his mouth better, a gentle, tentative exploration of his lips while her fingers made a gentle, tentative exploration of his cheeks and jaw, rubbing against his beard and up to trace the contours of his ears.

He fought to hold on, fought to deny the sensation burning through him.

He might have won had he not opened his mouth to let in air and her tongue darted through his parted lips. In an instant he was filled with the sweet heat of her kiss and the fingers he'd raised to yank her hands away from him were cradling her skull as he kissed her back as deeply as a parched man drinking from a cup.

She tasted sweeter than he could have dreamed.

Her arms wrapped around his neck while his arm hooked around her waist to crush her to him. She melted into him with a breathy sigh, charging his desire like a rocket.

He roamed her curves, finding her waist, her hips, her bottom, which was round and pert and felt delectable beneath his fingers. *She* was delectable. Soft and womanly beyond imagination.

Rising onto her toes had the effect of lifting her dress. When he skimmed down her thigh he came to bare skin that had him sucking in a breath at its satin sheen and holding her tightly so he could devour her mouth again.

It was her response that so blew his mind. Her hunger was as acute as his own and it fed his.

He could take her now if he wanted and she would welcome him with the breathy sighs that were growing in intensity. God knew, he wanted to take her, this craving like nothing he had ever known.

His exploring hands ran up her bare thighs to find her panties and he slipped a finger under the skimpy material and almost groaned aloud to feel the hot dampness there.

She squirmed against him, one foot running up and down the length of his leg, kissing him, licking him, her teeth grazing his neck then kissing up to brush her cheeks against his beard like a purring cat. He could taste her desire in her kisses, smell it in the heat radiating off her.

Tugging the panties down her hips, he pressed the palm of his hand over the soft, downy hair and felt the gasp that flew from her throat. She pressed her pubis into him but before he could explore any further, her nails suddenly dug through his shirt and into his flesh and she collapsed into him, crying out and shuddering.

And then she stilled.

For a long, drawn out moment Felipe couldn't find his breath. Francesca didn't seem to be breathing either.

The only sound he heard with any clarity was the roar of blood in his ears.

It was like the room was clearing of fog. Slowly they released their hold on each other and took wary steps back.

*What the hell did he think he was playing at? Had he lost his mind?*

Francesca put trembling hands to her mouth, covering it as if in prayer, her eyes wide and dazed.

He felt pretty dazed himself.

He breathed out deeply.

He'd been minutes away from making love to her. There were no excuses he could make.

For the first time in his life he'd let his desire guide him and his loathing for himself tasted like salt on his tongue.

He was a thirty-six-year-old man. He knew better than this. He *demanded* better than to behave like this.

He should never have followed her into the suite, not when his awareness of her and the desire in his loins had been simmering since the first moment he'd set eyes on her.

'I need to go.'

She jerked her head and took another step back. He took it as agreement.

His heart hammering, he backed away to the door and left.

Francesca put the pillow over her head to drown out the sound of the knocking on the door. She knew who it was and she did not want to see him. She didn't want to see him ever again. She couldn't. It was just too mortifying.

She'd rather dance naked through the streets of Caballeros with the lecherous Governor ogling her than see Felipe again.

Her cheeks scalded to remember how she'd come undone with one touch.

*One touch.*

Why didn't she know that could happen? How *could* she have known when she hadn't even kissed a man before?

His *face*. He'd been horrified.

No wonder he'd run from her suite.

And to think she'd gone into the restaurant hating him.

She'd just wanted to kiss him.

It was his smile that had done it, one unguarded curve of those gorgeous lips that had made her own lips tingle and her pulses quicken.

She'd spent almost their entire meal fantasising about the feel of his lips on hers.

Curiosity had certainly killed the cat.

She couldn't even blame it on the alcohol, although she wished she could. It had loosened her inhibitions considerably but she'd been the one to drive the kiss, not the Tequila Sunrises.

She'd played with fire and been burnt for her trouble. She certainly wouldn't open the door to the man who'd lit it.

The phone beside her bed rang.

She wanted to scream. *Just leave me alone!*

She snatched the receiver up. 'What?'

'You have one minute to open your door or I break it down.'

The dial tone played out before she could summon the words to answer back.

Throwing on her robe, she hurried to open the door a crack before Felipe could follow up on his threat.

He was already there.

He didn't wait for an invite, simply pushed the door open and strode in, glass of fizzing water in hand.

'Drink that,' he said, handing it to her. 'It'll help your hangover.'

'I don't have a hangover.' She was quite sure the sickness in her belly was nothing to do with alcohol. Her banging head might be, though.

'Just drink it.'

How could he look so fresh? He'd showered, his charcoal suit crisply pressed, his hair still damp.

Sulkily, she did as she was told and gulped the liquid down. It tasted much less disgusting than she expected.

He took a deep breath. 'May I sit down?'

*No. Go away and let me sleep away my mortification.* 'If you want.'

He sat on the armchair in the corner and indicated for her to sit on the sofa.

Perching herself gingerly, aware of the humiliation ravaging her, she tried to put on a brave face. Tried to show she didn't care what he thought of her.

*But she did care. She really did.*

'I must apologise for my behaviour last night,' he said heavily. 'I should never have taken advantage of you as I did.'

The last thing she'd expected was an apology.

His choice of words made her study him properly.

Her heart loosened to see he wasn't angry with her. Felipe's anger was directed at himself.

His self-recrimination also loosened her tongue. 'You didn't take advantage of me. If anything I took advantage of you. I started it.'

'You were drunk,' he refuted flatly.

'Not drunk enough that I didn't know what I was doing.'

Heat pulsed between her thighs as she remembered how wonderful it had been in that moment and how she'd ached to do so much more. She'd had no idea such feelings existed in her. Desire and curiosity had erupted into something she'd had no control over.

And he'd been a full participant. She'd been so busy castigating herself and so busy focussing on his abrupt departure from her suite that she'd pushed aside *his* response. She might not have had any prior experience but she'd felt his arousal pressed hard against her belly and known what it meant. He'd wanted her as much as she'd wanted him.

He dug his fingers into the back of his skull, a set look in his jaw. 'I run my company with strict rules. No relations with the client.'

'Is that what you call it? *Relations*?'

'We both know what it means.' Now he pressed his hand to his forehead. 'It's not just the rules I abide by. It's you. You're too young to be messing around with men old enough to be your…'

'Big brother?' she supplied.

His jaw clenched. 'Francesca, you are in my care for a very good reason. You're too young and too vulnerable to be party to a tawdry affair.'

'My mother got married at nineteen. She was pregnant with Pieta when she was my age. If my family had had their way, I would be married with kids by now. If I want to be party to a tawdry affair, then I'm more than old enough to make that choice.'

'But you *are* vulnerable and grieving. You can't argue with that.' He got to his feet. 'You're my client. There can be nothing between us. Do you understand that?'

She stared at him for a long time, taking in the tension radiating from him. He hadn't looked her in the eye since entering her suite.

'Answer me one thing,' she said. 'One of the questions I asked last night, and this time I want an answer. Are you attracted to me?'

'Whatever attraction I feel is irrelevant,' he answered roughly.

'It wasn't irrelevant last night.'

'Last night was a mistake that will not be repeated.'

'Says you?'

Jaw clenched, he strode to the door. 'This conversation is over. If you still want to visit the hospital site and meet up with the charity, then I suggest you get dressed. We leave in thirty minutes.'

He left her suite without further comment.

Alone, Francesca drew her knees to her chin and hugged her legs. She felt she could start dancing again.

For all her fears that she'd made another monumental mistake, Felipe *did* desire her and that knowledge took away the sting of his rejection. If he'd flat-out denied it she thought it possible she might be tempted to curl into hedgehog-like ball and hibernate until she could be sure of looking at him without toe-curling shame and embarrassment. That the attraction was mutual made it a whole lot easier to bear even if he was adamant that last night was a one off.

Eventually she straightened and took some long breaths, forcing herself to concentrate on what was important. She was in the Caribbean for a reason and that reason wasn't for a holiday or for a man.

The woman she was meeting from the Blue Train Agency had promised to discuss the hospital, the needs of the people and how Francesca should navigate her way around the additional bureaucracy she would find.

She needed to be alert and have her professional head on, not be fantasising about what it would take to wear down Felipe's defences.

The day passed quickly and much more productively than Francesca could have hoped. Eva Bergen from the Blue

Train Agency had been there to meet her at Caballeros' airport, as she'd promised, escorted by a couple of Felipe's men, and they'd spent the day visiting the site where they hoped to build the hospital and met some of the officials she'd have to deal with when the site was signed over to Pieta's foundation on Saturday. After arranging meetings with the other officials for the next day, they headed back to Aguadilla.

When they dropped Seb and James off at their lodging, she stayed in the back of the car to make more calls without the distraction of Felipe's strong thighs in her eyeline.

Her first call was to Alberto. It went to voicemail.

'Problem?' Felipe asked from the driver's seat when she cursed under her breath, adopting the same grim tone he'd used since he'd left her suite that morning.

Clearly his regret of their *relations* meant he was now determined to keep his distance as much as the situation allowed. Today he'd left it to Seb to stand at her side as principal protection but had still been close enough to listen in on every conversation, close enough to ward off any perceived threat that might come her way.

Not once had he met her eye.

In a way she was grateful for his distance as it had allowed her to concentrate on what needed doing.

'I've been trying to get hold of Alberto to arrange for the cash to be sent over in time for the Governor's party,' she explained. 'He'll know what to do about the bribe too without getting the foundation into trouble but he's not answering his phone.'

Until everything was sorted out with Pieta's estate and businesses, Alberto controlled the finances for the foundation. When she'd spoken to him at Pieta's funeral he'd assured her he would sign off the funds when a deal was brokered.

'It's already in hand,' Felipe informed her. 'My men will transport it. The money arrives in Aguadilla on Saturday.'

'How do you know that?'

'I made the arrangements.'

'What? *When*?'

'Yesterday.'

'But… How…? Why?' She couldn't get a coherent question to form.

'I decided the best way to get you out of the mess you'd got yourself into was to sort it out myself before you dragged yourself in deeper.'

It took a long time for Francesca to find her voice. 'This has nothing to do with you. You're here as my protection…'

'Exactly. A young woman with a suitcase of cash? Four hundred thousand dollars is a fortune to the people of Caballeros. You'll be a magnet for every thief out there and you're already a target.'

'How's anyone going to know about the money?' she protested. 'It's a private transaction between myself and the Governor.'

'A private transaction—or bribe—agreed in a residence I warned you was filled with cameras recording every word you said. This is damage limitation. The cash for the site will be paid in full from the foundation but the bribe money will come from a different source. There will be no trail leading it to you or your brother's foundation.'

'You've done all this? The damage limitation?'

'Yes. Don't ask me how. I have no wish to lie to you.'

Francesca clenched her hands into fists and forced herself to breathe. She knew she should be grateful to him for saving her from herself, not wanting to bash him over the head with her handbag.

'I thank you for thinking of my career.' She spoke carefully, struggling for breath. 'But don't ever go over my head like that again. If anything else occurs, speak to me before acting.'

'If you'd been thinking clearly in the first place I wouldn't have had to go over your head.'

'That was then,' she contested tightly. 'What happened to drawing a line under it all? I made one mistake...'

'My actions prevented you making another.'

'I made one mistake that I'm doing my best not to repeat and it's not fair to keep throwing it in my face. Have *you* never made a mistake? Or were you born perfect?'

He didn't answer.

They drove the rest of the route back to the hotel in silence and went to their respective suites without a further word.

# CHAPTER SEVEN

FRANCESCA CLOSED THE folder sprawled on her lap with a sigh and rubbed her eyes. It was gone midnight. She'd been in her suite since their return to the hotel, having another re-read of the foundation's files. She wished she'd brought some of the case files she was supposed to be studying for her traineeship with her, could kick herself for not even thinking about it. When she returned home to Pisa she would get her head down and get stuck back into her studies.

In the hours spent reading, she'd ordered room service and drunk nothing stronger than black coffee but even all the caffeine couldn't stop the heaviness of her eyes. All those Tequila Sunrises from the night before had finally caught up with her. She was exhausted.

She really needed to get some sleep but was terrified of closing her eyes, wondered if there was some magic pill out there that guaranteed a dreamless sleep.

Her thoughts, as always, drifted back to Felipe. As the night had gone on her fury at his high-handed behaviour had slowly evaporated.

She wondered where he was. Had he left his suite that evening or stayed in as she had done? The hotel's walls were so solid that no sound penetrated.

On impulse she leaned over, picked up the telephone receiver from the bedside table and dialled his room number.

He answered on the second ring. 'Yes?'

'It's me. Francesca Pellegrini.'

She pulled a disgusted face at herself. Why did she give him her *surname*?

There was a small pause before he said, a slight tinge

of amusement in his voice, 'What can I do for you, Francesca Pellegrini?'

His words sounded like a caress. He really had the dreamiest of voices.

'I wanted to say thank you…for digging me out of the hole I'd put myself and the foundation in…and…and…' She forced the word out. 'Sorry…for being so ungrateful about it.'

'Apology accepted.'

'Just like that?'

'Just like that.'

'You don't want me to crawl over broken glass to show my penitence?'

A low rumble of laughter blew into her ear and curled its way down her spine. 'An apology is enough. I'm not without blame. You weren't being ungrateful. You were right to be angry with me. I should have consulted with you before I went ahead with my plans.'

'Why didn't you?'

'I was angry with you and the whole situation. I thought you'd behaved insanely.'

'I *did* behave insanely,' she conceded. 'Do you normally try and fix the holes your clients dig for themselves?'

A small pause. 'No.'

'Do you often get angry with your clients?'

Another small pause. 'No. It's not my place to get angry with them or fix their problems. I'm paid to protect them, not have an opinion.'

His confession made the most wonderful warmth spread through her. She pulled her knees up and curled against the headboard and murmured, 'I must be special then.'

Another rumble of laughter. 'That is one way to describe you.'

'Am I the most annoying client you've ever had?'

'You're the most challenging,' he answered drily.

'I've always been challenging.'

'I'll bet.'

A silence formed.

'It's late. I should let you go,' she said, breaking it. But she didn't want to let him go. She wanted to have that glorious voice speak into her ear all night. A thought occurred to her. 'Did I wake you?'

'I'm watching a film in bed.'

'Is it any good?'

'It's bad enough to remind me why I hate television.'

'You can't hate television,' she said, feigning outrage.

He groaned. 'Don't tell me you're one of those television addicts?'

'I *love* television,' she informed him gleefully. 'If I was put on a desert island and only allowed to take one thing that would be it.'

'You're a heathen.'

'A heathen with a large collection of box sets.'

His laughter rumbled down the line again, warming her from her lobes all the way down to her toes.

To think Felipe was lying in his bed too...

'Did you go anywhere for dinner?' she asked.

'I had room service in my suite.'

'So did I.'

'What did you have?'

'Jambalaya. You?'

'The same.'

There was no reasonable answer as to why Felipe independently eating the same meal as her should make her glow.

Another silence formed, this time broken by Felipe. 'We should get some sleep.'

'I'm not tired.' A lie. She was exhausted. But speaking to Felipe had recharged her. She wanted more than a conversation down the phone. The easiness of their talk, the subtle undertones racing beneath it propelled her to say, 'Do you want to come to my suite for a nightcap?'

There was another prolonged pause with time enough to make her heart expand with anticipation.

'Goodnight, Francesca,' he eventually said in such a gentle tone her heart flipped over on itself and her unanswered offer didn't sting as much as it should.

She hugged the receiver to her chest for a long time after he'd hung up.

When Felipe strode into the hotel lobby the next morning, the first person he saw was Francesca, sitting on a sofa with her legs elegantly crossed, reading a newspaper.

As if she had a sixth sense to his presence, she tilted her head and immediately fixed her gaze on him. Her lips curved into a smile that made his chest compress.

He nodded a greeting in return.

He'd given himself a sharp talking to that morning, reminding himself of all the reasons he needed to keep his distance from this mesmeric woman. He'd put the phone down after their late-night conversation with an ache in his groin that had still been there when he'd woken.

Her call had caught him off guard. Her husky voice had played down the line, into his ear and into his veins before he could put the mental blocks in place to deflect it.

Her apology had taken him off guard too. Francesca was not a woman who found apologies easy.

That he knew such a thing about her disturbed him on many different levels but nowhere near as disturbing as the strength it had taken to refuse her suggestive offer of a nightcap. He hadn't been able to refuse in words, not when his tongue had been clamouring with the rest of his body to say yes.

He should have ended the call after she'd made her apology, not allowed that husky voice draw him into further, more intimate conversation.

They had five more days left together and in one respect he was glad they would now be able to get through it without a wishing well full of antagonism between them.

He could laugh at his optimism. He'd only known her a short time but knew perfectly well Francesca was not a woman one could expect to have an easy life with, not even for five short days. Everything she did, she did with passion. Everything she felt was with passion.

He'd felt that passion for himself and, *Dios*, he craved to feel it again.

He'd never met anyone like her. He'd never desired anyone as he did her. He'd never become aroused at a voice before.

He'd had to force himself to say goodnight.

'Ready to go?' he said briskly. He would not allow the spell they'd fallen into during their late-night call seep into the job in hand.

It had been one phone call, he told himself irritably. They'd hardly shared a naked sauna together.

But, naturally, his thoughts immediately turned to the image permanently lodged in his retinas of her sunbathing in that tiny yellow bikini.

Thankfully, today she was fully covered in a simple blue knee-length dress, black fitted jacket and black heels, her dark hair plaited and coiled. She looked ready to step into a courtroom. She also looked as sexy as a siren.

Her light brown eyes widened a little at his tone but her poise remained. 'I'm ready when you are.'

They collected Seb and James at their lodgings and then drove onto the airport, keeping conversation light and professional. If not for the gleam in her eyes every time she looked at him he could believe he'd mistaken the sensual undertone in her nightcap offer. But the gleam shone brightly. *She* shone brightly even though she was more together and composed than he had ever seen her.

When she met with the official in charge of the island's medical service, who in turn expected his own bribe, he was impressed with the way she used a combination of facts, charm and intelligence to deflect him and get him to agree to naming a wing of the hospital after him in lieu of a backhander.

'Weren't you tempted to use that technique when dealing with the Governor?' he asked on the drive back to the airport.

She shook her head and pulled her lips together ruefully. 'I wish that meeting could be scrubbed away so I could pretend it never happened. I was so excited to get his agreement that, frankly, if he'd asked me to serve him the moon on a dish I would have accepted. I didn't think the ramifications through clearly. I should have been a lot more prepared.'

He admired her ability not to pull punches at her own faults. The more he observed her, the more he found to admire, from her professionalism to that inherent zest for life she carried with her. 'You didn't make the same mistake this time.'

She met his eye and her lips curved. 'I make it a point to learn from my mistakes, not repeat them.'

That was so close to his own personal beliefs that for a moment he was tempted to pull her to him...

Ever since those crazy, heady few minutes in her suite he'd done his damnedest not to think of it, not to remember the sweet heat of her passionate kisses or the softness of her lips and silkiness of her skin. It was the cry of surprise she'd made when she'd come with virtually one touch that he couldn't eradicate. Remembering that sound made his every sinew tighten.

He knew he could never make the mistake of being alone in a room with her again.

'Boss?'

James's voice broke into his thoughts. They'd pulled into Caballeros airport where the pilot was waiting for them. 'Yes?'

'See that black Mondeo?'

Felipe followed his gaze. Roughly ten metres away from their Cessna sat the car that had followed them from the Governor's house three days ago.

He thought quickly as he scanned their surroundings.

'Stay here,' he told Francesca before getting out of the car. Seb and James, who'd already recognised the danger and armed themselves, didn't need to be told to stay with her or to keep the engine running.

Gun in hand, keeping the black car in his eyeline, he strolled with deceptive casualness to the Cessna. If this was an ambush he wouldn't have Francesca caught in any crossfire.

'How long has that Mondeo been there?' he asked his man who he'd left with the pilot.

'Three hours. Three men.'

'Any activity?'

'None. I've run a trace on the licence plate but you know what this island's like—even before the hurricane I doubt I'd have got any information from it. We're working on facial recognition as we speak.'

Felipe nodded grimly and said to the pilot, 'Get ready to leave.'

The small plane's engine was switched on before his feet hit the tarmac and he was heading back to Francesca.

'What's going on?' she asked when he opened the car door. 'Is it the men who were following us before?'

'It appears so.' He held out his hand, preparing to throw

her over his shoulder if she gave any resistance. 'Time to move.'

He gave her credit. She didn't hesitate or demand more answers. Her eyes held his—he could almost read her thoughts, Francesca saying 'Okay, I'm trusting you here,'   and she took his hand and held it tightly on the quick march back to the plane, James flanking her other side, Seb bringing up the rear.

Only when they were seated, their belts hardly buckled before the pilot had them airborne, did she quietly say, 'I assume those men mean trouble.'

'I have to assume that too.'

She nodded slowly. 'Them being at the airport can't be a coincidence. What do you think they want?'

'That's the million dollar question.' A question he'd give one of his kidneys to answer.

She didn't speak for the longest time. 'Do you think they know about the money?'

'I would put my savings on it.' He wiped perspiration from his brow. He already knew what he would have to do.

Unbuckling himself, he moved to the front of the plane to share his thoughts with his men.

He waited until they arrived at James and Seb's lodgings and the two men had got out of the car before sharing it with Francesca. She'd proved remarkably stoical about the situation. He must have made a dozen phone calls and she'd sat quietly beside him, not interrupting, not talking, letting him get on with what he needed to do.

'James and Seb are getting their gear together. They're coming with us.'

'To our hotel?'

'I've also arranged for three of my men staying in Caballeros to fly here. Between them they'll cover all entry points to the hotel and keep watch.' Now that the threat against Francesca was unequivocal he would not trust her safety in the hotel to the security guards. Guards could be bribed. His men could not. His men wouldn't miss anything.

The face she pulled was sceptical. 'You think those men at the airport are going to come here?'

'I don't know what those men are going to do so I'm preparing for any eventuality.'

'Aguadilla has really tight security. Our hotel has really tight security. They haven't got a hope of getting to us.'

'You may be right but I'm not taking any risks.' He wasn't prepared to leave anything to chance. Security at Aguadilla airport was as tight as any in the US or Europe, its waters heavily patrolled. In theory Francesca should be safe for as long as she remained in Aguadilla. In theory.

Felipe had learned a long time ago that 'in theory' didn't mean a damn thing. People were unpredictable, especially those under pressure.

His gut told him it was the money the men were after and not Francesca personally. They'd initially followed them from the Governor's residence. That had to mean they'd been tipped off about the money from a member of the Governor's personal staff.

But what if he was wrong? What if they wanted both, the cash *and* a hostage for ransom?

What if they weren't merely staking them out, waiting for signs of the cash, and were instead only waiting for an opportunity to snatch her? He'd been at the forefront of a hostage situation that had gone wrong. The thought of Francesca being held...

His stomach roiled violently.

He'd watched the light die in Sergio's eyes and the eyes of his other fallen comrades. He could not allow himself to imagine it draining from Francesca's eyes too. To protect her and keep her safe he had to keep his focus.

There were too many what-ifs. Far too many.

* * *

Francesca was quite sure she should be biting her nails in terror. That would be a normal reaction to being followed by unknown persons on one of the most dangerous islands in the world.

But she was safe in Aguadilla with Felipe and his army of warriors protecting her. Unlike Caballeros, Aguadilla was a true paradise.

She'd definitely experienced fear when she'd realised the men who'd followed them after her meeting with the Governor had been staking out their Cessna but one look into Felipe's dark eyes had been all the reassurance she'd needed. He hadn't needed to spell it out, his eyes had told her everything she needed to know. He wouldn't let anything happen to her.

Once they'd made the brief walk from the car to the plane without incident, she'd been able to breathe. If they'd wanted to take her, they'd had their chance.

It was the money they were after. The money she'd foolishly agreed to bring *in cash* into Caballeros.

So, no, it wasn't fear currently gripping her. It was guilt, and mingled with it a strange form of exhilaration, an awareness of her blood pulsing through her veins. She'd never been so aware of being *alive*, of the sun's rays beaming onto her skin, of the soft material of her dress caressing her body, of the sweet scent of the air filling her lungs, all the small things she took for granted in her daily life sharply in focus as if she were experiencing them for the first time.

The closest she had come to this feeling before had been two nights ago in Felipe's arms.

She followed him through the hotel, marvelling at the strength of his frame, noticed again the slight limp, the only imperfection she could find on this magnificent man whose arms she longed to be in once more.

When they reached their suites, she opened her mouth to thank him and to apologise—again—for all the trouble her actions had brought on them.

Before she could speak, though, Felipe said, 'Come into mine for a minute while I get my stuff together.'

'Why? Are we changing hotels?'

'I'm changing rooms.' His features darkened. 'I'm moving into your suite. Until we trace those men and know who they're working for and what their intentions are, you're not to be alone.'

Far from sharing the thrill that raced through her at the thought of them sharing a suite, he had the face of a man tasked with guarding a hungry Venus flytrap.

She tailed him into his suite, a mirror image of her own, and took a seat on the sofa, watching as he pulled a large khaki kitbag from a cupboard and put it on the bed. He then walked into his dressing room and returned with an armful of clothes.

'Do you normally do sleepovers?' she asked, trying to lighten the atmosphere.

She was rewarded with a biting glare. 'This isn't a joke.'

'I know.'

'Then don't act as if it is.'

'What do you want me to do? Cower in a corner? Hide under a bed? It's obvious that they're after the money. All they're going to do is watch us until they know the cash is here… When is the money due?'

'Saturday. And it's obvious, is it? I thought you were training to be a lawyer. There's no clear evidence for a scenario so we're going to act as if any scenario is a possibility.'

'If it's me they want then they would have tried to take me already.'

'How do you know that?' he said through gritted teeth.

'An educated guess.'

'But still a guess.'

But she wasn't saying anything Felipe hadn't already thought. Whoever these men were, they'd had the opportunity to make a grab for her if it was indeed Francesca they wanted. These were cautious people he was dealing with, not hot-headed druggies. Stupid too. Parking just feet away from their Cessna and waiting for three hours without attempting to give themselves a cover story was the height of stupidity, and stupid people were the most dangerous.

His gut agreed with Francesca that they were after the money.

He could stay in his own suite in good conscience, content that she was safe in hers.

But he couldn't take the risk. Not with her. Just thinking it was enough for him to break out in a cold sweat.

What if his gut instinct born from almost two decades of risk assessments in dangerous situations was wrong?

This was why one didn't mix business with pleasure, he thought grimly, storming into the bathroom to get his toiletries. It clouded judgement. It made one doubt oneself.

Like it or not, his attraction to Francesca and the weight in his chest from being around her was accelerating. All his senses were attuned as if she were a magnet they were straining towards.

It was a fight to contain it. To protect her effectively he needed his head clear, a task made harder by the way she kept looking at him. If he could tune her out he would be fine. But he already knew tuning Francesca Pellegrini out was near on impossible.

One night alone in a suite with her he could handle. Any longer than that...

'I'm taking you back to Pisa in the morning,' he told her as he placed his toiletry bag with the rest of his kit, bracing himself for the furious protest that was bound to follow.

'No way,' she snapped, her nonchalance gone in an instant, just as he'd expected.

'It's too dangerous for you here. Pisa is safe. If I could take you back now I would but the quickest I can get a jet here is for early tomorrow morning and there's no commercial flights leaving any sooner. We'll leave first thing.'

'I'm not abandoning the project. No way.'

'You won't be abandoning it.' He would not allow her to set foot in that country again. 'You've got the agreement for the sale and met with the government's health representative. I'll get the cash to the Governor. Everything else can be handled by Daniele—he's the one who'll be getting the hospital built.'

'I'm going to the Governor's party,' she told him obstinately. 'If I don't attend he will see it as an insult and withdraw his permission and the hospital will never be built.'

Felipe swore loudly.

Damn it, she was right.

He thought quickly. The party was four days away. Plenty of time to draw up effective plans to protect both Francesca and the money.

'I'll fly you back for the party,' he said with a curt nod. 'But we leave here first thing in the morning. You'll be a sitting target if you stay. I'm taking you home where you'll be safe and I will have no further argument about it. When I bring you back, you will have nothing to do with the handover of the money. You will do exactly as you're told.'

He zipped his kitbag with more force than necessary and waited for another onslaught.

He knew he sounded like a tyrant but didn't care. The cold fear he'd experienced when he'd recognised that car had been like nothing he'd ever felt before, not even when he'd realised too late he'd led his men into a trap.

But no explosion came.

When he next looked at her, Francesca's legs were

crossed, her fingers laced together, a thoughtful expression on her beautiful face as she studied him. Then her lips curved into a smile and she said, 'Does this mean we get to share a nightcap now?'

# CHAPTER EIGHT

'I'M HUNGRY.'

A whole hour they'd been in her suite. A whole hour in which Felipe had ignored her existence, setting himself up with his laptop on the bureau in the corner.

For her part, Francesca had sat herself on the huge bed and watched him as studiously as he'd ignored her.

She could sense his awareness of her. It was in his every move, as strong as her awareness of him. The only difference was his resolve to pretend it didn't exist. His ridiculous rule of no *relations* with the client meant he was determined to fight it.

He regarded her as his responsibility and was doing everything in his power to keep her in the box he'd cast her in.

Well, she was determined to do everything in *her* power to pull herself out of that same box.

'I'm hungry,' she repeated.

He didn't look up from his laptop. 'You're always hungry. Order room service.'

'I had room service last night. It's only seven o'clock. If I spend another evening stuck in here, I'll get cabin fever. I'm going to get something to eat—are you coming with me?'

Now his eyes darted to hers and narrowed.

'I've agreed to go home in the morning,' she said sweetly, 'and I understand why you feel I need your full protection tonight. But I'm not going to be a prisoner in this suite. If you don't want to eat with me, call one of your men stationed around the hotel to join me instead.' She knew he would never go for that. She also knew that trying to draw him into conversation while in her suite would be akin to drawing blood from a stone. Without a laptop to hide behind he would be forced to talk to her.

Fury mounted in his returning glare but Francesca kept her gaze steady.

Then his glare turned into a look that could solidify gel. 'We eat, we come back. No drinking and no dancing. Is that understood?'

'Why don't you write it on a piece of paper so I don't forget? I'll sign it for you if you like.'

'Don't tempt me,' he growled.

'I'm doing my very best there.' She rose to her feet. 'I'm going to take a shower and make myself look beautiful before we leave. Is that okay with you, my lord and master?'

Certain he was cursing her in Spanish under his breath, Francesca sauntered to the bathroom.

Felipe waited for the click of the bathroom door's lock. When it didn't come he swore again. She'd deliberately left it unlocked.

He rubbed a knuckle to his forehead, trying not to think about what was going on behind the unlocked door.

Making herself look beautiful? It wasn't possible for Francesca to be more desirable than she already was.

The sound of the shower running came through the walls.

*Do not think of her naked.*

An email pinged into his inbox and he seized on the distraction; a recce report by a team of his men in North Africa in preparation for a business trip by the head of an American petroleum company.

He'd almost finished writing his reply when the bathroom door opened.

He looked up before he could stop himself.

*Dios*, Francesca had only a towel around herself.

'Don't mind me,' she said demurely, brushing past him

and leaving a cloud of fruity scent in her wake, 'I'm just going to get changed.'

Gritting his teeth to counteract his thickening blood, he looked again at the email he was replying to.

She might as well have fired a bullet into his brain his concentration was so shot.

He blinked to refocus but, even when she disappeared into her dressing room, all he could see were bare slender arms and long black hair that, when wet, fell all the way to the base of her spine, almost touching the curvaceous bottom the white towel hugged so beautifully.

He knuckled his forehead and swore violently. She was taunting him. Tempting him. It was in her every look, her every movement.

The vows he'd made to himself in recent days were tested to the limit when she emerged some time later.

She'd changed into a Chinese-style red dress that was perfectly modest, not displaying any unnecessary flesh, falling to a decent length just above the knees, but…it clung to her every softly rounded curve…

And then he noticed she'd put make-up on. Not a huge amount but enough to make her light brown eyes even more seductive than they already were and her lips even more kissable. She'd blow-dried her hair and it hung like a silk sheet. On her feet were high black strappy sandals.

'Did you want to take a shower before we go?' she asked, appraising him with one of the gleams that fired straight into his groin.

He slammed the lid of his laptop down. 'Let's get this over with.'

Francesca swirled the white wine in her glass and watched Felipe study his menu.

He'd looked at her only once since they'd sat down, a

piercing glare when she'd ordered her wine. She'd given an unrepentant shrug in return.

They were in one of the hotel's outdoor restaurants on a patio area that encircled a large swimming pool aglow with soft lighting.

Her intention had been to get Felipe out of the suite and get him talking. Whenever they'd had a proper conversation together they'd proved things could be harmonious between them. She wanted to find that harmony again.

She knew he desired her but what good was that when he fought it every step of the way? She wanted him to desire her company as well, to see her as herself. Francesca. Not Pieta's little sister. Not Daniele's little sister. Not the foolish client who'd agreed to a bribe because she hadn't been thinking straight and who needed saving from herself as well as the bad guys, whoever they were.

She waited until their order had been taken before asking, 'Where are you going when this job's done with?'

'Back to the Middle East.'

'You're not going home for a few days or anything?'

'Why do you want to know?'

'I'm making conversation. Annoying, I know, but one of us has to make the effort.'

Felipe tore his gaze from the distance he'd fixed on to look at her.

She tilted her head, her features softening. 'Please, Felipe, can't we just have a normal conversation like normal people?'

He smothered a sigh. It was far easier for him to ignore the tightening of his loins that occurred just by being around her if he didn't have to listen to the husky voice that stroked his skin like a caress and stare into the beguiling eyes that had the power to hypnotise him.

Her request wasn't unreasonable.

*He* was the one being unreasonable.

She couldn't help it that every look made the yearning to touch her grow and his self-loathing ratchet up another notch.

'Do you still live in Spain?' she probed, taking his silence for assent.

'No.'

'Where do you live then?'

'Nowhere.'

'Nowhere?'

'Nowhere,' he confirmed. 'I have no home. I am of no fixed abode.'

'But…' She smoothed a long strand of hair behind her ear. A teardrop diamond earring winked at him. 'Where do you call home?'

He shrugged. 'Wherever I happen to be. I have a bedroom on my plane. Hotels are easy to come by. Everything I own is easily transported and as easily stored.'

She rocked forward slowly, a crease in her forehead. 'Where do your letters go? Bills? Bank statements? You have to have an address to have a bank account.'

'Not all banks require it if you know where to ask. My business isn't a typical one. My work is my life. It has been since I joined the army.'

She pulled a face. 'Yes, I get that. You're a macho man who runs around the world protecting the weak and helpless.'

A laugh crept up his throat. 'The majority of the people I protect are far from weak. It's generally business people, government officials and aid agencies. People who go to war zones and countries with high crime rates where they know they're going to be a target. My job is to let them do their jobs in safety.'

'Why does that stop you having a home of your own? Everyone needs a home.'

He shook his head. This was why he would have preferred to stay in the suite. There, he would have been able to work on his laptop, catch up on reports from his staff around the world, issue orders and directives, and ignore Francesca while ensuring her absolute safety. Here, there was nothing to do but talk while they waited for their food to be cooked and as he'd learned the other night in the hotel's main restaurant and their late-night conversation the night before, he enjoyed talking to Francesca far more than was good for him.

When they talked she became more than the alluring woman who made his blood thicken to look at her. She became flesh and blood.

The sooner this meal was finished the better.

'What about family?' she asked, oblivious to his wish—his *need*—for her silence. 'Do you see much of them?'

'No.'

'But you do have family?'

Felipe sighed. She didn't know when to give up. If Francesca made it to the bar she would be an excellent cross-examiner. 'I have a mother, grandparents, aunts, uncles, cousins. Yes. Family.'

'Do you see much of them?'

'No.'

'Why not?'

'I'm too busy.'

'Too busy to see your own mother?'

'I visit her whenever I can. The rest I was never close to so it's no loss.'

'No siblings?'

'I'm an only child.'

'Spoilt?'

He laughed harshly. Chance would have been a fine thing. 'No.'

'A father?'

'He died five years ago.'

The inquisitiveness on her features softened. 'I'm sorry. I lost my father last year. It's hard, I know.'

'It wasn't much of a loss. I hardly knew him.'

Seeing her open her mouth to ask another question, he leaned forward. 'My mother raised me as a single parent. They were married but my father was rarely there and rarely gave her money. She worked so many different jobs to put a roof over my head and food on the table that she was hardly there either, but she wasn't absent by choice as my father was. She didn't have the time or money to take me to Madrid to visit her family. We lived in Alicante, hundreds of miles from them. If my father hadn't been such a selfish chancer our lives would have been very different so, no, I didn't find his death hard. I went to his funeral out of respect but I am not going to pretend I grieved for him. I barely knew the man.'

His father had been unsuited to family life, a man always on the road searching for the next big thing, which had never turned into anything, but that next big thing had always been more important to him than his wife and child.

So unimportant was his father to his life that he rarely thought about him, never mind talked about him, but with Francesca seemingly keen to interrogate him about his life, it was simpler to give her the full impartial facts and be done with it.

'That must have been hard for you. And your mamma,' she said, her eyes full of sympathy.

Thankfully their food was brought over to them by the cheerful waitress, T-bone steak for him and seared tuna pasta salad for Francesca.

She dived into hers and for a while he thought he'd escaped further interrogation.

Wrong.

'How often do you see your mother?'

'I try and visit over Christmas and for her birthday.'

'Is that it? Two visits a year?'

He took a large bite of his steak and ignored the implied rebuke. He didn't need to justify himself to her.

'If I only saw my mother twice a year she'd kill me,' Francesca mused. 'She thinks I live too far from her as it is and I'm only a twenty-minute walk away.'

'You're her daughter. It's a different relationship.'

'Tell that to my brothers,' she said with a roll of her eyes that immediately dimmed, the vibrancy in them muting.

With a pang, he knew she was thinking of Pieta.

'Pieta was a good son to her,' she said quietly. 'He travelled all around the world but always remembered to call her every night. Daniele's the opposite—I'm always annoying him by sending reminders for him to call. She worries about us. Pieta's death has devastated her.'

'You're a close family,' he observed.

She nodded. 'I've been very lucky.'

Lucky until the brother she'd adored had been so tragically killed.

'Your life and background are very different from mine.'

'My life and background are different from most peoples. But, then, everyone's is. None of us are the same. We all have our worries.'

'You grew up rich and with a loving family. What worries did you have?'

'Me, personally? None that were serious. I was lucky and privileged but I know I'm one of the fortunate ones and it's why I want to go into human rights law.'

'You want to spread some of your good luck?'

'You may mock me but I'm serious. I could have settled down with a husband and babies by now but I want my life to mean something.'

He could only guess how hard she'd had to work to prove herself. He knew how old money worked—he'd protected enough of the people who lived in that world to know it was still male dominated. It couldn't have been easy for her to go against her family's expectations and wishes.

'You could run Pieta's foundation.'

Her pretty brow rose. 'Are you mocking me again?'

'Not at all. You were the consummate professional today. Pieta would have been proud of you.'

Her face flushed with pleasure. 'You think?'

'I'm sure of it, and I'm sure Alberto will be back at work soon. He could help and guide you. And keep you out of trouble,' he couldn't resist adding.

She half grinned and half scowled then shrugged ruefully. 'It isn't for me. I want to get the hospital on Caballeros built for Pieta's memory but his philanthropy isn't the route I want to go. That was his and once things have settled we'll work as a family to make sure the foundation continues, but it won't be me running it. Maybe Natasha will.'

She fell silent after that, eating her food quietly, her thoughts obviously thousands of miles away with her family.

He watched her carefully. Underneath the front she put on she was grieving. He'd caught snatches of it during their time together, moments when she'd be talking to someone and, just like that, her eyes would lose their focus and her brow crease as if in confusion. And then, just as quickly, she would pull herself together and snap her focus back to the person before her.

She did it now. 'When was the last time you spoke to your mother?'

He could laugh at her single-mindedness. 'A couple of months ago.' At her exaggerated incredulity, he felt compelled to add, 'We've never been close in the way you are with your mother. Her whole life revolved around me and making sure all my needs were met but to get that she had to work fifteen hour days. I hardly knew her.' He hardly knew her now.

He took a long breath.

He really needed a beer.

Felipe raised his palm before she could ask anything else and said, 'It was a long time ago. I haven't lived with her for almost twenty years. We respect each other but she's not like your mother. She's not the clinging sort.'

'My mother doesn't cling,' she said defensively, then covered her mouth to hide a snort of laughter. 'Yes, she does cling. But I don't mind. I like it.'

'And I like the relationship my mother and I have. It suits us both.'

She cast him with a look of pure disbelief then shrugged as if to say it was a point she couldn't bother arguing. 'Is her life easier now?'

'Much easier. I've bought her a house and a car, I send her regular money. She doesn't need to work. She has friends and goes on dates. She has a life now, which she never had before.'

That perked her up. 'You bought her a house?'

He groaned, sensing a new thread of his life for her to delve into. 'Can we not talk of something else?'

'Okay, tell me why you joined the army.'

'Because I was turning into a juvenile delinquent with no parental authority and no hope of getting a decent job because there was no one there to make sure I attended school.'

'How long were you in the army for?'

'Eight years in all.' And they had been the best years of his life. The camaraderie, the companionship…after a childhood spent alone the army had given him the family he'd always craved. In Sergio he'd found the brother he'd always longed for.

How could the woman sitting opposite him understand any of this? Her family was as close as a family could be. She'd never eaten her childhood meals alone with only the television for company. She'd never *been* alone. She'd never wanted for anything, not materially or emotionally. It had all been handed to her on a plate.

So why was he fighting his own tongue from spilling the rest of it out to her?

It was those eyes, the way they smouldered and hung on to his every answer.

Every time he stared into those honest eyes a pulse would flow through him. He'd scrubbed his hands over and over but could still feel the softness of her skin and the silkiness of her hair on his fingers as if they'd marked him. When she'd been standing with Eva, the charity worker, he'd distinguished Francesca's scent without even thinking about it.

He knew her *scent*.

During their conversation, without him realising how, they'd both cleared their plates.

It was time to bring to a close this ordeal he'd enjoyed far too much.

He got to his feet. 'We can go back to the suite now.'

She stared up at him with such hurt at his brusqueness that he felt much as he would have if he'd kicked a puppy. Like a heel.

Instead of obeying, she folded her arms, the obstinate look he was becoming accustomed to setting on her jaw. But her eyes were knowing as she said, 'I think I'll stay for dessert.'

# CHAPTER NINE

'You're welcome to share my bed,' Francesca said brightly as Felipe made a bed on the floor for himself close to the door, using the duvet, spare sheets and pillows from his suite.

He didn't look at her. He'd returned to ignoring her and speaking in monosyllabic grunts ever since she'd insisted on staying for dessert.

Her insistence on staying had been a deliberate kick-back. Felipe had relaxed over their meal and opened up to her, not by much but enough for her chest to lighten and hope to spring free. A proper conversation between two adults enjoying each other's company. There were times he'd looked at her as if he wanted to eat her, the desire in his eyes vivid... But then he'd withdrawn as quickly as if he'd pulled the trigger on a gun.

Now he was back to looking at her as if he'd like to chuck her in the sea.

'Why don't you stop talking and get ready for bed?' he growled. 'Tomorrow's going to be a long day.'

'I'm not tired.'

'Read a book.'

She wished she knew what it would take to pull his barriers down long enough for him to forget his reasons for resisting and simply treat her as a woman. That's all she wanted.

'I'll put my nightclothes on in the bathroom, shall I?'

'*Yes*!'

'Okay. I won't be long. Try not to miss me.'

It didn't take long for her to change into the over-sized T-shirt she slept in, wash her face and brush her teeth, all the while wondering if she had the courage to go for full-scale seduction.

She could hardly believe she was having these thoughts.

Pieta's death had brought home how short and fickle life could be. The dangers of Caballeros had reinforced that notion. All those years she'd spent studying, any thought of a romantic life pushed aside so as not to distract her from her dreams… It had stopped her *feeling* life rather than just going through the motions of living it.

Felipe was nothing like the rich, boring, single men her parents had brought in a steady trickle to the family home before she'd escaped to university, hoping their darling daughter would snare one of them and marry into luxury and be doted on. The only similarity he had with them was that he was fabulously rich.

Francesca hadn't wanted to be doted on. Her mother had married young and was content to live the life of a social butterfly where the biggest daily problem would be matching her nail varnish with her outfit. Francesca had wanted so much more. She had wanted to be like her brothers and cousin Matteo. They were also expected to settle down and breed but at a much older age. They were expected to have fantastic careers first, whereas she'd been expected to adorn her husband's fantastic career. She hadn't wanted to adorn or be beholden to a man. She'd wanted a fantastic career of her own and had known from a very young age that the only way to get it was by studying as hard as she could to get the highest possible grades so her parents had no choice but to take her and her aspirations seriously.

She had succeeded. There had been many fights and many tears but eventually they had accepted her wishes. That hadn't stopped them parading eligible rich men in front of her but the tone had changed; become hope rather than expectation.

If she continued working hard, in two years she would

sit her bar exams and qualify as a lawyer, then spend a few more years establishing herself in the career she'd devoted her life to achieving. Only then would she think of making a marriage, safe in the knowledge that, whoever she chose, her hard-won independence would not be compromised and the marriage would be conducted as equals.

That had been the plan.

What she hadn't expected was this awakening, this heady desire for a man that no amount of logic could explain.

She didn't want to explain it. She wanted to explore it, to reach out and touch it and experience these wonderful feelings that had soaked into her being, all of which were for Felipe.

He was not a man to dote on a woman. He was strong and protective but would never treat a woman as a pet.

And he didn't want a relationship either.

If anything were to happen between them it would be nothing but a short, sweet affair that wouldn't compromise either of their chosen paths.

The problem, Francesca acknowledged ruefully, came with the *if*.

It would help if she knew how to seduce a man, let alone one so determined to keep her at arm's length. And wasn't seduction supposed to be conducted wearing sexy lingerie? She wore pretty underwear but nothing that could be considered sexy or lingerie.

All she had was herself.

When she walked back into the suite she found Felipe kneeling by his huge khaki kitbag.

He looked at her briefly then closed his eyes and muttered something under his breath before pulling out his washbag. 'I'm going to take a shower.'

A moment later came the telling click of the bathroom lock.

Taking a deep breath, Francesca turned all the lights off

apart from her bedside one, giving the room a soft seductive quality. Then she got onto the huge bed and arranged herself into what she hoped was a seductive pose. Instead of making her feel wanton it made her feel like a fool so she tried a different pose. That made her feel a bigger fool. After trying a variety of others she settled for sitting with her legs stretched out and hooked at the ankles, her head resting on the headboard.

Felipe spent so long in the bathroom that doubts began to crowd her. Did she have his feelings for her all wrong?

Were those times when she looked in his eyes and saw pained desire burning back at her nothing but creations of her own tortured mind, like a child desperate to see Father Christmas swearing blind they saw him flying his reindeer past their bedroom window? Nothing but a hopeful, overactive imagination?

She sensed when he was ready to leave his sanctuary and swallowed, placing a hand to her rapidly beating heart.

The bathroom door opened. Their eyes met.

He held her gaze a beat too long then broke it, striding past her to the nest he'd made by her door.

She watched his every step with her heart in her mouth.

Francesca had seen Felipe with nothing but tight swim shorts on at the swimming pool but she had been some distance away. Up close his magnificence was stark enough to steal her breath and set her already ragged pulses soaring. Up close there was no escaping the bulge in the snug black boxers he wore.

Even a straight man would do a double take at him.

A silvery mark on his right calf caught her eye, pulling her out of the trance she'd slipped into. 'What happened to your leg?'

'Gunshot,' he answered gruffly.

His answer had her pressing the switch behind her to turn the corner light on.

Her hand flew to her mouth.

It wasn't just a silvery mark; there was a hollowed out section of flesh around his shin bone that covered half his calf.

Thick icy sludge crawled up her spine and through her veins, freezing her from the inside out.

She could hardly get her vocal cords working to whisper, 'What happened to you?'

'The perils of army life.'

'You were shot in battle?'

'Something like that.'

Feeling faint, she took a long breath, unable to look away from the ugly wound that made her heart hurt.

Felipe was a military man. She'd known that before she'd met him. It was his career in the army, including his time in the Special Forces, that made him so effective at what he did, that had given him the solid foundations to build the hugely successful enterprise he had now.

Yet whenever she thought about the armed forces—admittedly, before she'd met Felipe that had been rarely—she'd imagined it to be like those computer games she'd been banned from watching Daniele play when he'd been younger and she much younger still but, of course, had sneakily peeked in on. She hadn't seriously thought about what it must be like to be in a real war, to have people firing at you not for fun but because they wanted to kill you.

Someone had shot Felipe with the intention of killing him.

He must have noticed her horror for his expression hardened. 'I apologise if my wound disgusts you.'

'No.' She shook her head, trying to clear it, trying to refocus her eyes. 'Don't think that. *I* don't think that. Felipe…' She shook her head some more.

Now the limp she'd often noticed made sense.

As if to distract her attention from his wound, Felipe

slid into the makeshift bed he'd made for himself on the floor, thumped the top pillow and lay on his back, gazing at the ceiling with his arm crooked above his head.

Francesca turned the corner light off so the only illumination in the suite came from her bedside light.

She felt chilled to her core. If whoever had shot at him had had a better aim the vital, intense man who lay in a nest of bedding at her door would not be here. He would be gone from this earth like Pieta, nothing but a memory. But not a memory to her because she never would have met him.

She remembered Daniele—or was it Matteo?—saying Felipe had been discharged from the army on medical grounds.

'Was that the reason you left the army?'

Even with the limited light she saw his grimace. 'Yes. The wound meant I was no longer an effective soldier. It's standard procedure. It wasn't personal.'

'Would you have stayed if you could?'

'I would have stayed for as long as they'd had me. I loved the life.'

'You loved going into war zones?'

He let out a low rumble of laughter. 'Believe it or not, yes. I thrived on the danger. We all did. I loved everything about army life. Passing selection for the Special Forces was the best day of my life. Receiving my discharge was the worst.'

Felipe had known as soon as the bullet had hit him that it was the end of his army career and the end of everything he'd held dear. The bullet had splintered in his leg, shrapnel lodging in the bones. There had been talk of amputation.

The long months spent in rehabilitation, working into a sweat just to walk again, dealing with the pain of his wound and the darkness of what he'd lost…it had all brought home to him that he was meant to be alone.

When it was just you in the world the only threat of pain was the physical kind. He'd proven he could deal with that. Physical pain was mind over matter. Determination. It hurt but didn't leave you bereft and empty inside.

For once Francesca was silent. He knew it wouldn't be for long. He was right.

'Is that why you went into protection? So you could still get the adrenaline buzz?'

'The world is full of dangers and people still need to visit those danger zones. I knew I could provide the protection they needed and that there were many other soldiers like me who were fit and ready for the next challenge.' But not Sergio. The first bullet that had hit him had gone straight into his heart.

'Do you get the same fulfilment you got from the army?'

'It's a different kind of fulfilment.' Even though he'd thrown all his energy into it, he could never have guessed how successful his business would be. He had more money than he could spend in a thousand lifetimes, was on the speed dial of the world's most powerful people, but knew that given the choice of swapping his riches for a return to his army days he would discard his worldly goods without a second thought.

'Don't you ever wish for a normal life?' she whispered in the silence.

'What's your definition of a normal life?'

'One that's not completely nomadic.'

'No.' Yet as he spoke his rebuttal he found his mind meandering for the first time ever to a real home with an ebony-haired beauty…

He pushed the thought away. A normal, regular life was not for him.

'That's enough talk. We've an early start. Get some sleep.'

'But—'

'I mean it. No more conversation.'

But he knew the chances of his getting any sleep were slim, not when he was certain that beneath her oversized T-shirt Francesca lay naked.

He closed his eyes and willed his mind not to think of her naked.

*Dios*, this was torture. He ached to join her in that bed.

In his head he counted out the reasons why he needed to stay exactly where he was.

One. She was his client.

Two. She was grieving.

'It's not even ten o'clock. I'm not tired. I never go to bed this early.'

Just the sound of her voice was enough to make Felipe's loins tighten.

'Read your book,' he said through gritted teeth.

There was another long period of silence but he sensed a shift in the atmosphere, a change in her mood.

'*"Read your book, stop talking, go to sleep"*,' she mimicked suddenly. 'It's one step forward and two steps back with you, isn't it? One minute you're opening up and talking to me like a normal human being, the next you act like you're trying to forget my existence. Do you treat all your clients like this?'

He smothered a groan at the hurt echoing in her voice. 'Like what?'

'Like they're an encumbrance to be endured. Sometimes it feels that you don't even like me.'

He clenched his jaw. What did she want him to say? Mere *liking* had nothing to do with his feelings for her.

'It's different with my other clients.' He'd never struggled with professional detachment before. He'd never wanted to rip any of their clothes off.

'So it's true!' As quick as a flash she threw her covers

off and jumped off the bed. 'You don't like me. I thought it was the attraction between us you hated.' She stormed into her dressing room and slammed her hand against the switch, bathing the room in fresh light. 'I didn't realise the problem was that you actively dislike *me*.'

'I *don't*…' But his words fell from his lips when she pulled her T-shirt off. Even with the distance between them, he could see her clearly, from the divine weighty breasts with their dark aureoles to the soft womanly hair between her legs.

Oh, dear heaven…

*Francesca* was heaven. A taste of paradise wrapped up in beautiful, womanly form.

But then she grabbed the dress she'd been wearing earlier and he understood what she was doing.

Springing to his feet, he strode over and blocked the doorway of her dressing room. 'Where do you think you're going?'

'For a drink. Anywhere away from you.'

Fire blazed from her eyes, her whole body vibrating with anger. And, *Dios*, no matter how hard he tried he couldn't stop his eyes from devouring her, naked before him, not an ounce of embarrassment in her returning fury.

Then she tilted her chin and pulled the dress over her head. The delectable curves disappeared as she smoothed the dress down and tugged her trapped hair free. As it tumbled down her back he couldn't help but fantasise what it would feel like to have that hair tumble over *him* in all its silken glory.

'Get out of my way,' she said coldly.

'No.'

Slowly, her fiery gaze holding his, she stepped to him. When she was close enough for his senses to be hit with her scent, she put her wrists together and held them out to him. 'If you're intending to treat me as a prisoner you might as well tie me up because that's the only way you're going to stop me leaving this room.'

Electricity shot between them, so real he could almost hear the crackle. It heated him too, tiny jolts bouncing on his skin, his heart thrumming…

His hand rose by its own volition, his fingers stretching towards her.

A throb of need burst through him, so powerful he had to dig his feet into the floor to stop from hauling her into his arms.

'You are not leaving this suite.' His speech was long, drawn out, ragged.

'I'm not staying with someone who can barely look at me and gets irritated every time I open my mouth.'

Without him knowing how it happened, his fingers closed around the delicate wrists. A moment later he'd pulled her to him so their bodies were flush, her breasts pressed against his chest.

'I don't dislike you,' he ground out, gazing down at the spitting eyes, the luminous skin, the lips that begged to be kissed… 'Don't you see that? I like you *too much*.'

For long, long moments they did nothing but stare at each other until the anger that blazed so brightly in her eyes softened to blaze with something that struck straight into his loins.

Francesca stared helplessly at the man who had her in a grip so tight she could never break free yet which elicited not the slightest amount of pain.

The humiliation that had washed over her like a cold shower at the realisation she'd been longing for a man who hated her vanished as awareness filled her in its stead, awareness of his heat, of being held against this dangerously masculine man her body craved.

She had no conscious reckoning of the change in him, of how the fury deepened into something so dark and molten her chest filled, of the deepening of his breaths as he continued to gaze down at her...

'I can't hear your voice without becoming aroused,' he said, his voice low, pained. 'I can't look at you without wanting to kiss you. I can't breathe your scent without wanting to possess you. Wanting you like this is torture.'

'Then stop fighting it,' she whispered.

Later she would have no conscious remembrance of the moment his lips moulded onto hers. It was like a beast that lived inside them both suddenly became unleashed.

There was nothing gentle about his kiss or her response to it. It burned her, ravaged her. All her nerve endings exploded and leapt onto him. The hand that had been holding her wrists was now wrapped tightly around her waist, her arms now looped tightly around his neck, kissing as if they needed the other for air, lips parted, devouring each other.

She grabbed at the back of his head and raked her fingers through his hair, nuzzling, kissing, nipping, her senses filling with his very essence, all the hunger she had for him soaring free.

His arousal pressed hard and huge against her belly, his hands roamed her contours, kneading, fingers biting. The evidence of his desire for her was dizzying and heightened her own. The desire she'd experienced during the alcohol-induced fumble that had gone further than either of them had expected had been like a carnal dream but this... sober...everything felt gloriously, dizzily heightened and *urgent*, no slow sensual build-up, her body craving nothing less than full possession.

He broke the kiss to place his hands at her waist and lift her into the air like a ballet dancer lifting his partner. Her hair fell onto his shoulders and he turned his face to breathe the scent of it in. '*Dios*, I want you,' he muttered raggedly.

Without another word said he sat her on the edge of the

bed and pressed her down so he lay on top of her, crushing her, his heart drumming strongly enough for her to feel it against her own hammering heart. Their lips entwined in another deep, hungry kiss and he ran a hand up her thigh to take the hem of her dress and raise it to her waist.

Needing to touch him, she ran her fingers down his back and revelled in the smoothness of his skin, the muscles that bunched beneath her touch, then traced lower to the tight buttocks. Grasping frantically, she found the waistband of his boxers and tugged at them. Felipe's hand covered hers and together they shifted them down his hips, allowing his erection to spring free.

Her eyes flew open to feel the weight of his excitement against her inner thigh, a deep throb pulsing through her to know this was for her. Her own arousal had melted into a mass of heat and dampness, all concentrating in the one area he was so close to taking possession of.

Francesca had never dreamt she was capable of such wanton, reckless carnality, that her flesh could feel like a living being, that desire could beat like a drum with a rhythm felt in her every pore.

*This*, she thought dreamily… *This*…

Instinct had her raising her thighs and wrapping her legs around Felipe's waist, urging him on, her body speaking the language she had never learned.

The tip of his erection found where it needed to be with no guidance from either of them and in one driving thrust he was inside her.

It happened so quickly that it took a few beats for her brain to register the sharp pain and when it did register, the gasp of relief at his possession that had flown from her mouth turned into a gasp of shock and stilled on her lips.

Felipe froze.

The heady urgency of his desire deflated like a punctured balloon. He gazed down in horror at Francesca's whitening face.

*It wasn't possible…*

His head pounded loudly, bells clanging, sirens wailing.

*It wasn't possible.*

With as great a care as he could manage, he withdrew from her and swung his legs over to rest on the floor then grabbed the back of his neck and dug his fingers into it.

The beat of his heart was out of time.

She didn't move.

He didn't move.

For the longest time he sat on the bed staring incomprehensibly at the thick carpet while she lay on the bed gazing mutely at the ceiling.

He wanted to be sick. There was movement beside him as Francesca slowly sat up.

A trembling finger was placed lightly on his shoulder. 'Felipe…'

Slowly he raised his head and caught sight of himself in the mirror on the wall.

The reflection gazing back was a man he didn't recognise.

He didn't think he would ever recognise himself again.

# CHAPTER TEN

WHEN HIS THROAT had loosened enough so he could breathe, Felipe got to his feet and put his boxers on. Only then did he turn to the hunched figure in the centre of the bed. She still had her dress on.

Francesca's eyes were huge but when he met them he saw they were filled with defiance as well as misery.

With a sigh, he sank back onto the edge of the bed and buried his face in his hands. 'You should have told me.'

Her voice was low but steady. 'If I'd told you, you would have stopped.'

'Damn right I would have stopped.' He swore loudly as he remembered something else that made the hairs on arms lift. 'We didn't even use protection.' Not that they'd needed it. It had been over almost as soon as it had begun.

'I'm on the Pill,' she mumbled.

'Are you?' he demanded. 'You're not just saying that?'

A quick shake of her head. 'I used to have terrible pains every month. The Pill helped.'

'Francesca... *Dios*...' He raised his head and met her gaze. 'What were you thinking?'

She didn't answer.

'Was it your intention to make me hate myself?'

She shook her head and blinked rapidly. If she cried, he thought there was every chance he would lose the plot completely.

How was it possible she'd been a virgin?

'For God's sake, will you say something? Tell me what's going on in that head of yours?'

'I thought you wanted me to shut up,' she whispered with a forlorn smile.

His hands clenched into fists and he swore loudly.

She screwed her eyes tight shut.

He fought to control his tone, to soften it. 'Francesca, please, tell me why you didn't think fit to inform me you were a virgin. Don't you understand how sick I am at myself for what just happened? My self-loathing would have been high enough but discovering that...' He threw his hands in the air. His affairs had always been conducted with experienced women who knew better than to expect anything from him. Did Francesca giving her virginity to him mean she wanted more? 'Why didn't you stop me?'

'Because I wanted it to happen,' she said so quietly he had to strain to hear.

'But *why*? There can never be anything between us, don't you understand that? Even when this is all over and you're no longer my client, you and I can never be.'

'Why? Because I'm too young for you?' Her voice shook. 'I'm twenty-three, not thirteen, old enough to marry, to vote, to drive, to work, to make mistakes and be judged old enough to know better.'

'No!' His voice rose as he lost the battle with his temper. 'I don't do relationships. I told you this. You were a twenty-three-year-old virgin for a reason, I assume because you were waiting for the right man or for marriage. I could never be that man!'

'I don't want you to be that man!' Francesca shouted back. Her shame and Felipe's anger had pushed her to breaking point. 'Stop making assumptions about me. I wasn't *saving* myself. Haven't you listened to me? I've told you more than once I don't intend to settle down for years, not until I've set up my own law firm. I want a career first, thank you, and when I do marry it will be to someone who can treat me as his equal. You are *not* that man.'

'Then *why*?' He gripped the back of his head and breathed deeply. 'Please, explain it to me so I don't spend the rest of my life hating myself for taking advantage of your vulnerability. And do not deny that you're vulnerable, you buried the brother you loved only days ago and something like that does affect you even if you don't see it at the time.'

She dragged her fingers down her face and tried to control the violent trembling racking her body.

Whenever she'd imagined them together, and in the past few days it had seemed that was *all* she'd thought about, she'd blithely assumed he wouldn't notice she was a virgin and that she would have the wit to smother any pain because everyone said the pain only lasted a moment.

She'd known perfectly well he would reinforce the barrier he'd put between them if he knew she was a virgin and seeing his self-loathing horror at what they'd done made her feel more wretched and ashamed of herself than she had believed she could feel.

Had it been such a bad thing, keeping quiet about her virginity? It was her body. Wasn't she free to do with it as she wished?

Silence filled the room as she composed her thoughts and tried to compose herself, biting back the tears that were right there, waiting to be unleashed.

'I know Pieta's death's affected me,' she whispered. 'It's made me see how short life can be. I could get a terminal illness or get hit by a car or be the victim of a natural disaster... People die every day. You've walked the streets of Caballeros with me...you've been in battle, you must feel life's fragility.'

A tear leaked down her cheek. She wiped it away before continuing. 'I'm not trying to be morbid. Before Pieta died... I'm trying to make you understand what it was like. I knew from the time I could speak that I would never inherit anything and I remember my mamma stroking my hair when I was seven and saying what a pretty girl I was and how lucky I was that I would have my pick of rich husbands and always live a life of luxury. My looks and my family name were expected to be enough for me to have a great future but I remember feeling sick at the thought of it.

'Daniele wasn't going to inherit but he was expected to build a great life for himself—why should it be different for me because I was girl? Why should my future depend on what would, essentially, be the goodwill of a man I hadn't even met? Why should I be forced to beg for money to buy the clothes I need when I can earn it myself and control my own life? I think that was the moment I decided I would take my own path and prove that anything my brothers could do, I could do too, and do it better. I've spent my whole life working towards that. But I didn't live like a recluse. I partied and had fun but relationships…I saw how my friends were with their boyfriends and how their relationships consumed their lives and knew I couldn't afford that distraction.'

While she spoke, Felipe didn't say anything, listening with narrowed eyes without comment.

She met his gaze and tried to smile but instead found herself wiping away another tear. 'Until eleven days ago I never had the sense that it could all end at any moment. My father's death was awful but he'd been in his seventies and had been ill for years. In many ways the end was a relief for him. Pieta was only thirty-five, young, fit, recently married, a whole future to look forward to and it was all taken away in a moment by something as innocuous as fog. *Fog*!' She could laugh at the madness and cruelty of it.

To watch her father slowly disintegrate had been heartbreaking but his faculties, his sense of humour…they had all survived in him to the very end. They'd had time to prepare. Nothing could have prepared her or any of them for Pieta's death.

'All those people who died in the hurricane in Caballeros,

they'd had futures and family too, people who loved them. If it could happen to Pieta and to them, then why not me?'

Felipe made to speak but she raised a hand to stop him.

'Whether I have days left to live or years or decades, I want to live it to be the best I can but I want to *feel* it too. You make me feel things I've never felt before. Good feelings. Scary feelings. But *real* feelings.' Feelings she'd ached to explore to see where they would take her because *what if she never felt them again*? 'Do you understand that?'

His dark eyes held hers as he gave a sharp inclination of his head.

'I don't know if it was this new awareness of life and its fragility that woke these feelings up or if it was just the catalyst…' She attempted a smile. 'No, I do know. If I'd met you under different circumstances I still would have wanted you. What I don't know is if I would have had acted on it. I don't expect anything from you or want anything more than this. Don't think you took advantage of me. I gave my body to you freely as a consenting woman, just as you gave yours freely to me as a consenting man.'

She tried to smile again but her chin wobbled too much for it to form. 'And that's it.'

As Felipe listened, his fury with both Francesca and himself slowly seeped from him.

Curled on the huge bed, she looked so intensely vulnerable that his heart ached.

His pulses hammering, he shifted closer to her and took her cold hands, which just a short time ago had been warm, and rubbed them gently between his own then pressed a kiss to them.

She attempted another shaky smile that made the ache in his heart expand.

'I hurt you, didn't I?' he said quietly.

She drew her lips in and nodded. 'That was my own fault. If you'd known…'

'If I'd known it was your first time I would have taken it slowly, not taken you like a rutting bull.'

She pulled a face. 'If you'd known it was my first time you wouldn't have taken me at all. That's why I didn't tell you.'

He laughed, his chest lightening at her wry quip.

'You're right, I have made many assumptions about you, *querida*,' he said, reaching out to stroke her pale cheek. 'It's the nature of my life. I work with men, the people I protect are normally men too.'

Women had always been on the periphery of his life, even his own mother, too busy working to feed him for him to learn any feminine secrets. Women were a mystery. He'd shared his bed with many of them through the years but had no clue as to how their minds worked. Francesca was the closest he'd come to understanding.

'Women have always seemed like a different species to me,' he admitted ruefully. 'I accepted your family's description of you being a danger to yourself at face value, which I wouldn't have done if you'd been a man.'

'Maybe they were right,' she whispered.

He shook his head, knowing she was thinking back to her gung-ho response to the Governor's demand for a cash bribe. 'To begin with you were on the edge but you soon found the strength you needed. What I am trying to say in my clumsy way is that I've not been able to look past my initial assumptions and too busy fighting my attraction to you to see you as you really are.'

'How do you see me now?'

'As strong.' *And beautiful.* 'You're a fighter, *querida*.'

Another tear rolled down her cheek. She screwed her face up as he wiped it away with his thumb.

'Not very strong now,' she mumbled.

He leaned forward and cupped her face in his hands.

'I've seen men bigger than me cry. It's nothing to do with strength and nothing to be ashamed of.'

She sighed and nodded then seemed to gather herself together, her back straightening. 'I should put my night-shirt on.'

Her legs made a slight wobble as she padded to the dressing room and closed the door behind her, re-emerging moments later with her nightshirt on.

She stood in the doorway and tucked a stray lock of hair behind her ear. 'What happens now?'

His heart hurt to see her vulnerability. He couldn't turn his back on it, not yet.

'Now, *querida*, we get some sleep.' Sliding under the bedsheets, he opened his arms to her.

Tentatively she walked to him. When she climbed onto the bed he switched the bedside light off then gently laid her down so she was nestled against him.

Holding her tightly, he lay with her in silence, his mind still reeling from everything that had just happened, his loins still aching from unfulfilled desire.

Instead of acting on it, he did nothing more than stroke her hair and trace his fingers gently over the top of her back.

He'd never held a woman like this before. It was an intimacy he'd always steered away from.

He couldn't stay here holding her like this. Equally, he couldn't leave her. Not yet.

Only when Francesca's breathing had become deep and regular, her limbs weighty on him, did he extricate himself and settle in his makeshift bed on the floor, attempting to calm his racing head and thrumming heart enough to find some sleep of his own.

Felipe opened his eyes, instantly alert to any sound.

The suite was in darkness. All was quiet. But something had woken him.

Then he heard it again, the sound that had roused him from his sleep. A whimper.

He threw his covers off and climbed onto the bed where he found Francesca curled in a ball, crying into her pillow.

'*Querida?*' Tentatively, he put a hand on her head.

She stilled at his touch. After a moment she turned her face and opened her eyes. 'Felipe?'

He smoothed damp hair from her wet face. 'What's the matter?'

Her face crumpled and tears fell down her cheeks, silvery in the shadowed darkness.

'A bad dream?'

She gave a jerky nod.

He scooped her up to pull her to him and wrapped his arms tightly around her.

'Hush,' he whispered, kissing the top of her head. 'It's over now.'

Clinging to him as if he were a life raft, she sobbed into his chest.

'It's over now,' he repeated, feeling as ineffectual as it was possible to feel.

He'd held fellow soldiers in his arms when they'd sobbed over a fallen comrade, but never had he held them and heard the cracks of his own heart.

If he had the power, he would snatch out the terror that had taken her into its hold and bury it for ever.

'It's over.'

Her hair brushed against his chin as she shook her head. 'It will never be over.'

He held her until the shudders ceased and the tears dried up, then got under the covers and lay beside her, still holding her to him.

'It will get better,' he whispered, stroking her hair. 'Not yet, not for a long time, but one day.'

'How?' she asked dully into his chest.

'I know loss. Grief has to come out. You've been keeping yourself so busy during the day it's coming out at night.'

She was silent for a long moment before saying in a small voice, 'It's not grief. It's guilt.'

'Guilt over Pieta?'

She nodded.

'How can you feel guilt, *querida*? You weren't in the helicopter with him.'

There was another lengthy silence. When she eventually replied her voice was so low and muffled it was a struggle to hear clearly.

'When Mamma called me to tell me my brother had died, I thought she was talking about Daniele. He's always travelling by helicopter. I didn't realise it was Pieta until she asked me to go with her to tell Natasha.'

'Why would you feel guilty about that?'

'Because my first emotion when I realised it was Pieta was relief that it wasn't Daniele.'

Francesca waited for a reaction from him, a condemnation, however subtle.

His only response was to tighten his hold and rub his mouth into her hair.

'I haven't told anyone that,' she whispered. 'I tried to deny it to myself but he won't let me forget.'

'Who won't?'

'Pieta. He's haunting my dreams. He knows how I felt. He knows the truth and he won't let me forget it.'

'That's not possible,' he said gently, his breath warm against her skull. 'They say dreams are our subconscious talking to us and I know it to be true from my own experience. That's all it is.'

'My guilty conscience talking to me?' She swallowed back more tears.

'Yes. But you have nothing to feel guilty about.'

'I have everything to feel guilty about.'

'Did you wish Pieta dead?'

'*No!*' The idea was so horrific that she disentangled herself from his hold and sat up. 'No. Of course I didn't. He was my brother and I loved him.'

'And he knew that.' He took her hand and laced his fingers through hers. 'He was your hero.'

She smiled wistfully and squeezed his interlinked fingers. 'I did love him. I really did. But I was never close to him as I am to Daniele. He left home to go to university when I was six so I only have faint memories of living with him. He was this mythological being who would sweep into the family home at various times bearing thoughtful gifts. He would sit down with me and ask me questions and listen closely to all my answers. He encouraged me in everything I did. Truly, he was a brilliant big brother but...'

'But?' Felipe asked into the silence.

'He was detached. I never connected emotionally to him. Daniele's a lot older than me too but he was a *proper* brother. He teased me and tormented me, and I teased and tormented him back. When I went to university, he was always dropping in on a whim if he was in Pisa, taking me out in his newest car or jet or whatever expensive toy he'd recently brought. He took me shopping, brought me my first legal drink...'

'He was the fun one?' Felipe suggested.

'Yes. That. The fun one. That wasn't Pieta's fault. He was raised the eldest son, knowing the family's estate would pass to him, that keeping it intact for the next generation would be his responsibility. He was very serious. When I started working for him at his law firm I hoped we would get closer and I would see another side to him. I thought we would go out for lunch together and have after work drinks.'

'It didn't happen?'

'We never had the time. I only started my traineeship a few months ago and Pieta was rarely there as he was always travelling. I was put under the charge of one of his senior lawyers.'

She sighed and lay back down, resting her head next to his. All that time she'd thought she would have to finally get to know her oldest brother, all gone in an instant.

'Pieta was a hard man to get to know,' Felipe said quietly. 'I worked with him many times on his philanthropic missions. He was a good man and I enjoyed his company.'

'But?' she prompted, certain he wanted to say more.

He rolled onto his side to look at her, so close his nose brushed hers. 'He kept people at arm's length. I don't think there were many people he allowed to see his real self.'

'I wish things could have been different between us and that we'd been closer.'

'I know you do. Pieta was just a man doing the best he could with the hand he'd been dealt. I'm sure he didn't mean to shut you out.'

Francesca gazed at him, her chest feeling so much lighter yet, conversely, unbelievably full.

'Thank you,' she whispered.

'For what?'

'For listening and not judging.'

He kissed the tip of her nose.

She thought back to his earlier comment about the subconscious. 'What was it that gave you bad dreams?'

She caught the flash of pain in his eyes.

Palming his cheek, she stroked the soft beard. Tentatively, she probed, 'Is it from when you were shot?'

He covered her hand with his own. 'I lost my closest friend that day. I watched him die.'

'Oh, Felipe,' she breathed with a sympathy she felt right in the centre of her being.

'The Special Forces do many classified covert missions.

This was one of them. The most I can tell you about it is that a group of Spanish executives were taken hostage in a North African country by a guerrilla group. My unit was flown in to rescue them. Our intelligence was faulty. We were told there were three hostage takers but there were eight of them. It was a bloodbath. We lost ten of the hostages and I lost three of my men. Good men. Sergio was shot first. He'd been by my side since our basic training days when we were green eighteen-year-olds. We took selection for the Special Forces together...we were as close as brothers. I was best man at his wedding. I was to be godfather to his child. I lost everything that day—my brother, my army family and the career I loved.'

Francesca, her heart in her mouth, stared into the dark eyes and wished with all her heart that she could find the words to take his pain away.

No wonder he understood her pain so much. He must have been battling his own nightmares for the past decade.

His overprotectiveness and desire to plan for each and every eventuality suddenly made perfect sense. Even the business he'd formed, protecting civilians, ensuring they were as safe as they could be, never leaving anything to chance. She would bet her career none of his clients had ever been taken hostage while under his protection.

It also made sense of his solitude. Here was a man who'd spent his childhood alone but in the army had found a place where he belonged, only to have it all ripped away from him in one disastrous mission.

This time she was the one to wrap her arms around him and hold him close so his head was nestled in the crook of her neck, his beard scratching her collarbone.

She swallowed a lump away and closed her eyes, trying to process how everything had turned on its head.

This closeness she felt with Felipe right now...

Did sex always lead to such emotional intimacy?

How did men find it so easy to conduct meaningless affairs? How could Daniele and Matteo hop from one bed to another without a second thought?

She'd assumed it would be the same for her but what had happened between her and Felipe that night transcended way beyond sex.

Her head was so full that it took a long time to fall back to sleep. When she finally did, there were no dreams.

# CHAPTER ELEVEN

IN THE MORNING, Francesca awoke to find the bed empty and the sound of the shower running.

She looked at her watch. Seven o'clock.

The longest night of her life had passed very quickly.

When Felipe emerged from the bathroom, fully dressed in a navy suit and tie—she had no idea how he kept his suits so pristine—the strangest shyness passed over her.

'How are you feeling?' he asked, casting her that piercing, scrutinising gaze that made her belly flip.

'Like I could sleep the whole day.'

He smiled wryly. 'You can sleep on the plane. We're running late so you'll have to eat breakfast on the plane too. I don't want to rush you but we need to be at the airport within the hour.'

'I'll get a move on then.' Scooting out of bed, she brushed past him and locked herself in the bathroom.

She looked in the mirror, expecting to see a different face reflecting back.

She felt different. She felt as if her world had changed.

Everything that had passed in the night felt like a dream, her nightmare a dream within it.

Felipe had caught her at her lowest moment and carried her through it.

He'd listened without judgement. He'd held her. He'd comforted her.

And then he'd shared the darkest part of himself with her. He'd trusted her with that.

She couldn't begin to describe what that meant. All she knew was that it meant everything…

Her heart thumped erratically against her chest.

*Oh, Dio, Dio, Dio.*

This wasn't good. This was bad. Very bad.

She rubbed shampoo into her hair vigorously, scratching her nails into her skull.

She *couldn't* be falling for him. It wasn't possible. She'd only known him for five days.

That settled her.

Breathing a little more easily, she squeezed conditioner onto her palm and spread it through her hair.

This was her grief talking. Felipe had said so many times that her grief made her vulnerable and now she got what he'd meant.

A bad case of lust mixed with his tenderness and shared secrets were clouding her feelings. If she'd met him in different circumstances she was quite sure she'd still want him but her feelings wouldn't be so extreme. She wouldn't feel that she was standing on the edge of a precipice, waiting to fall into terrifying unknown depths.

Her grief, the situation they were in…it had all converged together to make her feel things that weren't true.

She wasn't falling for him.

She was still telling herself that when she hurried from the bathroom to her dressing room.

She was still telling herself that when she was fully dressed, had packed her stuff into her case and joined him in the suite.

And she was still telling herself that when he flashed her the smile that made her stomach melt into liquid butter.

'My men are all in position,' he told her.

It was time to go.

Francesca stared at the sleek white jet waiting on the runway in the distance. 'I thought we were going back on Pieta's plane.'

'It couldn't get to us until the afternoon so I had one of my own flown over.'

'I've always wanted to travel by private jet and now I get to go on two different ones in the space of a week? I'm being spoiled.'

'You didn't travel on the family jet when you were growing up?'

'What family jet?' she snorted. 'There was lots of family money, enough for us to be privately educated and see a lot of the world, but the *castello* needs a fortune to maintain it…'

'Your family has a castle?' he asked with surprise.

'It's in the middle of the family estate. I thought you knew that?'

'Pieta never spoke of it.'

'I don't think he liked it much. We used to spend summer holidays there but we never lived in it. Mamma found it too draughty. It's currently hired out for corporate functions and to ghost hunters.'

'Ghost hunters?'

'It's supposed to be haunted.'

'Did you ever find a ghost?'

'No, and I looked *everywhere*.'

He laughed.

'Daniele hid behind a gravestone in the cemetery once and jumped out on me, pretending to be a ghost, when I was about eight.'

'He would have been eighteen?'

'Yes. He was very mature for his age.'

He laughed even louder and shook his head. 'Your family has its own cemetery? That's quite an unusual thing to have, isn't it?'

'And a chapel. Until fifty years ago it had its own priest too. All the family on my father's side are buried there dating back to around the fifteenth century.' She attempted a smile even though her humour had drifted away from her. 'We buried Pieta next to my father. I suppose Daniele and I will end up there one day too.'

'It's a very different world from what I grew up with,' Felipe said, thinking of the plot in the packed cemetery in the middle of Alicante he'd paid for his father to be buried in. 'I can trace my lineage back only four generations.'

'Have you looked into it?' she asked, eyes lighting with curiosity.

'My mother did last year. There was nothing exciting to be found so she gave up.'

'There's always something exciting to be found in the past,' she insisted, 'but it's when people live in the past that there become problems. We have to respect the past but look to the future or everything stagnates.'

'Speaks the voice of experience?'

She pulled a face. 'If generations of my family had thought to maintain the *castello* rather than close rooms off when they became uninhabitable, it wouldn't be in the state it's in now.' Then she shrugged and gave an evil grin. 'Still, if Natasha isn't pregnant it'll be Daniele's problem now. Let him deal with it.'

'Didn't Pieta do anything to it?'

'He got builders and local craftsmen in to repair one wing, which is the part that's hired out, but...' She sighed. 'He never had the chance to follow it through.'

The car had come to a stop beside the plane, which was ready for boarding.

When they entered the cabin she stopped to take it all in, then nodded her approval. 'It's beautiful.'

This, his favourite of his planes, was the closest Felipe had to a home, with a bedroom and fully functioning bathroom, dining and study area. He'd long ago decided that as he spent so much time travelling from one country to the next, he might as well do it in comfort and style.

They took their seats either side of a mahogany table and five minutes later they were airborne.

'I've just thought—aren't James and Seb coming with us?' Francesca peered out of the window as if she expected to see them flying up with jetpacks on to join them.

'They're staying in Aguadilla with my other men to prepare for our return on Saturday.'

'What preparations are needed?'

'Only the small matter of making sure we get you and four hundred thousand dollars of cash on and off Caballeros without you being kidnapped or the money stolen.'

'Oh. That.'

Oh. That. As if her safety meant nothing to her when it meant everything to him.

'Aren't you going to ask about any of the details?'

She raised her shoulders with utter nonchalance but her tired eyes were steady. 'Felipe, I am one hundred percent certain you will have every eventuality covered. I don't need the details. You just tell me what to do and when, and I'll do it.'

Something warm flowed into his veins at this and expanded, his blood flowing thickly into his every crevice.

People put their lives in his hands every day of the week but Francesca's utter faith in him meant more to him than all those people's trust combined.

He'd put his life on the line more times than he could ever count in the past eighteen years, had accepted it from the outset as a part of his job. But for the first time he knew he would gladly, not just willingly, lay down his life if meant keeping someone from harm. Her. Francesca. He would have his legs riddled with bullets if it stopped her being hurt.

And then the dreamiest of smiles crept over her cheeks. 'You can always fill me in on anything important while you're protecting me in Pisa.'

'Protecting you in Pisa?' he asked, raising his brow.

'Of course. What if those men who have been following me decide to fly out to Italy and hunt me down? You wouldn't leave me to that fate, would you?'

Even Felipe, who saw danger in everything, had to laugh at the absurdity of the notion, even as his blood thickened to treacle.

He'd planned to fly on to his headquarters in London after refuelling in Pisa.

But…

Did he really want to give up the chance to spend some proper time with this captivating woman, away from the dangers of Caballeros?

He no longer cared that he'd broken his rules and given in to his desire for her. He was beyond that.

He'd awoken with Francesca's leg draped over his thigh, her warm body pressed against him, and a powerful erection. He'd had to drag himself out of bed when all he'd wanted was to roll her onto her back and make love to her again, this time properly and with the tenderness that had been missing from their almost angry coupling before he'd discovered the truth that she'd been a virgin.

But getting her home to safety was his priority. Making love—if he was to make love to her again—would have to wait until they had the time and leisure to make it everything her first time should have been.

They'd shared with each other intimacies that went beyond their bodies. That in itself should have been enough to stop him making love to her again too.

In his younger years he'd had thoughts of settling down once his army days were done with but since Sergio's death and his own discharge the only life he could contemplate was one spent alone. He'd learned to fend for himself in his childhood and be content in his solitude. For Felipe, it was the natural way to be. Those long dark days spent fighting his injury to be able to walk again had made him see that.

But Francesca wasn't looking for anything heavy either. Neither of them wanted a proper relationship and he'd already broken all his rules with her…

In Pisa she wouldn't be under his protection. It would be just them, two consenting adults enjoying each other in a brief window of their lives.

For all his rationalising, it came down to one simple fact. He didn't want last night to be their only night.

'I can show you round the *castello*, if you like?' she added temptingly, hitching her knees to snuggle more deeply into her seat.

'Now there's an offer I can't refuse.'

'And, of course, I'll make sure to obey your every command.'

'My *every* command?'

She covered her mouth and yawned widely. Her sparkling eyes were getting heavier by the second.

*Dios*, she was beautiful even with dark circles under her eyes.

The throbbing ache in his groin had him tempted to carry her straight into his bedroom but the moment was interrupted by a member of the cabin crew entering the cabin with the tray of coffee he'd asked for when boarding.

By the time she'd bustled out again, Francesca was fast asleep.

Francesca's heart pounded as she led Felipe into the elevator that went to her apartment floor.

He'd insisted on carrying her cases along with his own kit bag.

She still couldn't believe she'd found the nerve to invite him to stay with her. It had been the look in his eyes, the desire and tenderness she'd seen there as the jet had lifted through the clouds that had given her the courage.

They both knew it was only until their return to Caballeros. It didn't need to be vocalised. Neither wanted anything heavy or permanent.

But now that they were here, she found her nerves shredding her.

She'd never invited a man into her home before who wasn't related by blood.

Unlocking the front door, she took a deep breath. 'Coffee?'

He was staring around the apartment with evident interest. 'That would be good, thanks.'

She led him through to the kitchen, whispering a prayer of thanks to herself that the place wasn't a complete mess.

'I'm afraid I haven't got any milk.'

'Black's fine.'

'Give me a minute to call my mamma and let her know I'm back.' Fortunately, her mother's phone was switched off so she left a message to let her know she was home safely.

She put her phone on the kitchen island and swallowed. Felipe's presence in the large space seemed to have shrunk its proportions.

'This is a nice place,' he said, nodding approvingly. 'Much bigger than it looks from the outside.'

'Thank you.' She poured water into the pot and tried to control the tremble of her hands. Her movements felt awkward and stilted, as if she'd forgotten how to use her limbs. 'I can't take any credit for it—it belongs to Daniele. I just rent it off him. At a discount rate,' she added with the flash of a grin.

'What happened to your independence?' he teased.

'I'm independent, not stupid.' She strove to keep her tone light but it was so hard when she was massively aware that she was alone with Felipe in her apartment. Excitement thrummed through every part of her but the nerves were thrumming along with it. 'Daniele's got lots of properties. If he wants to rent one out cheaply to his little sister while she completes her education then his sister would be an idiot to say no. I moved in when I started university.'

'You did your law degree here in Pisa?'

She nodded and opened the fridge. 'Oh. I forgot. I haven't got any milk...I already told you that, didn't I?' She felt her cheeks burn to know she sounded like a bumbling idiot.

He stepped over and closed the fridge for her then trapped her against it, his large warm hands curving around her hips, his fingers biting into her flesh, his spicy scent sending her senses buzzing.

'Relax, *querida*,' he murmured, staring down at her. 'I'm not going to bite you.'

And then his lips came down on hers and she was swept into a kiss of such intoxicating hunger that she felt utterly dizzy when he finally let her go.

'Better?' he asked with a gleam.

'No,' she answered boldly.

With a sound that was a cross between a laugh and a groan Felipe dipped his head and kissed her again.

Her answering sigh loosened the tightness that had been coiled in his chest since he'd awoken. When she sank into him and kissed him back with the passion that was pure Francesca, a feeling he'd never known filled his heart to replace it.

How could he have ever thought himself capable of resisting her?

Francesca Pellegrini was a woman like no other, an intoxicating combination of strength and vulnerability he would lay down his life to protect.

Breaking the kiss, he took her face in his hands to gaze at her.

Light brown eyes shone back at him, then she took his hands from her cheeks and, holding them tightly, stepped backwards, taking him with her, her gaze not leaving his as she guided him back into the living room and through to her bedroom.

The shutters were closed, sunlight shining through a few of the slats to bring some relief to the duskiness, but he took no notice of anything else as she led him to large bed abounding with soft pillows and lay back on it.

So quickly he had no memory of his feet moving, he was on top of her, pinning her down with his hands holding hers tightly either side of her face, drinking in the beauty of what lay beneath him.

And then he kissed her. Slowly. Deeply. Relishing the softness of her lips. Breathing in the sweetness of her taste and her jasmine perfume.

When he pulled away to stare again she smiled and placed a hand on his cheek, rubbing the palm over the bristles of his beard, then raised her head to kiss him.

Her hands moved from his face to his neck and to the collar of his shirt. Her fingers played with the buttons with such clumsiness he couldn't believe he hadn't noticed her lack of experience that first time.

He put his hands to her waist and raised her up so they were both propped up facing the other.

Not a word was said.

Not a word needed to be said. Everything she wanted to say was right there in her eyes and from the expression in them she was reading his as well as he read hers.

Taking her hand, he placed it to his chest and held it there.

Had his heart ever beat as strongly?

Eyes now screwed with concentration she tentatively,

but with growing confidence, unbuttoned his shirt until it fell open and he could shrug it off.

Now her eyes dilated and she pressed a kiss to the base of his neck and rubbed her cheek against his skin. Her gentle hands moved slowly across his chest, exploring him. He closed his eyes at the sensation of her touch firing through his veins.

His breathing became ragged as her fingers drifted down to his abdomen and rested on the band of his trousers.

She marked his shoulder with the gentlest of kisses while she found the button to his trousers and popped it open after only the smallest of fumbles.

Last night he'd taken her in a madness of rage-filled lust. Now his desire burned as strongly as it had then but there was nothing else to compromise the thrills burning through him. Now it was just the two of them and the attraction that had been there from the very first look.

He stretched up higher so she could unzip him without constriction and with heightened colour blazing across her cheeks she pulled the zipper down. Then she swallowed before pinching the edges of his trousers and pulling them down to his thighs, taking his underwear with it.

Her eyes widened as his arousal sprang free.

'Can I touch it?' she asked tentatively.

He'd never had a woman look at him—all of him—with such unabashed desire. But there was shyness too and the whole mixture was intoxicating.

He brushed his hands through her hair as he'd spent what felt like for ever dreaming of. 'You can touch and do whatever you like to me.'

Francesca was certain he must be able to hear her heart beating. It echoed through her ears, a rhythmic thrum that was almost painful.

Everything felt so different this time round.

Yesterday, she'd been too full of hurt and fury to care about being naked in front of him.

This time round she felt very much the virgin she had been.

She could hardly believe he was here and that this was happening.

Taking a breath, she raised herself to kneel too and lifted her dress over her head. Throwing it onto the floor, she then removed her bra and, with hands that now trembled wildly, tugged her panties down.

She was glad she'd forgotten to open her shutters before she'd last left her apartment. She could see him clearly and he could see her too but there was a haze that softened it. Romanticised it.

She swallowed her fear and forced herself to meet his eyes.

The desire pulsating from his stare was a look she knew she would remember for the rest of her life.

He shifted to remove his trousers and underwear, then knelt back so they faced each other, the tips of her breasts jutting against the hairs of his chest sending further tingles racing through her.

She put her hands to his chest as she'd done before and explored him with her fingers then followed that exploration with her mouth. His skin was smoother than she remembered from the night before and as she tasted and breathed in his muskiness she could feel her excitement building.

She heard the intake of air as she took his erection into her hand. It too was smoother than she'd expected but every bit as hard. It throbbed at her touch.

When they'd both lost their heads the night before, everything had been so urgent and immediate she'd not seen his erection before he was inside her.

Like the rest of him, it was magnificent, not at all ugly as she'd always imagined the male member to be.

His hands wove into her hair again but he made no further gesture of encouragement or expectation, letting her take things at her own pace, letting her go as far as she wanted, as far as she dared.

Dipping her head, she pressed her lips to the tip.

His groan was the encouragement she needed and she opened her mouth and covered the head.

And then he pulled away from her before she could take it any further.

'I'm sorry,' he said hoarsely, cupping her face in his hands. 'That feels too good. I don't want to come yet.'

The thought sent more pulses through her. He must have read her thoughts for he covered her lips with his.

'You can do it another time, *querida*, when I have more control over myself,' he murmured heavily into her mouth. 'But this time is for you.'

It thrilled her more than anything to know she had the power to make Felipe lose his control.

It thrilled her more to think of all the other moments they would share.

She wasn't after anything heavy or permanent, she reminded herself, knowing she *needed* to remind herself of this.

She wasn't in love with him, she was in lust. And if she felt as if she were under some kind of enchantment where all she could see and hear was Felipe then...

And then he laid her back down and kissed her so passionately that she stopped thinking at all.

Slowly, reverently, he made love to her.

There wasn't a part of her body left untouched or without the mark of his lips or the trail of his tongue. Every caress melted her a little more and soon she was nothing but a helpless mass of burning, sensual nerves.

He seemed to know exactly what she wanted and needed, rough and biting in places, tender and gentle in others, between her thighs and *there*, right in the very centre of her pleasure, coaxing her with his tongue until the explosion she'd felt at his hand on their drunken night happened again but this time deeper, longer, *more*…

When he snaked his way back up to kiss her deeply on the mouth, her head was spinning, her heart racing, the world around her gone to be just her and Felipe and her overwhelming need for his possession.

This time when he slid inside her she was more than ready for him.

The feel of him there, filling her, *completing* her…

And then he began to move and she lost what little of herself she'd had left.

It was too much. Overwhelming.

There was nothing she could do to stop it, to stop herself riding the waves, Felipe with her, and before she knew what was happening she was no longer riding it but soaring high off it into a world that dazzled her with the brilliance of its colour and the brightness of its stars, a world made purely of pleasure.

She didn't know how long she spent there. The journey back to earth was gentle, like a feather falling slowly through the breeze.

When she landed and opened her eyes, Felipe lay deliciously heavy on her, his breath hot on her neck.

After a long, long time he shifted his weight and moved his head onto the pillow beside hers and gazed at her with the same dazed look she knew must be in her eyes.

And then his gorgeous face widened into a grin and he laughed, though there was a shaky timbre to it. 'That was…'

'Better?' she supplied in the same shaky voice.

'No. It was incredible.' The grin faded. 'I didn't hurt you, did I?'

She palmed his cheek and slid a thigh between his. She'd never imagined it was possible to feel such closeness to someone. To feel as if she'd been one with them. 'The only way you can hurt me now is if we never do that again.'

# CHAPTER TWELVE

THEY SPENT THE rest of the day in bed. By the time night fell, hunger of the more traditional kind took its hold and they ordered takeout. Francesca found a bottle of wine and they consumed it all it in her bed.

She was quite certain she'd fallen into a dream. None of it felt real and yet the intensity of her emotions were incredibly vivid.

She didn't want to probe what it all meant. All she wanted was to enjoy it for as long as it lasted before she returned to her real life.

Night turned into morning and she woke to crumpled sheets and an empty bed.

Immediate panic clutched her throat and she jumped out of bed at the same moment Felipe entered her room carrying two take-away cups and a fat brown paper bag.

'I couldn't find any food in your kitchen so I've brought breakfast,' he said with a grin, handing her one of the cups. 'This is a nice neighbourhood you live in. I always thought Pisa was nothing but its famous tower but it's surprised me.'

She took in the faded jeans and black T-shirt with the album cover of a punk band printed on it.

She hadn't seen him in jeans before and had had no idea he liked punk music.

'I also bring news—those men who were following you have been caught.'

'Have they? When? How?'

'I have a lot of contacts. One of them runs the foreign department for a country that will remain nameless. They in turn contacted Caballeros' president and made certain threats about foreign aid budgets. I got confirmation an

hour ago that the men have been taken into custody. One
of them was an employee in the Governor's house, the
other two his cousins. The Governor has been warned that
if anything untoward happens to you on Saturday night
then he might find himself kicked out of office.' He gave
a wry smile. 'Unfortunately corruption is everywhere. I
have a feeling that the President will be sharing the bribe.'

'Threats, blackmail, bribery and corruption,' she said
in awe. 'So that's how to run a country.'

He laughed but his eyes were serious. 'It happens to
degrees everywhere but Caballeros is more extreme than
others. Don't think it means Saturday will be plain sail-
ing. We're still going to take every precaution.'

'I know you will.' From Felipe she expected nothing
less. The threat those men had posed hadn't scared her as
much as they should have simply because she'd known he
would do everything in his power to keep her safe.

'Does this mean you don't have to stay and protect me
any more?' she asked with a flutter of her lashes, although
her heart was skipping all over the place in panic.

His eyes blazed as he opened the paper bag and offered
first pick of the contents to her. 'It wouldn't do to take
chances, would it?'

'Definitely not.'

'And you did promise me a tour of the *castello*.'

'I did.' She nodded solemnly. 'I'd be much safer there
so maybe we should stay at the *castello* until we have to
go back.'

'You're not afraid of the ghosts?'

Placing a hand to his chest, she pressed her lips to his
neck. 'With you there to protect me, the ghosts wouldn't
dare haunt us.'

Later that morning, they set off to the *castello* in a shining
sports car Felipe had had delivered to them. Francesca had

spoken to her mother, thinking she would drop in to check on her on the way, but had been relieved to hear she'd gone out for the day with her sister, Francesca's Aunt Rachele. It would have been hard explaining what she was doing with Felipe and she could hardly ask him to wait in the car.

Her mother was one of the strongest, most stoical people she knew. She'd nursed her husband through years of ill health and had buried her eldest child whilst making sure her roots were touched up first, but for the first time ever Francesca heard her mother's voice and thought how old she sounded.

Her poor mamma was suffering.

Thank God her mamma's younger sister lived with her. The two women rattled around the rambling villa on the Pisa Hills, driving each other slightly mad, but both would be lost without the other. It helped to know her mother had Rachele there.

Francesca hadn't mentioned she would be taking a guest to the *castello*.

Although she had no right of inheritance to the estate, tradition had always dictated that immediate members of the family had their own rooms and could have full use of the *castello*. Pieta hadn't changed that and she had her own key to the family wing.

Located on the Tuscan hills twenty short miles away from Pisa, Francesca felt the familiar curls of excitement in her belly when she caught her first glimpse of it, and couldn't resist staring at Felipe to watch his reaction.

He turned to her for a moment with a raised brow. 'Now, that is what you call a castle.'

She laughed. 'Wait until we get closer. You'll see how dilapidated it is.'

Encircled by a high wall Felipe estimated to be at least twenty feet high that had sentry towers at each corner, the castle dominated the countryside. Geometrically perfect, he couldn't begin to count the number of arched windows.

As they got closer, he began to see what Francesca meant about generations of Pellegrinis letting it fall into disrepair. Closer inspection revealed a crumbling fascia; what would once have been vibrant stonework faded into blandness.

He drove them into a courtyard where only three other cars were parked. At the furthest point his eye could see, scaffolding had been erected. He guessed this was the latest part of the renovations Pieta had embarked on.

'Where are all the builders?'

'The renovations have been halted for a couple of weeks out of respect,' she explained with a sad shrug. 'There's staff here, I've let them know to expect us.'

'Does your family know you've brought me here?'

'No. They only come here to visit the cemetery. Papa and I were the only ones who liked staying here.' Her gaze cast off into the distance. 'Do you mind if I go to the cemetery?'

'Of course not. I'll come with you if you like.'

Leaving their stuff in the car, they set off to the salmon pink chapel that, unlike the rest of the castle, was in wonderful repair, proving Francesca's assertion of a family rooted in the past. She'd been the first to break free of the expectations built over generations. He admired her more than he could say.

The cemetery itself was chillingly beautiful, row upon row of highly glossed tombs and gravestones, all lovingly tended.

They stood in silence, hands clasped and heads bowed at the spot where Pieta lay buried next to his father. Vases of flowers sat in abundance.

What must it be like, he wondered, to be a part of a family that loved each other so dearly and protected each other almost mercilessly? And it didn't just extend to their blood-line. Natasha, Pieta's widow, was as much a Pellegrini as if she'd been born one. From everything Francesca had said, she'd been embraced into being a part of them.

For the first time he thought of his father with regret rather than indifference. He'd been someone who'd flitted in and out of their lives. Standing here now, he felt the loss of what his childhood could have been and wished that he could grieve for him the way a father should be grieved for.

He thought of his mother, now living a life of comfort and luxury but as remote in his adult life as she'd been in his childhood. He admired her enormously, knew the admiration was mutual. But how could they forge a true relationship when the foundations had never been properly built?

And then he thought of Sergio, who he'd mourned as if he'd lost a true brother.

'Shall we go to the *castello* now?' Francesca asked, her sombre voice cutting through his private reverie.

He pulled his lips in and nodded.

Being with Francesca felt different from anything he'd known before. Their time together was limited. He wanted to make the most of it before they said goodbye for good.

The family rooms were in the south of the *castello*, where renovation work had yet to begin. Francesca led him down a wide corridor that was so dark it brought to mind the horror films he'd watched on occasion as an unsupervised child. He could quite see why tales of it being haunted had been so believable to the impressionable Pellegrini children.

Francesca's room was something else.

'You slept in here as a child?' he asked with amazement.

'Yes. Not exactly child-friendly, is it? I loved it, though. I used to feel like a princess sleeping in this room.'

'Aren't the Pellegrinis descended from royalty?'

She shrugged. 'We haven't used the titles for generations. It's silly. How can you call yourself a prince or a duke if the title isn't recognised as meaning anything any more?'

Amply proportioned, the room had what would once have been vibrant gold and green wallpaper lining the walls but, like the *castello*'s fascia, it had faded into blandness. The ceiling, like the surrounding corridors, was of dark wood panels, laced with gold leaf. The same wood had been used to carve the enormous four-poster bed and headboard, and all the furnishings. Deep red velvet curtains hung on the tall windows, matching the inviting bedspread.

'If I ever get around to buying a home, I'd be tempted to have a bedroom like this.'

'Buy your own *castello*; you can afford it.'

'It would have to be warmer than this.' The early autumn sunshine that blazed down so brightly outside hadn't penetrated the thick stone walls. Given the choice, Felipe liked to be outdoors in the sun. He didn't like to think how cold the *castello* would be in the depths of winter.

'I told you it was draughty.' Throwing herself onto the bed, she rolled onto her belly and rested her chin on her hands. 'Shall I call a member of staff and get them to light the fire?'

'If you're cold I've got a much better method of warming you.'

Her eyes gleamed. 'I am *freezing*.'

And with that he proceeded to warm her more effectively than a dozen blazing fires.

Their time in the *castello* passed far more quickly than Francesca wanted. The live-in chef, thrilled to have something to do, produced delicious meals for them and in between eating and making love they explored the *castello* and its grounds. The only areas other than the chapel that had been maintained through the generations were the busy vineyards and cellar.

Felipe also had to spend time preparing for their return to Caballeros, liaising with his staff, approving plans... she didn't want to know the details. She would leave that to the professionals. Leave it to him. She had no concerns about that at all. Indeed, it was kind of wonderful not having any concerns. Except...

'This all feels so strange,' she said to him while they paddled in the lake on the Friday afternoon. The cool water sloshed around her ankles, making her wish they'd been here the month before when the water had been warm enough to swim in. The seasons were changing. The leaves on the trees were thinning. Soon they wouldn't be green but autumnal reds and browns and yellows.

And she was changing with it.

She had to keep reminding herself there was no future for her and Felipe. These few days were the most they could have. She had her future to think of, the future she'd fought so hard to get. She was so close to qualifying she could almost touch it.

But a thought kept pushing itself to the fore.

*Why* did a relationship have to compromise her career or her independence?

Hadn't she made that promise to herself to feel life and embrace all it had to offer?

What was to say that once she'd established her career and was ready to settle down she would meet a man for whom she felt a tenth of what she felt for Felipe?

She'd never imagined she could feel such closeness to someone, a closeness that stretched far beyond desire.

She hadn't even known him for a week but it felt as if he'd been a part of her life for ever.

'What does?'

Francesca forced her mind back to the conversation.

It didn't matter how deeply her feelings had developed or how her outlook on life had changed, nothing could come of it. It didn't matter how tenderly he treated her now, Felipe had given no indication that his own feelings or outlook had changed. For him, their time together in Pisa was a short, sweet interlude before he resumed his real life, and she would be wise to remember that.

'This…doing nothing. I feel like I should be studying case files or working on one of the boring draft proceedings Roberto gave me. I can't remember when I last went this long without studying *something*.'

'Who's Roberto?'

'The senior lawyer Pieta put me under.'

'And why is it boring?'

She pulled a face. 'It's corporate law.'

After a few moments, Felipe said quietly, 'You don't have to stay at Pieta's firm.'

She glanced up at him.

'You don't enjoy it there.' It wasn't a question.

'It doesn't matter if I enjoy it or not. I'm committed.' She found corporate law as dull as dirty dishwater.

'You committed to working at Pieta's firm because you wanted to get closer to him.'

'What, and now he's dead I should abandon that commitment?'

'Did he think you would stay with him once you passed your bar exam?'

'No. He knew human rights was my long-term goal.'

'Did he try and talk you out of joining his firm and encourage you to go to a firm that specialised in human rights?'

She thought about it. 'Not really. It doesn't matter where I do my traineeship.'

'So he knew you joined his firm for him?'

'We never spoke of it in such terms but, yes, I suppose he must have known.' She remembered Pieta's genuine delight when she'd asked to do her traineeship with him. She remembered her disappointment when he'd put her under the wing of another senior lawyer and his explanation that she would need consistency while she did her traineeship. With all the travelling he did for his foundation he couldn't provide that consistency for her but was glad to be her mentor.

'So if he knew you were there for him, do you think he would think less of you if you were to move on now he's no longer here?'

'I can't think of this right now. It feels too disloyal.'

'All I'm suggesting is you think about it. It wouldn't be disloyal. Pieta would understand, I am certain of it. He wouldn't want you to waste two years working somewhere that didn't fulfil you.'

'Do not presume to tell me what my brother would have thought,' she snapped. 'If I, his own sister, wasn't privy to his private thoughts then I'm as sure as hell you wouldn't have been either.'

'Don't be so defensive. I'm not presuming anything.' He wrapped an arm around her waist and pulled her close.

Francesca sighed and rested her head in the crook of his arm, her sudden burst of guilty anger soothed by his touch. She *mustn't* allow herself to get used to it. 'I'm sorry. I know it's something I need to think about. And I will. There's a lot for me to consider. I'll probably have to go to Rome to practise if I want to make a success of it so if I were to make the change now then it would be silly not to go to Rome for my traineeship too.'

'You don't like Rome?'

'I love Rome, but it's a four-hour drive. I'm not like you. I'm happy to go away for a week or two but I always like coming home. I've never lived away from my family before. I thought I had another two years to get used to the idea.'

'Get Daniele to buy you a jet. That will make the distance seem closer.'

She laughed. 'He probably would if I asked nicely. There's a lot to think about—finding a firm to take me on, finding a place to live and all the small things that come with it. I will do it, though, whether now or when I've qualified for the bar. I've not worked so hard all my life to let it go to waste.'

He tilted her chin up and kissed her. 'Let's go back to the *castello* and I'll help clear your mind so you can think properly.'

'And how do you intend to do that?'

His hand found her bottom and squeezed it. 'I'm sure I can think of a few ways.'

Felipe sat on the Gothic armchair, watching Francesca get ready for their last meal in the *castello*.

He'd never watched a woman dress before. And the woman doing the dressing was determined to put on a show.

They'd showered together and then he'd donned his suit while she had sat at the dressing table with a towel around herself and blow dried her hair.

He'd watched her moisturise her face and then skilfully apply her make-up, which to his mind did nothing but enhance the natural beauty she'd been blessed with. Then came the jewellery, a gold choker with a black sapphire that rested at the base of her slender neck, and matching earrings.

And then she had dressed.

First went on the underwear, functional and black, nothing in the least erotic about them, but…the way she slid the panties up her legs and thighs…

*Dios*, it was enough to raise his blood pressure to alarming levels.

Then she'd stared at him with challenge in her eyes.

She'd bet him he wouldn't be able to keep his hands to himself until after their meal.

'You're playing dirty,' he said when she cupped her breasts to make sure they were perfectly encased in her strapless bra.

She flashed a wicked smile and then turned her back to him, bending over seductively to straighten her high black shoes before sliding her feet into them.

He smothered a groan.

Finally, she took the black dress off the hanger and slowly stepped into it.

When she turned round to face him a smile played on her lips. 'So, Señor Lorenzi, are you ready to escort me to dinner?'

Felipe swallowed back the lump in his throat that was as hard as the ache straining between his legs.

She'd never looked more beautiful. Or sexy. Her dress just begged to be ripped off, and she knew it. Strapless, like her bra, her cleavage sitting like ripe peaches, it was diagonally slashed, one side falling to her knee, the other to the top of her thigh.

She had done all this for him.

He cleared his throat.

Never mind keeping his hands off her until after their meal, he had no idea how he was going to walk away from her permanently.

# CHAPTER THIRTEEN

THEY ATE IN the *castello*'s armoury, seated at the end of a polished oak table that could comfortably seat fifty people. Serena, the woman who managed the *castello* and was delighted to have guests in, had turned the enormous room with its frescoed ceiling, checked flooring and walls lined with bronzes and weaponry into a romantic fool's dream.

The chef had surpassed himself too. They'd been served an appetiser of beef carpaccio, followed by an aubergine tortellini. Their main course had been an exquisitely cooked boneless duck thigh in a berry and red wine sauce. Now they were making their way through their coffee and amaretto *semi-freddo*.

Francesca was thrilled with it all. The food had been dreamy, the service discreet. A fitting finale, she thought, to what had been the best few days of her life.

Tomorrow they would return to Caballeros then stay the night in their hotel in Aguadilla. On Sunday morning they would go their separate ways...

She didn't want to think of that. If she blanked it out she could pretend there wasn't a clock frantically counting down the seconds until they had to say goodbye.

She peppered Felipe with questions about the music he liked and the places he'd been, asked for stories of his childhood escapades, drinking in his answers, committing them to memory because all too soon that would be all she had left of him. In return she regaled him with tales of summer holidays here in the *castello* and its long notorious history.

'How did you find the time to learn so much about it when you were always studying so hard?' he asked admiringly. He took the last bite of his *semi-freddo*, placed his spoon on the plate and pushed it to one side.

'Papa knew far more than me. He would tell me bedtime stories about the *castello* and our ancestors—some of them were *really* bloodthirsty.' She remembered the old tales with glee, not just the stories themselves but those happy times with her father. 'It was hard for him watching it fall into such disrepair but he was ill for a long time. He spent as much of the income as he could on maintaining it but the priority was paying for full-time nursing care for him.' Her father had had motor neurone disease, which had gradually worsened through the years until in the months before he'd died he'd become immobile. It had been hard on all of them to see the strong man who had loved and raised them slowly disintegrate. Of all of them, she thought Daniele had suffered the most. She'd spent a lot of time with her father and when he'd died she'd had peace and acceptance as well as pain in her heart. Daniele's relationship with him had been difficult. He travelled even more than Pieta had and had rarely been there in those last few months. She didn't think he'd found either peace or acceptance.

'Was your father's illness the reason you chose to study in Pisa rather than further afield?' he asked, swirling Chianti in his wineglass.

'It was part of the reason but I think even if he hadn't been ill I would have stayed. I love my family. I wanted my independence but I wasn't ready to cut the apron strings completely. Moving into Daniele's apartment gave me the best of both worlds. It meant I could study and lead an independent life but be close enough that I could see my parents whenever I wanted and be there if they needed me.'

'And now?'

'And now I take stock and decide whether to make the move to Rome now or in two years.' She breathed deeply then admitted, 'I'm leaning towards doing it now. You were right earlier that Pieta wouldn't want me to spend the next two years unhappy and we both know life's too short. Mamma has Aunt Rachele living with her so she won't be alone.'

Felipe swirled his glass some more, nodding slowly. She recognised the expression. She'd learned to read all the expressions on his handsome face and knew this one meant he was thinking of something. She wished they had the time for her to learn everything about him.

'I can help you out with the living arrangements,' he said eventually.

'What do you mean?'

'Your surprise that I don't own my own home has got me thinking that it's time I invested my money. My life is always so busy I never think long term other than with the business and it's time to change that. I'll start by buying a house in Rome and when you're ready, you can move into it.'

His words were so unexpected that she gaped at him.

'Do I get a discount on the rent?' she asked cheekily when she'd regathered her wits. She must not read anything into his offer. She couldn't. Assumptions were dangerous.

That didn't stop her heart from setting off at a trot and for hope to start bashing at her chest.

'I wouldn't ask my lover to pay rent.'

She cleared her throat, the trot turning to a full-blown canter. 'Your lover? Does this mean…?'

His eyes holding hers steadily, he took a drink of his wine. 'I'm not ready to say goodbye. Are you?'

The ticking countdown in her head that had been beating like a drum in her ears suddenly exploded inside her, but instead of the misery she'd been dreading, unremitting joy burst through. All the dreams that had been building but which she'd shoved away from her mind, too scared to look at them, sprang free.

Her and Felipe. Together.

He wanted it too!

He didn't want to say goodbye either.

Was it possible, could it *be* possible, that he'd fallen in love with her as she had fallen in love with him…?

Love?

*Oh, Dio, Dio, Dio.*

Love?

Lightness filled her.

The truth had been staring her in the face for days.

Somehow, in this crazy week, she had fallen irrevocably in love with Felipe Lorenzi, and admitting it to herself was as heady and thrilling as it was terrifying.

She loved him.

Francesca swallowed, managing to produce a nod that could have been a shake of her head. 'I'm not ready to say goodbye either,' she said, her chest rising and falling so rapidly the words fought for release.

His eyes gleamed. 'Then a house in Rome is the perfect solution for us. An investment for me and a home for you.'

She loved the way *us* rolled off his tongue, how natural and right it sounded.

Us. Them. Together.

He drained his wine. 'Once I've bought it I'll give you the money to decorate and furnish it to your tastes.'

Her mind immediately careered to the land of soft furnishings and huge carved beds. 'We can have a bedroom like my one here,' she said, thinking aloud, beaming her delight.

He refilled his glass and topped hers up with it. 'That will be up to you. You'll be the one living in it.'

She stared at him blankly, not understanding. 'Just me? What about you?'

'I never know from one week to the next where I'm going to be but I'll visit whenever I can.' Another gleam flashed in his eyes. 'I will be there to keep the bed warm when time allows, so make sure it's a big one.'

*Visit?*

*When time allows?*

The unfettered dreams that had been let off the leash came to a crashing halt.

'Right…' She nodded slowly, trying hard not to leap to conclusions, not to panic, to get straight the basic facts of what he was offering and what he wanted from her. 'So I'll be living in the house alone?'

He nodded. 'Mostly.'

'How often would we see each other? Weekly? Monthly?'

'You know I'm not in a position to answer that. You know the life I lead. If we weren't returning to Caballeros tomorrow I'd be back in the Middle East already. We'll see each other whenever I can.'

She swallowed before asking the question she most needed the answer to, trying to affect nonchalance. 'What kind of commitment will you want from me?'

His brows drew together before a wide smile broke over his face. 'We won't be in a relationship, *querida*. Don't worry, you'll still have your independence.'

His words were like a slap in the face.

That he seemed so pleased with himself only made it worse.

Sharp pain squeezed its way through at the crushing realisation she had got everything wrong.

She'd misread him entirely.

'It sounds like the kind of arrangement a man makes with his mistress,' she said slowly, trying to keep a hold of her wildly veering emotions, clamping on the nausea roiling violently in her belly.

'Mistress?' He made it sound as if he'd never heard of the word. 'A mistress is a woman kept by a married a man.

I'm not married and I won't be keeping you. I'll have an investment, you'll have a home to live in and your independence, and we'll be able to see each other. It's the perfect solution.'

'No rent. No commitment. Sex whenever you fancy it. I'd be a woman kept for your convenience.'

He stared at her for too long. His dark eyes narrowed and glinted dangerously. 'That is not how it is.'

'That's what it sounds like.'

He'd made love to her like she meant something to him, he'd listened to her, he'd comforted her...and now all he wanted from her was sexual release when he could fit her in his schedule?

'You allow Daniele to help you. There is no difference.'

'There's *every* difference. He's my *brother*.' She pushed her chair back, the nausea growing. Bile had lodged in her throat. 'He charges me minimal rent because he loves me. He would let me have it for nothing.'

'I'm offering you a whole house for nothing.'

'No, not for nothing.' Now on her feet, legs shaking, Francesca jutted her chin in the air, no longer able to feign nonchalance. 'I thank you for your kind offer but I can't accept. I will not be your whore.'

And as she spoke, she looked down at what she was wearing and felt a wave of self-loathing.

She'd dressed like this to tantalise and torment him, had spent most of their meal imagining him peeling it off.

Wearing it like this now made her feel like a whore as much as his words did.

'My *whore*?' He shook his head as if clearing his ears of water, distaste etched on angry his face. 'How can you say such a thing? I thought you'd be pleased.'

Pulling the top of her dress up so it covered her cleavage and made it the respectable dress it should have been, she spat, 'Pleased to be your *concubine*? Pleased to be beholden to you, pleased to have you flit in and out of my life whenever it's convenient to you? How can I be pleased in a relationship that gives you all the power and when you won't even call it a relationship? Have you not learned anything about me?' She tugged the skirt of the dress down so the slash didn't ride so high.

Felipe was breathing heavily, staring at her with eyes that had turned to steel. Any tenderness that had been on his face earlier had been wiped away.

'You insult me,' he said, putting the palms of his hands on the tables and getting slowly to his feet. 'I have tried to help you. I have offered you more than I have ever offered anyone and you throw it back in my face.'

'I've insulted *you*?' she asked, outrage sweeping through her misery. 'You've just insulted everything we've shared together. You've cheapened it and you've cheapened me.'

'No, *you've* done that. I thought we understood each other but clearly I was wrong. I've offered you all I can. I will not be offering more. I live my life on *my* terms, *querida*. I've never lied to you. You know I don't have space in my life for anything permanent and you've told me enough times that you're not ready for anything permanent until you're established in your career. Or was that a lie?'

She tugged a weighty earring off her throbbing earlobe and threw it on the table, wishing she could throw it in his face. It hit her wineglass with such force it knocked it over, smashing it, the remnants of her wine spilling onto the oak.

She barely noticed.

'No, it wasn't a lie but my perspective's changed. I want to be happy and to feel life, and you make me feel *so much*.' She gazed at him, silently pleading for him to see the truth; that she loved him and that if he could only bring himself to give *something* of himself to her, something they could build on, something she could cling onto with hope in her heart, then her answer would be different. 'Having a relationship doesn't have to compromise my future, I see that now, but I still want a relationship of equals. What you're suggesting for us gives you all the power. I'd be at your mercy for the roof over my head. I can't be happy with a one-sided arrangement where the only commitment I'd get from you is that there will be no commitment. I want more than to be your concubine, Felipe. I want…'

But she couldn't continue. The words wouldn't come, not with Felipe's nostrils flaring as he breathed deeply, staring at her as if she were a stranger.

She'd heard many tones of voice from him but never had she heard such steely coldness as when he said, 'My offer is the most I'm prepared to give. Take it or leave it.'

The rip in her heart was so acute her knees almost buckled beneath her.

Somehow she managed to hold on, to keep herself upright, to eye him squarely. 'I choose to leave it.'

Total silence filled the room.

For a long time they did nothing but stare at each other.

Felipe was the one to break it. He nodded curtly. 'Then there is nothing left for us to say. I thank you for your hospitality. I will be in touch with instructions for tomorrow.'

Then he turned on his heel and strode out of the armoury, leaving her with nothing but the shattered remains of her wineglass and her head spinning at how quickly everything had disintegrated between them.

Francesca woke on her bedroom's sofa. The fire she'd lit had burnt to cinders, the room cold enough for her breath to mist.

Swinging her legs round, a pain shot through her neck. Great. She'd cricked it.

Her phone had fallen onto the floor. Holding a hand to her neck for support, she picked it up to check the time. Four o'clock in the morning.

She hadn't thought she would sleep. She'd curled up on the sofa unable to face getting in the bed that would have still been warm from their lovemaking, thinking she would wait it out until the sun came up.

Then she noticed a text message had come through.

She hesitated before swiping her thumb to open it.

A driver will collect you at your apartment at one p.m. to take you to the airport. Change into your dress before landing. You will be flown directly to Caballeros from Aguadilla.

It came from a number she didn't recognise but she didn't need to recognise it to know it came from Felipe. She'd shown him the dress she'd planned to wear to the Governor's party, anxious that he approved, not from a fashion point of view but from a safety aspect. Whatever promises had been made to him regarding her safety, the Governor's lecherous stares had given her the creeps. She wouldn't give him an inch of flesh to leer at.

She turned her phone off and staggered to the unmade bed.

She closed her eyes and swayed, the spinning in her head returning with a vengeance.

As she counted to ten, a pain, much like she imagined a punch in the stomach would feel, hit her, making her double over.

It took a long time to pass.

When she opened her eyes something black caught her eye, poking out from under her bed.

It was Felipe's black T-shirt with the punk band's album printed on it.

Felipe checked his messages.

Nothing new had come in since he'd last looked a minute ago. That was good.

All his men were in position. They'd run through the drill for all eventualities enough times that if anything should happen their reactions would be automatic.

He didn't expect anything to happen now. The Governor had called him personally to apologise for what the men had been planning and given his assurances that Francesca's safety and her entire project in Pieta's memory was guaranteed.

Felipe would not take anything for granted. The cash still needed to be handed over. Until that was done he knew he wouldn't be able to breathe easily.

A car appeared.

He checked his watch.

She was exactly on time.

James, who'd been waiting with Felipe by the Cessna, for once keeping his mouth shut, opened the back passenger door.

Francesca stepped out.

She'd shown him the dress she intended to wear. On the hanger, he'd thought it imminently suitable for the occasion, with its high rounded neck and long sleeves. Professional and elegant was the look she wanted to achieve, dressing for a party that was, for her, purely business.

She'd achieved it.

The black dress had delicate embroidered colours running the length of it and fell to her knees, lightly caressing her body. On her feet she wore electric blue high heels and carried a matching clutch bag. Her hair gleamed and hung loose like a waterfall.

His throat closed.

She looked stunning.

She met his eye. There was a moment of total stillness where not even the breeze stirred. He caught the briefest flash of emotion in her gaze before she inclined her head in greeting and walked the few paces towards him.

He turned and extended a hand to the open door of the Cessna, indicating for her to get in.

She obeyed the wordless gesture and climbed the stairs, her heels clanging on the metal steps, a cloud of her perfume trailing behind her.

Felipe gritted his teeth and followed her on board.

He had come close to bowing out of the whole operation and letting Seb take the lead on it. He'd got as close as calling Seb to tell him of the new plan but had found himself unable go through with it.

Despite the dark bitterness that curdled his insides at their angry parting, he could not bring himself to put her safety in someone else's hands.

The accusations she'd thrown at him…

He couldn't think of that now. He never wanted to think of it or think of her again.

When she was seated he showed her a tiny gold pin, no bigger than a centimetre in diameter.

'Wear this as a brooch. It has a tracking device in it.'

He dropped it into her open hand and watched her pin it securely.

James, who was sitting in front of them, watching his phone for the pin's signal, gave the thumbs up.

The Cessna rumbled down the runway and was soon in the air, flying high over the Caribbean Sea.

During the short journey from Aguadilla to Caballeros, he once again ran through the game plan with Seb and James.

Francesca didn't join in with the conversation.

If it wasn't for her perfume, filling the small cabin with its heady scent, filling him, he could tune her out entirely.

All he had to do was get this evening over with and then he could wash his hands of Francesca Pellegrini for ever.

# CHAPTER FOURTEEN

TWINKLING FAIRY LIGHTS hung round the perimeter of the Governor's residence. Francesca looked at them, distaste rising through her as she thought of how half the island's electricity was still down almost three weeks on from the hurricane.

Her disgust grew when they entered the residence and discovered hundreds of people dressed to the nines. Squeals of laughter and raucous laughs echoed throughout. In the centre of the first room they were taken through to, was an enormous champagne fountain.

They found the Governor outside by his swimming pool wearing a white tuxedo, surrounded by a group of giggling women in bikinis young enough to be his granddaughters. The tall woman who'd first led her to him a week ago stood a short distance behind them, keeping guard, wearing a different white outfit than she'd worn then.

The Governor saw them and excused himself from his eager sycophants.

He greeted them like long-lost friends but with a wary eye at Felipe and asked about their journey, in English, polite talk that made Francesca think that whoever Felipe had got to put the screws on this man had tightened them like a vice.

She had to bite her cheek to prevent laughter escaping. She didn't doubt it would have a hysterical quality to it.

She *had* to keep her focus.

The Governor led them to his study, refusing even to let his all-in-white female shadow enter the room.

'Before we get down to business, a drink?'

He produced a bottle of brandy from the cabinet behind his desk.

'Why not?' she said before Felipe could say anything.

She might despise the Governor but she saw little point in antagonising him. The hospital still needed to be built and she would prefer his goodwill while it was being done.

He poured three hefty measures and handed them round. 'To new friends.'

Without meaning to, she caught Felipe's eye, then quickly looked away and took too big a sip of the brandy.

It was easier to manage the entire situation if she kept him in the periphery of her vision rather than look at him directly.

She'd discovered that when she'd stepped out of the car at the airfield. She'd taken one look at him and had wanted to throw herself into his arms and beg him to never let her go.

She hadn't allowed herself to think of him since she'd got back to her apartment soon after the sun had come up, his T-shirt chucked in a bag which she'd intended to give back to him. Then she'd set to work. She'd stripped the bedsheets and boil-washed them, cleaned and polished, vacuumed every inch of flooring, all the while refusing to allow the nausea and dizziness that kept racking her to derail her from her mission.

Then she had packed her evening dress and some clean clothes to change into for the return flight home and waited to be collected.

She hadn't expected him to be the one to collect her but that hadn't stopped her belly dropping with disappointment when she'd opened the door to find Seb there.

She hadn't expected him to be on the plane either but, again, unmistakable disappointment had punched her to find she would be making the flight with only Seb and the cabin crew for company.

By the time they landed in Aguadilla, with no sign of Felipe at the main airport, she'd convinced herself that he wouldn't be there at all, so to see him when they entered the airfield, standing in front of the Cessna, had hit her like another punch.

At least she'd had a minute to compose herself before having to get out of the car and face him looking so sickeningly handsome in a black tuxedo. He could wear anything and he would still be sexiest man in a thousand mile radius.

She didn't know what she'd expected to see in his eyes when she faced him. Acrimony? Disgust? But apart from one brief flash of emotion, which she could quite easily have imagined, there had been nothing there. His eyes were blank.

He'd reverted back to the authoritative, arrogant man she'd first met a whole lifetime of a week ago.

The brandy burned then numbed her throat. She welcomed it. If she drank the whole glass it might numb the rest of her twisting insides too.

'I wish to apologise for the behaviour of my staff member,' the Governor said, settling on his captain's chair. 'I was very shocked when I heard.'

*I just bet you were.*

'I have your assurance it won't happen again?' she asked pleasantly.

'You have my word.' He said it as if his word should mean something. Then his left eye twitched. 'You have the money?'

She glanced at Felipe without fully looking at him.

He placed the briefcase he'd been carrying since they left the Cessna on the desk. Only then did she notice the glint of metal around his wrist.

She'd been avoiding looking directly at him so effectively that she'd failed to see he'd handcuffed the briefcase to his wrist.

He pulled the key out of his pocket and unlocked the cuffs.

The briefcase sprang open. He twisted it around and pushed it to the Governor.

The older man flicked through the case, nodding his approval, then pulled open a drawer and removed a stack of papers. He handed them to Francesca.

'The deeds to the site. We both sign them.'

Tempted though she was to read them quickly, she made herself sit down and read it through properly.

Written in English, it was concise and unambiguous. When she put her name to it the site would belong to Pieta's foundation.

Thirty minutes after entering the Governor's study the job was complete.

Before they left his office, Felipe turned to him and fired off something in Spanish.

She didn't have a clue what he said but the Governor's face went as white as his teeth.

She had a feeling the hospital would be built without any problems whatsoever.

Felipe rode up front with James on the drive back to the airport, leaving Francesca in the back with Seb.

The stars twinkling in the black sky reminded her of a purer version of the Governor's fairy lights. Thank God she'd never have to see him again.

Soon she would never see Felipe again either. Her part in the project was over.

His jet waited on the runway exactly where they'd left it.

She would travel back to Pisa alone. Felipe and the others had another plane coming to collect them in the morning, taking them on to whatever dangerous part of the world they were working in next.

Fighting a closing throat, Francesca said, 'Thank you, gentlemen, for everything you've done for me.'

James turned his head to look at her.

'No worries,' he said. Was that sadness she saw in his grin? 'It's been fun.'

She gave a hollow laugh. 'I think that's enough of that kind of fun for me. Keep safe.'

With James and Seb's farewells echoing in her ears, she got out of the car.

Felipe, who hadn't exchanged a direct word with her since giving her the tracking pin, got out with her and shut the door behind him.

They stood by the car in a silence that grew tauter with every passing second.

He was close enough for her to raise her hand and touch him but the distance between them was greater than it had ever been.

She wished he'd never made his offer of a house. She wished she'd never had that leap of joy when she'd misinterpreted the offer as one of a home for them both. She wished she was still ignorant of the extent of her feelings for him.

Felipe was a lone wolf without roots, roaming with his pack but apart, never breaching the distance he'd created with them. He would never settle down, not in one place and not with one person. His wounds from his past were too deep.

She was more of a homing pigeon. She needed her roots and her family.

Telling herself all this didn't stop the crushing weight in her chest at all that could have been and all that had been lost.

'I congratulate you on getting the deeds,' he said stiffly. His eyes rested in the distance over her shoulder. 'You did well.'

'Thank you,' she whispered. She put her fingers to her neck and to the pulse beating frantically in it. It felt like her heart was crying.

The door to the jet opened and one of the cabin crew put his put his head out. 'Control's been on the radio. We have ten minutes to get airborne.'

Now Felipe did meet her eye, and in that glance she thought she saw a glimpse of all the misery and pain she felt inside herself.

And then he turned and got back in the car.

Felipe wouldn't allow James to drive away until the plane carrying Francesca was indistinguishable from the stars themselves.

'We can go now,' he said bleakly.

In silence, James pulled away.

Felipe rested his head against the window and closed his eyes. He could still feel her breath on his face.

His heart had never felt heavier.

*Dios*, he could still hear her laughter ringing in his ears, like an echo.

He had to stop this. She'd made her choice. What he had to offer and what she wanted were worlds apart.

'Are you okay, boss?' James asked. For once his tone was serious.

'Why wouldn't I be?'

'No reason. You look like you have something on your mind, that's all.'

'Well, I haven't.'

'Funny job we do, isn't it?' James said, ignoring the 'shut up' warning tone Felipe had just given him. 'Putting our bodies on the line every day for people we don't know and half the time don't even like, preparing to take a bullet for each other, but ask us to put our hearts on the line for someone special and we run away screaming like frightened schoolboys.'

'James?'

'Yes, boss?'

'Shut up.'

Two weeks later and Felipe could still hear James's words as fresh and as painful as when he'd first uttered them.

*'Ask us to put our hearts on the line for someone special and we run away screaming like frightened schoolboys.'*

Is that what he was doing? Running away?

He'd been upfront with Francesca from the start. She was the one who'd changed. He'd never lied about his feelings. He'd offered her an inch and she'd wanted a mile. She'd wanted more than he was capable of giving. Much more.

He'd seen it in her eyes, a hope for something he could never give her.

He wouldn't even be thinking of her if Daniele hadn't just called him to discuss protection for his men during the hospital's construction.

They'd come to the end of the conversation before he'd asked the question that had played on his lips since he'd first heard Daniele's voice. 'How's Francesca? Keeping out of trouble?'

Daniele hadn't sounded surprised at the question. 'She's doing okay on the surface. Getting ready for her move to Rome...'

'Rome?'

'Didn't you know?' He'd sounded surprised that Felipe wasn't privy to all Francesca's private doings. 'She's transferring her traineeship to a firm there. She starts in January.'

A spark of pride had flickered in his numb chest. She was doing it.

Daniele continued speaking. 'But to be honest with you, I'm worried about her. I don't think she's sleeping and I'm sure she's not eating properly, which is not like her at all. I'm taking her out to lunch in an hour to try and get some food into her.'

'She's grieving,' Felipe had said automatically. 'You all are.'

'I hope that's all it is.'

And Felipe hoped that's all it was too.

At least Francesca had her family watching her, ready to catch her if she should fall too far.

He rubbed the back of his neck with both hands.

*Dios*, he was tired. Like Francesca, he was having trouble sleeping.

He had no appetite either. All the food he'd consumed recently had been for the purposes of fuel.

He felt like he'd spent the past two weeks in a form of limbo, going through the motions of his life but with no real animation.

There was an emptiness inside him he'd never known before.

'I *am* eating,' Francesca hissed. She speared a gnocchi and popped it in her mouth, making a big deal of chewing and swallowing it. 'See?'

Daniele did not look impressed. 'Eat another one.'

She complied moodily. It was as tasteless as the first.

'I spoke to Felipe Lorenzi earlier,' he said casually.

Hearing the name spoken was as painful as climbing into her empty bed.

'That's nice,' she managed after a pause that went on long enough for Daniele's eyebrows to rise.

'He asked after you.'

'Did he?'

Oh, God, her pathetic heart was battering her ribs again.

'What happened between you two?'

'Nothing.' Her lie was automatic. She couldn't talk about Felipe to anyone. Somehow she knew that if she started to talk about it she would start to cry and if she started to cry there was a danger she would never stop. Desperate to divert his attention, she said, 'Have you received the hotel bill yet?'

Her diversion worked.

'What hotel bill?'

'From when I was in Aguadilla. I hope you scrutinised it. I made sure to have all the most expensive items off the menus.' It was a struggle to keep her voice light to the end of her sentence.

Aguadilla and Caballeros would always be bound in her mind with Felipe.

'I didn't pick up the tab,' he said, looking confused. 'I had nothing to do with it.'

'Then who…?'

But as she asked the question she realised she knew who'd paid.

'Daniele, did you pay the bribe?' She'd gone through the foundation's accounts. The site bill had been paid but there was no evidence of the bribe money leaving the accounts. Alberto had taken leave again and wasn't answering her calls so she hadn't been able to check with him where the money had come from.

'What bribe?' His face darkened. 'What have you done?'

'Nothing,' she said hastily. 'I nearly did but Felipe stopped me. He sorted it.'

And he hadn't told her family.

Felipe hadn't only saved her from killing her career before it had even started but had saved her from the humiliation of her family's disappointment in her.

He must have paid the bribe from his own money.

'Francesca, what's wrong?'

With a start she realised she was crying, tears pouring out of her so thickly her brother's face blurred before her.

She'd been right to fear them because now they'd started she couldn't stop them.

She'd lost him. Her big, strong, arrogant protector, who had done everything in his power to save her from herself, had comforted her, shouted at her, laughed with her and made love to her.

She'd lost him and there was nothing she could do about it. He would never love her.

He couldn't stop thinking about her.

The call with Daniele had made it worse.

Now he couldn't stop himself worrying that she was eating.

When he retired to bed that night in another opulent but generic hotel room, this one in Dubai, he closed his eyes and thought of her.

Was she thinking of him?

Could he be the reason she couldn't sleep? Or was that just the arrogance she'd often accused him of coming out? Or wishful thinking?

He pulled a faded photo from his wallet. Him and Sergio in their army gear, shades on, arms slung around each other's shoulders, wide grins on their faces.

Sergio had had an infectious zest for life. He'd thrown himself into every part of it, his enormous smile never far from his face. In that respect he'd been similar to Francesca, who never committed to anything half-heartedly. With Francesca it was all or nothing.

He sat up straighter and dug his fingers into his skull.

All these years he'd been on his own…

It suddenly dawned on him that if Sergio could see him now he would slap him round the head.

James had been right that they put their bodies on the line every day, for people they didn't know as well as for each other. It had been the same in army. They'd all known the risks from the moment they'd signed on. Sergio had known it, his other fallen comrades had known it.

Sergio's wife had moved on. She'd remarried and had another child. Sergio would have wanted that for her.

So what was stopping *him* from moving on too? Why had he retreated to the familiar childhood loneliness he'd joined the army to escape?

He'd kept to himself all these years because the loss of Sergio and the family he'd found in his army career had been so great it had been safer for him. No attachments meant he couldn't be hurt again. But how was this any safer, sitting in a room sick to his guts missing the only woman in the world who could make him laugh and drive him to fury in the space of one conversation?

When he'd made his offer of the house to her he'd believed he was offering the most he could give but now, twisting it round, he could see he hadn't offered her anything, not of himself.

He'd been alone for the greatest part of his life but only now, without Francesca in his life, did he truly feel lost.

If her brother didn't take his finger off the intercom Francesca was going to throw something at him.

Couldn't he take the hint? She didn't want to see him.

She'd cried in the restaurant for a good fifteen minutes. Luckily her back had been turned on most of the other diners so no one other than Daniele had seen the silent waterfall pouring down her cheeks. He'd wanted to take her to their mother's house but she'd dug her heels in and insisted he take her home.

She'd needed to be alone. She'd told him that. She'd thought he'd respected that.

Fine, he wanted to check on her, but at six o'clock in the morning? So what if she hadn't been to sleep yet.

He wasn't giving up. He must have decided to just leave his finger on the buzzer until she gave in.

Throwing the bedcovers off, she stomped to the intercom. She picked up the receiver and yelled, 'Come in then!', pressed the button to admit him, and then flung her front door open.

She might as well make a coffee now that she was up. If Daniele was lucky, she might not throw it in his face.

But the man who entered her apartment wasn't her brother.

She stared from the kitchen door in disbelief, unable to speak, unable to move, unable to even breathe.

It was *him*. Felipe. There. *Here*. In her apartment.

Blood rushing to her head, she had to grind her bare toes into the floor stop herself from swaying or running to him, had to blink frantically to stop the tears that had welled in her eyes like a tap being turned on from falling.

He closed the door behind him and gazed at her with an expression she didn't recognise, his throat moving but no words coming from his mouth.

'Why are you here?' she whispered, breaking the silence.

His shoulders rose, a huge sigh escaping him. 'I'm sorry to turn up like this.'

'What's wrong?' He looked so haggard, something terrible must have happened.

'Nothing's wrong. No...' He cleared his throat. '*Everything's* wrong. I can't go on like this. I've been a fool. The biggest fool. I'm lost without you. I'm here to say sorry. I'm here to ask you… No, to *beg* you to forgive me.'

Her heart pounding, head spinning, Francesca stared in disbelief at the face she had missed with a desperation she hadn't thought possible.

'You were right. Everything you said. What I offered was an insult to everything we'd been together. I thought I was meant to be alone, I've spent so long telling myself that I had come to believe it as fact. I thought it was the way nature had made me but it wasn't. I was just protecting myself from being hurt again but you slipped into my heart without me realising and I can't bear to be without you a minute longer. I want to be with you. I know I don't deserve it but I am begging you, please, give me the chance to make things right. I love you, *querida*.'

His words filled her head with a dazed amazement.

He loved her?

Was she dreaming? Had the sleep that had been so impossible to find these past few weeks finally enveloped her and given her what she yearned for?

'Please, *querida*…' His voice broke. 'Say something. Shout at me. Hit me if you must. Whatever you need. I deserve it. If it's too late for us then tell me and I'll leave but if you can find it in yourself to forgive me I swear I will give all of myself to you. Whatever you decide, know that I will always be yours and my heart will always belong to you.'

She continued to stare, taking this all in, slowly starting to believe that this was really happening, and then her feet ungrounded themselves and her legs moved for her, towards him, running the steps needed to throw herself into his arms.

He caught her and held her tightly, close enough for her to feel the beating of his heart through the hardness of his chest and feel his breath in her hair, so solidly *real*, and she buried her face into the open collar of his neck and inhaled his scent and warmth.

She wasn't dreaming. He was here.

And he loved her.

Felipe closed his eyes tightly as he breathed her in and nuzzled into the soft cheek he had thought he would never feel again.

He hadn't known what reception he would receive and this…it was more than he had dared hope for.

Once he'd acknowledged to himself just how deeply his feelings for her ran, madness had taken its grip. All he could think was that he needed to get to her, no cares for the people he'd had to wake to get him there. He would have dragged a thousand people out of bed to get to her.

After the longest time he shifted so he could take her face in his hands and examine her closely. His heart lurched. Her beautiful face had a haunted quality to it, her eyes hollow with dark circles running under them. '*Querida*, are you ill?'

'I've been… I've not had an illness. I've…' A solitary tear fell down her cheek and she closed her eyes.

'Look at me, *querida*,' he commanded gently.

When she opened them he wiped another falling tear with his thumb before taking her hand and pressing it to his thundering heart.

'Do you feel that? It hasn't beaten the same since I met you. It's yours.'

'Oh, Felipe,' she whispered. 'I've been so unhappy without you. I go through the motions but I can't sleep. I'm struggling to concentrate. I have to make myself eat. I never knew what it meant to be heartsick but that's how it's been, like my heart's been broken.'

Something so strong filled him, threatening to burst out of his chest.

Her hand found his cheek and rubbed the bristles of his

jaw lovingly then the widest, most beautiful smile lit her face. 'I love you, Felipe.'

Even though her feelings shone out of her eyes he still didn't dare believe it. 'You do?'

She nodded, her hand still stroking his face. 'I don't want to be without you and if you mean what you say and if there's a chance we can make it work then I want to take it because being here with you right now... I can breathe again.'

Hearing those words was like being handed a gift-wrapped box of happiness.

'Oh, my love,' he breathed, and finally allowed himself to kiss her. 'Marry me.'

'Marry you?'

'Marry me. No half-measures. I want everything with you. The full commitment. A marriage of equals. If you say no then I will accept that without—'

'Yes,' she interrupted.

'You don't want to think about it?'

'No.'

'No, what?'

'No, I don't want to think about it. I want to marry you.'

'Are you sure?' He searched anxiously into her eyes, which were bright again with tears. 'You look as if you're about to cry.'

'Yes! And I'm about to cry because you've just made me the happiest woman alive!'

'I have?'

'You have a lot to learn about women.' And with that she pulled his head down to smother his mouth and face with kisses.

It was only when he lifted her to carry her into the bedroom that he noticed what she was wearing.

'Is that my T-shirt?'

She beamed. 'It *was* your T-shirt.'

'You sleep in it?'

'Every night. It was the only thing of yours I had left.'

That one thing convinced him more than anything else that Francesca Pellegrini loved him as much as he loved her.

He carried her to the bedroom, reflecting that he was the luckiest man who had ever lived.

# EPILOGUE

TWO YEARS LATER, Francesca Lorenzi waddled through the front door of her beautiful house in Rome holding onto her huge belly and hoping her husband had beaten her home. She hadn't seen him for two days and had missed him dreadfully. With their first child due in four weeks, they were both clearing their desks—Felipe metaphorically— so they could spend some time together alone to prepare.

Instead of finding a quiet home, she walked in to find her entire family there, mother, mother-in-law, siblings, cousins, aunts, uncles and, of course, her husband standing there with an indulgent expression on his handsome face.

'Surprise!'

'I haven't had the baby yet,' she said, laughing, allowing herself to be engulfed in a wave of careful hugs and wet kisses.

'This is to celebrate you qualifying for the bar,' her mother explained.

'I tried to stop them,' Felipe said.

'Liar.'

'He is a liar, it was his idea,' Aunt Rachele said.

Felipe pulled her into an embrace and whispered, 'You've worked so hard for this. We all wanted to show you how proud we were.'

'I couldn't have done it without you,' she whispered back before kissing him.

He'd been her rock.

After that dream morning when he'd turned up at her apartment declaring his love for her, he'd set about putting into motion all the changes needed for them to be together properly. The first thing he'd done was hire a PA for himself. The second thing had been to promote Seb to Chief Executive of all operations.

He'd opened a base in Rome on the same street as the human rights law firm she'd joined, and restructured the way things were run so he could be home at night with her the vast majority of the time. Seb now ran all the operations with James as his deputy. The two men were here now, and she greeted them warmly while keeping a tight hold of her husband's hand. She always kept a tight hold of it.

Felipe sometimes felt he should pinch himself to make sure he hadn't slipped into a dream.

He'd never had any doubts that stepping back from the operational side of the business was the best thing for him and Francesca. He'd expected to miss the adrenaline and excitement that had come with it, but…nothing. He hadn't missed it at all. His passionate, open-hearted wife was all the excitement he needed.

Finally, he had the family he'd always craved but had stepped away from seeking. Her family had embraced him so deeply as one of their own that often he thought he should have been the one to take her surname rather than the other way round. Francesca had been the one to encourage him to get closer to his own mother, surprising him by inviting her to stay with them for a long weekend. Loving Francesca had given him a greater understanding of the love his mother had for him. She'd sacrificed everything for him, just as he would gladly sacrifice everything, his wealth, his business, his life, for Francesca. Slowly they were building towards a proper mother-son relationship and now he felt the love for her in his heart like a pulse. She adored her daughter-in-law.

As he led the toast to his wife and all her amazing accomplishments, he marvelled for the thousandth time that he was indeed the luckiest man to have ever walked the earth.

* * *

Two weeks later, Sergio Pieta Lorenzi was born, weighing seven pounds and one ounce.

Everyone said he had his father's looks and his mother's temper.

* * * * *

*If you enjoyed the first part of Michelle Smart's*
BOUND TO A BILLIONAIRE *trilogy look out for*

*CLAIMING HIS ONE-NIGHT BABY*
*Coming September 2017*

*BUYING HIS BRIDE OF CONVENIENCE*
*Coming October 2017*

*In the meantime why not explore another*
*Michelle Smart trilogy?*
THE KALLIAKIS CROWN
*TALOS CLAIMS HIS VIRGIN*
*THESEUS DISCOVERS HIS HEIR*
*HELIOS CROWNS HIS MISTRESS*

*Available now!*

## 'Tell me you want me.'

'I want you, but there's—'

Emily stepped back from Loukas with what little willpower she had left, but she stumbled over the pedal bin behind her left foot and it tipped over and spilled its contents in front of his Italian-leather-clad feet.

An unpinned grenade would have had a similar effect.

Loukas's face drained of colour as if *he* was the one with morning sickness. He stood frozen for a moment. Totally statuelike. As if someone had pressed the 'pause' button on him.

Emily watched as if in slow motion as he bent to pick up not one but seven pregnancy test wands. He examined the telltale blue lines, clanking the wands against each other like chopsticks.

His eyes finally cut to hers—sharp, flint hard with query. 'You're…*pregnant*?'

# One Night With Consequences

*When one night…leads to pregnancy!*

When succumbing to a night of unbridled desire
it's impossible to think past the morning after!

But, with the sheets barely settled, that little blue line
appears on the pregnancy test and it doesn't take long
to realise that one night of white-hot passion
has turned into a lifetime of consequences!

Only one question remains:

How do you tell a man you've just met
that you're about to share more than just his bed?

Find out in:

*The Greek's Nine-Month Redemption* by Maisey Yates

*Crowned for the Prince's Heir* by Sharon Kendrick

*The Sheikh's Baby Scandal* by Carol Marinelli

*A Ring for Vincenzo's Heir* by Jennie Lucas

*Claiming His Christmas Consequence* by Michelle Smart

*The Guardian's Virgin Ward* by Caitlin Crews

*A Child Claimed by Gold* by Rachael Thomas

*The Consequence of His Vengeance* by Jennie Lucas

*Secrets of a Billionaire's Mistress* by Sharon Kendrick

*The Boss's Nine-Month Negotiation* by Maya Blake

*The Pregnant Kavakos Bride* by Sharon Kendrick

Look for more **One Night With Consequences** stories,
coming soon!

# A RING FOR THE GREEK'S BABY

BY
MELANIE MILBURNE

First Published in Great Britain 2017
By Mills & Boon, an imprint of HarperCollins*Publishers*
1 London Bridge Street, London, SE1 9GF

© 2017 Melanie Milburne

ISBN: 978-0-263-92532-6

Printed and bound in Spain
by CPI, Barcelona

**Melanie Milburne** read her first Mills & Boon novel at the age of seventeen, in between studying for her final exams. After completing a master's degree in education she decided to write a novel, and thus her career as a romance author was born. Melanie is an ambassador for the Australian Childhood Foundation and a keen dog-lover and trainer. She enjoys long walks in the Tasmanian bush. In 2015 Melanie won the HOLT Medallion—a prestigious award honouring outstanding literary talent.

### Books by Melanie Milburne

### Mills & Boon Modern Romance

*The Temporary Mrs Marchetti*
*Unwrapping His Convenient Fiancée*
*His Mistress for a Week*

### *Wedlocked!*

*Wedding Night with Her Enemy*

### *The Ravensdale Scandals*

*Ravensdale's Defiant Captive*
*Awakening the Ravensdale Heiress*
*Engaged to Her Ravensdale Enemy*
*The Most Scandalous Ravensdale*

### *The Playboys of Argentina*

*The Valquez Bride*
*The Valquez Seduction*

### *Those Scandalous Caffarellis*

*Never Say No to a Caffarelli*
*Never Underestimate a Caffarelli*
*Never Gamble with a Caffarelli*

Visit the Author Profile page
at millsandboon.co.uk for more titles.

To my darling father, Gordon Luke,
who passed away during the writing of this novel.

You were an amazing father, grandfather and
great-grandfather, brother, uncle and friend.
You have touched so many lives with your
funny stories, your generous spirit and
strong work ethic. I will always treasure the memories
I have of our relationship. The world would be a better
place if everyone could have a dad like you.

Rest in peace. xxx

# CHAPTER ONE

When the seventh test came back positive, Emily knew it was time to face the truth. Face it or spend a fortune on pregnancy tests until there wasn't a pharmacy she could walk into in the whole of London without blushing with an 'it's me again' grimace. She'd thought buying a jumbo box of tampons was embarrassing, but a basket full of pregnancy tests was way worse. There was no avoiding it. Those little blue lines weren't lying even if she wished they were.

She. Was. Pregnant.

Not that she didn't want to have a baby. Some day, with some nice guy who was madly in love with her and had married her at a big, white wedding first.

Her first ever one-night stand and look what had happened. How could she be so fertile? How could condoms be so unreliable? How could she have slept with a man so out of her league? Emily was all for aiming high in life, but a Greek billionaire? And not one of those short, fat, balding middle-aged ones, like those in her local deli, but a six-foot-four heart-stoppingly gorgeous man who had eyes so brown you could lose yourself in them.

Which she had promptly done. Completely and utterly lost herself in a sizzling sexual encounter unlike anything she'd experienced before. Which, truth be told, was not saying much, because her experience could hardly be described as extensive given she'd wasted seven years with her ex-partner Daniel. Seven years. *Argh!* Why couldn't the number seven be lucky for her like everyone else? For seven long years she'd waited for a proposal. It had got so bad that every time her ex had bent down on one knee to pick something up off the floor she would get all excited thinking this was it—the moment she'd been waiting for.

It had never happened.

What had happened instead was she'd got cheated on. The ignominy of being betrayed was bad enough, but to be left for a male lover was a whole new level of humiliation. How could she have been the last to know Daniel was gay?

But it wasn't the betrayal that hurt her the most. It was the loss of being a part of a couple; the shock of being single for the first time in so long she had forgotten *how* to be single. Going out at night without a partner by her side felt weird, like going out with only one shoe on. Or eating in a restaurant on her own, working her way through a meal, wondering if everyone was speculating if she'd been stood up or something.

She used to love going out to dinner with Daniel,

who was a bit of a food and wine connoisseur. They would try different restaurants and cuisines and sit for hours over a meal, discussing the food, the presentation, the wine and even the other diners. She used to love coming home from work knowing she had someone to talk to about her day. Daniel had been her 'guess what happened to me today' person, her sounding board, her back-up, her anchor. The person who'd provided the stability she'd craved since she was a child.

She hadn't had much luck since with dating. Her New Age relationship-therapist mother said it was because she was subconsciously sabotaging her male relationships because of her father issues. Father issues. And whose fault was it she didn't have a father? Her mother hadn't managed to get his name and number when she'd had sex with him under a rain-soaked tarpaulin at a music festival.

Emily looked at the pregnancy test again. No. She wasn't having a nightmare. Well, she was. A *living* nightmare. A nightmare that involved fronting up to commitment-phobe Loukas Kyprianos and telling him he was going to be a father.

*Oh, joy.*

Such a task would be a whole lot easier if he had called her in the month since their night of bedwrecking, pulse-throbbing sex. Or sent a text message. Or an email. A carrier pigeon, even. Given her some tiny thread of hope he might want to see her again.

Although, come to think of it, she hadn't exactly

done herself any favours in that department. She could write a book on how to get a guy to lose interest in one date. When she was nervous she talked too much. Way too much. When she gushed like that, she didn't just wear her heart on her sleeve but on every visible part of her body. A couple of drinks down and she'd mentioned her dream of marriage, four kids and a dog—an Irish Retriever, no less. To a man who had a reputation as an easy come, easy go playboy.

What was *wrong* with her?

Emily walked out of the bathroom and picked up her phone. No missed calls. No text messages… apart from four from her mother with links to her prescribed daily meditation and yoga practices. It was easier to let her mother think she used the links than to argue why she didn't. She had learned a long time ago that arguing with her mother was a pointless and energy draining exercise.

Emily didn't have Loukas's number even if she could summon up the courage to call it. She could get it from her friend Allegra, who was married to Loukas's best friend, Draco Papandreou, but somehow telling Loukas over the phone didn't seem quite the way to go. *Hey, guess what? We made a baby!* would probably not be such a great opening gambit.

No. This called for a face-to-face conversation. She needed to gauge his reaction. Not that he was an easy person to read. He had one of those faces that gave little away in terms of expression. His facial muscles were into energy saving or something.

It was like trying to see what was behind a curtained stage. But he had an aura of quiet authority she'd found overwhelmingly attractive. His aloofness had intrigued her at the wedding. He didn't seem to necd people the way she did. She was like a too-friendly puppy at a garden party, moving from group to group, trying to win approval.

He, on the other hand, was like a statue.

Emily's phone rang and she almost dropped it in surprise. She didn't recognise the number and answered it in her best legal secretary voice. 'Emily Seymour speaking.'

'It's Loukas Kyprianos.'

Her heart kicked her ribcage out of the way, leapt to her throat and clung there with hooked claws.

*He'd called her. He'd called her. He'd called her.*

The words were beating in time with her panicked pulse. She needed more time. She wasn't ready for this conversation. She needed to rehearse in front of the mirror or something, like she used to do as a kid with a hairbrush as a pretend microphone. She tried to calm herself but her breathing was so choppy it felt as though she was having an asthma attack.

*Breathe. Breathe. Breathe.*

She could do with some of her mother's mindfulness techniques right about now. 'Erm…hi. How are you?'

'Fine. You?'

'Erm…good, thank you. Great. Super. Fantastic.'

*Apart from a little morning sickness.*

There was a tick-tock of silence.

'Are you free this evening?'

Emily swallowed. Free for what? Hook-up sex? She didn't want to sound too available. A girl had her pride and all that. But she had to tell him about the baby. Maybe over dinner would be the best way to do it. No. No. No. Not in a public place. She would have to do it in private. Private was best. 'I'll have to check my diary. I seem to remember I have something...'

He gave a soft sound that could have passed for an amused chuckle. 'You don't have to play hard to get with me, Emily.'

Yes, well, it was a little late for that, she had to admit. The way he said her name with that subtle Greek accent made the base of her spine go all squishy. *Em-il-ee*. It wasn't a name when he said it. It was a seductive caress, as if he had circled each and every bump of her vertebrae with a slow-moving fingertip. 'Look, I think you should know, I'm not usually like that...like I was the night of the wedding. I don't normally drink so much—'

'Have dinner with me.'

Emily took umbrage at the way he said it, like a command instead of an invitation. Did he think she'd been sitting by her phone waiting for him to call? Well, she had, but that was beside the point. She wasn't going to let him think he could call her out of the blue and get her to drop everything to have dinner with him—even if she had nothing to drop. 'I'm not free this evening so—'

'Cancel.'

*Cancel?*

What the hell? Why should she cancel something at his say-so? 'I don't think so.'

She was quite proud of the haughty I-haven't-been-Superglued-to-my-phone-waiting-for-you-to-call tone in her voice.

'Please?'

Emily let a small silence pass. Let him sweat it out, as she'd been doing for the last month.

'Why do you want to have dinner with me?' she finally asked.

'I want to see you again.' His voice was rough and smooth. Gravel dipped in honey.

He wanted to see her again? Why? He had a reputation as a playboy, perhaps not as wild and loose-living as some rich men, but he hadn't had a relationship lasting longer than a few days.

Or, at least, none the press knew about. Since his best friend's marriage, the media interest had shifted from Draco to Loukas. Before that, Loukas had been able to fly below the radar but now everyone was speculating on whom he would date next. Emily privately had been dreading seeing him with another woman in the weeks since the wedding. If he were involved with someone else then the task of telling him he was to be a father would be even more difficult.

'Is that code for "sleeping with me"?' she asked. 'Because, if so, I think you should know I'm not that sort of girl. I've never had a one-night stand before and I—'

'It wouldn't be a one-night stand if we did it again.'

It was a good point. But she couldn't sleep with him before she told him the result of their last encounter. Even thinking about that night in his arms made her insides do cartwheels of excitement. Listening to his voice was as good as foreplay. If he kept talking to her, who knew what might happen? 'Just dinner, okay?'

'Just dinner.'

'Will I meet you somewhere?'

'I'll pick you up. What's your address?'

Emily gave it to him while part of her mind was worrying about what to wear. Little black dress or colour? No. Not too much colour. Not red. Definitely not red. Red was too 'come and get me'. Pink was too girl-next-door. Did she have time to do her hair? Should she wash and blow-dry it or just scoop it up and hope for the best? Not too much make-up. Subtle and classy was best. Which heels? She needed heels because he was tall—a pair of stilts, even. A night of craning her neck to maintain eye contact would send her muscles into spasm.

'I would've called you before this but I was away on business.'

*You still could have called me.*

Was his 'business' a svelte blonde like the one she'd seen hanging off his arm when she'd searched him online? 'Really?'

'Yes. Really.'

Emily chewed at one side of her lower lip. Why

*had* he called her? Hadn't she put him off with her 'marriage and kids' manifesto? Why had she blurted that out anyway? It was a first date no-no. Although, strictly speaking, it hadn't been a date at all. It had been a chance hook-up. An impulsive act she still couldn't explain. 'Why? I mean, it's not as if I'm your type.'

'Given your relationship with Allegra and mine with Draco, I wanted to make sure there wasn't any uncomfortableness about that night, in case we run into each other again because of our connection with them.'

There was going to be a whole heap of uncomfortableness when Emily told him what had resulted from that night. 'Right…good thinking.'

'I'll see you at seven.'

Emily didn't get a chance to say anything in reply for he ended the call. She stared at her phone, wondering if she should press redial, but then she realised he had a withheld number.

Her mother would say it was a sign.

Loukas clicked off his phone, placed it on his desk and leaned back in his office chair. He was breaking a rule by contacting Emily Seymour but he hadn't been able to get her out of his mind, or the memory of her touch out of his body.

One-night stands were meant to be exactly that.

One night.

He had occasional relationships but he always kept things casual. Casual worked for him. Casual meant no emotional investment. Casual meant no promises he couldn't keep. He kept his relationships short, simple and based on sex.

But the sex didn't get much better than what he'd had with Emily. He wasn't sure what it was about her that had got him so worked up that night. She was cute in a girl-next-door way, with her petite frame and wavy shoulder-length hair that was neither blonde nor brown but a combination of the two. 'Bronde' she'd laughingly called it.

Her eyes were like a fawn's. Bambi eyes. Toffee-brown and dusted with dark spots that looked like tiny iron filings sprinkled over pools of honey. Her skin was peaches-and-cream and silk, with a scattering of freckles over the bridge of her retroussé nose that reminded him of a dusting of nutmeg. She had a sunny smile, bright and cheery with an endearing little overbite, and well-shaped lips built for kissing…and other things. Those other things had just about blown off the top of his head.

It was true she wasn't his type. But in another lifetime she might have been. In a parallel life where he didn't carry guilt like convict's chains. A life where every day he didn't relive the stomach-churning moment that had changed everything for his half-sister Ariana and had made him even more of an outcast in his family than he had been before. Even after seventeen years, every time he saw a child's bike his breath would stop and his guts would turn to gravy. If he heard the sudden squeal of brakes his heart would bang against his sternum like a wrecking ball. The siren of an ambulance sent his pulse sky-rocketing. He still lay awake at night hearing the crunch and crumple of metal and the piercing scream of a critically injured child…

Loukas knew he shouldn't be seeing Emily again. He shouldn't have hooked up with her in the first place. But, after having gone straight to the wedding from visiting Ariana in hospital after her latest bout of orthopaedic surgery, those chains of guilt had dug in with a cruel bite. He couldn't undo the past. It didn't matter how many times he relived that day. He had ruined his sister's life and destroyed his mother's second marriage in the process.

Emily's smile had been like a bolt of sunshine at the wedding. Her creamy cheeks had blushed when she'd first met his gaze. It had been a long time since he had been with a woman who blushed when he looked at her. He avoided that type usually. But something about Emily had drawn his interest, with her dancing eyes, neat little ballet dancer's figure and her cute clumsiness. Not to mention her adorable little bunny rabbit twitch where her nose would wrinkle up as if she had an invisible pair of glasses on and was trying to hitch them back up on the bridge of her nose.

He wasn't going to offer her anything but a temporary fling. He was only interested in the here and now. He was in London for a week working on some software for one of the government's security agencies. It was too good an opportunity to waste. A week-long fling to enjoy a little more of what they'd experienced that night. He would be upfront and honest about it. He wouldn't dress it up as anything other than what it was. He would offer her a no-strings, no-promises fling and leave it at that, just as he did with any other woman he took a fancy to.

And he had taken rather a fancy to Emily.

His mind kept going back to that night like a tongue going back to a niggling tooth. Loukas still wasn't sure why he'd taken her back to his room after Draco and Allegra's wedding. Emily had been staying on the same floor of Draco's private villa and he could easily have left her at her door after accompanying her back from the reception. But somehow the impersonal 'it was nice to meet you' kiss he'd intended to plant on her cheek had turned into something else. It was as if his lips had had their own agenda. They'd moved from her cheek to her lips like a missile finding a target.

*Wham.*

One kiss hadn't been enough. Her soft lips opening under his unleashed a ferocious desire from somewhere deep inside him. A desire that had swept away to some far-off, unreachable place every reason not to sleep with her.

They hadn't talked much—or at least, he hadn't. But then, that was his way. Talking had never been his currency in relationships. He was the strong, silent 'get on with the job' type. Emily, on the other hand, had talked of her fairy-tale dreams as though he'd been auditioning for the role of handsome prince.

As if that was ever going to happen.

*But once it might have...*

Loukas pushed out of his chair and turned to look out of the window to the motherboard-like grid of London's streets below. Crowds of people bustled about like busy ants. He was content with his life as it was...more or less. He had more money than he knew what to do with, a career that was global and a lifestyle that was enviable. It wasn't like him to leave it a month between lovers, but he hadn't been with anyone since Emily. He'd been over-the-top busy, certainly, but that didn't usually stop him from engaging in a bit of sex to relieve the tension with someone who was agreeable to his terms. Terms that didn't include anything long-or even mid-term. Short-term suited him because he could leave before things got too intense.

However, he didn't care for the term 'playboy' the press labelled him with because it suggested he was shallow and exploitative with women. In reality it was because he wanted to spare his partners unnecessary hurt. He wasn't like his father who moved from woman to woman with no regard for their feelings, promising them everything and then leaving them with nothing.

Loukas was the opposite. He promised them nothing and left them with generous gifts to soften the end of the affair.

But now the press's interest in him had gone up a notch. With his best friend now off the market the focus had switched to him. Everywhere he went he had to be mindful of who was watching. The paparazzi were bad enough, but everyone had a camera phone these days, hankering after the money shot, so it was harder and harder to escape the intense interest in his private life.

Was it risky to see Emily again? Probably. But it was only for a week while he was in London. Seven days of sex without strings. The sex had been so damn good that night after the wedding. Good was an understatement. Everything about that night still reverberated in his body like a plucked cello string. He had only to think of her soft little hands with their butterfly touch to feel an aftershock roll through him. Just hearing her voice gave him goose bumps along the flesh of his spine. The soft breathlessness of it, the way she talked too much when she was nervous. The way she chewed at her lower lip and shielded her gaze with those spider-leg-long lashes. The way her cheeks pooled with pink as delicate as the blush of a rose.

He normally steered clear of sweet homespun girls like her. He always kept his head in relationships. Always. But just this once he wasn't listening to his head. His body was telling him to go for it.

And just this once that was exactly what he planned to do.

# CHAPTER TWO

EMILY WAS JUST ABOUT to put her lip-gloss on when the doorbell rang. She grimaced at the state of her bathroom counter. Nearly every item of make-up or skincare treatment she owned was strewn about, some with the lids still open. Her bedroom was even worse. Clothes were on just about every surface, including the floor. It looked as if her room had been ransacked by an addict in frantic search of a fix.

She closed her bedroom door on the way past and opened the front door with a smile that fell a little short of the mark. 'Hi.'

Loukas's deep-brown gaze met hers in a look that sent a current of awareness through her body like a lightning strike on metal. 'Hello.'

How could a one-word greeting create such havoc with her senses? How could one man have such a potent effect on her? He was dressed in dark-blue trousers and a white shirt with a silver-and-black-striped tie and a navy-blue blazer, giving him an air of sophisticated man about town that was lethally attractive. Her pulse skipped and tripped at the mere sight of him. She opened the door wider, inching her feet back against the wall of the narrow hallway to give him more room. 'Would you like to come in for a bit? I'm not quite ready.' A hundred years wasn't enough time to get ready.

He stepped through the door without touching her but Emily felt as if he had. Her body tingled when he moved past her in the doorway, as if he had sent out a radar signal to every cell of her flesh. His tall frame shrank her hallway, the carriage-light fitting only just clearing the top of his head. The citrus notes of his aftershave swirled around her nostrils, the clean, sharp scent taking her back to that night in his arms. She had smelt him on her skin for hours afterwards. Felt his hard, male presence in her tender muscles for days. Every time she moved her body it reminded her of the glide and thrust of his body within hers.

The intimacy they'd shared that night was like a presence hovering. The air was charged with it. Electrified by it. Humming with it.

His bottomless brown gaze moved over her body like a caress. 'You look beautiful.'

Emily wished she didn't have such a propensity to blush. She could feel it crawling over her cheeks like a spill of red wine on a cream carpet. She tucked a strand of hair back behind her ear. Shifted her feet. Smoothed her hands down the front of her dress. 'Would you like a drink or...?'

He stepped closer, placing his hands on her waist and bringing his mouth down to within a breath of hers. 'Let's get this out of the way first.'

With a willpower Emily hadn't even known she possessed, she placed her hands against his chest and took a faltering step backwards. 'Can we have dinner first? It's just, it's been a month, and I feel a little...'

He gave one of his rare smiles. It was little more than an upward movement of his lips but it made something quiver on the floor of her belly like autumn leaves rustling in a playful breeze. 'You don't need to be nervous.'

*Yes, I flipping well do.*

Emily couldn't quite meet his gaze and focussed on the knot of his tie instead. 'Would you like to sit down? I just have to get my...my bag.'

*And my courage, which seems to have left the building. Possibly the country.*

'Take your time. The booking isn't till eight.'

'Right, well, then, I'll just be a moment.' She backed away but bumped into the lamp on the table behind her. 'Oops. Sorry. Won't be a tick.'

Emily dashed back to the bathroom and gripped the edge of the basin.

*You can do this. You can do this. You can do this.*

She glanced at her reflection and stifled a groan. Was it her imagination or did she look a-vampire-just-left-me-for-dead pale? Maybe a bit more make-up would help. A bit of bronzer or something. She reached for her bronzer pad and brush but her hand knocked her bottle of perfume to the tiled floor with a glass-shattering crash. She looked at the shards of glass for a split second before she bent down to scoop them up, slicing one of her fingers in the process.

Blood oozed down over her hand and wrist as if she was on the set of a horror movie. Footsteps sounded outside the bathroom, each one of them stepping on her flailing heart.

*Boom. Boom. Boom.*

'Are you okay in there?' Loukas asked, opening the door.

Emily grabbed the nearest hand towel and wrapped her hand in it. The smell of honeysuckle and vanilla was so strong and cloying it was nauseating. His nostrils quivered as if he thought so too. 'I—I broke my perfume bottle.'

He stepped closer and gently took her hand. 'Let me have a look. You might need stitches.'

She watched with one eye squinted while he carefully unpeeled her makeshift bandage. He held her hand to the light, his eyes narrowed in focus, his strong eyebrows drawn together in concentration. 'No stitches needed, but I think there's a sliver of glass in there. Do you have some tweezers?'

What a question to ask a girl with eyebrows that grew faster than weeds. 'In the cupboard above the basin.'

He opened the cupboard and took the tweezers from the bottom shelf next to her jumbo pack of tampons.

*Won't need those for a while.*

He rinsed the tweezers under the hot tap and then ran some antiseptic he'd found on the middle shelf over them.

Emily braced herself for the sting but his touch

was so gentle she barely noticed anything except the way he was standing close enough for her to feel his body warmth. Close enough to smell the sharp notes of citrus in his aftershave, redolent of sun-warmed lemons and limes. Close enough to see the pinpricks of dark stubble peppered over his lean jaw, hinting at the potent male hormones surging in his blood.

*Stop thinking about his surging blood.*

*I can't help it!*

He glanced at her. 'I'm not hurting you too much?'

'No…' Emily looked at his mouth, the way it curved around his words, the way the stubble surrounded it, making her fingers ache to reach up and trace it.

He went back to work on her finger, gently removing the shard of glass and cleansing the wound with another wash of antiseptic. He reached back to the cupboard for a plaster and a small crepe bandage, which he placed on her finger. 'There you go,' he said with another heart-stopping, upward movement of his lips. 'Good as new.'

Emily was so dazed by his almost-smile and his closeness she didn't register what he was doing for a moment. It was only when he stepped past her to place the plaster and bandage wrappings in the metal pedal bin next to her that her heart came to a screeching standstill. She quickly blocked him from accessing the bin, as if she were guarding the Hope Diamond. 'D-don't put it in there.' She held out her good hand, not one bit surprised it was shaking. 'I'll take it and put it in the bin in the kitchen.'

One of his eyebrows rose like a question mark. 'Why not this bin?'

She forced herself to hold his gaze, her heart beating so hard it was as if there were panicked pigeons and a handful of hummingbirds trapped in her chest. 'This one's…erm…full.'

His eyes moved back and forth between each of hers. 'What's wrong? You seem a little jumpy.'

'I'm not jumpy.'

*Probably shouldn't have answered so quickly.*

He reached out his hand and trailed the backs of his bent knuckles down the slope of her cheek, making every nerve fizz and whizz. His eyes went to her mouth, lingering there as if he was reliving every time he had kissed her that night a month ago. 'Why do I make you so nervous?'

Emily swallowed loud enough to hear it. 'I'm n-not nervous…'

Loukas inched up her chin, the pad of his thumb moving in slow mesmerising circles, his eyes holding hers. 'I couldn't stop thinking about that night. How good it was between us.'

She sent her tongue out to moisten her lips that were as dry as the crepe bandage on her finger. 'Isn't it always good between you and your lovers?'

He gave a shrug but there was no hint of arrogance about it. 'Mostly. What about you?'

Emily tried but failed to suppress a snort. 'I can count my previous lovers on half a hand. My mother's had more sex than me. She's *still* having more than me.'

He continued to look at her without speaking, his eyes holding hers as if he found her fascinating. But then, maybe a twenty-nine-year-old almost-virgin was something of an enigma to him.

'She's a relationships therapist,' Emily said into the silence. 'She teaches people how to have better relationships by working on their sex lives. Ironic that her daughter's sex life is practically non-existent.'

*Here you go again. Telling him all your stuff.*

*So? I need to break the ice a bit. I can't just tell him he's going to be a dad without a bit of a lead up.*

*You are so unsophisticated!*

His hands came to settle on her waist, his eyes sexily hooded. 'Maybe I can help you with that.'

The warmth of his hands seemed to be travelling right through her clothes, through every layer of her skin, sending electric pulses down her nerves until they were twitching in excitement. Her inner core registered his proximity like a scanner recognises a code. It was as though she were micro-chipped for him and him alone. Her intimate muscles were clenching, contracting, wanting.

'I haven't had a lot of luck with men,' Emily said. 'I had one lover before my ex, but it hardly counts, as it was over before I blinked. I was with Daniel seven years so it's left me a little out of the game, so to speak.'

*Argh! What are you doing? You're making yourself sound like some sort of relationship tragic.*

*But I don't want him to think I've been jumping every man I meet.*

His hands went from her waist to skim up her arms and rest on her shoulders. His eyes had a lustrous depth to them that reminded her of a bottomless lake. 'You haven't had a lover since Daniel? Apart from me, I mean?'

'No. I dated a few times but it never came to anything. I suspect that was why I was so...so enthusiastic when you kissed me outside my room,' Emily said. 'I hope I didn't shock you.'

Loukas brushed his thumb over her lower lip. 'You delighted and surprised me.'

*That's me. Full of delightful surprises.*

She stretched her lips into a rictus smile. 'Erm... there's something we need to discuss...'

'I'm not in this for the long haul, Emily.' His mouth had an intractable set to it. 'I want you to be clear on that right from the outset. I'm only here in London this week, so if we have a fling that's all it will be. A fling. Nothing else.'

'I understand that. It's just there's some—'

'I want you.' His voice hummed in her core as deep as a bass chord.

Emily placed her hands flat against his chest, her hips bumping into his, sending a shockwave of tingly awareness through her body. She couldn't think when he was this close. Her body went on autopilot. Wanting. Craving. Hungering. Her breasts tingled with the memory of his touch, the heat and fire of his lips and tongue and the sexy scrape of his teeth.

He was so magnetic. So irresistible. So tempting her inner core was contracting with little pulses of lust, as if recalling the sexy thrust of his body within hers.

How could she possibly be thinking about sex at a time like this? But it seemed her body could only think about sex when Loukas was within touching distance. His chest was hard and warm under her hands, the clean, laundered scent of his shirt filling her nostrils. The length and strength of his thighs so close to her own reminded her of how those muscle-packed legs had entrapped hers in a tangle of sheets, taking her to a sensual heaven she hadn't known existed. Her body remembered everything about that encounter. Remembered and begged for it to be repeated. The drumming of her pulse echoed in her core, making her aware of every inch of her body where it was in contact with his, as though all the nerves on those spots had been supercharged.

His mouth came down to hover above hers, his warm, minty breath sending her senses reeling. 'Tell me you want me.'

'I want you, but there's...' Emily stepped back from him, using what little willpower she had left, but she stumbled over the pedal bin behind her left foot and it tipped over and spilled its contents in front of his Italian-leather-clad feet.

An unpinned grenade would have had a similar effect.

Loukas's face drained of colour as if he were the one with morning sickness. He stood frozen for a moment. Totally statue-like—as if someone had pressed a pause button on him. Then he swallowed.

Once.

Twice.

Three times.

Each one of them was clearly audible in the pregnant silence—*no pun intended*. Emily watched as if in slow motion when he bent to pick up not one, but seven test wands. He examined the tell-tale blue lines, the wands clanking against each other like chopsticks.

His eyes finally cut to hers, sharp, flint-hard with query. 'You're…*pregnant?*'

He said the word as though it was the most shocking diagnosis anyone could have. Up until a few hours ago, she had thought so too.

Emily wrung her hands like a distraught heroine from a period drama, wincing when her damaged finger protested. 'I was trying to tell you but—'

'Is it mine?' The question was a verbal slap.

She double blinked. 'Of course it's yours. I—'

'But we used condoms.' The suspicion in his voice scraped at her already overwrought nerves.

'I know, but condoms sometimes fail, and this time one must have—'

'Aren't you on the pill?' His brows were so tightly drawn above his eyes it gave him an intimidating air.

'I—I was taking a break from it.' Emily could feel tears welling up. The concentrated smell of her spilt perfume was making her feel queasy. Her fingertips were fizzing as if her blood were being filtered through coarse sand. The tingling sensation spread to her arms, travelling all the way up to her neck, making it hard to keep her head steady. The room began to spin, the floor to shift beneath her feet as though she were standing on a pitching boat deck. She reached blindly for the edge of the bathroom counter but it was likc a ghost hand reaching through fog. Every one of her limbs folded as if she were a marionette with severed strings. She heard Loukas call out her name through a vacuum and then everything faded to black…

'Emily!' Loukas dropped to his knees in front of her slumped form, his heart banging against his chest wall like a bell struck by a madman. Her face was as white as the basin above her collapsed form, her skin clammy. He brushed the sticky hair back from her forehead, his mind still whirling with the news of her pregnancy.

*Pregnant.*

The word struck another hammer-like blow to his chest. A baby. *His* baby. How had it happened? He was always so careful. Paranoid careful. He never had sex without a condom. He never took risks. Never. How could he have got her pregnant? It had been a bit low of him to suggest it wasn't his, but panic had blunted his sensitivity.

A father?

Him?

Why hadn't he asked her about contraception? If he'd known she wasn't on the pill, or using a hormone implant device, he would have taken extra caution. He couldn't be a father. He didn't want to be a father. He had never planned to be a father. Panic drummed through him like wildebeests in stampede. He tried to picture himself with a baby and his mind went blank, his chest seizing with dread, vice-like. His intestines knotted as though they were being sectioned by twine.

No. Not him. Not now. Not ever.

He looked at Emily's slumped form and another dagger of guilt jabbed him. Hard. He had done this, upsetting her to the point of collapse. She had been trying to tell him something but he'd been so intent on squaring up their fling he hadn't given her a chance. No wonder she had acted so nervous and on edge.

She was pregnant.

With *his* baby.

What was he going to do? What was the *right* thing to do? Hands-off provision for his child seemed a little tacky somehow. There was no way he could walk away from this. He would have to be involved with his child as he wished his father had been for him. He would have to be responsible for the child. To provide for and protect it. The thought of protecting a child was enough to make Loukas break out in another prickly sweat.

How could *he* keep a child safe?

He had got Emily pregnant. Some would call it an accident, a freakish trick of fate, or destiny or whatever, but he blamed himself. He had slipped up. He had done what he had sworn he would never do.

He was to become a father, unless she chose to get rid of it.

He allowed the thought some traction, but as escape hatches went it wasn't one he felt comfortable with. It would be Emily's decision, certainly, but he hoped she wouldn't feel pressured into it because of their circumstances. He would have to make it clear he was okay with her keeping it. More than okay, even if he harboured more doubts than a sceptics' conference. Not doubts about keeping the baby— doubts about himself as a father.

His own father had insisted a recent partner have an abortion after she'd fallen pregnant, and when she'd refused he'd summarily dumped her. The young woman had subsequently attempted suicide and lost the baby as a result. She had recently been paid a large sum of money by a gossip magazine for a tell-all interview about how Loukas's father had caused her so much distress. The interview, by association, had put the spotlight on Loukas and the way he conducted his relationships, especially now he was attracting more media attention than ever before.

But there was no way he would ever put that sort of pressure on any woman. Emily's pregnancy was a shock, a surprise and an inconvenience, but there was a tiny human life in the making, and he would not do or say anything to compromise that development, nor the mental health of its mother.

He was angry with himself for putting Emily in this situation. Furious. Ashamed. Deeply, thoroughly ashamed that he had acted on impulse and slept with her when normally he would have steered clear of an unworldly woman like her. He'd been the one to make the first move. He hadn't been able to keep his eyes off her, much less his hands. He had foolishly thought he could have a one-night stand and walk away. He should have walked away from her at her bedroom door at Draco's villa—that was what he should have done.

What had he been thinking, sleeping with a cute little homespun girl like her? She wasn't his type and he certainly wasn't hers. He wasn't a rake, but he was no altar boy either. It had been a night of out-of-character madness and now it had come to this. A life had been created that would link them together for ever.

How could he walk away from this? This was his doing and he would have to face it even though it was like facing his worst nightmare. Panic wrapped steel cords around his chest, squeezing the very breath out of him. Sweat broke out over his brow. The roots of his hair prickled as if ants were playing hide and seek on his scalp.

Why couldn't he press replay on his life and do everything differently? How many times had he wished that? Every time he saw his sister's damaged body he wished he could turn back time. Now he had another regret to hang on his conscience. But, unlike with his sister and mother, whom he kept at a respectful distance, given the dreadful impact he'd had on their lives, he could not so easily distance himself from his own child.

A child who would grow up and call him Daddy. A child who would look up to him. A child who would expect certain things of him—things he wasn't capable of giving. How could he be trusted with a child's welfare when he had already ruined one innocent child's life?

Emily groaned and slowly opened her eyes. She looked at him blankly for a moment and then she captured her lower lip with her teeth and lowered her gaze. 'I'm sorry...'

'No.' His voice caught on the word and he had to clear his throat to continue. 'I'm the one who's sorry. Are you okay? Shall I get you a glass of water?'

She made to get up and Loukas helped her into a sitting position to allow time for her blood pressure to go back to normal. 'I'm fine. I just need a minute.'

'Should I call a doctor?' He began to reach for his phone but she put a hand on his arm.

'No, I'm fine, really.' Her hand melted away from his arm and went back to her lap. The sound of her fingertips flicking against each other made him realise how nervous she was.

'Have you seen a doctor at all?'

She shook her head. 'Not yet. I wanted to do a few tests first.'

Loukas glanced at the seven test wands, wondering how many more she'd planned to take.

When he looked back at her she gave him a self-deprecating grimace. 'I know,' she said. 'Overkill.' After a moment she added, 'We can do a paternity test if you'd—'

'No,' Loukas said, surprising himself with the strength of his conviction. 'That won't be necessary.'

Her eyes shimmered and her throat rose and fell over a swallow. 'Thank you for believing me. It means…a lot…'

He brushed his hand over her hair and then tucked a couple of strands back behind her ear as if she were six years old. She gave him a tremulous movement of her lips that loosely could have been described as a smile. 'You can't be very far along,' he said. 'Isn't it too early to be sure one way or the other?'

'The tests are pretty accurate these days. They can pick up the slightest change in hormonal activity within a few days of conception.'

'What do you plan to do?' As soon as he asked it he wished he hadn't phrased it quite that way. It sounded as if he considered the baby to be a problem to be removed. Eradicated. Deleted like an incorrect digit in a code.

Her eyes took on a determined spark, her normally plump mouth now a tight line. 'I'm keeping it, so please don't try and convince me otherwise, because I don't need your help. I'm perfectly able to do this on my own. I just thought you should know, that's all.'

'I'm sorry. I wasn't suggesting you should get rid of it,' Loukas said.

She angled him a look that reminded him of a detective nailing a suspect. 'Weren't you?'

He released a jagged breath. 'I can't deny I'm a little shocked by the news. More than shocked. If I'm not acting with the sensitivity and enthusiasm of a normal father-to-be, then you'll have to forgive me. I never planned to be a father.'

Emily clambered to her feet, brushing off his offer of assistance. 'Then why haven't you had a vasectomy? Then you could rule a line under the subject permanently.'

He'd thought of it. Several times. He hadn't avoided it out of cowardice, or squeamishness, or out-dated notions on masculinity. He didn't know what it was but something had made him shy away from the decision to render himself infertile. 'I haven't got around to it yet.'

'Maybe you should before someone else ends up pregnant.'

Loukas was ashamed he hadn't yet thought of what this was like for her. Sure, she'd said she wanted marriage and kids, but he'd got the impression she wanted them in that order. Marriage first. Kids later. Having a child was a huge responsibility for a woman under any circumstances—a life-changing responsibility. 'Emily…are you okay with this? With being pregnant?'

Her eyes fell away from his as if she couldn't bear to look at him. 'I wasn't at first. I was in denial until I did the seventh test. I didn't want to be like my mother. Pregnant outside of marriage to a guy she had a one-night stand with. It was like a nightmare.'

'And now?'

Her good hand crept to her abdomen, resting on it as though she were protecting a baby bird. 'It's not the baby's fault it wasn't planned. I'll cope. Somehow.'

'I'll support you in any way I can. You know that, surely? You and the baby will want for nothing.'

'I'm not after your money, Loukas.' Her eyes came back to his. 'I just wanted our baby to know its father. I've never met mine. I don't even know who he is and he has no idea I even exist. Even my mother isn't sure who he is.'

Loukas could hear the regret in her voice. He wasn't close to his own father but at least he knew who he was and he shared his surname. Which brought him up against another huge stumbling block. Marriage. The only way his child could legally have his name would be for him to marry Emily. He wasn't against marriage per se. It was an institution he believed in—for other people. People unlike him who didn't have the sort of baggage he was lugging around. Baggage that still gave him sweat-slicked nightmares. Baggage he couldn't get rid of because his half-sister Ariana lived with the consequences of what he'd done every single day of her life.

A sharp-clawed fist clutched at his gut.

*Marriage?*

To a girl he had only met a month ago? A girl who was now carrying his child? A girl he hadn't been able to get out of his mind because she was sweet, clumsy and shy.

Could he do it? Could he sacrifice his freedom for the sake of a child he had never planned to have?

He had a responsibility towards his child. He

wasn't the sort of man to shirk responsibility. That was what his father was like, but not him. He faced up to problems. Assessed them. Dealt with them. Conquered them.

He could provide money without marriage, plenty of money, although having contact with the child would be tricky if he wasn't living under the same roof. He wanted to be involved but had no idea how to go about it without marrying Emily. He had seen too many fathers, including his own, who provided everything money could buy but gave nothing of themselves. He didn't want to be that sort of father, but he didn't know how to conduct a relationship— any relationship—except at arm's length.

'We should marry as soon as possible.'

'Don't be ridiculous,' Emily said. 'No one has to get married because of pregnancy these days. Even couples in love don't always get married when they have a child together.'

'I want to be a part of my child's life,' Loukas said. 'I want him or her to have my name.'

'They can still have your name. But I'd only like you to be involved if that's what you want. A child can tell if its parent wants to be around them or not.'

Loukas wondered about the dynamic between Emily and her mother. There seemed a subtext to her words that hinted at some tension. 'I'll do whatever I can to support you, Emily. You can trust me on that.'

Her gaze met his. 'Will you publically acknowledge the baby as yours when it's born? Or would you prefer me to keep it a secret to protect your privacy?'

Loukas frowned. There was no way he was going to disown his own flesh and blood. Not like his father, who had insisted on a paternity test and then, when it had come out positive, still insisted the poor woman get rid of his baby. 'Of course I'll acknowledge it. This is my mistake, not the child's. I accept full responsibility for it.'

'Then please don't insult me by asking me to marry you,' she said with a look hard enough to crack a nut.

Loukas wondered what had happened to the girl who couldn't wait to get married and have babies. Four kids and an Irish Retriever, if his memory served him correctly. Why then wasn't she grasping at this chance to land herself a rich husband? Though he hadn't taken her for a gold-digger. That was what had most appealed to him about her the day of the wedding. She had a guileless innocence about her. She reminded him of a friendly puppy who wanted to be loved by everyone.

But what was insulting about his proposal of marriage? He could think of hundreds, possibly thousands, of women who would jump at the chance of a proposal from him. The more he thought about it, the more he felt that marriage was the best option all round. It would give him the best chance of supporting her and the baby. It wasn't as if it would have any of the toxic elements of his parents' marriage. Emily and he were not in love with each other, so the marriage could be drawn up as a parenting contract. A formalised parenting contract that gave them the benefits of marriage without the emotional baggage of a normal relationship.

He would broach the topic again once she was feeling a little better, but this time he would lay out what was going to happen: a convenient mid-term marriage to parent their child. Perfect solution. 'Do you need anything now? Some money to buy baby stuff or—'

'No, I haven't needed to buy anything yet...' The colour drained out of her face again and she wobbled on her feet as if the floor was uneven. She put a hand to her forehead. 'I—I think I might have to give dinner a miss. I'm going to lie down for a bit...'

Loukas lunged forward and caught her before she hit the floor. Emily folded like a rag doll in his arms, her chalk-white face lolling to rest against the wall of his chest. 'Are you okay?'

'Feeling a bit faint...'

He reached for his phone with his free hand, the other keeping her close. 'I'm going to call an ambulance.'

She pushed back against him, her eyes troubled. 'No, please don't do that. I'll be fine in a minute or two.'

What about in half an hour? Later that night? The following morning? Who was going to take care of her, to watch over her, to make sure she didn't faint and hurt herself? He couldn't leave her like this. What if she had a fall? She could end up with a brain injury or worse. She was his responsibility now. The knowledge cemented his decision to marry her. How else could he keep a close eye on her if he lived in another country, or even a few streets away? No. This was the only way forward. 'Do you want to lie down? Here, I'll carry you.'

He scooped her up and carried her to her bedroom. It looked like someone had ransacked the room or got dressed for a night out in the middle of a hurricane. The wardrobe was open and a variety of clothes strewn about, some on the end of the bed, others draped over a chair and more on the floor. The dressing table was scattered with make-up detritus: brushes, pots, hair products and a hair straightener. He laid her slight figure on the bed.

She lay back, folded her bandaged hand over her forehead and closed her eyes. 'I'm so sorry about this.'

Loukas took her good hand and stroked her slender nail-bitten fingers. 'Don't be silly. It's not your fault.'

*It's mine.*

# CHAPTER THREE

IN THE END Loukas decided against calling an ambulance. But, as soon as Emily's dizziness passed, he insisted on taking her to hospital. Hospitals were not his favourite places, with their palpable sense of urgency. The lights, the sounds, the smells, and the nerve-jangling scream of sirens as the ambulances came rocketing into the receiving bay, made his heart threaten to beat its way out of his ribcage. It brought back the memory of the afternoon when his sister had been rushed to hospital, clinging to life.

But he wanted Emily checked out.

She, however, was not so keen on the idea.

She stood with her arms folded and her heels dug into the carpet beside her bed as if someone had glued her to the floor. 'But I don't need to go to hospital.'

'You fainted twice in the space of half an hour,' Loukas said. 'I'm not leaving you on your own until I get you checked out. What if you fainted in the middle of the night and hit your head and got a brain injury?'

She pouted like a small, obstinate child. 'You're being ridiculous. First suggesting marriage and now a trip to the emergency department. The staff will think I'm crazy. Pregnancy isn't a disease, you know.'

'I want that finger checked out,' he said, trying another tack. 'It needs to be looked at under ultrasound in case there are any fragments in there. If you got blood poisoning it would be disastrous for the baby.'

Her face suddenly fell. 'Oh…'

He held out his hand and she silently slipped hers into it. He closed his fingers around her hand, privately marvelling at how small it was compared to his. But everything about her was tiny. He felt like a giant next to her. She barely made it up to his shoulder in heels and he could just about span her waist with his hands. Not that he would be able to do it once her pregnancy started to show. He still couldn't get his head around the fact she was pregnant. Inside her womb his DNA was getting it on with hers and making a baby.

*His baby.*

The thought of bringing a child into the world that he would be totally responsible for made his head pound with dread. What if he screwed up? It wasn't easy being a parent even when you planned to be one. He had no idea how to be a father. He was hopeless at familial relationships. He kept people at a distance. Even the people who mattered to him he kept at arm's length.

That was why casual relationships worked so well

for him. There were no emotional expectations. No closeness. No bonding. No one got hurt. What if he hurt his child? Not physically, but emotionally? Didn't kids need close emotional bonds with their parents to thrive and reach their full potential? He had been close to his mother until his father got sole custody of him in a bitter divorce, only to dump him in an English boarding school when he got tired of being a single parent. After years of living so far away from his mother, Loukas hadn't been able to rebuild the relationship to the way it had been before. He knew it hadn't been his mother's fault. She had done everything in her power to make him feel loved and wanted.

It was he who was the problem.

He'd never wanted to be that vulnerable again. To need someone so much, only to have them ripped away from you. He had taught himself not to need. These days the only needs he had were physical, and he dealt with them efficiently and somewhat perfunctorily, which was probably why the sex with Emily had stood out in a long list of impersonal hook-ups. Stood out so much he could still feel it in his body, the erotic echo of it moving through his flesh like aftershocks if he so much as touched her.

But, while marrying her would solve one problem, he was too well aware it could stir up others. He would offer commitment but not love. The concept of loving someone made all those childhood demons come back to haunt and taunt him: *you love them, you lose them. You love them, you hurt them.*

He would be committed for as long as their marriage lasted but he would not—*could not*—promise anything else.

Loukas tucked Emily into his car and made sure she was comfortable before he took his place behind the steering wheel. 'I haven't finished with the topic of marriage,' he said, glancing at her as he turned over the engine. 'It's the best option going forward.'

She flicked him an irritated glance. 'You know what? I'm going to ignore that. I did not hear you say the M word.'

Loukas had never felt more serious about something. It was the perfect solution and he wasn't going to back away from it. 'We'll make a formal announcement after we get you checked out.'

'You can't force people to marry you, Loukas. You just can't do that.'

*Don't be so sure about that.*

Emily was embarrassed about turning up at Accident and Emergency when there was essentially nothing wrong with her. The waiting room was full of sick and injured people much worse off than her, but Loukas had insisted, and had all but bundled her into his top-of-the-range hire car, casting her worried glances all the way to hospital as if she was going to expire right there in front of him. Not only had he insisted on taking her to hospital, but he'd also returned to the subject of marriage with a steely determination that was a little terrifying, to say the least. Surely he wasn't serious? She hadn't had the energy to argue with him back in the car. The nausea and dizziness had made it impossible for her to string two lucid thoughts together, and the thought of marrying Loukas Kyprianos was a thought a long way from being lucid.

But, when they walked into the reception area, it looked as if Loukas was the one who was ill. He went a ghastly grey colour and his hand where it was holding hers became slick with sweat. 'Are you all right?' Emily asked, glancing up at him.

'I'm fine.' He spoke the words through lips that barely moved, as if he was trying to conserve energy.

'You look awfully pale.'

He slanted her a wry look. 'You should talk.'

'Can I help you?' asked the weary-looking receptionist.

'My…er…fiancée needs to see a doctor,' Loukas said.

*Fiancée?*

Emily rounded her gaze on him and mouthed, *'What the hell?'*

The receptionist glanced at Emily's bandaged finger. 'For your finger?'

'That and…something else,' Loukas said, pulling at his shirt collar as if it was too tight.

Emily moved closer to the reception window. 'I didn't want to come in but Loukas insisted.'

'What seems to be the problem?' the receptionist asked.

'I'm…pregnant.'

'Are you bleeding?'

'No.'

The receptionist handed Emily a form on a clipboard and a pen dangling on a string. 'Fill out the patient details and someone will be with you shortly.'

Emily sat beside Loukas and painstakingly filled in the form, but she was conscious of him sitting there in a state of barely disguised agitation. He shifted his feet, crossed and uncrossed his ankles. Pushed them back underneath the chair, only to bring them out again. He rubbed at the back of his neck. He loosened his tie. Then he sat forward with his elbows on his knees and his head in his hands.

And so he should sweat. What was he thinking, pulling that *'my fiancée'* stunt on her? Did he think she'd be too embarrassed to correct him?

*Then why didn't you correct him?*

*I was too embarrassed.*

*You could correct him now.*

*In front of all these people in the waiting room?*

*Better do it sooner rather than later.*

Emily anchored the pen under the clip on the clipboard with a resounding click and placed it on the vacant seat on her left. 'Can you sit still, or is that your conscience niggling at you?'

He swivelled his head to look at her. 'I hate hospitals.'

'Well, maybe if you hadn't told the receptionist we're engaged, you wouldn't be feeling so rotten.' She kept her voice at a stage whisper because she was conscious of the other patients sitting nearby. 'But I suppose you only did that because you knew I'd be too embarrassed to make a scene. But once we get out of here I'm going to give you a piece of my mind.'

He glanced at the clock on the wall and gave an exaggerated eye roll. '*If* we ever get out of here.'

Emily winced at the time that had already elapsed. Where had the last hour and a half gone? 'I hope it won't be too long. You can go if you like. I can catch a cab after I'm—'

'No. I'm staying with you and that's the end of it.' He jerked his sleeve up to glance at his watch, presumably to check if the one on the wall was lying, and then sat back against the plastic chair with a thump. 'How long is "shortly", for God's sake?'

'I once waited six and a half hours for a splinter in my foot to be removed when I was ten,' Emily said. 'My mum left me for most of it to go to an astrology workshop. I got the nurse to call her when I was done.'

Loukas turned to look at her, his brows drawn together in a tight frown. 'Are you close to her?'

Emily shrugged and shifted her gaze to stare at the linoleum on the floor. 'Aren't all girls close to their mums?'

'Have you told her about the—'

'Not yet. But she's not the maternal type, so the prospect of being a granny won't have her rushing off for a pair of knitting needles any time soon.'

Emily suddenly noticed that the two women sitting opposite them in the waiting room were glancing in their direction. The woman on the left nudged her friend and pointed at Loukas. Emily wasn't game enough to look at Loukas but she sensed him stiffening in the chair beside her. She sank a little lower in her chair, wishing she could disappear before the women asked for verification. How much had they heard of her conversation with Loukas? She'd kept her voice low, but what if they'd overheard her talking about their 'engagement' or the baby? She wasn't used to being examined. Was this what Loukas had to live with? The constant scrutiny of his private life would be torture for someone as reserved as him.

The woman's companion pulled up something on her phone screen and seemed to compare it to Loukas. 'It's Loukas Kyprianos all right,' she said, loud enough for half the waiting room to hear. 'The Greek billionaire friend of Draco Papandreou. Did you hear the girl with him say she's pregnant? Quick—take a photo.'

The click of the camera phone was as loud as a rifle shot.

Loukas didn't move. Emily cast him a covert glance but his features were schooled into an impassive mask, except for a tiny muscle in his jaw that was twitching as if it was being randomly zapped by an invisible electrode.

The woman who had taken the photo spoke again. 'Let's hope he doesn't do what his jerk of a father did when he got his young girlfriend pregnant.'

'Yeah, I read about that. Awful business, wasn't it? But the girl got paid a fortune for that interview. Good on her, I say. Who wouldn't want to be compensated after what that lowlife put her through?'

*What awful business?*

Emily's ears weren't just out on stalks but on scaffolding and in a high-wire harness too. What had Loukas's father done to his pregnant girlfriend? He sounded like an absolute cad. Was that why Loukas was making such a big deal about marrying, so no one would think he was anything like his disreputable father?

The nurse called Emily's name at that point and Loukas stood and guided Emily out of the waiting room with brisk efficiency. 'What happened with your—' she began.

'Later.' The word was clipped out through white, tight lips and he led her into the cubicle to wait for the doctor.

The curtain twitched aside and a doctor came, who did a double-take when she saw Loukas. 'Oh, my God, Loukas? Fancy seeing you here.'

Was there anyone in the whole of London who *didn't* know who Loukas was? Emily glanced at him to see if he was as excited as the young doctor but his face was blank. 'I'm sorry, do I know you?' he said.

The doctor's smile faded a little. 'We had a drink together at a charity function last year here in London. Don't you remember? Maida Freeman's my name. We were going to catch up later but I got called away to an emergency. I was on call.' She rolled her eyes. 'Story of my life.'

'Of course I remember,' Loukas said with a polite movement of his lips that didn't involve his eyes or his teeth.

Dr Freeman turned to Emily. 'Such a small world.'

*Not small enough if I'm going to run into a host of his ex-or would-be lovers.*

'What can I do for you?'

'I didn't want to bother anyone but Loukas insisted on—' Emily began.

'Emily fainted this evening. Twice,' Loukas said. 'She's…pregnant.' He swallowed audibly between the two words.

'That's quite common in early pregnancy,' Dr Freeman said. 'Dizziness, light-headedness, fainting, nausea and vomiting, as the hormones do their thing. I'll get the nurse to do some obs and we'll take some blood to make sure you're not anaemic.' Her gaze honed in on Emily's bandaged finger. 'What happened to your finger?'

'I cut it on some broken glass.'

The doctor's gaze seemed to sharpen. 'How are you feeling about the pregnancy?'

'What do you mean?' Emily asked.

'Was it planned or…?'

'Not planned but very much welcomed,' Loukas said, reaching for Emily's good hand and holding it within the warm cage of his.

*Welcomed?*

Emily did her best to disguise her shock.

But then the doctor looked between Loukas and her and, finally settling her gaze on Loukas, smiled again. 'I'm really happy for you, Loukas. I'm sure you'll make an excellent father.'

*Unlike your own.*

The doctor didn't say it out loud, probably because she was too much of a professional, but the words seemed to hover there in the silence all the same. Emily felt as though she were on stage in a play on opening night, but having been given the wrong script. She didn't know anything about Loukas other than he was Draco Papandreou's best friend. She didn't know what his favourite colour was. She didn't know what books he liked to read or what movies he watched. She didn't know what political persuasion he had or anything about his childhood other than his parents had divorced when he was a kid. And she had learned that from Allegra.

'How long have you been a couple?' Dr Freeman asked.

There was another beat of silence. 'We've been keeping it a secret for a while,' Loukas said before she could answer. 'I met Emily through my best friend from university.'

The doctor smiled again. 'Ah yes, he got married recently, didn't he? I read about it in the press. I guess you two will be getting hitched too, now you're going to be parents?'

'We don't—' Emily began.

'Yes,' Loukas said, squeezing Emily's hand. 'The plans are already afoot.'

'Oh, that's lovely,' the doctor said. 'I'm a bit old-fashioned in that way. I reckon kids need to know their parents are committed enough to marry each other. It gives them a sense of security, in my opinion. Now, let me have a look at that finger of yours.'

The doctor examined the wound and ordered an ultrasound to make sure there was no further debris. The machine came in on a portable trolley with a radiology attendant. 'Just the hand at this stage,' the doctor said. 'It's a little early to see the baby unless we do a vaginal ultrasound. If we weren't so busy tonight I'd order one for you.'

'No, that's okay,' Emily said. 'I'll wait until later.'

The hand was given the all-clear and the radiology staffer wheeled the trolley out. A nurse came in and took blood while the doctor saw to another patient in the next cubicle. There wasn't enough privacy to talk to Loukas but Emily sent him a speaking look. If he thought he could railroad her into marriage, then he was in for a big surprise.

The doctor came back a short time later with a bottle of iron supplements and an information sheet for maternal health and maternity services. 'You're all good to go. Have plenty of rest and try to eat small meals when you can. If the nausea and vomiting increase or become chronic, then see your GP as soon as you can.' She smiled again at Loukas. 'You did the right thing, bringing her in. It shows how much you care about her. Believe me, I see all types in here, and the behaviour of some fathers-to-be towards their partner would make your hair fall out.'

'Thanks for taking care of her,' Loukas said. 'I appreciate it.'

Emily walked out of the hospital with Loukas beside her. 'I can't believe you told her we're getting married,' she said once they were clear of the busy entrance and on their way to his car. 'Not only Dr Freeman, but the receptionist as well. Are you nuts? What if they tell someone?'

'They're meant to keep patient information confidential,' he said.

She stopped walking to look up at him. 'And what about everyone else in that emergency department? What about those women in the waiting room? They recognised you. They took a photo of you. They've probably sold it to one of those media sites by now.'

His features gave a tight spasm. 'If it happens, it happens.'

'But why say we're engaged when we're—'

'We're what?' he said. 'Virtual strangers? How do you think that would've made you look?'

Emily blinked. 'Oh…'

'Exactly.' He let out a short breath. 'You've come out of a long-term relationship only to get pregnant after a one-night stand. It's not fair, but women still get frowned on for stuff like that. I figured it was best to let Dr Freeman think we've known each other for a while and were planning to marry.'

Emily could see his point and was unexpectedly touched he'd considered the impact on her reputation. But she suspected his motives were not entirely about protecting her reputation. Loukas wanted to marry her and was refusing to take no for an answer. She hadn't taken him for a my-way-or-the-highway guy, but then she was hardly an expert when it came to reading men. She had been with Daniel for seven years and had never once suspected he was interested in men instead.

Once they were inside Loukas's car and on their way, she swivelled in her seat to look at him. 'So, what was the business with your father those women in the waiting room spoke of?'

His mouth tightened as if invisible stitches were being tugged from inside his jaw. 'Nothing.'

'It can't have been nothing if those strangers know about it,' Emily said. 'And Dr Freeman didn't say anything but I could read the subtext. Don't you think I should know too, since I'm now apparently—' she made air quotes with her fingers '—engaged to you?'

He blew out another breath, longer this time, and his hands gripped the steering wheel firmly, as if he was worried it was going to be snatched away from him. 'He got a partner pregnant earlier this year. She was nineteen years old. He insisted she have an abortion and when she refused he dumped her.' His knuckles and tendons showed white through the tan of his skin. 'She tried to kill herself by slashing her wrists soon after. Someone found her in time but not in time to save the baby. There was too much blood loss. She miscarried on the way to hospital.'

'Oh, that's terrible…'

'My father is a high-profile businessman here and in the US, and of course the press love salacious stories like that,' he said. 'The young woman got offered a large sum of money for a tell-all interview. I can't say I blame her, but it's made my life difficult, because everyone's waiting to pounce on a "like father, like son" follow-up story.'

Emily could see the invidious position Loukas was in with her pregnancy. No wonder he'd insisted on marriage. He would be keen to avoid any remote comparison with his father. But marriage was meant to be a sacred commitment between two people who loved each other. How could he possibly think a marriage between them would work? They barely knew each other. 'Loukas, it's terrible what happened to that poor girl—shocking and awfully sad. But you're not your father, and shouldn't be judged by his standards or lack thereof.'

'Try telling the media that.'

Emily sat quietly for the rest of the journey back to her flat. Loukas seemed disinclined to talk and she could hardly blame him. In the space of the evening, he had found out he was to become a father, had had to deal with her cutting her finger and fainting and take her to hospital and deal with an inquisitive public and hospital staff. She would discuss the marriage thing when they had both had a decent night's sleep and were in a better frame of mind.

But, when Loukas turned the corner to the townhouse her little flat was housed in, she realised the night wasn't over yet. Loukas slowed down to swing into the parking space two spots behind her car. 'Are you expecting visitors?' he asked.

'No.' Emily shrank back down in the seat as a man wielding a camera came rushing towards the car. A woman with a recording device was close behind.

Another person hopped out of a car further along the street and came towards Loukas's side with a camera poised. Emily sent Loukas a panicked glance. 'How did they find me?'

'Someone must have tipped them off at the hospital,' Loukas said. 'Let me handle it.' He wound down his driver's side window to the approaching journalist.

The man leaned down. 'Mr Kyprianos, a source tells us you and Miss Seymour are engaged and expecting a baby. Do you have any comment to make?'

'Only to say we're thrilled to be getting married and starting a family,' Loukas said. 'Now, if you'll excuse us, we have things to do.'

He got out of the car and came around to Emily's side, but the female journalist was already at the passenger window. 'Miss Seymour, how does it feel to be engaged to one of Greece's most eligible bachelors?'

Emily got out of the car and slipped her hand into Loukas's. 'It's…great. Wonderful. Amazing. I mean, *he's* amazing. Truly amazing and so kind and thoughtful and…'

Loukas's arm went around Emily's waist, drawing her close to his side. 'That's it, everyone. Emily's had a big day. So if you'll excuse—'

'What happened to your hand, Emily?' the same journalist asked.

'I—I broke a perfume bottle and cut my finger.'

'What does your father think of becoming a

grandfather, Loukas?' one of the other journalists asked. 'Have you told him yet?'

'No, but I'm sure you'll take care of that for me,' Loukas said with an on-off movement of his lips. He led Emily to her front door and gestured for her to hand him the key. She rummaged in her purse, handed the key to him and Loukas unlocked the door and led her inside.

'How quickly can you pack a bag?' he asked once they were safely inside with the door closed.

Emily looked at him blankly. 'A bag? What for?'

'I'm taking you back to my hotel,' he said. 'It will be safer than here until this blows over.'

'So much for patient confidentiality,' she muttered, not quite under her breath.

'It wouldn't have been Dr Freeman. As you pointed out, it could've been anyone at the hospital. My money is on those two women. They probably got your address off the form you filled in.'

Emily folded her arms, casting him a look that would have done a jealous wife proud. 'If Dr Freeman hadn't got called away that night would you have slept with her?'

He gave her an unreadable glance. 'Maybe. Maybe not.'

'She was up for it,' she said. 'In fact, if you hadn't told her we were engaged, I reckon she would have asked for your number to hook up with you after work. You could be with her right now, having smoking-hot sex, instead of stuck here with—'

'Emily.' There was a strong note of calm reproof in his tone.

Emily was close to tears and spun away from him to pull the curtains across the windows to block the paparazzi from seeing inside her flat. Her life was spinning out of control. How could this be happening? One day she was anonymous, the next she was being hunted down like a famous celebrity. When would it stop? *Would* it stop?

'I reckon she's wondering how on earth you could have chosen me over her. I bet those journalists out there are wondering it too. And so will everyone who reads tomorrow's gossip. A man like you choosing a boring, unsophisticated legal secretary from Tottenham over an emergency doctor from Knightsbridge? What a joke.'

He came up close and turned her to face him, flinching when he saw her shimmering eyes. He lifted a hand to her face and gently tucked a strand of hair behind her ear, brushing away a couple of tears from the side of her left eye. 'Please don't cry.'

'I—I'm not c-crying.' Emily sniffed.

Loukas handed her a clean handkerchief that smelled of his aftershave and was warm from being housed close to his body. She buried her head in its citrus scented folds and allowed herself a couple of noisy sobs. One of his hands went to the back of her head and moved in slow, soothing strokes from the top of her scalp to the base of her neck, sending shudders of reaction through her body. Then he lifted her hair and brought his hand against the nape of her neck, his fingers warm and gentle as they moved through the fine hairs there, sending delicious currents of electricity to the core of her being.

When had anyone ever comforted her like this? Daniel had never been the cuddle-and-comfort type, which was understandable, now she knew how awkward it had made him feel. But even her mother wasn't great at affection. The best she got from her mother was an air kiss and a hug that lasted no longer than a blink. When had anyone ever just sat with her and held her? Loukas's hug made her feel safe and protected from the crazy world outside.

Emily slowly lifted her head out of the handkerchief and focussed her gaze on his dark inscrutable one. She bit her lower lip. 'Hormones. Sorry.'

A ghost of a smile flickered at one side of his mouth and his hand moved to cradle her cheek, his thumb stroking back and forth in a barely touching movement that set her facial nerves dancing. His eyes became hooded and he slipped his gaze to her mouth, lingering there for an infinitesimal moment. Emily sent the tip of her tongue out over her lips in a darting movement, unable to stop the impulse even though she knew it was a primary signal of arousal.

The air tightened. Crackling with possibilities. Erotic possibilities that made her blood tick and her heart trip.

His thumb moved to her bottom lip, stroking along it like someone smoothing out a tiny crease in silk. It was as if every nerve in her lip rose to the surface, swelling, pulsing, heating against the pad

of his thumb. 'You have the most beautiful mouth.'
Loukas's voice was so deep it sounded as though it
had come from beneath the floor.

Emily touched his face with her uninjured hand,
losing herself in the depths of his deep-brown gaze
with its fringe of inky lashes. His eyes were so dark
she couldn't tell where his pupils began and ended.
'What are we doing, Loukas?' Her voice was not
much more than a whisper.

His warm breath wafted over her lips. 'This is
what we're doing.' And his mouth came down on
hers.

His lips moved with sensual expertise over her
mouth, rediscovering its contours, drawing from her
a response that made her blood sing in her veins.

Emily's hands crept up his chest and then linked
around his neck, her body pressing closer to the
warm, hard heat of his. His tongue stroked over the
seam of her mouth and she opened to him on a sigh
of pleasure. The glide of his tongue was just as intoxicating as the first time he'd kissed her. It sent
every female hormone in her body into paroxysms
of excitement. His tongue found hers and cajoled it
into play, teasing it, stroking it, chasing it. Seducing
it. Loukas's hands settled on her hips, holding her
close to his body, where his blood pumped and his
flesh surged. She moved against him instinctively,
driven by primal urges she had no control over. He
angled his head to deepen the kiss, one of his hands
coming up from her waist to cup the side of her face,
his fingers splaying through her hair.

He nudged against her lips and then nibbled the lower one until she was whimpering against his mouth. She sent her hands through the thick silk of his hair, tugging and releasing the slight curls, delighting in the way he made deep, guttural sounds of approval.

One of his hands went to her breast but their hormone-induced sensitivity sent her jerking back from him. 'Ouch!'

He looked down at her, frowning in concern. 'Did I hurt you?'

She winced. 'My breasts are really tender. It's the hormones.'

His hands settled back on her waist as gently as if she were made of gossamer. 'I'm sorry. I didn't realise. Are you okay?'

'I'm fine…'

Loukas stepped back from her with a rueful grimace. 'It's probably a good time to stop before things get out of hand.' He rubbed a hand over his face as if trying to recalibrate himself. 'This is turning out to be one hell of a night.'

*Tell me about it.*

Emily watched as he moved across to the window to check the street outside. 'Are they still there?'

He let the curtain drop back into place. 'No, but I still think you should come back to my hotel with me.'

'Surely that's not necessary?'

Something about his expression made her realise once he made up his mind it would not be changed without a fight. Even *with* a fight. 'Humour me, Emily. I know what the press are like. They'll be here first thing and hounding you for an exclusive.'

'I won't speak to them so—'

'You won't be able to help yourself.' His mouth had a wry slant to it. 'You'd be too worried about being rude. Before you know it, you'll be inviting them in for coffee and home-baked cookies and telling them your life story.'

Emily pressed her lips together, not sure she cared for his summation of her character. So she had a loose tongue at times? So what if she over-shared occasionally? It was only when she was nervous. And how did he know she had home-baked cookies in the house? He was making her out to be some sort of nineteen-fifties throwback, complete with frilled pinafore and polka-dotted headscarf. 'I'm not going to be able to avoid them for ever. I can't stay at your hotel indefinitely. You're only here for a week in any case.'

He looked at her for a long moment.

'Why are you looking at me like that?' she asked.

'I want you to come back to Corfu with me.'

Her stomach dropped like an anchor. 'What?'

'Just until the press interest dies down,' he said. 'My villa is secure from media intrusion. You can rest up without the constant threat of having a camera or microphone thrust in your face. We can stay there until the ceremony.'

Emily turned away, holding her arms across her middle. 'Now you're being ridiculous again.'

He came up behind her and turned her to face him, his hold gentle but firm—a bracelet of warm male fingers overlapping on her wrist, reminding her of his superior strength and essential maleness. His eyes held hers prisoner. 'I'm trying to protect you, Emily.'

The thought of someone offering to protect her was tempting. Way more tempting than it should be for an emancipated woman of nearly thirty. But for so long Emily had craved security and stability. Would Loukas be that go-to person she'd thought she had in Daniel? The person who would stand up *for* her as well as *by* her? She allowed her mind to drift with the possibility of marrying him. She wouldn't have to be a single mum. She wouldn't have to worry about bringing up a baby alone. Loukas would be there as back-up, involved with the baby and always on hand if she needed extra support. She would be part of a family unit: mum, dad and baby. A unit of stability and belonging that she had longed for since she was a little girl.

*You're thinking of marrying him? You took longer to choose that dress you're wearing.*

*But I like the thought of being protected.*

*You definitely need protecting—from your traitorous hormones, that's what.*

If Emily went anywhere with Loukas who knew what might happen? One kiss a month ago and she'd ended up pregnant. A week or two at his private villa was just asking for trouble. She tried to ease out of his hold but his fingers countered the move by gently tightening. 'I can protect myself.' Somehow her voice didn't come out as stridently as she'd hoped.

One of his dark brows rose in a sceptical arc and he glanced pointedly at her bandaged finger. 'How's that working out for you so far?'

*Clearly not well.*

Emily compressed her lips again, shooting him a glare cold enough to freeze vodka. 'I can't just walk out on my job without notice.'

'Allegra's your boss, right? She'll understand. In fact, she'll encourage you to get away somewhere safe.'

Emily frowned. 'But what am I going to say to her?'

'Does she know about the pregnancy?'

'Not officially—I only told her I was late. You're the first person I've told.'

Something moved through his gaze, softening it. Darkening it. 'Thank you.'

'You're welcome.'

'You'd better call Allegra before she reads about us over breakfast,' Loukas said.

'Are you going to call Draco?'

He released her hand and stepped back from her. 'It's not something I've been looking forward to.'

'I can imagine it must be galling for you to admit to having knocked up the bridesmaid.' Emily's voice was so tart it was as if she were speaking through a mouthful of lemons. 'Especially since she's not your type.'

He shifted his lips from side to side as if monitor-

ing his response. 'Someone's done an excellent job
on your self-esteem.'

She sent him her best nose-in-the-air, haughty
look. 'I'd like you to leave.'

'I'm not leaving without you,' he said with an intractable set to his features. 'Now, go and pack a bag,
otherwise I'll pack it for you.'

Emily planted her feet, pushed her chin up higher
and folded her arms. 'You're not the boss of me.'

*You're not the boss of me? What are you? Six?*

*He's not telling me what to do.*

*Yes, he is, and by the look on his face you'd bet-
ter do it.*

Loukas held her gaze in a silent tug-of-war that
did strange, fizzy things to the backs of her knees,
like someone was trickling sand down her legs.
Emily would have stuck it out to show she wasn't a
pushover but a wave of nausea rose in her throat and
she threw a hand over her mouth and made a mad
dash to the bathroom.

She heard him come in behind her but she was
beyond caring about having an audience to her
wretchedness. Right then and there, an entire foot-
ball stadium of fans could have crammed in and
she wouldn't have cared. She flushed the toilet and
dragged herself upright but Loukas already had a
face cloth rinsed and ready for her. 'Here you go.'

She covered her clammy face with the cloth and
then washed her face at the basin. She was acutely,
intensely aware of him. Her bathroom was already on

the phone-box-size side, but with him in there with her it shrank to the size of a tissue box.

Loukas placed his hands on the tops of her shoulders from behind, his hips close to her butt cheeks. If she moved half an inch she would come into intimate contact with him. The temptation to lean back into his fortress-like body was nothing short of overwhelming. She gripped the edge of the basin to stop herself from doing it. She met his gaze in the mirror and a jolt of something sharp and electric shot through her system. His hips brushed her from behind.

*Oh, God. Oh, God. Oh, God.*

How could she be thinking about sex when a minute ago she'd been yodelling over the toilet?

'Let me take care of you, Emily.' His voice had a note of determination. The note that made her want to forget all about female emancipation, park herself behind a picket fence and don a pinafore and oven mitts.

Emily turned to face him, her teeth sinking into her lower lip. 'Corfu does sound kind of nice…'

He tipped up her chin and for the first time she saw a glimmer of a smile tugging up the corners of his mouth. 'That's my girl.'

# CHAPTER FOUR

LOUKAS WAS STAYING in Chelsea at one of the hotels Emily had never expected to go into for a drink, let alone stay the night in. Uniformed attendants with top hats greeted them when Loukas pulled into the bay in front of the stately entrance. The car doors were opened and she stepped out on to the strip of red carpet that led into the dazzling foyer. Her bag was whisked away and Loukas took her arm and looped it through his. 'We'll leave for Corfu after lunch tomorrow. I have a couple of things to see to first thing, but you can rest up here until it's time to head to the airport.'

Emily's eyes rounded to the size of dinner plates when she stepped into the hotel. Corinthian columns divided the foyer, sprouting out of a sea of black-and-white tiles. A central crystal chandelier hung from the impossibly high ceiling and other glittering lights were placed strategically upon the walls. An ornate gold-framed mirror the size of her bedroom hung above a marble fireplace where some classic sofas and wing chairs were nestled to create a cosy setting.

On the other side of the room was a black grand piano, so glossy the chandelier above was reflected in its surface in dozens of sparkles that looked like scattered diamonds. White-columned archways divided the massive space into sections and the reception was at the far end where more uniformed staff were in attendance. Loukas informed them Emily would be joining him in his suite and then led her to the bank of lifts through another archway.

He held her hand while they waited for the lift, glancing down at her. 'How are you doing?'

Emily tried not to show how awestruck she was but she was pretty sure she was doing the kid-in-a-candy-store thing. Everywhere she looked was luxury beyond anything she had seen before. Even the lift call-button looked as though it was pure gold. 'I'm fine, but I could do with something to eat.'

'I'll order some room service for you.'

A short time later, Emily sat propped up with several cloud-soft pillows on the acre of bed. She had a silver service meal on a tray table parked over her stretched out legs. Loukas was seeing to emails on his smart phone and had so far not touched his own meal set on a table beside him. She picked at her dinner, not wanting to overdo things in case she had another attack of nausea. In between cautious mouthfuls, Emily took the time to study him while he was preoccupied with business. His forehead was creased in a frown of concentration, his shoulders hunched forward as he scrolled through his messages. Evening stubble surrounded his nose and mouth and flared either side of his jaw in a rich, dark swathe that made her itch to run her fingertips over it.

She remembered how that bristly skin felt against her smoother skin. After that night in his bed, it had taken days for the marks to fade from her face. And other more secret places. She'd had to use concealer to disguise it on her face and, every time she'd applied it, her stomach would free fall as she remembered the way the marks had got there.

Loukas glanced up from his phone to catch her looking at him. 'All done?'

Emily hoped she wasn't blushing but it sure felt like it. At this rate she could have moonlighted as a *bain-marie*. No dinner could ever go cold balanced on her cheeks. 'I'm done. Thanks, it was lovely.'

He rose from the chair and came over. When he leaned down to lift the tray off the bed, Emily put her hand on one of his arms and met his dark gaze. 'You're being awfully good about all this…I mean, this must be your worst nightmare, and here you are waiting on me and looking after me like I'm some sort of princess.'

His eyes moved between each of hers, then he glanced down at her mouth. Loukas took a steadying breath, lifted the tray away and placed it on the table next to his untouched meal. He stood with his back to her and pushed a hand up his face and over the back of his hair but, rather than straightening it, it made it even more sexily tousled. He turned back around but his expression was impossible to read. 'You'd better get some sleep.'

'Where are you going to sleep?'

He nodded towards the sitting room next door. 'I'll take the sofa.'

Emily rolled her lips together and began to fiddle with the edge of the sheet. 'You don't have to do that. I mean, this bed is practically bigger than my flat.'

'Emily.' The way he said her name in that stern schoolmaster tone made her feel like a child who'd been told she wasn't allowed in the drawing room with the grown-ups.

She couldn't hold his gaze and focussed on the hem of the sheet instead. 'Right, well, goodnight, then.'

She saw his long trouser-clad legs appear beside the bed. He placed a gentle fingertip beneath her chin and elevated her gaze to meet his. 'I shouldn't have touched you in the first place,' he said. 'I was out of line. Way out of line.'

Emily couldn't peel her eyes away from the dark intensity of his. 'Why did you make the first move that night, after the wedding?'

His hand fell away from her face and he thrust both hands into the pockets of his trousers as if to keep them out of the way of temptation. 'I was… on edge.'

'On edge?' Emily asked. 'About what?'

'Stuff.'

'What stuff?'

He drew in a breath and released it in stages. 'Family stuff.'

'Your father?'

Something passed over Loukas's features, like a tide of tension stiffening his facial muscles in degrees until his entire face was a mask set in stone. 'That's enough talking for now. I'm keeping you up. You look done in. I'll see you in the morning.'

Emily frowned as the door closed behind him. She considered going after him to pump him for more information but the long day was finally catching up with her. She was almost too tired to remove her contacts and place them in the solution container she drew out of her bag beside the bed, but remove them she did. Then she sighed and leaned back against the downy-soft pillows and within seconds her eyes drifted closed...

Loukas gave up on sleeping on the sofa, even though it was reasonably comfortable. He sat staring sightlessly at the view from the windows, barely noticing the beads of rain dripping down the glass. He'd cancelled all but one of his work commitments so he could get Emily out of London and safely on Corfu, where hopefully they would be left in peace until he got a ring on her finger.

He hadn't yet given his mother or his sister the heads up about Emily. Not that he was in regular contact with them. He'd visited Ariana after her recent surgery, but mostly he kept his distance, because every time he phoned or visited he was conscious of how it reminded her of what he had done to her. He figured, out of sight, out of mind worked best for all of them. Ariana, thankfully, remembered nothing of the accident, and she accepted the years of operations and physical therapy with admirable if not downright astonishing fortitude.

But, even though they never talked of that day, it was something he could never forget. He had caused so much damage to his family, injuring his sister and destroying his mother's marriage as well. Her husband had left just over a year after the accident, unable to cope with his wife's absences while she helped Ariana in hospital and then the start of the long months in rehab.

Loukas had watched in despair as the people he loved most in the world had lost everything that was dear to them. His sister had lost her ability to run, play and dance, her future stolen from her, never to be regained. Her mother had lost the love she had found after her bitter divorce from his father and had become a shadow of herself, physically gaunt and emotionally fragile, only managing to survive out of her fierce determination to claw back her daughter from death's greedy jaws.

Their lives had improved a lot over the years—Loukas had seen to that, providing them with everything they needed—but at the end of the day it still came down to the painful reality that Ariana was never going to do all the things her peers took for granted. His mother was never going to get those lost years back and, because she was Ariana's full-time carer, there was no way she could have a life of her own.

And it was his fault.

How was he going to call his sister and mother to tell them about this new hurt he'd caused? He hated the thought of them opening a newspaper or news link and hearing about it that way, but how did you tell your family you'd got a girl you should never have slept with pregnant? Not that his mother would mind. If anyone was a frustrated grandmother it was she. He saw the way she looked longingly at passing prams and advertisements with babies and children in them. It was like a knife twisting in his gut to see how hard she tried to disguise it. But, because of his sister's on-going health issues, there would be no grandkids other than his.

Knowing he had taken away his sister's chance of becoming a mother made his guilt about the accident all the harder to bear. It was one of the reasons he had never planned to marry and have a family— because why should he have that privilege when his sister could not? Every milestone of his would be a guilt trip instead of a celebration.

Loukas got up from the sofa and crossed the suite to creak open the bedroom door. The light from the streetlights outside cast the bed in a beam of silver. Emily was curled up like a comma on the bed, barely taking up any space at all. Her brown-blonde hair was spread out over the pillow like a halo and her hand with its bandaged finger was tucked up near her chin, the other splayed on the sheet beside her head. She made a soft murmuring sound, rolled over and stretched like a cat, her small but perfect breasts rising under her top, the darker nipples showing through the fabric.

Emily suddenly opened her eyes and saw him standing there. She sat bolt-upright and reached for a pair of glasses beside the bed, pushed them up her nose and then grabbed at the sheet to pull it up to her chin. 'You gave me such a fright!'

'Sorry. I was just checking you were—'

'You could have knocked first.' Her mouth was just shy of a pout. 'How long have you been there?'

'Not long.'

She hugged her bent knees, giving him a look over the rim of her tortoiseshell glasses that reminded him of a child pretending to be a starchy librarian. 'How's the sofa working out for you?'

'Great.'

'Liar. I bet your legs hang over the edge.'

Loukas glanced at the bottle of contact lens solution beside the bed and the little container she housed them in. 'I didn't know you wore contacts. Were you wearing them the night we—'

'Yes, but I didn't take them out because...' Her cheeks went a delicate shade of pink. 'I didn't have time.'

'We were in a bit of a hurry, weren't we?' He came to sit on the edge of the bed next to her bent legs. 'Can I get you anything? A drink?'

'No, I'm good.'

'Not sick?'

She lifted her good hand and crossed her middle finger over her index finger. 'So far, so good.' She uncrossed her fingers and then, after a brief moment, reached out to touch his jaw, her soft fingertips catching on his stubble. Her eyes behind the glasses looked big and luminous, her mouth so soft and kissable he had to pinch his lips together to stop himself from leaning forward to kiss her. 'I had beard rash for four days after that night we slept together. It cost me a fortune in concealer.'

As she dropped her hand, Loukas lifted his own and traced a fingertip down the creamy slope of her cheek all the way to her mouth. He slowly circled its Cupid's bow contours, watching as her lips trembled and quivered in response to his touch. 'Kissing you was my first mistake.'

Her pupils flared into dark pools of ink. 'Your second?'

'I'm about to make it right about now.' He brought his mouth down to hers and tasted her lips. Once. Twice. Three times. She gave a soft, breathless sigh and he touched down again, lingering longer this time, feeling the suppleness of her mouth melding against his, making the blood thunder through his body and charge south to his groin. He had never tasted a mouth as sweet as hers. Sweet and yet smoking hot. Heat exploded from her mouth to his, lighting fires all over his flesh, making him gather her closer, desperate to feel her body against his.

She wound her arms around his neck, her fingers

playing with the ends of his hair, her soft mouth torturing his self-control.

*What self-control?*

Did he have any when it came to her? Every time he put his mouth on hers his willpower took leave without pay. Her little whimpers of encouragement made it impossible to pull back from her temptation. He deepened the kiss, exploring every corner of her mouth, enticing her tongue to play, flirt and mate with his. Loukas cupped her face in his hands, angling his head to gain better access, relishing the scent and texture of her skin.

Her fingers were on his scalp, massaging him into a stupor. Her touch unhinged him, unloosed in him a primitive urge to lose himself in her like he had done with no one else before. He always kept control. Always. But, with her mouth fused to his and her hands moving over him, his need for her was almost frightening.

He pulled back from her but kept his hands cradling her face. 'You are a dangerous young woman.'

Emily's toffee-brown eyes were guileless and she quickly straightened her crooked frames with her finger. 'Why?'

Loukas brushed the pad of his thumb over her kiss-swollen bottom lip. 'Because I can't seem to keep my hands off you no matter how much I tell myself to.'

Her hand came to rest on one of his wrists, her fingertips light as fairy feet. 'I have the same problem.' She moved her fingers to his mouth, circling it as he had done hers. 'Should we be doing this?'

'This?' Who was he kidding? He knew exactly what *this* was. *This* was magic. *This* was irresistible. *This* was the only thing he could think about. The only thing he wanted.

She leaned forward and pressed a feather-soft kiss to his mouth. 'Touching and kissing and...stuff.'

'Isn't that what engaged couples do?'

Her hand fell away from his wrist and her teeth began to work at her lower lip. 'I waited seven years for my ex to propose and he never got around to it. I only met you a month ago and you never *stop* mentioning marriage. When are you going to take no for an answer?'

He kept his gaze trained on hers. 'We can't retract our statement now without looking like fools. We don't have to be married for ever. Just long enough to get the press off our backs. I'm not offering you the fairy-tale. Just a convenient arrangement so that our child gets a good start in life. After that, we'll reassess if things aren't working out.'

Doubt flickered on Emily's face and her eyes became downcast. 'I don't know... It seems weird to be marrying someone I hadn't even met a month ago.'

'You will never want for anything. I will make sure of that.'

Twin pleats of worry divided her smooth brow. 'It's not about the money. We're not in love with each other.'

'Neither were Draco and Allegra but that seems to have turned out all right.'

'But Allegra was always a little bit in love with

him,' she said. 'We, on the other hand, are practically strangers. I hardly know anything about you and you expect me to marry you?'

'This is the only way forward. We should get married as soon as possible and then the press attention will go away, just like it did with Draco and Allegra.'

She narrowed her gaze. 'You'd seriously get married to a stranger just to stop a little press attention? *Really?*'

'We're doing this for our child, Emily. Why wait? Do you want to be hounded for the next eight months, having cameras and phones and recording devices thrust in your face every time you step out the door? Strangers taking photos of you while you're eating in cafés or restaurants or simply walking down the street? No. I didn't think so. We'll marry quickly and quietly and that will be the end of it. Problem solved.'

Something passed over Emily's face—a flash of panic followed by resignation. 'Okay, we'll do it your way. I'll marry you.' Her teeth kept going back to her lower lip. 'How soon were you thinking of—' she gave a tiny gulp '—doing it?'

'The end of the month.'

Her eyes widened. 'But that's only two weeks away!'

'So? It shouldn't take too much time to plan a simple ceremony with a handful of witnesses.'

'But won't people expect someone of your status and wealth to have a big church wedding?'

'I don't do things just because people expect me to,' Loukas said.

'No?' One of her brows rose in a wry you-can't-fool-me arc. 'Only marry a perfect stranger so people won't compare you to your father? Sure, I believe you.'

He pressed his lips together for a moment, determined not to be triggered by her little dig. It wasn't just about being compared to his father. He genuinely wanted to protect Emily and this was the only way he could see to do it. 'Do you *want* a big wedding?'

She gave an offhand shrug of one slim shoulder. 'Not particularly.'

'If you and your ex had married, what would the wedding have been like?'

Emily folded her arms and sent him a resentful glare. 'Could we talk about something else apart from my disastrous relationship with my ex?'

'Were you in love with him?'

Her gaze slipped out of reach of his. After a moment she released a short puff of a breath. 'I thought so, but I realised later I wasn't. Not the way other people describe being in love. I think I was in love with the idea of being in a relationship. Being a couple. Of having a base to come home to—of belonging to someone.'

'It's an easy mistake to make.'

Her eyes came back to his. 'Have you ever been in love?'

'No.'

'Never?'

'Never.'

She searched his gaze some more. 'Not even a teensy-weensy bit?'

'No.'

Her frown deepened. 'So you just sleep with women for the sex? You don't actually feel anything for them but pure and simple lust? Doesn't that seem a little…shallow?'

'No.'

'Well, it does to me.'

'Are you saying you felt something for me other than lust that night?' Loukas asked, drilling his gaze into hers.

She blew out another gust of a breath, her slim shoulders going down. 'Okay, you win. Point taken.'

Loukas put a hand at her nape and brought her head forward to press a soft kiss to the middle of her forehead. 'Go back to sleep, *glykia mou*. I'll see you in the morning.'

Emily lay staring at the ceiling once Loukas had left. So, she was going to marry him. Not that he'd given her much choice, but still. It wasn't exactly the most romantic proposal in the world: *we'll marry quickly and quietly and that will be the end of it*.

Sleep was out of the question, knowing he was in the next room tossing and turning on the sofa. Should she have asked him to stay? Asked him to make love to her?

*What are you thinking?*

*I want him.*

*So? You had him and look what happened.*

*He wants me. I'm sure of it.*

*For sex, yes, but forget about anything else.*

Emily didn't want anything else…did she? The marriage would be an arrangement, not a relationship in the truest sense. She wasn't in love with Loukas. This was a lust thing, and no doubt the pregnancy hormones were making it worse. His kiss had unravelled her. Again. As soon as his lips had touched hers she'd become a boneless, whimpering mess of need.

Emily turned over and hugged the nearest pillow but it was a poor substitute for his virile male body. But why hadn't he taken it further? Especially since he was so determined to marry her. Was he holding back from her until he got a ring on her finger? His ability to stop a kiss in its tracks made her self-doubts flash like warning lights. Daniel had always been able to pull away from a kiss. Always. It had made her feel undesirable, resistible. What if Loukas was only kissing her to keep her sweet about the marriage deal? What if he could resist her? *Would* resist her? Why was she signing up for such an arrangement? A marriage without love? A contract drawn up between two virtual strangers to live together until such time they didn't want to any more. How could she have agreed to that?

She'd had to because it wasn't just about what *she* wanted any more.

It was about what was best for their baby.

# CHAPTER FIVE

THE NEXT MORNING Emily showered and changed into fresh clothes, and came out to the sitting room to find Loukas staring out of the rain-splattered windows with his hands in the pockets of the same trousers he had been wearing the night before, which were looking a little worse for wear. He must have heard her soft tread on the carpet as he turned to look at her. His features looked as tired as his trousers. 'How did you sleep?' he asked.

She glanced at the rumpled sofa. 'Probably a whole lot better than you.'

He acknowledged that with a wry quirk of his lips. 'The news of our engagement has gone viral.'

'Your mission is accomplished, then.'

He came over to her and took her gently by the upper arms, his gaze meshing with hers. 'I know this is a big step for you. It's a big step for me too. I never intended to marry anyone, but—'

'Why not?'

He released her from his hold and took a step back, his gaze shifting to avoid hers. 'It was never on my list of things to do.'

'You must have a reason why it's not on the list,' Emily said. 'Marriage hasn't exactly gone out of fashion. Most people aspire to settle down and raise a family at some stage of their life. Why not you?'

He pushed out his mouth on an expelled breath. 'My parents had a messy divorce.'

'So? That doesn't mean you would too.'

'True, but I preferred not to risk it.'

'So you'd rather spend your life drifting from one shallow hook-up to the next without really connecting on any level but the physical?'

'I've seen what it can do to kids when couples divorce,' he said. 'It's not pretty.'

'Is that what happened to you when your parents broke up?' Emily asked. 'You got caught in the crossfire?'

His expression gave little away and yet Emily sensed this was a difficult and painful subject for him. Maybe she'd picked up a bit of her mother's mind-reading ability after all.

*Scary thought.*

But then, she'd gleaned enough about his father to realise things might not have been too easy for Loukas and his mother. 'Talk to me, Loukas,' she said softly. 'If we're going to get married then surely I should know a little bit about your background?'

He took a deep breath and then released it in a slow stream, as if he was letting go of something that had long been tied up tightly inside him. 'My parents divorced when I was six. I moved with my father to the States soon after. It wasn't a good experience. But then divorce rarely is for the kids involved.'

Emily frowned, thinking of him as a small boy travelling to new place, a new culture, without his mother. How had he coped with the separation? What little kid didn't want their mum at the ready? Why had his father got sole custody? 'Why with your father and not your mother?'

Loukas gave her a lopsided grimace. 'My father wanted to punish my mother for having the audacity to ask him for a divorce. He got an attack-dog lawyer to tear her reputation to pieces. After he was finished, there wasn't a court anywhere in Greece who would have awarded her custody of a stray dog, much less a child.'

'But that's awful! Your poor mum. And poor you. You must've been distraught to be separated from her so young.'

The taut line about his mouth made her wonder if he had ever forgiven his father. 'My father soon lost interest in bringing up a small child. I spent time with a number of nannies before I was packed off to boarding school in England. And it wasn't just because I was too young to go to an American boarding school. He didn't want me coming home for weekends and generally getting in the way.'

Emily decided she didn't like Loukas's father one little bit. His treatment of women was appalling. How could a man be so cruel as to separate a small boy from his mother, only to dump him in a boarding school thousands of miles away for the sake of convenience? No wonder Loukas wanted to do everything he could to avoid being compared to his father.

A marriage between Loukas and her didn't seem so outrageous now she understood a little more about his background. Of course he would want to do the best thing for his child, and protect and provide for the mother of his baby so he wouldn't be linked in any way to his father's shocking behaviour. 'Did you ever get to see your mother?'

'Once I was at boarding school I spent holidays with her. My father didn't seem to care about her having custody by then.'

'Did your mother ever remarry?'

Something passed over his face: a shadow in his eyes, a tensing of muscles, his locked jaw. It was as if what he had released moments ago was now being reined back in and locked down tightly again. 'Yes, but it didn't work out.'

Emily knew lots of second marriages failed but she wondered if there was more to Loukas's mother's story than he was prepared to share. She sensed his guardedness whenever she touched on the subject of his family. But then, with a jerk of a father like his, no wonder he was a little reticent about talking about his family. 'Just because your parents and subsequent partners' relationships didn't work out doesn't mean you'll suffer the same curse,' she said. 'I haven't had the best role model in the world but it hasn't stopped me wanting the fairy-tale.'

*Which you will be giving up if you marry him.*
*Don't remind me.*

*Just saying.*

'The break-up of any relationship where feelings are involved is difficult.'

'Is that why you never do long-term relationships?'

'I hate hurting people,' he said. 'I see no point in giving someone false hope. I've made it a policy to be scrupulously honest about what I'm prepared to give.'

Which he had been with her that night. Brutally honest.

*No-strings sex. No phone numbers. No follow-ups.*

His words hadn't been all that important to her back then. All she had thought about was how his mouth felt on hers, how he made her body sing with delight when he made love to her. 'But how long do you think our marriage would last? Are you expecting it to—'

'I don't expect you to commit to me for life,' he said. 'That's why I don't see the point in making a show out of the wedding. But I think we should remain married for the sake of the baby for three or four years at the very least. It will give our child a secure base before they go to school.'

Three or four years. It wasn't exactly a lifetime. And she would be fully supported and the baby would have everything it needed. Besides, Emily found Loukas increasingly intriguing. He was like a secret code she wanted to solve. Was a short-term marriage a stupid move on her part or the best thing under the circumstances? 'So...you're not worried about marrying a virtual stranger?' she said.

'We might not know much about each other but we do know we have the right chemistry,' Loukas said.

But would it be enough? Emily wondered if she was being a fool even considering it, let alone accepting his proposal. She had longed for one from her ex for seven years, longed and prayed for it every single day, and it had never been forthcoming. Now she'd had a proposal from a man she was fiercely attracted to but hardly knew. And she was having his baby. 'I wish you'd given me a little more time to think about this...'

'What's to think about? Most girls would jump at the chance to marry a rich man.'

Emily lifted her chin. 'If you think I'd marry a man simply because he's rich then you're very much mistaken. I'm not a gold-digger. Your money doesn't mean anything to me. It certainly wasn't why I slept with you.'

'Wasn't it?' Something dark and cynical glinted in his gaze.

'No.'

'Then why did you sleep with me?'

Emily forced herself to hold his gaze. 'You kissed me, that's why.'

He closed the distance once more and traced the line of her jaw with an indolent fingertip, his eyes holding hers in a sensually charged lock. 'Do you sleep with every man who kisses you?'

'No.'

'So...' His fingertip traced the vermillion border

of her lower lip, his body so close to hers she could feel the warmth of him, and smell the intoxicating citrus notes of his aftershave. 'If I kissed you right now would you sleep with me?'

Emily's lip was buzzing from his touch, her inner core already contracting at the thought of his hot male mouth coming down on hers. Her heart was racing so fast, if there'd been a cardiologist handy they would have sent for an immediate EEG. Or defibrillator paddles. What was it about this man that made her turn into a wanton woman with no measure of self-control? He only had to touch her and she trembled with need. 'But you don't want to sleep with me,' she said in a voice that sounded nothing like hers. It was too husky. Sexy husky. Phone-sex husky.

Loukas sent his fingertip over her top lip, making every nerve scream for him to replace it with his mouth. 'What makes you think that?'

'You didn't want to share the bed with me last night.'

His fingertip did another round of her mouth. 'I was concerned about you. You were sick, exhausted. It would have been insensitive of me.'

*I'm not sick now.*

Emily didn't say it out loud but her hands going to the front of his chest communicated it anyway. She gazed into the depths of his eyes, her insides stretching, stirring with the same need she saw reflected there. She lowered her gaze to his mouth, studying its contours, the way his dark, urgent stubble surrounded it. Had she ever seen a more fascinating mouth? That mouth had pleasured every inch of her body, done things to her secret places no one had ever done before. Her body thrummed even now with the memory of it.

Loukas brought her chin up with his fingertip, his lower body brushing against hers pelvis to pelvis. 'I want you. You can't be in any doubt of it, surely?'

Emily felt the hard contour of his growing arousal, the surge of blood so similar to the way her body swelled and moistened in secret. 'I want you too.' Desperately. Feverishly.

His hands cradled her face, his fingers splaying through her hair, his mouth coming down to hers in a searing kiss that spoke of primal urgings of his body that echoed her own. His tongue entered her mouth in a slow, silky thrust that made her inner core pulse and pound with lust. Her hands slid further up his chest to encircle his neck, her fingers caressing the tousled curls that brushed his collar. He groaned and deepened the kiss, his tongue exploring the recesses of her mouth with increasing fervour. A hot fizz filled her core as he brought her closer to his body, one of his hands settling in the small of her back to keep her in place.

Emily kissed him with the same blistering passion, her tongue duelling and dancing with his in little flicks and darts that made him murmur deep sounds of approval, making her feel more of a woman than she had ever done before. Desire rose in her like a swirling current, moving through her flesh with unstoppable force.

Loukas left her mouth to kiss his way down her neck, lingering over the pleasure spots he'd discovered that night a month ago. He came just shy of her breasts, his hands cupping her ribcage below them. 'I don't want to hurt you.'

'I'll be fine if you don't squeeze them.'

He moved her top aside and brushed his lips over the upper curve of her left breast. Then he sent his tongue in a rasping lick down the valley between her breasts. Well, maybe 'a valley' was stretching it a bit. Her pregnancy hormones had a little catching up to do, but she lived in hope. 'Tell me if I'm being too rough.'

Emily was fast moving beyond speech. She was having enough trouble breathing as it was. His tongue moved over the top side of her right breast before he unclipped her bra and stroked each of her nipples with his tongue. He kissed his way back up to her mouth, subjecting it to a long, slow kiss that fuelled her desire to a point where she was whimpering.

Emily could barely recall the steps of how she got there, but somehow she was lying on her back on the bed and Loukas was kissing his way down past her belly button to the triangle of cotton she was wearing. Yes, white, boring cotton. Why wasn't she wearing sexy black, cobwebby knickers?

He peeled the cotton down and gently traced the seam of her body with his tongue. The sensations tingled through her flesh, her nerve fibres shuddering as the strokes increased in pressure and intensity when he encountered the most swollen, tender part of her. She sucked in a sharp breath as the tension in her body gathered to one point as the wave approached. It seemed he knew her body better than she knew it herself. Within seconds she was convulsing with an orgasm that left her not just shaken and stirred but with her senses reeling.

But, just when she thought he was going to take things a step further for his own pleasure, he gave her a rueful grimace and stood, stepping away from the bed. 'Maybe we should save this until I have more time,' he said. 'I have a meeting in half an hour and I don't want to rush this.'

Emily wondered if it was the time factor or whether he didn't fancy her half as much as she'd thought. There had been no hesitation that night a month ago. No pulling away from kisses, no half measures of pleasuring. It had been full-on I-want-you-right-now sex. She'd got off. He'd got off. Or they'd got off together. Had she imagined how good it had been that night a month ago? Had the glasses of champagne she'd had that night blurred her memory?

Or was he a bit squeamish about her pregnancy? Some men found it a turn-on; others found it confronting to make love to a pregnant woman, worried they might hurt the baby or something. She pulled her knickers and top back into place, bundling her bra into one hand. 'I guess you've proved your point.'

Loukas frowned. 'What do you mean?'

'I have zero self-control around you.'

He grazed her cheek with his fingertip. 'Will you

be all right here on your own? Don't leave the suite. Call room service if you need anything. I won't be long—two hours, tops. It's a meeting with a government security agency and people have flown in from all over the country for it. I couldn't cancel it at short notice.'

'I'll be fine.'

'Do you want me to call Allegra for you, to tell her you won't be in for a few days?'

'No. I'll do it. I'm surprised she hasn't already called to ask me what's going on. But she's in the process of moving her practice to Greece, so is probably a bit distracted just now and hasn't seen the newsfeed yet.'

He bent down and brushed her hair back from her forehead. 'Be good while I'm away.'

Emily had barely straightened her clothes and hair when she heard her phone ringing from where it was plugged into a charger next to the bed. She knew it was her mother because she had set her number to ring with a particular ringtone. 'Mum, I was going to call—'

'Why am I the last person to know my one and only daughter is engaged and having a baby? What on earth is going on? I didn't even know you were dating someone.'

'I'm sorry, but it's all happened so quickly, I didn't have time to—'

'I hope you've established if he's gay or not,' her mother said.

'He's definitely not gay.' Emily placed a hand on her still flat tummy. It seemed unbelievable to think a tiny embryo was growing inside her womb, a combination of Loukas's DNA and hers making a little person who would, in a few months' time, be in her arms.

'Anyway, I knew you were pregnant well before I saw it splashed all over social media this morning,' her mother said.

Emily didn't really believe her mother could read minds, auras or tealeaves, but who knew what maternal sixth sense was at work? Not that their mother-daughter bond was particularly strong or anything. It was currently running on about two bars of signal strength. 'How could you have possibly known I was pregnant?'

'You haven't had PMS this last month. You always get crabby with me when you're due. Crabbier than usual, I mean.'

'That might've been because I took that vile-tasting liquid supplement you gave me.'

Her mother gave a snort. 'You haven't taken any of it. I checked the bottle last time I was over at your place.'

Emily had always thought her mother had missed her calling as a forensic detective. Which was why she'd been avoiding her until she'd told Loukas about the baby. Her mother would have ferreted out that stash of pregnancy tests like a sniffer dog on a drug bust. 'I'm hopeless at remembering to take medication—you know that.'

'Clearly you've neglected to take your contraceptive pill. How far along are you?'

She let out a jagged breath. 'I wasn't on the pill—I was taking a break after all those years on it. I'm four weeks or thereabouts.'

'You didn't think about terminating?'

'No.' It shocked Emily that it hadn't been the easiest decision to make. She'd always thought she would be thrilled about one day falling pregnant. But when she'd missed her period the panic had consumed any sense of thrill. The doubts and worries had rained on her like arrows: how would she cope with a baby? What if Loukas didn't want to have anything to do with their child? What if he hated her for keeping it? Or, worse, hated the child? She had worked at a law firm long enough to know there were men out there who began to hate their children because they'd been conceived with a partner they now detested.

It wasn't the way she had pictured her life panning out. She had pictured a white wedding to a man she loved and who loved her back, and then raising a family with him, a dream family, as she had longed for during her peripatetic childhood.

'Well, having a kid is one thing, but marrying the guy is another,' her mother said. 'Who marries because of a baby these days? It wasn't mandatory even in my day.'

*All the same, it would have been nice to find out the guy's name, even if you didn't end up marrying him.*

Emily didn't say it out loud because every time

she said anything about her mother's casual approach to sex she ended up sounding like a nineteen-fifties Sunday School teacher. 'I want my baby to have a father in its life.'

'I know you think you've missed out on having a father but not every man is cut out to be a dad,' her mother said. 'Some men can't cope with the responsibility.'

*Nor can some mothers.*

Emily sometimes felt her mum didn't enjoy being a mum and had only given birth to her so she could tick the box marked 'Mother'. Her approach to motherhood was the same as her approach to everything else. She would do it with great passion for a period of time and then the novelty would wear off and she would abandon it to sign up for something else that had seized her interest. Emily had barely been out of nappies when her mother had started offloading her to other people whenever she could to go on yet another yoga, mind or body retreat. Most of her school holidays had been spent in holiday care because her mother had always had better things to do than hang out with her.

'Why are you marrying this man?' her mother asked. 'Do you love him?'

Emily had no choice but to lie. She couldn't tell her mother the truth. She would never hear the end of it. 'Of course I love him.'

'You said you were in love with Daniel and look how that turned out,' her mother said. 'I told you he was hiding something the first time I met him. He gave off a furtive vibe. You wasted years on him. Years and years and years.'

*Don't remind me.*

'Look, I really have to go now, as—'

'You always do that,' her mother said. 'You run away from stuff that cuts too close to the bone. That's why you stayed with Daniel so long. You refused to face up to what was staring you in the face. If you'd listened to me from the get-go, you would've saved yourself a heap of heartache. His chakras were blocked. I knew it from the first time I met him but did you listen to me? No.'

'I'm marrying Loukas, Mum, okay? We're in love and can't wait to be a family.'

'When do I get to meet him?' her mother asked. 'I'll do a chart for him. What's his birth date?'

Emily mentally gulped. 'Erm…'

Her mother made a sound that had a broad hint of 'got you' about it. 'You don't know, do you? How well do you know this man if you don't even know when his birthday is?'

'I do know him,' Emily said. 'I know enough about him to know he's a good man who'll stand by the baby and me no matter what.'

'He's pretty wealthy according to the press,' her mother said. 'Funny, but I never took you for a gold-digger. You didn't trap him, did you?'

'How can you even *think* that?' Emily asked. 'Surely you know me better than that?'

Her mother gave a long-winded sigh. 'Sometimes I wonder if I know you at all, Emily Grace.'

*Likewise.*

'Look, I have to go—I'll talk to you some other time. Bye.' Emily clicked off the phone and then turned it to silent in case her mother called back and began another lecture. She sat on the edge of the bed and took a few seconds to calm herself. Not an easy task after a conversation with her mother.

Not an easy task, period.

Emily picked up her phone to call Allegra but then decided she would go in to see her at the office instead. Loukas had told her not to leave the suite, but surely she could dash out to see Allegra, who was coming in that morning after spending a few days with Draco on his private island in Greece? Besides, who would recognise her without Loukas by her side? He was the one who was the press magnet, not her. She could nip to the office and back and no one would even notice.

Emily slipped out of a side entrance of the hotel and jumped in a cab, arriving at the office a short time later. When Allegra saw her she signalled for Emily to come into her office out of the hearing of the junior staff. She closed the door and came over to where Emily was standing. 'I've been calling for the last hour but you haven't answered. What's going on?'

Emily had forgotten she'd turned her phone to silent after she'd spoken with her mother. 'Well, firstly the test was positive. All seven of them were.'

'Oh, Em. I don't know what to say. Congratulations?'

'Congratulations twice over,' Emily said. 'I suppose you've read the news about us being engaged?'

'I did, and you could have knocked me down with a finch's feather,' Allegra said. 'He actually *asked* you to marry him?'

'*Told* me would be more appropriate,' Emily said with more than a touch of wryness. 'I thought you said he was dead set against marriage? I swear to God, if there had been a priest or an Elvis impersonator handy Loukas would've demanded he marry us on the spot.'

'But is that what you want?' Allegra asked. 'I mean, you only met him a month ago. Are you sure you're doing the right thing? You hardly know each other.'

'I'm not at all sure; in fact I've never felt more confused in my entire life. But I want my baby to have a father and Loukas wants to be involved. He's worried about everyone thinking he'll be like his waste-of-space father. Did you know what a jerk his dad is?'

'Draco mentioned something about a scandal with a girl Loukas's father got pregnant but he didn't discuss it in too much detail,' Allegra said. 'Apparently Loukas doesn't like too many people knowing about it.'

'Can't say I blame him,' Emily said. 'Loukas wants me to fly to Corfu with him today. I know it's hideously short notice, but can you spare me for a couple of weeks?'

'Of course, but I'm worried about you rushing into this. You've barely had time to get used to the idea of being pregnant and now you're talking about marriage.'

'Yes, well, you can blame the press for that,' Emily said. 'We were at the hospital last night—'

'The hospital?' Allegra suddenly noticed Emily's bandaged finger. 'What happened to your finger?'

'Long story.'

'Tell me.'

'I was working up the courage to tell Loukas about the baby when I broke—'

'So he came to see you? In person?'

'Yes. He finally called. I didn't think it was right to tell him over the phone, so when he came round to take me out to dinner—'

'He asked you out to dinner?' Allegra asked, eyes wide. 'Before he knew anything about the baby?'

'Yes.'

'I can't wait to tell Draco. Why did he call you?'

'He wanted to see me again. He was only offering me a fling, mind you. Nothing permanent. But when I knocked over the bin and he saw all the pregnancy tests—'

'You mean you didn't actually tell him? He found out by default?'

Emily bit her lip. 'I know, I know, I know. I'm the world's biggest coward. I was trying to tell him but couldn't quite work up the courage.'

Allegra pulled out the chair for Emily to sit on and then, once Emily was seated, she perched on the edge of her desk, facing her. 'You don't have to marry him if you don't want to, Em.'

'Funny, but I seem to remember me saying something similar to you not that long ago,' Emily said with a pointed look.

Allegra did a self-effacing little eye-roll. 'Yes, well, I'm lucky it all worked out in the end.' Her frown snapped back. 'But Loukas isn't Draco. Draco told me no one gets close to Loukas. Think about it, sweetie. You're an open book, but he's as tight as a bank vault in a recession. Are you sure you'd feel comfortable marrying someone like that?'

Emily averted her gaze to focus on her hands resting on her thighs. 'I know he's a little locked down, but I'm just starting to peel back his layers. He's my baby's father and he wants to marry me, and with everything else that's been going on I can't see how I can say no now. I don't want him to be compared to his father.'

She looked back up at Allegra. 'I want people to see the Loukas I see. The one Draco knows as his best friend. He's a good man, a decent and honourable man. I want to get closer to him, and marrying him would be a good way to do it. Does that make sense?'

Allegra leaned down to press one of her hands on Emily's, her gaze warm with concern. 'Are you in love with him?'

Emily did her bunny-rabbit twitch, a habit she'd

had since childhood when she'd first started wearing glasses and had to winch them back up her nose. She wore contacts now but the habit remained. 'I like him, otherwise I wouldn't have slept with him. I'm not a one-night-stand person. But I'm not in love with him.'

*But how long before you are?*

*I'm not going to fall in love with him.*

*Ha-de-ha-ha-ha.*

Allegra gave her hand a little squeeze. 'I hope it works out for you, Em. I really do. But, just in case it doesn't, remember I'm always here for you. Whatever you decide to do.'

'Thing is, Loukas doesn't want a big wedding, so we're having a quiet ceremony to keep the press interest down.'

'Won't you be terribly disappointed?' Allegra asked, frowning again. 'You've been talking about weddings ever since you first came to work for me. You were so excited about being my bridesmaid. Surely you want to have more than a civil ceremony?'

Emily shrugged to disguise her niggling sense of disappointment. She had been picturing her dream wedding since she was a small child. Being the only child of a single mother who was staunchly against the notion of marriage had had the opposite effect on her. But if she married Loukas that dream would have to be relinquished. One of many she would have to let go. 'A big wedding will take months to organise and by then I'll be showing. No, it's better this way.'

'What does your mother think of all this?'

Emily grimaced. 'I told her I was in love with Loukas.'

Allegra's brows lifted. 'Did you, now?'

'It was easier than explaining everything. She wanted to do an astrology chart for him but I didn't know his birthday. I felt like such an idiot.'

'Was she excited about being a granny?'

Emily snorted. 'Can you picture my mother knitting booties? One thing I do know. There's no way she'll want to be called Granny or Nanna. She'll want to be called Willow.'

Allegra's brow furrowed. 'I thought her name was Susannah?'

Emily gave her a welcome-to-the-crazy-world-of-my-mother look. 'She did a "Names and Their Influence on Your Success" workshop a couple of months back. Apparently Willow has a better vibe or something. I just count myself lucky she didn't do that workshop before naming me. I dread to think what she might have come up with instead of Emily Grace.'

Allegra gave a wistful smile. 'At least you still have her.'

Emily felt a jab of remorse for harping on about her wacky mother when Allegra had lost hers when she was twelve. Allegra's children would only have one grandfather, Allegra's father, to whom she wasn't all that close, as Draco had lost both his parents when he was young. 'Sorry. That was a bit insensitive of me.'

'It's fine,' Allegra said with a closed-mouth smile.

'My mother and I weren't all that close anyway. Have you got time for a coffee and a choc-chip muffin?'

Emily put her hand over her mouth and gulped. 'Ack! Don't mention food.'

# CHAPTER SIX

LOUKAS GOT BACK to the hotel to find the suite empty. He went through every room, even going so far as to open the wardrobes, but there was no sign of Emily. He whipped out his phone and dialled her number but it went through to the message service. Panic gripped him by the throat, tightening his airway until he could barely snatch in a breath. Where was she? Was she ill? Had she been taken to hospital? Had she gone outside and been hounded by the press? Perhaps chased down the street? Got hit by a bus? Kidnapped? The list of possibilities rushed through his brain like a toxic fever. His heart hammered so hard it was as if a construction site were inside his chest.

He called the front desk, asking if anyone had seen his fiancée. He felt a fool for having to ask it. 'No, Mr Kyprianos,' the receptionist said. 'Perhaps she's gone shopping for the wedding. There are three bridal stores and two florists on this block. This area's very popular for brides-to-be.'

Loukas put down the phone and wiped the back of his hand over his clammy brow. He had to get a grip on himself. There was probably a perfectly good explanation for why Emily had disobeyed his instruction to stay in the suite. The sense of powerlessness was sickening, reminding him of the day of the accident when so many lives had careened out of control.

Why had Emily gone? Where had she gone? Was she coming back? Or had he scared her with his insistence on marriage? Sure, it was a big step to get married. He might not be perfect husband material but it wasn't as if he was some boorish oaf who wouldn't look after her. He tried her phone another time but it went to message service again. His hand tightened on the phone until he thought the screen would crack. Should he do a ring-around of the hospitals to see if she'd been admitted? Ask the hotel to run the CCTV tapes to see if she'd left the hotel with someone?

The door suddenly opened and Emily came in. 'Oh…you're back.'

Relief collided with anger that she'd put him through such a hellish few minutes. 'Where the hell were you?' Loukas asked. 'I've been out of my head with worry. I thought I told you to stay put until I got back?'

She slipped her bag off her shoulder and placed it on the table near the door, her movements slow and measured, as if she was frightened of setting off a loaded bomb. 'I went to work to arrange for some leave.'

'You could have phoned to do that.'

Her brown eyes contained a hint of defiance. 'I

preferred to do it face to face. Allegra's my best friend. I wanted to explain what was going on between us in person.'

'What did she say?'

'She has some misgivings about us rushing into marriage.'

'That's rich, coming from her.'

'Yes, I said much the same thing,' she said. 'But at least she knew the man she was marrying.'

Loukas let out a long breath to bring down his crazy heartbeat. 'We'll get to know each other in time, Emily. This is an unusual situation and it calls for an unusual solution. Did the press follow you?'

'Nope, I went out a side entrance and caught a cab to work,' she said with an element of smugness in her voice. 'I came back in the same way.'

'You scared the hell out of me, disappearing like that,' he said. 'Why didn't you leave a note or send me a text?'

She shifted her weight from foot to foot, like a child caught out in some misdemeanour. 'I thought I'd be back before you.'

'I would appreciate it if you would obey my instructions in future,' Loukas said. 'I didn't insist you stay here to punish you. I was genuinely concerned about you. The paparazzi can be ruthless in hunting down a target. You can get injured trying to escape.'

'As you can see, I'm perfectly fine and, just for the record, I'm not in the habit of taking orders from the men in my life,' she said with an uppity tilt of her chin.

'I'm the only man in your life from this moment. Understood?'

Twin pools of colour collected on her cheeks, either from embarrassment or anger, he couldn't quite tell. 'Am I the only woman in yours?' she asked.

'Yes.' Loukas was surprised at how good it felt to say it. Shocked, even. He normally found relationships claustrophobic but somehow being connected to Emily didn't feel like that. It felt like a discovery. An adventure. Every day he learned something new about her. 'I expect nothing less than absolute fidelity while we are together. Are you okay with that?'

'Yes, of course,' she said. 'I wouldn't agree to marry you if you didn't promise me that.'

'Fine.' He studied her for a moment. 'How are you feeling?'

'I was a bit queasy when I was with Allegra but I'm okay now.'

Loukas slipped his hand into his pocket. 'I bought this on the way back to the hotel after the meeting. I hope it fits.'

She took the designer ring-box from him and nudged it open. 'Oh, my goodness, it's gorgeous!'

He hadn't had much time to choose after the meeting, but he figured she wasn't the flashy big ring type. He'd gone for a more subtle design with a high-quality diamond and a classic setting that would enhance her small hand rather than swamp it. He took the ring from the velvet lining and slid it along her ring finger, privately pleased he'd got the size spot-on. 'Do you like it?'

Her toffee-brown eyes were shining so much they were dazzling. 'It's beautiful. But you shouldn't have spent so much money. What if I lose it? I'm hopeless with jewellery. I've lost three pearl earrings and a diamond stud in the last year.'

Loukas suppressed a smile. 'Don't worry. It's insured.'

She held the ring up to the light, turning it this way and that. 'I'll be super-duper careful, I promise.' She lowered her hand and gave him a smile. 'Thank you, Loukas. It was awfully generous of you.'

Loukas thought her smile gave the diamond a run for its money in terms of brilliance. He had never seen a smile so engaging as hers. When the edges of her mouth tipped up, two dimples appeared in her cheeks. 'You're welcome.'

There was a little silence.

Emily brushed back a loose strand of hair from her face. 'What time are we leaving?'

He wished he hadn't booked the lunchtime flight. Right then, he could think of nothing he'd rather do than spend the next couple of hours in that bed with her to show her his self-control wasn't in as good a shape as she thought. But he wanted to get out of London, away from all the attention of the press. 'Our flight is at one p.m., which doesn't leave us much time. Do you need a hand packing?'

'No. I'm all good.'

The flight to Corfu was direct from London and it seemed no time at all before they arrived at Loukas's villa set on a hilltop overlooking the stunning view of the ocean. The villa was Venetian-style with formal gardens out the back leading to woodland filled with pines, Holm oaks and wild olives. At the front of the villa was a sun-drenched flagstone terrace with a swimming pool that beckoned to Emily in the shimmering heat of the late afternoon.

The housekeeper came out of the villa and greeted Emily with a wide smile, her hands clasped together, as if giving thanks to the divine being who had orchestrated her boss bringing home a bride-to-be. 'So happy to meet you, Dhespinis Emily,' she said after Loukas introduced them. 'I have waited a long time for this day. I was wondering if it would ever come. And a baby too! It is a dream come true.'

Emily painted on a smile. 'Thank you. It is very nice to be here.'

The housekeeper beamed at Loukas. 'I have a lovely surprise for you.'

Loukas's tightly compressed expression gave the impression he didn't much care for surprises. 'Oh, really?'

Chrystanthe's expression, on the other hand, was not unlike that of a doting fairy godmother who had just waved her magic wand and pulled off the grand wish of the century. She kept looking from Loukas to Emily with a wide smile on her face and her black button eyes twinkling. 'Your mother and sister are here. They arrived half an hour ago. They're waiting in the drawing room.'

*His sister?* Since when had Loukas had a sister?

Why hadn't he mentioned her? She'd thought he was an only child of divorced parents. He had only been six years old when his parents had broken up. He had never said anything about a sibling, either older or younger. Allegra hadn't mentioned anything about him having a sister, either, which made Emily wonder if even Draco knew about her existence.

If not, why not?

Emily glanced at Loukas to find him frowning darkly. 'That's…nice,' he said, but the way he hesitated over the word 'nice' suggested he considered it far from so.

'They came off the luxury cruise you sent them on because they heard the news of your engagement,' the housekeeper said. 'They said they wanted to congratulate you in person.'

'Right,' Loukas said, taking Emily's hand. 'We'd better go see them.'

Emily waited until the housekeeper had gone ahead before asking, 'Is there anything else I should know about you that you haven't yet told me? Why didn't you tell me you had a sister?'

'Half-sister.'

'That's beside the point. You gave me the impression you were an only child,' she said. 'What sort of fool will I look if I don't know everything there is to know about you? I don't even know when your birthday is.'

'December twenty-eighth.'

'Capricorn.' Emily rolled her eyes. 'I should have guessed. You climb to the top and let nothing get in

your way of a goal. You have trouble expressing feelings and do rather than say—or so my mother will
tell you. She's done a course.'

'When's yours?'

'March second—Pisces. Apparently I'm selfless
to a fault, unassuming and naïve and deeply emotional. Go me.'

Loukas led Emily inside the villa's foyer. If she
had thought the hotel last night was spectacular, then
this more than topped it. It wasn't a showy, over-done
expression of wealth, but rather an understated sim-
plicity of design and décor that spoke of a man with
good taste and an excellent eye for detail. The walls
of the foyer were adorned with priceless works of
art, the polished marble floors covered strategically
here and there with ankle-deep Persian rugs, and a
staircase with glossy black balustrading led to the
upper levels.

He took her to the main sitting room where a
collection of plush sofas in brocade the colour of
milky coffee sat around a rug beneath a central crystal chandelier. Lamps sat on side tables, their muted
light giving the vast room a cosy atmosphere. The
walls were bone-white with soft green-grey wain-
scoting and feature trims that continued the Vene-
tian theme.

A steel-grey-haired woman in her fifties rose
from a wing chair near the marble fireplace and, to
her left, a younger, frail-looking woman in her early
twenties, presumably Loukas's sister, was sitting in
a wheelchair with a light throw rug over her knees.

'Loukas,' his mother said without approaching him, her tentative expression giving every indication she wasn't sure of the reception she would receive. 'I hope you don't mind us dropping in without notice, but we were so delighted by your news, we couldn't stay away. We won't stay long. We don't want to be in the way, but we just wanted to meet Emily.'

'It's nice to see you both,' he said. 'This is Emily.' He brought her forward with a hand on the small of her back. 'Emily, this is my mother, Phyllida Ryan, and my half-sister, Ariana.'

'I'm delighted to meet you both,' Emily said, taking his mother's hand and then his sister's.

Ariana smiled shyly up at Emily. 'Loukas is such a dark horse. He never tells us anything about his private life. We didn't know he was seeing anyone regularly. When did you meet?'

Emily wished she'd talked this through in a little more detail with Loukas. What if she said something that contradicted something he'd already said? Had he told them about their engagement or had they found out via the media? He didn't appear all that close to them. His manner towards them was polite but distant, almost to the point of being cold. 'Erm… we met through mutual friends.'

'I'm so thrilled for you both,' Phyllida said. 'I never thought he was ever going to get married. You must be a very special person.'

'She is,' Loukas said, slipping his arm around Emily's waist.

Emily smiled until her face ached. What was it with Loukas and his mother and sister? They didn't exchange hugs or kisses with him like a normal family would do. She wasn't sure what to say or do to ease the stilted atmosphere. She'd thought her relationship with her mother was a little awkward at times, but even a stiff broomstick hug and an air kiss was better than nothing.

'It's wonderful news about the baby,' his mother said. 'I wasn't sure I was ever going to be a grandmother. Are you keeping well?'

'I'm having a bit of trouble with nausea but otherwise I'm okay.'

'We won't stay long,' Ariana said to Emily. 'We just wanted to meet you in person.' Her gaze moved to Loukas. 'I know you don't like impromptu guests but we couldn't stay away this time.'

'You are welcome here any time.' Loukas's voice was unusually husky.

Emily couldn't help noticing the way Ariana kept glancing at Emily's abdomen with an almost wistful expression on her face. Was she worried she might never have the opportunity to marry and have children herself? How bad was her disability? Would it be rude to ask?

'I'm really happy for you, Loukas. I mean that,' Ariana said.

His expression gave little away but his voice still contained that deep, gravelly note. 'Thank you.'

'So when's the wedding?' Phyllida asked with an expectant air.

'In two weeks' time,' Loukas said. 'We're not having a big ceremony, so don't feel you have to attend.'

'But of course we'd love to come, wouldn't we, Ariana?' his mother asked.

'I wouldn't miss it for anything,' Ariana said. 'Although, if you'd rather not have us there…?'

'I would love you to be there,' Emily said. 'In fact, would you be my bridesmaid, Ariana? My best friend Allegra will be my maid of honour but I'd love it if you would be my bridesmaid.' The invitation was out before she had time to think about it. Why was she organising a bridesmaid when, strictly speaking, this wasn't a real wedding? Or at least, not the normal kind. Loukas didn't want a big ceremony, but she couldn't imagine having a wedding without a bridesmaid or two. And who better than his half-sister?

'Are you sure?' Ariana asked with a look of such longing it made something in Emily's chest squeeze, like it was being pinched. 'I've never been in a wedding party before. Are you sure I won't ruin all the photos because of my chair? I can stand for short periods with a bit of support but—'

'Of course you won't spoil the photos,' Emily said. 'How long have you been…? I'm sorry. Am I being rude to ask what happened to you?'

Ariana glanced briefly at Loukas, her teeth momentarily snagging her lower lip. 'Hasn't Loukas told you?'

Emily's stomach shifted like a shoe on a slippery surface. 'Told me what?'

Phyllida put her hand on Ariana's shoulder, her

gaze troubled. 'Come on, love. It's time you had a rest. Emily too must be exhausted after the flight. We've taken up too much of your time already.'

'No, no, of course you haven't,' Emily said, glancing at Loukas, but his expression was in its customary locked-down position. What hadn't he told her about his sister's disability? Why hadn't he told her he even had a sister? What was going on? Why was the atmosphere between him and his mother and sister so strained and awkward?

Phyllida and Ariana left the room, the whisper of the wheelchair's tyres over the carpet the only sound in the cavernous silence. Emily turned back to Loukas once the door closed quietly behind them. 'I've felt elephants in the room before, but that one was a woolly mammoth.'

'Leave it, Emily. Please.' He made to leave the room but she caught up to him just in time and snagged him by the arm.

'Tell me what I'm supposed to know,' she said, looking up into his tightly set features.

He put his hand over hers to remove it but she dug her fingers in. 'It's no concern of yours,' he said.

Emily raised her brows until they threatened to disappear past her hairline. 'No concern of mine? How can you say that when in two weeks I'm going to be your wife?'

His mouth was so flat his lips had all but disappeared. But then he let out a long breath that sounded as if it had come from some deep, dark place inside him. 'I was the one who caused the accident.'

Emily couldn't swallow her gasp of shock in time. He had caused the accident that had maimed his sister? She clutched at her throat with one hand, her heart shuddering at the thought of the burden of guilt he must feel. 'Oh, no...'

'I ran into Ariana with my car. I didn't see her in time. She lost control of the new bike she'd got for her birthday and careened down the driveway and on to the road straight in front of me.' His throat rose and fell before he continued. 'I slammed on the brakes but I...I'd only had my licence a few weeks. I didn't have the experience or the skill to avoid her.'

He had been so young himself—a teenager on the threshold of adulthood—only to be assailed with guilt that would last a lifetime. How devastating for him to be responsible for causing such hurt and suffering, even if it had been an accident. 'Oh, Loukas, that's so awful and tragic. I'm so sorry for your sister and for you. It must have been a nightmare.'

Long remembered anguish was etched in the landscape of his face. 'I thought I'd killed her at first. But then she started screaming.' He took another deep breath and released it in a staggered stream. 'She was in an induced coma for a month and spent a year in hospital and another six months in rehab. I've lost count of the number of surgeries she's had. The most recent one was the week before Draco's wedding, in an effort to get her walking again, but so far it's failed.'

'And all this time you've been blaming yourself,' Emily said, seeing it written not just on his face but also in the way he held his body. Was that why he avoided commitment? Why he had avoided marriage and kids of his own—because of the guilt he carried over that terrible day?

The look he gave her was grimly resigned and he removed her hand from his arm. 'Wouldn't you blame yourself?'

She ran her tongue over her carpet-dry lips. Of course she would if she had been in the same situation. Who wouldn't? No decent person wanted to hurt another person and see them suffer and struggle for years and years with the physical damage. The guilt would gnaw away at even the toughest, most resilient personality. 'Yes, but it was an accident. You didn't mean to hit her. Little kids are accident magnets. They run in and out of danger all the time. It could've happened to anyone coming along that road at that moment. And maybe, if someone else had been coming faster than you, then she wouldn't have survived at all.'

His gaze was ghosted with bone-deep sadness. 'If I had been even five seconds earlier or later she wouldn't have been hit at all.'

Emily reached out to comfort him. 'You have to stop blaming yourself, Loukas. It happened and she survived—that's the main thing.'

He eased away as if her touch made him uncomfortable. Or maybe it was because he wasn't used to talking about the accident. Emily was sure Allegra knew nothing about it, which meant Draco probably didn't either. Why hadn't Loukas told his best friend about the most tragic event of his life? Or was his guilt too burdensome to share? His aloofness had struck her from the first moment she'd met him at the wedding. But now she understood why he kept himself separate from other people. An invisible wall of guilt locked him in his own private prison.

'My mother's marriage broke up the year after the accident,' he said after a moment.

Emily frowned. 'But surely you're not blaming yourself for that too?'

'They were fine until the accident. Her husband Frank couldn't forgive me for what I'd done, and my mother couldn't forgive him for saying it to my face at every opportunity he could.'

'But lots of marriages break up when there's a sick or disabled child involved,' she said. 'It strains the steadiest of relationships. You shouldn't have been blamed for it. Your mother was right in standing up for you. I would've done the same in a heartbeat.'

He dragged a hand down his face as if to wipe away the memory of that time. 'My mother has been through two bitter divorces because of me. Firstly with my father and then with Frank.'

'Is that why you've always avoided marriage?' Emily asked. 'Because you think you'll somehow jinx it?'

'I hurt people without even trying,' he said. 'I've been doing it all my life.'

She put her hand back on his arm, firmer this time, so he couldn't so easily shrug her off. 'You haven't hurt me, Loukas. The pregnancy was an accident. You're doing all you can to support the baby and me. That's not the behaviour of man who intentionally wants to hurt people. That's the behaviour of a man who's mature and stable enough to face even the toughest of responsibilities.'

His expression had gone back to its default setting of inscrutable mask. 'Since you've asked Ariana to be your bridesmaid, I take it you've finally come to terms with our marriage going ahead?'

A part of Emily wished she hadn't been quite so impulsive in offering his sister the role of bridesmaid. It was like passing a point of no return. She hadn't realised he would use it as a way to bend her to his will if she'd had second thoughts. But the streak of ruthlessness in his personality was a reminder of the lengths he would go to achieve a goal. He wanted to be an involved father to their child. He wanted to provide for and protect it, as any decent dad worthy of the title would want to do. But why shouldn't she give him this chance to move on from his tragic past, to help him heal, by sharing the parenting of their accidental baby for as long as they stayed together?

Besides that, she cared about him. The more she learned about him, the more she cared. He was a complex man with hidden depths she wanted to explore. Hadn't she sensed that the first time she'd met him? Why else had she spent that crazily out-of-character night with him? Something about him had spoken to her on a level no one else had ever reached before. 'I know you don't want a big wedding, but I could see how much she'd love to be involved. I really like your mum and your sister. But you seem so stilted with them, even though they don't seem to blame you for the accident.'

He put some distance between their bodies, turning his back to stare at the view of the ocean below. It was as if a wall had come up around him. An invisible, impenetrable wall that had 'Keep Out' written all over it.

'They are nothing but gracious. But I'm aware every time I'm around them I remind them of my part in Ariana's disability. She's in a wheelchair, for God's sake. I put her there. She can't have the life every other young woman her age takes for granted.'

Emily came up behind him and stroked her hand down his stiffly held shoulders to the small of his back. 'It's tragic she's not able to walk but it might not be for ever. There are medical breakthroughs happening all the time. And she does have a life. It might not be the one she would have chosen, but that doesn't mean it's not fulfilling and worthwhile.'

He turned his head to look down at her. 'Look, I know you mean well, but it's not just Ariana's life that's been ruined. My mother is stuck in the role of full-time carer.'

'But maybe that's what she wants,' Emily said.

His eyes contained a bleakness that reminded her of a lonely and deserted moor. 'Maybe, but her life would've been better if she'd had a choice. I took that away from her.' He brushed past her to leave the room, almost colliding with his housekeeper coming through the doorway. 'Excuse me,' he said to Chrystanthe. 'I have some business to see to. Can you settle Emily into my room?'

The master bedroom Chrystanthe led Emily to was decorated in muted greys and stark white with subtle touches of blue. The king-sized bed had a velvet and studded Venetian-style headboard in a deeper shade of mushroom-grey, and there was a collection of plump pillows, both standard and European, and a velvet throw over the foot of the bed. Twin bedside tables balanced the massive bed, and the lamps with their dove-grey shades were a nice counter to the crystal chandelier above. The large windows were festooned with gorgeous white drapes with grey velvet piping featured on the pelmet above.

But, while supposedly it was Loukas's bedroom, at first glance there was little to tie him to it. It didn't have any personal touches such as photos or family memorabilia. While his clothes were arranged neatly in the walk-in wardrobe, and his toiletries in the *en suite* bathroom, the bedroom itself looked more like a luxury hotel suite than anything else. How much time did he spend at his villa? She knew he travelled a lot for work but if this was his base then it sure could do with a few little homey touches. It was almost *too* perfect. She couldn't imagine a sticky-fingered toddler coming in here... Well, she could, but it wasn't a pretty sight.

'Loukas is always working too hard,' Chrystanthe said, smoothing down the already impossibly smooth throw on the end of the bed. 'Maybe you will teach him to relax and enjoy life a bit more, *ne*?'

'I'll try,' Emily said. 'How long have you worked for him?'

'Five years. He is a good boss. Very generous. I want for nothing and neither do any of his staff.'

'Do his mother and sister visit often?'

'This is the first time in nearly four years,' Chrystanthe said, giving the pillows a quick plump. 'He is often travelling, you know? But he more than makes up for it by spoiling them with wonderful gifts. The cruise he sent them on was an exclusive one with their own private butler and chef. He flies them wherever they want to go in a private jet so Ariana doesn't have to suffer any delays or discomfort flying on a commercial airline. Her chair is custom-made. He pays for every medical expense and he lavishes them both with gifts at Christmas and on birthdays.'

Emily suspected Loukas would have been generous even without the guilt that plagued him. He was that sort of man. He didn't use his wealth to build himself up but to help others. But what if his mother and sister wanted less of his gifts and more of him? Could she help him with that? Perhaps build a bridge so he could be more comfortable around them and they with him?

Chrystanthe put the last pillow in place. 'Now, can I get you a cup of tea or a cool drink?'

'No, I'm fine,' Emily said, glancing longingly at the bed. 'I'll just have a lie down for a bit.'

The housekeeper closed the door softly behind her as Emily lay down. She closed her eyes, promising herself she would only have forty winks…

Loukas walked out of the villa to the olive grove he'd planted when he'd first bought the property. His mother and sister showing up like that had rocked him so much he had barely been able to talk. He had never encouraged them to call on him. He occasionally called on them, but he never stayed longer than an hour or two at the most. He provided them with everything they needed and more but, as to spending extended periods of time with them, well, that was asking too much of them, let alone him. He had only invited them to Corfu once, the year after he'd bought the villa, but it had been more out of duty than any desire to play happy families. He'd sent them on a ridiculously expensive cruise of the Greek Isles because he'd thought Ariana needed a distraction after the last bout of surgery that hadn't achieved the result she'd hoped. He knew he should have contacted them before they found out the news online, but any contact with them always made the guilt come back with a cruel vengeance.

He embodied Ariana's lost potential. Every time she saw him she was reminded of what he had done. How could she not be reminded? He was reminded every time he looked at her sitting in that chair. It didn't matter that it had been an accident. His actions had caused irreparable harm and he couldn't undo it. Not one little bit of it. He had seen the wistfulness in his sister's eyes when she'd glanced at Emily's abdomen. Ariana might never have children. The doctors had already warned her the internal damage had all but removed the possibility of having a family. How difficult must it be for her to see him marry Emily and have the family he knew she longed for, as most young women her age did?

Emily had generously invited Ariana to be a bridesmaid and he'd jumped on her gesture to secure even more firmly her agreement to marry him. It was a nice gesture on her part, but it would only intensify his guilt. Would his sister ever get to be a bride? And she couldn't shuffle more than a couple of steps without support. How then would she walk down the aisle of a church? As far as he knew, she hadn't even been on a date. Ariana lived a life of medical appointments and gruelling exercise programs to maintain what little mobility she had left.

Loukas snapped off an olive leaf and tore it into shreds, tossing them to the ground in a parody of tossing confetti. Even the late-afternoon sun seemed to be glaring at him accusingly. He had brought Emily here hoping it would keep her out of the way of the press and instead it had put her smack-bang in the middle of the train wreck of his family.

No matter what he did, he seemed to make things worse.

Emily hadn't realised she'd been asleep until she heard the faint clicking sound of the bedroom door opening. The tall figure of Loukas was framed in the doorway. He softly closed the door and came over to the bed. 'I'm sorry, did I wake you?'

She sat up and pushed the tangle of her hair away from her face. 'I was just dozing. I get so tired, it's unbelievable. How do women have more than a couple of kids? It must be exhausting.'

He sat on the edge of the bed next to her legs. 'Can I get you anything? A drink? Something to eat? Dinner won't be for a while but I can get Chrystanthe to rustle up something if you'd—'

'No, please don't fuss. I'll wait for dinner. I'm looking forward to chatting some more to your mum and Ariana.'

'They won't be joining us, I'm afraid.'

Emily frowned. 'Oh? Why not? Is Ariana not well?'

His eyes shifted from hers. 'They were keen to get back to their cruise. They only got off for a couple of hours so they could meet you.'

'That's a shame. Maybe I could visit them at home to discuss the bridesmaid dress. Where do they live?'

'In Oxfordshire in England.'

'Not in Greece?'

Loukas's expression had a hint of ruefulness. 'After the divorce from my father, my mother went off all things Greek. I bought her and Ariana a house in a village close to the hospital and physical therapy centre Ariana goes to. The house has an indoor therapy pool and a gym so she can continue her exercises at home.'

'You sound like a very generous person,' Emily

said. 'Chrystanthe was telling me what a great boss you are and how good you are to Ariana and your mum.'

His lips gave a humourless on-off movement. 'Let's hope I can be a good husband and father too.'

She placed her hand on his hair-roughened wrist. 'You will be. I'm sure of it.'

His brown eyes meshed with hers, his hand coming over her hand and holding it against his warm, hard thigh. Sensual energy pulsed and throbbed with every beat of Emily's heart. It was as if her blood was speaking to his blood through the skin-to-skin contact of his hand pressing hers to his thigh. She moistened her lips, her gaze slipping to his mouth, watching in breathless anticipation for him to close the distance.

He brought his head down, his lips nudging hers in playful little touches that made her mouth tingle. 'I should let you rest some more.' His deep, husky voice acted like another caress on her fevered senses.

'But I'm not tired now.' She bumped his lips with hers, using her tongue to glide over his lower lip.

Loukas made a groaning sound and gathered her closer, crushing her to him and bringing his mouth down on hers in a drugging kiss that made her insides quake with want. His tongue came in search of hers, teasing it into a sexy samba that mimicked the passionate love-making they had done a month ago. His hands cupped her face, his fingers splaying over her hair as he feasted on her mouth, like a starving man does a long anticipated meal.

Emily returned his kiss with just as much fervour, her senses reeling with each heart-stopping flicker and glide of his tongue. She set to work on his shirt, desperate to get her hands on his bare skin, but with her finger still heavily bandaged she didn't get very far. Loukas took over the task for her and hauled his shirt over his head and tossed it to the floor. He then began on her clothes, undoing buttons, sliding her top off her shoulders, kissing her as he went, drawing out the process until she was squirming with impatience. He left her bra in place and kissed the upper curves of her breasts with gentle barely touching presses of his lips. His concern about her tenderness touched her deeply.

He laid her back against the pillows and kissed his way down from her mouth to her décolletage, his hands cradling her as if she were priceless porcelain. It was different from their first encounter when clothes had been all but ripped off and bodies hard pressed together in an almost animalistic coupling. This was a slow but sure celebration of her body, a worshipful discovery of every curve and contour with his gentle hands, lips and tongue. Every nerve in her body vibrated with the pleasure of his touch, the sensations rippling through her in escalating waves.

It was the most thrilling experience of her life to be touched with such exquisite care. He helped her out of the rest of her clothes, every hair on her head tingling at the roots when he came to the final barrier of her knickers. Not white cotton this time, but dark blue lace, as she'd changed before she'd left to visit Allegra. He traced the seam of her body through the lace of her knickers, the touch so sensual it made her back arch off the bed.

He gently eased her knickers away, her senses so heightened the glide of the fabric against her skin made her sigh in pleasure. Loukas brought his mouth down to her feminine mound, stroking the outside of her form with his tongue just as he had with his finger against the lace. Every cell in her body throbbed with longing, her flesh swelling and delicately scenting with the musk of arousal. He separated her with his fingers, caressed her with his tongue in soft strokes that were slow and measured, before gradually upping the pace in response to her whimpered signals. The ripples started deep and low in her body and then spread out like a tide, coursing through her body in convulsive waves. Goose bumps rose on her flesh and hot, fizzing tingles shot up and down her spine until finally the sensations faded, leaving her in a blissful afterglow that made all her muscles feel like melted wax.

Emily opened her eyes to see his glittering with his own anticipation. She ran a hand down his sternum, past his wash-board abdomen, to her prize below. His features gave a spasm of pleasure when she took him in her hand, stroking and caressing him the way she knew he loved best. 'I guess we won't be needing a condom,' she said.

Dark heat flared in his eyes. 'I want you.'

'So I can tell.' She gave him another stroke, running her fingertip over the head of his erection.

He pressed her back down, taking care not to let her take his weight, their legs finding their preferred positions as if they had been making love together for years. That was what had struck her about that night after the wedding. There hadn't been any awkwardness between them. Her body had expressed her desire, as had his, and together they had created an explosive choreography of intimacy.

He kissed Emily thoroughly, his tongue duelling with hers in another slow tango that ramped up her desire all over again. She caressed Loukas's back and shoulders, delighting in the play of his taut muscles as they responded to her touch. She went lower to cup his buttocks, encouraging him to take his pleasure, opening her legs even further, her body on fire for the deep, silken thrust of his.

He made another guttural sound, as if his self-control was teetering at the limit, and then he entered her with a long, smooth surge that made her gasp out loud in relief. The feel of him moving inside her rocked her senses. He was gentle and yet thrillingly male, taking her on a tantalising journey of sensory delight that made every inch of her flesh go into raptures. Her intimate muscles gripped him with each thrust and retreat, the sexy rhythm in perfect tune with her body. He slipped a hand between their bodies, knowing exactly how to intensify her pleasure to give her the extra strokes of friction that would send her over the edge. The orgasm exploded like a massive firework, sending rivers of sensations through her body until she was shaking with the impact.

His low grunt of pleasure followed close behind, the dual rocking of their bodies in that penultimate moment sending another wave of delight crashing through her flesh.

Loukas slowly withdrew, but not before brushing her hair away from her face. 'Are your breasts okay? I didn't crush them too hard with my weight?'

Emily touched his face with her fingertips. 'I forgot all about them, to be honest.'

A smile ghosted his mouth. 'So, I guess that clears that up, then.'

'What? My breasts?'

He coiled a tendril of her hair around his finger. 'It was just as good between us as I imagined. Better, even.'

Emily sent her fingertip around his mouth. 'You were amazingly gentle with me.'

'I've never made love to a pregnant woman before. It's a bit nerve-racking, actually.'

'You don't have to treat me like I'm made of glass.'

He stroked his finger down between her breasts. 'Does this hurt?'

'No.'

He moved his finger to her right breast and traced a lazy circle around her nipple. 'This?'

'No…'

He brought his mouth to her breast, using his tongue to follow the earlier pathway of his finger. The feel of his warm tongue on her sensitive flesh made her skin shiver. 'You have beautiful breasts.'

'Glad you think so,' Emily said. 'I was about to send out a search party when I was a teenager but thankfully they showed up before my fifteenth birthday.'

This time his slanted smile made his eyes sparkle. 'You have nothing to be worried about, Emily. You are one of the most naturally beautiful women I've ever met.'

She couldn't help basking in the glow of his compliments. Who wouldn't feel beautiful, the way he looked at her? She wasn't a vain person—how could she be with an overbite and freckles and bad eyesight? But every time Loukas looked at her she felt as if she was the most stunning creature in the world. 'I'm not holding out for a *Vogue* shoot any time soon, but thanks anyway.'

He picked up a tendril of her hair again and wound it around his finger, his eyes holding hers in a smouldering lock that made her insides clench all over again with need. 'I want to make love to you again but I don't want to tire you.'

Emily pinched his chin between her finger and thumb and brought his face down to hers. 'Did I say I was tired?'

His lips moulded themselves to hers in a leisurely kiss that had a blistering undercurrent of lust. She opened for him, making a sound of sheer pleasure when his tongue circled hers. His afternoon stubble grazed her face when he changed position, but it only heightened her awareness and need of him. He turned her so she was lying over him, giving her more control and less of his weight to worry about. He placed his hands just below her breasts, offering them gentle support.

Emily swept her hair back over one shoulder, straddling him with her thighs, her body flaring with incendiary heat as his erection rose in front of her mound. She moved against him, letting him feel how ready she was for him.

He sucked in a harsh-sounding breath and groaned. 'You're killing me.'

She leaned over him, planting her hands either side of his head, letting her hair fall forward and tickle his chest. 'Kill me right back.'

Loukas's hands gripped her by the hips and he pushed up into her with another deep groan of satisfaction. The movement of his body in hers incited her to be more daring and adventurous. She moved her body in a circular motion, delighting in the way the friction changed with each movement. Each time his body surged and withdrew, waves of pleasure built in tantalising ripples and coursed through her flesh. She was so close to flying, but couldn't quite lift off, until he came to her rescue by massaging the swollen heart of her, sending her soaring into the abyss on an orgasm so intense she could barely register anything but the sensations ricocheting through her body.

His took his pleasure with a series of thrusts, each one sending a vicarious wave of delight through her intimate flesh. His whole body relaxed back against the mattress, and he brought her down to rest her head against his chest, one of his hands moving in a slow stroke up and down the curve of her spine.

Never had Emily felt so physically close to another person. Love-making with Daniel—when it had infrequently occurred—had often been quick and unsatisfying, for which she had mostly blamed herself. And, because Daniel had gone to any lengths to hide his secret from his overly conservative parents, he too would often allow her to feel it was her fault. For seven years she had felt hopelessly inadequate.

But ever since sleeping with Loukas she'd realised she was more than capable of experiencing earth-shattering orgasms—of being a sexually competent partner who could give and receive pleasure. The chemistry she shared with Loukas wasn't just in bed but in every aspect of her contact with him. She was attracted to his intellect, his quiet strength of character and his dry sense of humour. His sense of responsibility impressed her, the fact that he was prepared to do whatever he could to provide for his child, even though it pushed him out of his comfort zone.

Loukas's hand settled on the small of her back, creating a warm, soothing glow that threatened to melt her bones. Emily lifted her head and, leaning on his chest, toyed with the line of his lower lip with her fingertip. 'I think my mother might be on to something.'

One of his brows lifted. 'Oh? What's that?'

She traced the shallow dip below his lip. 'She

teaches couples how to communicate better through having great sex.'

His hand began another slow stroke of her spine, his dark eyes glinting. 'Sounds like the homework could be fun.'

Emily sent her finger over his top lip, playing special attention to the firm philtral ridge running beneath his nose to his mouth. 'Not that it ever worked with my ex.'

'So what happened between you and him?'

*You're talking about your ex while you're in bed with Loukas?*

*I have to tell him some time, don't I? Anyway, it's called communication.*

*It's called being a gauche idiot, that's what it's called.*

Emily focussed on Loukas's stubble-coated Adam's apple rather than meet his gaze. 'In the seven years I dated and lived with Daniel, he forgot to mention he was gay.'

Loukas frowned. 'You didn't suspect anything?'

Emily sighed. 'On reflection, there were lots of indications, but I disregarded them. He comes from a really conservative background. He didn't feel he could ever come out to his parents in case they disowned him, so he hid it since he was a teenager. I think that's why I never suspected anything at the beginning, because he was romantic and attentive and made me feel special. It was only after we started living together that things went downhill. For all of that time I blamed our patchy sex life on myself. We seemed to only ever have sex when he'd had a few drinks. It made me feel he wasn't attracted to me unless he had wine-or beer-goggles on. It wasn't great for my self-esteem, that's for sure.'

'You didn't think about leaving him sooner?'

She gave a self-deprecating grimace. 'I can be pretty stubborn when I know I'm in the wrong. I dig myself in deeper and deeper because I don't want to admit I've made a mistake. Don't get me wrong— we were good friends…really good friends, but the chemistry wasn't right. Once five years had passed, I got even more desperate to pretend everything was fine. Looking back now, I can see how I'd convinced myself everything was okay with the relationship when in fact it was anything but. The more time that passed, the more determined I was to ignore the signs. All of them were there but I point-blank refused to acknowledge them. I would've made a great attendant on the *Titanic*. I would've had those deck chairs repainted and handed around drinks and conducted the brass band to boot.'

'So how did you find the courage to leave?'

'Here's what I'm really ashamed about,' Emily said. 'I didn't find the courage. Not really. It was only when I found Daniel in bed with his lover when I came home unexpectedly from work one day, I realised I had to finally face up to what was right in front of me. He begged me to stay in the relationship to keep his cover for his parents. He even said we could have kids and the dog I've always wanted as long as I kept his secret. I was angry at first but then I felt so sorry for him. I knew his parents well and I knew exactly what would happen if he came out to them.'

Loukas's forehead was still deeply furrowed. 'You surely weren't going to stay with him after that?'

She pulled at her lip with her teeth. 'I thought about it for a day or two. It was so hard, because I actually loved him, and I truly believe he loved me in his way. But I ended things and moved out and within a few weeks he finally told his parents.'

'How did they take it?'

Emily let out another sigh. 'They haven't quite disowned him but they refuse to accept he's gay. They think it's a stage he's going through or something. They even blamed me for turning him to "the other side". I got the most horrible phone call from his mother accusing me of being such a rubbish partner he had no choice but to look elsewhere for comfort. They refuse to meet his partner, Tim, and they'll only see Daniel if he comes to the house alone. It's terribly sad.'

He touched her face again, his expression suddenly wistful. 'You're a good person, Emily.'

'So are you,' Emily said, holding his gaze.

A shadow moved through Loukas's eyes before he gently moved her aside to vacate the bed. He picked up his trousers and, stepping back into them, zipped them with a sound that sounded suspiciously to Emily like a punctuation mark.

'Let me guess,' she said, sitting upright. 'You have some urgent work to see to?'

A frown flickered over his forehead. 'Emily...' His voice had that note of reproof in it that made her feel like a child who had overstepped the mark. 'You don't understand...'

'I understand more than you give me credit for,' she said. 'I know how guilty you must feel. I can't imagine how painful it must be to—'

'Do you?' he asked, eyes glittering. 'Do you really know what it's like to ruin someone's life and never be able to do anything to fix it?'

Emily swallowed a tight lump as big as a pineapple. 'You can't fix it, but you're not going to help your sister or your mother by keeping your distance. They love you, Loukas. They want to be connected to you, but you seem to prefer to keep them at arm's length. They shouldn't have left this afternoon. They shouldn't have felt they had to go. They shouldn't have had to ask if you wanted them at your wedding. You should've insisted they stay for the rest of the weekend at the very least.'

He dragged a hand down the length of his face, the sound of his palm against his stubble overly loud in the silence. 'When I got back to the villa from a walk they'd already left. Chrystanthe informed me the butler from the cruise had collected them moments earlier.'

'But would you have asked them to stay?'

He let out a long stream of air. 'No, probably not.'

Emily got off the bed and, without bothering to cover herself, came up close to wrap her arms around his waist. She craned her neck to look up at him.

'Perhaps we can ask them to stay a few days before the wedding so I can get to know them better, plus get Ariana's dress sorted. Would you mind?'

His arms came around her to hold her closer. 'It's impossible to deny you anything when you stand naked in front of me. But then, I guess you know that, don't you?'

Emily gave him an impish smile and lifted her mouth to his descending one. 'I was counting on it.'

# CHAPTER SEVEN

WHEN EMILY CAME DOWNSTAIRS the following morning, Loukas had already been up for several hours. He had left her to lie in bed, giving her tea and toast and making her promise to rest as long as she wanted. She found him in his study, working at his computer, but he pushed his chair back when she walked in and came over to take both her hands in a gentle hold. 'How are you feeling?'

'Pretty good, actually,' she said. 'I think having that tea and toast first thing really helped.'

He gave her hands a tiny squeeze, his expression guarded. 'Emily, I've made an appointment with my lawyer to see to a pre-nuptial agreement. He'll be here in an hour.'

Emily rolled her lips together, her gaze slipping out of reach of his. A pre-nuptial reminded her of how everything was different about their relationship. She knew it was an insurance policy, and it made sound financial sense for him to insist on one, as it would for any person in a couple who had independent wealth or assets they wanted to protect.

But it was an unnerving reminder of the step she was taking—a step that was a long way from her dream of happy-ever-after. 'Fine. That's good. Makes sense to get things on the level from the get-go.'

He lifted her chin with the tip of his finger. 'I know how that must make you feel, but I will be very generous in the event of a divorce.'

'Don't you mean *when* we divorce?'

His mouth tightened for a brief moment and his hand fell back by his side. 'It would be wrong of me to expect you to stay with me indefinitely. It's not what either of us want.'

*But what if I do want it?*

*Uh-oh. I knew this was going to happen.*

*What?*

*You're falling in love with him.*

Emily pushed away the thought as if she were shoving something to the back of her wardrobe. She would sort it out later. Much later. Of course she wasn't in love with him. How could she be? Just because they had smoking-hot sex didn't mean they were Mr and Mrs Happy Ever After. It meant they had awesome chemistry—that was all. 'Right, of course,' she said. 'But it just sounds a little weird to be going into marriage with the idea of a divorce being a given rather than a possibility.'

'There is no need for our divorce to be anything but civil and entirely mutual.'

He made it sound so polite and clinical. How far away from her dream of a fairy-tale relationship was this heading? But she had to remember the baby.

She was only agreeing to this because of the child they had made together. She owed it to their baby at least to give Loukas a chance to be a present and actively engaged father. She had seen too many fathers distanced from their children in messy break-ups. Even the most devoted fathers were often thwarted by custodial arrangements in the event of a separation or divorce. This way she could give Loukas a chance to build a solid relationship with their child, but she wouldn't be tying either herself or Loukas down indefinitely.

His phone rang in his pocket and he fished it out, mouthed, 'Excuse me,' and answered it. He spoke in fluent Greek and she listened with one ear while her gaze drifted to his immaculately tidy desk. Unlike hers, which always looked like a child with a temper tantrum had taken to it. She was close enough to see what was open on his computer screen. Her heart gave a funny little skip. It was a popular and informative pregnancy site she had looked at herself. It touched her that he was showing an interest in the development of their baby. It was easy for fathers to feel shunted aside by the process of pregnancy and childbirth but he obviously wanted to equip himself with as much knowledge as he could.

Loukas put away his phone. 'Sorry about that. I was waiting on an important call.'

Emily pointed to the screen. 'Have you found that site helpful?'

His expression was too inscrutable to be described

as sheepish but she couldn't help feeling he'd been caught a little off-guard. 'Yes and no.'

Emily frowned. She had found it the most helpful of all the sites she'd checked. 'Why no?'

He looked as though he was trying to swallow something too big for his oesophagus. 'Things can go wrong during pregnancy.'

'Like miscarriage?'

His eyes flinched, as if blinking away a horrible thought. 'Women still die in childbirth. It might be not as common as a hundred years ago but it does still happen.'

Emily wondered what had triggered him looking at the website. Was it concern for *her*, rather than interest in the baby's development? 'Why did you look at the website?'

His face got that boxed-up look about it she had come to know so well. 'It has been a long time since I sat in a Sex Ed class.'

She fought back a smile. 'Me too. I don't think I heard anything about morning sickness and extreme fatigue. I just remember condoms and courgettes and squirming with embarrassment at the snickering boys.'

A smile tilted his mouth, transforming his features and bringing life to his eyes. But then a shadow passed over Loukas's face, dimming his gaze. 'Are you worried about what could happen to you?'

'Well, I guess I'm not so keen on getting stretch marks.'

He was still frowning in that I'm-being-serious-

and-this-is-no-time-for-jokes manner. 'I read about a condition where the amniotic fluid leaks into the mother's bloodstream and it's virtually always fatal. Then there's post-partum haemorrhage. A mother can bleed out in minutes if help isn't available.'

'I'm not going to die, Loukas,' Emily said, in a joint effort to reassure herself as well as him. She had skated over the risks section on the site. Her image of childbirth was a pink-faced, bunny-rug-wrapped infant in an exhausted but blissful mother's arms with a doting husband and father present. Nowhere in her imaginings had there been any emergency blood transfusions, crash trolleys and panic-stricken doctors.

Loukas didn't look all that convinced. 'And the risks actually escalate if it's a twin birth.'

Emily laughed. 'Will you stop it? It's bad enough accidentally falling pregnant with one baby, let alone two.'

A beat of silence passed.

'Give me your hand,' she said.

Loukas held it out and Emily placed it on her tummy, which was a little podgy for someone who was only a month into a pregnancy. But, given she was a comfort eater from way back, that was not so surprising. A family block of fruit and nut chocolate had to go somewhere and her tummy seemed to be where it had chosen. 'In a couple of months you'll be able to feel knees and elbows wriggling around in there.'

A look of awe passed over his face. 'Can you feel anything yet?'

'No, it's way too early,' she said. 'It's weird to think a new life is in there getting its act together, isn't it?'

He removed his hand after a long moment. 'We should discuss names at some point. And if we want to know the sex of the baby before it's born. Would you like to know?'

'Would you?'

'You can make the decision, Emily. You're the one doing all the hard work, so surely you deserve that privilege.'

She gave him a rueful look. 'I used to think I'd want to be surprised when it's born, but I figure you're a little over surprises, right?'

One corner of his mouth twitched. 'You can say that again.'

The lawyer arrived a short time later and the business of the pre-nuptial agreement was over soon after. As if to soften the blow, Loukas took Emily for a short walk through an olive grove to have a picnic in a secluded cove not far from his villa. The fringe of cypress pines provided some much-needed shade from the intensely hot sun, and she sat on the rug he'd laid down on the sand and looked longingly at the view of the sparkling ocean just metres away.

'I wish I'd brought bathers,' Emily said when he came down beside her on the rug. 'I was in such a mad dash to pack the other night, I didn't think to put some in.'

'You won't need them here,' Loukas said. 'I own this cove and it's completely hidden from the top of the cliff. The nearest road is at least three kilometres away.'

She turned to peer over her shoulder at the cliff path they'd come down, as if expecting to see a cluster of paparazzi with long-range lenses. 'Are you sure?'

He slid a warm hand down from the middle of her shoulder blades to the dip in her spine, making every muscle in her body sigh with pleasure. 'I've swum down here heaps of times.'

'Naked?'

'Yes.'

'Alone or with someone?'

He picked up a small twig off the rug and tossed it onto the sand near his crossed ankles. 'Alone. I haven't brought anyone down here with me before you.'

Emily glanced at him but he was staring at the twig he'd tossed with a part-frown on his face. 'Why did you bring me?'

He turned his head to look at her, his expression difficult to read. 'How about that swim? Do you want to have lunch or cool off first?'

Emily chewed at her lip. 'I've never swum naked before. What if something bites me? And I have to take my contacts out, unless you happen to have a pair of swimming goggles handy.'

He rummaged in the bag where he'd packed towels and sunscreen and handed her a pair of blue goggles. *'Voilà.'*

\* \* \*

Loukas walked hand in hand with Emily to the water, making sure she didn't lose her footing on the hot sand. She kept grinning up at him like a kid who had been given permission to do something that was decidedly wicked. 'Are you absolutely sure no one can see me? Scout's honour?'

He gave her hand a gentle squeeze. 'You're perfectly safe with me.' As soon as he said the words, his gut clenched. Was she safe? He had made sure she stayed in bed and rested that morning because he'd read on that website how pregnancy nausea hit hard first thing on an empty stomach. That wretched website was giving him nightmares. So much could go wrong when a woman was pregnant. He had gone online out of curiosity about the process of pregnancy...or so he'd told himself. It was only after he realised how obsessed he was becoming that he understood it had more to do with Emily than with the baby. The baby was important to him in a distant sense, but Emily was present, and had such a potent effect on his senses. Not just his senses. That was the scary part. He was developing a thing about her.

*What the hell was a thing?*

He had never felt this way before. He kept putting it down to the fact she was pregnant but he couldn't help feeling it was more than that. He genuinely liked her. She made him smile. Who had ever done that to him before? She was fresh and honest and didn't live on the surface of life, like some of the women he'd dated. She dug deeper. A little too deep for his liking, but in a way it had been a relief to tell her about the accident. Telling her hadn't eased his guilt but it had eased his burden. Someone else knew what he felt. Empathised with him.

He had been careful how he'd broached the subject of the pre-nup because he hadn't wanted to upset her. He had never brought anyone down to his cove before because it was his private sanctuary, but it seemed fitting to share it with Emily and their developing child. He'd had some qualms about her walking down the cliff path but she had done it without even drawing breath. The sun was scorching, and her skin was a lot lighter than his, but he'd lathered her with sunscreen and only just stopped himself from making love to her on the rug because she was feeling so hot.

That was another thing he'd read about pregnancy—the mother shouldn't let her core body temperature get too high because it could harm the baby.

*The baby.*

Every time he thought of those two words he would start to imagine their child. Would it look like him? Would it be a girl or boy? Emily wouldn't show for weeks, if not months, but he couldn't help wondering what it would be like to see their baby on an ultrasound. Would that make it seem more real to see those tiny developing limbs and body? That tiny heartbeat? He wondered what it would be like to see his child born. To hear that first cry. To hold it in his arms for the first time.

What sort of father would he be?

Loukas hadn't expected to feel anything for the baby at this stage and yet, the more he thought about that tiny developing body, the more he got a warm feeling in his chest.

Almost as warm as the feeling he got when he thought of Emily…

Emily smiled up at him once they were waist-deep in the water. 'You can let me go now. I won't fall over.'

'In a minute.' He brought her closer so her body was slick and cool and wet as a seal's against his. 'There's something I want to do first.' He pressed his mouth to hers and she gave a soft whimper of pleasure—the same little whimper that had wreaked such havoc on his control the night of the wedding. Her mouth was like a flower opening, soft and fragrant, and sweet as nectar. Her tongue shyly met his and then became bolder as he deepened the kiss. He held her by the hips, holding against the pounding heat of his body, wanting her so badly it was an ache that dragged at his flesh. She pushed herself even closer, her arms going around his neck, her fingers tugging and releasing his hair as her mouth stayed fused to his.

After a long, blissful moment, he moved his mouth from hers to kiss a pathway down the side of her neck, to the spot below her earlobe that never failed to get a breathless gasp out of her. He used the tip of his tongue around the shell of her ear, tracing the delicate whorls, until she turned her head to press her mouth back to his in a hungry 'I want you' kiss that made the blood roar through his veins like a freight train. She reached for him, her soft little hands massaging and stroking him before she brought him to her entrance, raising herself on tiptoes to give him access.

He needed no other invitation.

Loukas was inside her with a thrust that made every hair on his head tingle, her body clutching at him, rippling around him as tight as a fist. She moved with him, her little moans and gasps spurring him on, ramping up his desire until he was fighting not to lose control before he made sure she was satisfied. He slipped one of his hands beneath the water to find the heart of her, taking her over the edge with a few strokes of his fingers. She came apart around him, her body convulsing with pleasure that triggered his own.

The sun beating down on his back, the cool water lapping at their bodies and Emily's gasping cries of ecstasy brought to the experience an earthy, elemental quality he had never experienced before.

She gave a long, shuddering sigh and met his gaze with a sparkling look. 'Wow. Swimming has never been so much fun before.'

Loukas gave a soft laugh and brushed a droplet of seawater away from her cheek. 'Likewise.'

She planted her hands on his chest, her lower body snug against his, her toffee-brown eyes luminous. 'Do you know, that's the first time I've ever heard you laugh?'

He had never felt like laughing before he met her.

She was a fun person to be around with her sunny, optimistic disposition. When he was around her, he felt alive in a way he hadn't in years. He looked forward to being with her. Wasn't that why he'd sought her out in London? He'd wanted to feel that kick in his blood, that spring in his step, and that fire in his belly that he only got when she was near. He looked down at the soft bow of her mouth and gave a crooked smile. 'Maybe there's some hope for me after all.'

# CHAPTER EIGHT

EMILY SPENT THE next few days with Loukas, looking at some of the sites on Corfu. At first he wasn't keen on the idea of going to the most popular tourist places, in case they were spotted by members of the press or public, but Emily was keen to see more of the beautiful island he called home. They had lunch each day in quaint little restaurants or cafés and wandered around the ancient streets, archaeological museums, art galleries and churches, such as the spectacular Church of St Sypridion. There was a visit to the magnificent Mount Pantokrator, the highest mountain on the island.

After they came back from the mountain, Emily spied an antique shop in the Old Town. 'Can I have a look in there?'

'Sure.'

She walked in and smelt the passage of time. Lots of time. Whole centuries of it. She browsed through the shop, stopping to pick up pieces that snared her interest. While Loukas was occupied with a phone call, she caught sight of a faded blue velvet jewellery box sitting on a shelf next to a collection of early Greek coins. The box was probably more trash than treasure, but Emily couldn't help thinking of the woman or women who had stored their jewellery in it. It had a lock but no key, and when she opened the lid she felt sure she could smell history. She closed the lid and put it back on the shelf. It wasn't expensive at all but she didn't have her purse with her and she couldn't imagine Loukas buying something so unsophisticated.

'So why did you choose to live on Corfu?' Emily asked over coffee a little while later. 'You're not originally from here, are you?'

Loukas stirred his coffee even though she knew he didn't take sugar. 'No, but I liked it from the first time I came here as a kid on a holiday with my parents before they divorced.'

'Were they ever happy together?'

His mouth turned down at the corners. 'No. My father wasn't ready for marriage—he still isn't, to be frank. But it's a long-held custom in Greece that gaining parental blessing of your marriage partner is essential to a happy union. My father's parents knew my mother and stated their approval.'

'So it was an arranged marriage?'

'Strictly speaking, no. He let my mother think he was in love and then, once he had a wedding ring on her finger and got his parents off his back, he had affair after affair with other women.'

Emily frowned. 'But she loved him?'

He gave her a grim look. 'Not for long. But it took

years for her to convince him to give her a divorce. He didn't want his parents to think it was his fault, of course, so he cooked up a whole lot of lies and made her life a miserable hell.'

'And yours too, by the sound of it,' Emily said. 'Do you see much of him these days?'

He pushed his coffee away. 'No. I limit my contact to cards at Christmas and for his birthday.'

'What about Father's Day?'

He gave her a speaking look. 'I never seem to be able to find one that has the most fitting message. "You're a terrible father" isn't usually available.'

Emily couldn't help a giggle escaping. 'And here I was thinking my mother was bad. She's not, by the way. Annoying at times, but definitely not bad.' She frowned and went on. 'I hope she doesn't embarrass you at the wedding. You don't mind if she comes, do you? I know you said it's a quiet ceremony, and to be perfectly honest there is nothing about my mother that's quiet, but I'd like her to be there.'

His mouth slanted in one of his rare smiles. 'Of course she must come.'

Emily played with her teaspoon for a moment. 'Thing is…my mum is a bit of a detective when it comes to relationships. She reckons she can tell at twenty paces if a couple are well suited or not. Apparently, it's all in their body language or something.'

His long, tanned fingers reached for hers, sending a warm tide of longing straight to her core when he stroked the fleshy part of her palm in slow, tantalising circles. 'It kind of makes sense when you think about it.'

She looked at his hand and a frisson went through her at the thought of what magic those fingers could make her feel. 'I told her we're in love. I had to, otherwise she would've gone ballistic about throwing my life away on another dead-end relationship.'

His fingers stalled their movement for a brief second. 'Are you worried about lying to her?'

'Yes. No. Maybe.'

*I'm more worried about lying to myself.*

He gave her hand a light pat and then sat back in his chair, signalling to the waitress for the bill. 'Come on. It's time we got you out of this sun before you melt.'

*I melted a month ago, when you first kissed me.*

Emily was waking from a rest a couple of days later when Loukas came in with a silver-wrapped rectangular package tied with a black ribbon in his hand. He sat on the edge of the bed next to her and handed it to her. 'Remember that antique shop we visited the other day?' he asked. 'I went back to get this for you.'

She took the package and unwrapped it to find the faded antique jewellery box she had admired. She hadn't realised Loukas had even seen her looking at it, as he'd been on the phone to one of his clients while she'd been browsing the shop. It touched her he'd not only noticed but gone back to purchase it for her. Not that it was expensive. It was probably worth less than the price tag stated, but the fact he'd noticed she'd been taken with it moved her deeply. 'Oh, how sweet of you,' she said, stroking the velvet.

'Open it.'

Emily lifted the lid to find two sets of earrings inside: a set of creamy pearl droplets and two winking diamond studs. She didn't need to see any price tags to know they were hideously expensive. 'Oh, they're so beautiful!' She picked up the droplet earrings and draped them over her fingers. Then she picked up the diamond studs and turned them to allow the light to catch their brilliance. She glanced at Loukas, suddenly feeling shy. 'You're too generous. They look terribly expensive.'

'You said you kept losing your jewellery, so I figured the box will help you keep it safe,' he said. 'It has a lock and a tiny key. See?' He pointed to the miniature lock on the base of the box. 'The original key was missing but I've had another one made up.' He fished in his shirt pocket and, taking out a miniscule key, placed it in the centre of her palm and closed her fingers over it to keep it secure.

Emily met his gaze, wondering if he would ever hand her the key to his heart for safekeeping. 'I don't know what to say, other than thank you. No one has ever given me such gorgeous things before.'

'Then it's time someone did.' He brought her hand up to his mouth and pressed a soft kiss to it, holding her eyes with the dark intensity of his.

Emily placed the key next to the jewellery box and then tiptoed her fingers along his lean jaw. 'I've never met anyone like you before.'

*Argh! Don't do this!*

*I have to. I can't deny it any longer. I love him.*

*Don't say I didn't warn you.*

Something flickered through his eyes, like a lightning flash of regret. Then he gave a slow blink, as if preparing to deliver an unpleasant lecture. 'Emily...'

She put a finger over his mouth as if she were pressing a pause button. 'No. Please don't say it. I can't help feeling the way I feel. I love you.'

Loukas let out a long sigh and took her hand away from his face. 'Look, the gifts are just gifts, okay? They don't mean anything.'

Emily refused to believe it. The jewellery box might be worth nothing but the earrings, as well as the engagement ring, were worth more than she earned in a year. *Two* years. How could he say they didn't mean anything? 'Do you buy everyone you sleep with gifts?'

He got up from the bed to stand a few feet away, his eyes so masked they were like the boarded-up windows of a deserted building. 'Yes.'

Her heart shrank away from her chest wall as if it had been punched. 'So...you're saying I'm nothing special?'

He closed his eyes and leaned his head right back, as if searching the heavens for guidance. Then he let out a long breath and returned his gaze to hers. 'No. I'm not saying that. You're incredibly special.'

'But you don't love me.'

He came back to the bed and sat beside her again. He took her nearest hand and held it in his. Her cut finger had recently healed but now a new wound was opening up inside her heart and it was a thousand times more painful. 'I'm not sure I'm capable of feeling that way about anyone.' He gave her hand a gentle press, the set of his mouth rueful. 'I know it's a cliché, but it's not you, it's me.'

Emily looked down at their joined hands. Why had she blurted out her feelings like that? What had it achieved? A big, fat nothing. She'd made a fool of herself yet again. When would she ever learn?

*Told you so.*

What was she doing, settling for a relationship that was less than perfect? How could she marry him, in the vain hope he might change at some point in the future? He was only marrying her out of duty, not because he loved her. He desired her, but how long would that last? How long before he called time on their marriage? She would have to live with the threat of it ending instead of the joy of building up a long and lasting relationship together. That wasn't what she'd planned for her life. She wanted to be loved for who she was, treasured and adored the way she had dreamed of for so long. Having a family was supposed to be born out of enduring love. How could she bring a child into a relationship that wasn't based on mutual love?

Emily pulled out of his hold and got off the bed. 'I'm sorry, Loukas, but I can't go on with this a moment longer.'

A frown made a map of lines across his forehead. 'What are you talking about?'

She met his gaze head-on. 'This marriage you're proposing. I'm not comfortable with it. Not any of it. I don't care if it's a small ceremony or a big one. I don't care if no one is there, or every relative and person we know and half of Greece is there. The one thing that should be there and won't be is your love for me.'

He made to reach out to her but she held up her hand like a stop sign. 'No. Don't try and talk me out of it. You're the one who talked me into this ridiculous plan in the first place. I should never have agreed to it. I'm going back to London. Our engagement is over.'

A muscle clenched at the side of his mouth as if he was trying to control an involuntary tic. 'This is crazy. You're not thinking straight—'

'That's exactly what I *am* doing,' Emily said. 'I'm thinking how wrong it is to bring a child into a relationship that has a clock ticking on it. Who *does* that? It's not what I want for my life. I want the fairy-tale; I'm not ashamed of wanting it, either. It's what most people want—to be loved. I stayed in a loveless relationship for seven years. Every one of those years I lived in hope, wishing things would get better, but they never did. I can't afford to give up any more of my life to a relationship that isn't working for me.'

'I told you from the start what I was prepared to give you,' he said. 'I haven't made promises or pretended things I don't feel. I want to be involved in my child's life. I don't want my child to be punished because of my mistake.'

That was how he saw his relationship with her—as a mistake. Loukas had offered her a one-night fling and it had come with consequences. Consequences he had been prepared to take responsibility for but with conditions she couldn't accept. Not now she loved him. She knew he felt wretchedly guilty about the accident, but it didn't mean he had to punish himself for the rest of his life, denying himself normal human feelings in a quest to right the wrongs of the past. Who had control over love anyway? It happened no matter what you did to avoid it. She hadn't expected to fall in love with him, it had crept up on her. Each kiss, each touch, each time he made love to her, the feelings had blossomed and grown until she could no longer ignore them.

Emily shook her head at him. 'That's the kicker right there. You see me as a mistake. That's how you see our baby. An accident you're now dutifully dealing with, just like you dutifully deal with your mother and sister. I don't want to be dealt with dutifully, Loukas, I want to be dealt with devotedly. I deserve it and so do you.'

His expression was as stony as one of the ancient walls of the Old Town they had walked past a few days ago. 'You say you love me, so why are you leaving?'

'Because in the long run it will hurt you if I stay,' Emily said. 'It will hurt me and it will hurt our baby too. I won't stop you being involved. You can come to the twelve-week scan, if you like, and of course the birth, if you want to.'

His hands were shoved in his trouser pockets as if he was determined not to touch her, although she sensed there was a struggle going on inside him, for a tiny muscle in his jaw was working overtime. 'What about the press? They'll hound you for a statement.'

Emily started packing her things but her hands wouldn't seem to co-operate. She couldn't fold a thing but had to scrunch her clothes into creased balls. She would not cry. She would not cry. She *must* not cry. The tears welled in her eyes but she stoically blinked them away. Her chest ached as though someone had wrenched apart her ribcage and torn out her heart but she continued to snatch her belongings from wherever she had last left them: her watch from the bedside table. Her phone charger from the power point next to the bed. Her make-up bag from the bathroom. She worked like an automaton—a robot programmed to complete a task. But inside she wanted to throw herself to the ground like a hysterical child and pummel the floor with her hands and heels.

*Why don't you love me? Why? Why? Why?*

'I would never say anything bad about you,' she said at last. 'I'll simply tell them the truth. I've changed my mind about marrying you, but we will be co-parenting our child, and look forward to its birth, like any other parents.'

'Leave that,' he said, jerking his head towards the things she'd thrown in a jumble on the bed. 'I'll get Chrystanthe to pack them for you.'

She looked at the pile of clothes and the jewellery he'd given her and swallowed a thick knot in her throat. 'I can leave the jewellery and the box. You might like to give it to someone—'

'Take it,' he said, turning away as if it no longer concerned him what she did.

In the end she took the box but not the jewellery. She left the ring and earrings on the bedside table, locked the box with the little key to keep the lid secure and slipped it into her handbag while he had his back turned to her.

'I need to get a flight,' Emily said, brushing her hair back with her hand, suddenly a little overwhelmed at what she was doing. This was the problem with not being single for so long. You didn't know how to do stuff any more. When was the last time she had booked a flight for herself? Daniel had always done the flights when they'd gone anywhere. It had been his job, just as it had been his job to take out the garbage and empty the dishwasher. Even the flight to Allegra's wedding had been booked for her by Draco. She fought down the panic.

*Breathe. Breathe. Breathe. You can do this.*

She glanced at Loukas and saw he already had his phone out. What did that mean? That he was keen to see her go?

'I'll book you a flight,' he said in a curt, business-like voice, which she took as a sign she was doing the right thing by leaving. If he loved her he would have been on his knees begging her to stay. He would have been smothering her with kisses and caresses, telling her he couldn't live without her. He certainly wouldn't be whipping out his phone to book her on the next available flight.

She kept her expression composed but inside she was screaming, *Don't let me leave!*

Emily didn't get the chance to say goodbye to Chrystanthe because it was the housekeeper's night off. She scribbled a short note, thanking her for everything, and left it propped on the kitchen counter while Loukas carried her bag out to the car.

The drive to the airport was painfully silent.

Even to the point where Loukas helped her check in to the private jet he'd organised, she hoped he would say something. Anything. But it was as if he was seeing to the departure of an acquaintance. He didn't touch her. He barely even looked at her and, when he did, his expression was as locked down as hers.

When it was time to board, she held out her hand but he coldly ignored it. 'Really?' he said with a cutting edge to his voice.

Emily dropped her hand along with the last of her hopes. Her heart was so heavy it felt as though it were towing the jet she was about to board. Couldn't they at least part as friends? How were they supposed to be parents of their child if they could barely speak to each other? 'I'll let you know the date of the scan.'

'Fine.'

She searched his face for a sign that he was finding this as difficult as she was but there was nothing there. It was as if he had wiped every emotion from the hard drive of his personality. There wasn't even a flicker on the screen of his face. 'Goodbye, Loukas.'

He didn't answer.

Emily turned and walked down the boarding corridor, but when she glanced back for one last look at him he had already gone.

Loukas walked out of the airport before he created a scene. Anger, disappointment and some other nameless emotion were boiling inside him in a toxic mix the like of which he had never quite experienced before. The sense of powerless was overwhelming. He wanted to pick Emily up and carry her fireman-style back to his villa—to give her no choice but to stay with him. He could be ruthless when he needed to be, but her confession of love had stunned him.

Why had she had to throw *that* in the mix? Surely it was just fanciful on her part? Good sex did that to women. To be fair, it did it to men too. But just because the sex was great didn't mean he was in love with her. He had never been in love with anyone. Her confession shouldn't have surprised him so much. She was an affectionate and giving person. Loving came naturally to her. She didn't have to think about it. Guard against it. Block it. It wasn't that he wasn't capable of love. He loved his mother, his sister and his friends but in a remote and hands-off way. Getting close to someone didn't come naturally to him. Maybe it was the way his personality was wired, or maybe it was because of the trauma he'd gone through with his parents' acrimonious divorce and custody battle, not to mention the harrowing guilt he felt over the accident with his sister.

Loving someone scared the hell out of him.

It scared him to be that vulnerable. The odds of losing someone escalated the more you cared about them. The odds of hurting them were even worse.

He remembered how he used to lie in bed at night as a small child listening to his parents argue bitterly. The sense of insecurity had been sickening but he had always comforted himself that no way would his mother ever leave him. His father, yes, but never his mother.

He still remembered the day when his father had taken him roughly by the hand and all but dragged him to the waiting car. Loukas had fought against the tears, not wanting to make it any worse for his distraught mother but, more importantly, not wanting to let his father know how upset he was at leaving his mother behind. His father would have enjoyed that too much. He would have relished in the pain and suffering he was inflicting. Loukas had schooled his features into a mask, just as he had done just now with Emily. But he could still picture his mother running after the car, her hands reaching out to him, her hair flying in disarray about her tear-ravaged face.

Such intense emotion had terrified him then and it terrified him now. He sought refuge in anger because anger was something he could control. He could lock it down and tie it up like a wild animal. He could wait it out. Let it cool off before he looked at it again.

What had Emily been thinking, offering her hand

to him like some mild acquaintance? They'd had smoking-hot sex together. They'd made a baby together, for God's sake. How dared she reduce their relationship to an impersonal press of hands at a gate lounge? She had no right to do this when he'd offered her more than he'd offered anyone.

He didn't want to hurt her but how could he pretend to feel things he had never felt for anyone? That was why he had given her the get-out option on their marriage. He had never promised her 'for ever'.

He wasn't that person. He could never be that person.

He wondered now if he ever had been.

# CHAPTER NINE

EMILY HAD BEEN back in London a week when the doorbell rang. Her heart leapt as if it were bouncing off a trampoline. Could it be Loukas? Had he changed his mind? Did he love her after all? She had heard nothing from him other than a brief text to make sure she'd got home safely. She had thought about texting him, especially since she couldn't find the little key to the jewellery box, but she didn't want him to think she was using it as an excuse to contact him. The key probably had been lost at the security checkpoint at the airport or when she'd dug out tissue after tissue from her bag on the flight home.

But in a way the box symbolised her despair over Loukas's inability to love her. His heart was as locked as that box. Day after day had gone by and she had watched her phone with bated breath, hoping the next time it rang it would be him. But he never called.

She rushed to the front door of her flat but her heart sank to her feet when she opened it. 'Oh... Mum...I can't talk right now...'

'I just got back from my eight-day yoga retreat and turned on my phone to read your engagement's been called off! What's going on?'

Emily found it hard enough dealing with everyone else's disappointment, let alone her own, so she had only sent the text the day before because she hadn't wanted her mother to counsel her as if she were one of her clients. She had told Allegra about her decision to leave Loukas as soon as she'd got back home and, while Allegra was concerned and sad for her, she knew Loukas well enough to know it was pointless hoping he might change.

She couldn't stop her bottom lip from trembling. 'Oh, Mum. My life is such a terrible mess.'

Her mother stepped inside and closed the door then, after a brief hesitation, held her arms out. 'Tell me everything.'

Emily stepped into her mother's hug that for some reason didn't feel as stiff and awkward as normal. She sobbed her way through the story of the last few days. 'He was only offering to marry me out of a sense of duty. But I love him. How could I marry him, knowing he doesn't love me back?'

Her mother patted her back and made soothing, cooing noises as though she were settling a fractious baby. 'You can't. You did the right thing in putting an end to it.'

They moved to sit together on the sofa and her mother kept handing her a steady supply of tissues. 'It'll be okay, poppet. You'll get through it.'

'But I'm so unhappy!'

'I know, I felt like that when I broke up with my fiancé. I literally wanted to die.'

Emily lifted her head out of her hands to stare at her mother. 'Your fiancé? When were you engaged?'

Her mother gave her a sad, twisted little smile. 'It was a couple of months before I went to the music festival. His name was Mark. We were madly, passionately in love—or at least, I was. He clearly wasn't. We were getting married but then he broke it off a week before the wedding. He married another girl a few weeks later. She was from money—heaps of money. I didn't take it well. I kind of…lost myself there for a while.'

She let out a long sigh. 'Drugs, sex, rock and roll—you name it. But then, getting pregnant with you turned my life around. Sort of.' She squeezed Emily's hand. 'I know I'm not the best mother in the world. But after Mark broke my heart I couldn't settle to anything for long. I lived with a constant fear of it being snatched away from me. So I became the one who moved on before someone could do that to me again. I even kept you at arm's length because I was frightened I might lose you too.'

'Oh, Mum.' Emily hugged her mother close. 'I had no idea. Why didn't you tell me about him before now?'

Her mother eased back to look at her. 'I was ashamed of being such a naïve fool over him. How could I have not known he was not as invested in the relationship as me? One minute we were planning the wedding, and then the next I was calling everyone to say it was off. It was the most embarrassing thing, having to hand back all those presents. For years I only had to look at a wedding dress and I'd want to throw up. It infuriated me that I hadn't seen what was right before my eyes. That's why I was so worried about you and Daniel. I could sense he wasn't the one for you. I want you to be happy. I want you to have the "for ever" love I can't seem to find no matter how hard I try.'

Emily frowned. 'But I thought you were happy with your footloose and fancy-free lifestyle?'

Her mother let out a puff of air. 'Why do you think I teach all this couples' intimacy stuff? Because I'm rubbish at it in my personal life.'

Emily's shoulders drooped. 'Yeah, well, it seems I'm not too great at it, either.'

'So the sex wasn't good?'

She couldn't believe she was discussing her sex life with her mother. 'No, it was amazing. It was the one thing we were good at—better than good. Perfect.'

Her mother shifted her lips from side to side in a thoughtful manner. 'If only I'd met him and seen him with you I could have told you for sure if he was the one for you. Body language doesn't lie.'

'I already know he's the one for me,' Emily said, taking another tissue and sighing deeply. 'Thing is, he doesn't think he's the right one for anyone.'

*Six weeks later...*

Loukas was glad his work called him away to the States for a few weeks because he was sick to death of his housekeeper casting him How-could-you-have-let-her-go? looks that grated on his nerves like a file on a bad tooth. He was doing his best not to think about Emily so he didn't appreciate Chrystanthe reminding him at every opportunity that he hadn't gone after her.

What would have been the point? She had made up her mind. He would only be lying to her if he got her back by telling her what she wanted to hear. That was the sort of thing his father would do. She had made her decision and he had to respect it. At least she was allowing him access to his child, but it stung a little that he wasn't there twenty-four-seven so he could see the changes in her body as the baby grew. Was she still nauseous? Did she still feel faint? What if she was sick and needed help? Who would she call? She didn't seem all that close to her mother, in spite of her words to the contrary.

He had thought about calling or texting but he hadn't trusted himself not to plead with her to come back. He wasn't the sort of man to beg. That was a lesson he'd learned a long time ago. He'd once begged his father to take him back to his mother. He'd been sent to his room and only allowed out once he'd apologised for being ungrateful. He had stayed in his room for two weeks, only coming out for meals and bathroom visits. His begging had given his father even more power over him and he had sworn he would never allow anyone to do that to him again.

But it wasn't just his housekeeper on his back. Draco and Allegra had been at him as well. He'd told them to back off. He was in London to see Emily at the twelve-week scan today, and that was all he was prepared to do in terms of contact before the scan. The press had noted he and Emily were currently living apart, but apparently they had other much more scandalous couples to follow now, and had left both of them alone.

The only people who hadn't said anything to him were his mother and sister. A month ago that wouldn't have been all that unusual. Sometimes several months went by without any contact from them. But, since they knew of Emily's pregnancy and his intention to marry her, why hadn't they contacted him and offered commiserations at the very least? It said a lot about his relationship with them. They were as distant with him as he was with them.

Or was it because Ariana was disappointed she wasn't going to be a bridesmaid after all? His sister's one chance of being part of a bridal party and he had ruined it. Or maybe they had sided with Emily since they had met her and seen her warm and generous personality for themselves.

He could hardly blame them for shifting loyalties. How could they not prefer her to him? She was all he was not. She was love, laughter and hope while he was an emotionless wasteland. They would probably think she'd had a lucky escape from a loveless union with him.

*But would it have been loveless?*

The thought kept at him, catching him off-guard at odd moments. He already loved his child even though it was still only a tiny foetus. He'd been on that pregnancy website every day. It was almost like an obsession now. First thing in the morning—if he had even been to sleep, that was—he would check it out. He'd even been on a baby-name site, trawling through names, wondering whether his baby was a girl or boy. He had even been checking out baby wear and toy shops. He'd bought a hand-made teddy bear while he'd been in New York and, when the shop assistant had asked him if it was for his child, he'd been ridiculously proud to say yes.

But along with that pride was a niggling sense of disappointment Emily hadn't been with him to help him choose it. Weren't they supposed to be doing this together? Wasn't that part of the joy of welcoming a child into the world? Preparing the nursery, buying a pram and car seat, a high chair and a cot? How was he supposed to do it without her? What was the point of anything without her?

Loukas didn't like admitting it but he missed her. He missed her smile with its adorable dimples, her cute little rabbit-twitch, her soft hands and how it felt when they touched him. He couldn't imagine making love with anyone else. The thought hadn't even crossed his mind.

He only wanted her.

His gaze drifted to the tiny gold key on his hotel room's desk. He had found it on the floor by the bed after Emily had left. She must have dropped it when she stuffed the jewellery box in her handbag. She'd thought he hadn't noticed but he'd seen her in the reflection of the mirror. He couldn't understand why she had bothered taking it. He picked up the key and turned it over a couple of times. It had cost more than the silly little box. Way more. Why had she left the most expensive gifts and taken that old box that wasn't even worth the money he'd paid for it?

He put the key back on his desk, but every few minutes his gaze would go back to it. She couldn't open the box without the key and the key was useless to him without the box. He suddenly realised Emily was like that tiny, golden key. She had come into his life and picked the lock on his heart. He'd thought it was lust that had driven him to seek her out, but now he wondered if something else had been going on. Something he had never encountered before. Something that dismantled all the barriers he'd put up over the years.

It was easy to lust after someone. It took no courage at all. But loving someone was different. It opened you up to hurt, to vulnerability.

But it also opened you up to healing.

Loukas had never considered himself a coward. He had prided himself he'd always faced up to responsibility and never shirked from a task because it was unpleasant or inconvenient. But hadn't he been hiding away from love? Lacking the courage to explore the emotions he had locked down deep inside him?

Emily had found the key to him. Her bright, cheery smile had shone on all the dark, shuttered and shadowed places in his soul, illuminating him with a beam of hope for the first time in years.

His professional reputation was built on his ability to keep places, people and top level security systems secure, and yet a cute little clumsy Englishwoman had stumbled into his life and cracked his code.

He *loved* her.

Wasn't that why he had sought her out in London a month after Draco and Allegra's wedding? He hadn't been able to get her out of his mind. But it wasn't just his mind that was captivated by her.

It was his heart.

Loukas had a couple of hours until he met with her at the hospital for the scan. Should he wait till then or go and see her now? How could he wait two minutes, let alone two hours?

He could and he would, because there were things he had to do before then so that she would be absolutely convinced he loved her.

Emily had a full bladder and an empty heart when she arrived at the hospital for the scan. Her mother had offered to come with her but Emily had decided against it. She didn't trust her mother not to give Loukas an earful about his 'love' issues. Emily had texted him the time and place and he'd responded with a curt 'Thanks'. It seemed so impersonal and clinical; nothing like she expected it would be when having a child with someone she loved. She placed a hand over her abdomen. She had ballooned over the last week. Not a party balloon, either. A hot-air balloon. Surely it wasn't normal to show this much so soon? She could barely do up the top button on

her cotton trousers. Or maybe it was nerves. Maybe
it wasn't butterflies in her stomach but bats—big
spiky-winged ones, beating around in there in panic
at the thought of seeing Loukas again.

Oh, God, why had she said he could come to the
scan? Maybe she should've just sent him the photo.
No. That wouldn't be fair. He was the baby's father.
He had a right to be here if he wanted to be.

A nurse directed her to the cubicle to wait for the
sonographer. 'Is anyone going to be with you?'

'My…erm…the baby's father said he'd be here.'
Emily glanced out at the reception and waiting room
area but there was no sign yet of Loukas. Surely he
would turn up? Or had he changed his mind? He
hated hospitals, but surely he wouldn't let that get in
the way of seeing his child for the first time?

'No problem,' the nurse said. 'We'll get you set up
and then when he arrives I'll send him in.'

Emily lay on the table and waited with her hands
over her rounded belly. She hoped Loukas wouldn't
be too long otherwise her bladder was going to have
something to say about it. Where was he? She'd told
him the right time. Surely he wouldn't let her down
on this day of all days?

The plastic clock on the wall mechanically clicked
its seconds. Tick. Tick. Tick.

Laughter came from the reception area and the
sound of someone squealing with delight. 'Oh, how
cute are you two little darlings?'

Emily assumed a mother had come in with a toddler or two. She wondered if the mum had a partner,

someone who loved her as much as she loved him. She tried not to cry, but her emotions were on shaky ground as it was. This wasn't the way she'd thought it would be. She'd pictured this day when she was younger, imagining how exciting it would be to be holding hands with her partner as they met their tiny baby *in utero*. Now she was a frazzled mess of nerves because the only partner she wanted didn't love her. He liked her. He desired her. But he didn't love her. Why wasn't he here? Had he got more important things to do than meet his baby for the first time?

The curtain was suddenly swished back and Loukas came in. The cubicle had seemed spacious until he entered it. Or maybe that was because, this close to him, she ached to reach out and touch him. She curled her fingers into her palms to stop herself. She could smell the fresh citrus scent of him and longed for him to lean down and press a kiss to her mouth. 'Sorry I'm late,' he said. 'I got held up with…something.'

'Work?' She couldn't quite remove the barb in her tone in time.

His expression registered her comment with a tiny flinch near the edge of his mouth. She noted he had cut himself shaving for he had a little scratch on his cheek. But then she noticed he had two or three scratches on his hands as well.

'How are you?' He swallowed and glanced at her bulging tummy. 'Growing by the minute, by the look of things.'

'Yes, well, some of that may well be my bladder,' Emily said. 'If you make me laugh then things could get pretty awkward around here.' Not that he was likely to make her laugh any time soon. All she wanted to do was cry.

'How's the nausea?'

'A little better.'

'That's good.'

God, how stiff and formal they sounded! Like two people who had only just met and were making idle chit-chat to fill in the time. 'So, how are your mum and sister?' Emily asked. 'Have you seen them lately?'

'I haven't seen them but I spoke to them an hour ago. I thought you might like to visit them with me after this.'

She frowned. 'Why would I do that?'

The sonographer came in just then and began setting up the ultrasound equipment. A generous layer of gel was smeared over Emily's belly and the sonographer angled the screen so both Emily and Loukas could see. 'So, here we have the placental sac… Hang on a minute.' She fiddled with the dials on the machine for a few moments, a frown of concentration pulling at her forehead.

Emily's heart pounded as though she had just bolted up ten flights of stairs. What was wrong? Why was the sonographer peering at the screen so intently? She glanced at Loukas. He too was frowning and his hand suddenly reached for hers and squeezed it. 'What's wrong?' he asked.

The sonographer turned on her stool and smiled at

them both. 'Have a look.' She pointed to the screen with the cursor. 'Here is your baby's heartbeat. See that? And here is another one.'

*Another heartbeat?*

Emily met Loukas's stunned gaze. 'Twins?' he asked.

'We're having *twins*?' Emily echoed him.

'You are indeed having twins,' the sonographer said. 'And they're identical, from what I can see. Congratulations. I'll print out the pictures for you while you sit here and get acquainted with your babies for a while. I won't be long.' The curtain swished closed.

Emily couldn't stop staring at the screen where their babies were curled up like two peanuts. 'Oh. My. God.'

Loukas brought her hand up to his mouth and kissed it. His eyes were moist and he seemed to be having trouble speaking. He opened and closed his mouth a couple of times but didn't get any words out.

'I'm sorry,' Emily said, her bottom lip beginning to tremble. 'Trust me to not do anything by halves. You didn't even want one baby and now I've given you two.'

'No, don't say that,' he said when he was finally able to speak. 'I do want the baby—I mean, babies. I want you too. I love you, Emily. So, so much.'

Emily wasn't sure if she should believe him. He had just been informed they were having twins. He might be able to let her walk away from him with one baby, but two was something else again. If he was so sure he loved her, why wait until today? Why not some time over the last six weeks? She narrowed her gaze. 'How do I know you're not just saying that because we're having twins?'

He held her hand against his chest where she could feel the thud of his heart. She was no cardiac doctor but it seemed to be racing as hard and fast as hers. 'I only realised it a couple of hours ago. I know how unlikely that sounds—I should have realised the moment I met you that you were the only woman for me. I'm sorry for putting you through hell these last weeks, but I've been a coward. I didn't want to fall in love because everyone I've loved in the past I've hurt. I convinced myself I hadn't fallen for you, but I think I did at Draco and Allegra's wedding when you caught the bouquet and smiled at me with those gorgeous dimples of yours showing.'

Emily wanted to believe him but she had been so hurt by his distance these last few weeks. 'I don't know…it seems a little too convenient to me.'

'I can prove it, *agape mou*,' he said. 'I have a surprise waiting for you in the waiting room. The reception staff are minding them for me. That's what all that laughter you can hear is about. I bought you a present to convince you I love you and want to spend the rest of my life with you.'

'You buy presents for everyone,' Emily said with a little scowl. 'It doesn't mean you love them.'

'I know, and that's been my mistake in the past,' he said. 'But when you took everything but the jewellery box key I realised how much I loved you. You're my key. You've unlocked my heart and wriggled your way into my life to such a degree I can't bear to be without you.'

'I wondered where that key went,' Emily said. 'I haven't been able to open the box. I locked it after I took the earrings out before I left your place. I tried picking the lock with a nail file but it didn't work.' But despite Loukas's words she still wasn't convinced he was truly in love with her and she kept frowning at him.

'Will you at least come with me to visit Ariana and my mother once we're done here?' Loukas asked. 'I have a present for Ariana as well as you. Please? Will you just come and see, and then you'll know I'm not lying?'

Emily climbed off the bed with his help. 'Maybe I should go to the bathroom first.'

'Good idea.'

When she came out of the bathroom, Loukas took her by the hand and smiled down at her. 'Ready?'

Emily walked with him to the reception area to find two adorable Irish Retriever puppies being babysat by the reception staff. She promptly burst into tears and turned blindly into Loukas's chest, hugging him tightly. 'I can't believe you bought me a dog. Two dogs! Are you even allowed to bring them in here?'

He smiled down at her tear-stained face. 'I told the staff they're therapy dogs. One is for Ariana. It will give us a good excuse to visit for play dates. Will you help me build my relationship with my mother and sister? They already love you and can't wait to see you.'

Emily leaned back to gaze up at him. 'You really do love me, don't you?'

His eyes were glistening with moisture. 'I love you more than I can say. Will you marry me, my precious love? Will you be my wife and help me raise our family?'

She touched his face as if to see if he was really standing there in front of her. Not just in front of her, but all the patients and staff as well, who were watching with avid interest, faces beaming. 'I will marry you. I love you. I can't wait to spend the rest of my life with you. I've been so lonely and sad without you these past weeks.'

He held her close. 'Me too. What a fool I've been for waiting so long to tell you. And then, when I did tell you, you didn't believe me. That was a bad moment.'

'But saved by those adorable little puppies,' she said, slipping out of his arms to go to cuddle them and having her face thoroughly licked in the process. 'Do they have names?'

'Not yet, we have to choose them. While we're at it we'd better get working on our babies' ones as well.'

Emily handed him one puppy to hold while she cuddled the other. 'You've made me so happy, darling. I feel like pinching myself to make sure I'm not dreaming this.'

Loukas stretched his neck to avoid a wet puppy

tongue aiming for his chin. 'Forget about pinching yourself. These little guys have needle-sharp teeth that will more than do the job for you.'

Emily laughed. 'And here I was, thinking you'd cut yourself shaving. Although, I did wonder how you scratched your hands.'

Loukas grinned. 'I'm dying to kiss you but I'm worried it might turn into a foursome if I bend down while we're holding these little rascals.'

'Kiss her. Kiss her!' the reception staff and patients chanted.

Loukas's eyes twinkled. 'Are you up for it?'

Emily lifted her face to his. 'You bet.'

# EPILOGUE

LOUKAS STOOD AT the end of the aisle at the St Sypridion Church on Corfu. He could barely see through the blur of moisture in his eyes when he saw Ariana coming down the aisle in her chair behind Allegra. It had only been a couple of weeks but already his relationship with his sister and mother was in a better place. A good place. A place where they could talk about the accident and how it had impacted on all of them. His mother had even confessed her own crushing guilt over not watching Ariana in that split moment when she'd gone off to ride her bike. Because he had been so focussed on his own guilt, he hadn't realised his mother had been in her own private hell for all these years.

But seeing Ariana now, filled with joy for him, he felt a sense of peace she too one day would find the love and happiness he had found with Emily.

He looked at his mother, who was in the front row, mopping tears from her eyes, and another wave of emotion rolled through him. She smiled and gave him a little wave and he smiled back, full of love and admiration for her, for how she had supported his sister and now welcomed Emily to the family as if she were her own daughter.

Emily's mother was in the front row on the bride's side and she winked cheekily at him. He genuinely liked Willow, especially since he'd passed the Body Language Intimacy test, whatever the hell that was. Not that he needed anyone's approval, other than his beloved Emily's, but it was nice to know her mother was part of his family now.

And then, just when he thought he had his emotions back under control, in came Emily. Nothing could have prepared him for that moment. She was dressed in a beautiful French lace dress that couldn't quite hide the swell of her belly where their twin babies were continuing to thrive. She was glowing with good health and radiant with love. The same love he could feel beaming out of him as she took her place by his side. He took her hands and gave them a gentle squeeze. 'You look so beautiful, you took my breath away.'

Her dimples appeared when she smiled. 'Didn't Ariana look amazing?'

His heart gave a spasm of happiness. 'You've given me back my family, *agape mou.*'

She leaned a little closer to whisper. 'Speaking of families. Allegra has some news.'

Loukas glanced at Allegra but she was looking dreamily at Draco, one of her hands pressing against her abdomen underneath the bouquet she was holding. Loukas smiled at Emily. 'Looks like we're not the only ones starting a family.'

'I know. Isn't it exciting?'

'Ready?' the priest asked, stepping forward to begin the service.

'Are we?' Loukas asked, winking at Emily.

Her sparkling brown eyes twinkled back. 'We're ready.'

\* \* \* \* \*

*If you enjoyed*
*A RING FOR THE GREEK'S BABY,*
*why not enjoy these other*
ONE NIGHT WITH CONSEQUENCES
*themed stories?*

*THE GUARDIAN'S VIRGIN WARD*
*by Caitlin Crews*
*A CHILD CLAIMED BY GOLD*
*by Rachael Thomas*
*THE CONSEQUENCE OF HIS VENGEANCE*
*by Jennie Lucas*
*THE BOSS'S NINE-MONTH NEGOTIATION*
*by Maya Blake*
*THE PREGNANT KAVAKOS BRIDE*
*by Sharon Kendrick*

*Available now!*

# MILLS & BOON®

# MODERN™

**POWER, PASSION AND IRRESISTIBLE TEMPTATION**

## A sneak peek at next month's titles...

**In stores from 10th August 2017:**

- **The Tycoon's Outrageous Proposal** – Miranda Lee *and* **At the Ruthless Billionaire's Command** – Carole Mortimer
- **Claiming His One-Night Baby** – Michelle Smart *and* **Cipriani's Innocent Captive** – Cathy Williams

**In stores from 24th August 2017:**

- **Engaged for Her Enemy's Heir** – Kate Hewitt *and* **His Drakon Runaway Bride** – Tara Pammi
- **The Throne He Must Take** – Chantelle Shaw *and* **The Italian's Virgin Acquisition** – Michelle Conder

*Just can't wait?*
Buy our books online before they hit the shops!
**www.millsandboon.co.uk**

**Also available as eBooks.**

# MILLS & BOON®

## *EXCLUSIVE EXTRACT*

Natasha Pellegrini and Matteo Manaserro's reunion
catches them both in a potent mix of emotion, and they
surrender to their explosive passion. Natasha was a virgin
until Matteo's touch branded her as his and when Matteo
discovers Natasha is pregnant, he's intent on claiming his
baby. Except he hasn't bargained on their insatiable
chemistry binding them together so completely!

*Read on for a sneak preview of Michelle Smart's book*
CLAIMING HIS ONE-NIGHT BABY
The second part of her Bound to a Billionaire trilogy

'For better or worse we're going to be tied together by our
child for the rest of our lives and the only way we're going
to get through it is by always being honest with each other.
We will argue and disagree but you must always speak the
truth to me.'

Natasha fought to keep her feet grounded and her limbs
from turning into fondue but it was a fight she was losing,
Matteo's breath warm on her face, his thumb gently moving
on her skin but scorching it, the heat from his body almost
penetrating her clothes, heat crawling through her, pooling
in her most intimate place.

His scent was right there too, filling every part of her, and
she wanted to bury her nose into his neck and inhale him.

She'd kissed him without any thought, a desperate
compulsion to touch him and comfort him flooding her, and
then the fury had struck from nowhere, all her private thoughts
about the direction he'd taken his career in converging to
realise he'd thrown it all away in the pursuit of riches.

And now she wanted to kiss him again.

As if he could sense the need inside her, he brought his mouth close to hers but not quite touching, the promise of a kiss.

'And now I will ask you something and I want complete honesty,' he whispered, the movement of his words making his lips dance against hers like a breath.

The fluttering of panic sifted into the compulsive desire. She hated lies too. She never wanted to tell another, especially not to him. But she had to keep her wits about her because there were things she just could not tell because no matter what he said about lies always being worse, sometimes it was the truth that could destroy a life.

But, God, how could she think properly when her head was turning into candyfloss at his mere touch?

His other hand trailed down her back and clasped her bottom to pull her flush to him. Her abdomen clenched to feel his erection pressing hard against her lower stomach. His lips moved lightly over hers, still tantalising her with the promise of his kiss. 'Do you want me to let you go?'

Her hands that she'd clenched into fists at her sides to stop from touching him back unfurled themselves and inched to his hips.

The hand stroking her cheek moved round her head and speared her hair. 'Tell me.' His lips found her exposed neck and nipped gently at it. 'Do you want me to stop?'

'Matteo…' Finally, she found her voice.

'Yes, *bella*?'

'Don't stop.'

Don't miss
CLAIMING HIS ONE-NIGHT BABY
By Michelle Smart

Available September 2017
www.millsandboon.co.uk